The Copperfield Affair

The Copperfield Affair

Roberta Marlow

Copyright © 2007 by Roberta Marlow.

ISBN 10:	Hardcover	1-4257-3851-6
	Softcover	1-4257-3850-8
ISBN 13:	Hardcover	978-1-4257-3851-8
	Softcover	978-1-4257-3850-1

All rights reserved. No part of this book may be reproduced or transmitted in any form or by any means, electronic or mechanical, including photocopying, recording, or by any information storage and retrieval system, without permission in writing from the copyright owner.

This is a work of fiction. Names, characters, places and incidents either are the product of the author's imagination or are used fictitiously, and any resemblance to any actual persons, living or dead, events, or locales is entirely coincidental.

Several historical persons are a part of this account. When using their real names, actions and words have been recreated by the author from news stories of the time. Other characters are the work of the author's imagination. Any resemblance to real persons among these characters, living or dead, is coincidental.*

*One exception is the District Attorney. Because of his interconnection with the actions of Governor Oswald West, his characterization does include information from news stories of 1913-1914. However, because the majority of his role is imagined, his name and many details are fictitious.

This book was printed in the United States of America.

To order additional copies of this book, contact:
Xlibris Corporation
1-888-795-4274
www.Xlibris.com
Orders@Xlibris.com

Contents

Prologue 11

PART 1

A Troubled Cowboy 21

Gambler' Luck 28

A Cowboy in Trouble 34

The Sheriff Investigates 43

Friends on the trail 50

Ridin' on Down the River 56

Settling In 63

Meeting the Community 72

On the Job 82

A Hot Time in the Old Town 88

Dancing the Night Away 100

The Second Fire 111

The Sheriff Calls on Copperfield 118

Meanwhile Back at the Courthouse 131

Booster Night 135

A Sunday Stroll 141

Meeting in the Back Room 150

Slipping on Ice 158

The Town Council Meets 168

PART II

Ribbons, Bunting and Martial Law 179

The Party's Over 191

On the Road Again 198

The Injunction and its Aftermath 210

Be My Valentine 221

The Red Ball Gown 230

Martial Law Continues 238

PART III

To Jail or Not to Jail 247

Getting Ready to Come Out 255

The Best of the Best 262

Salem Visit 269

At Champoeg 275

The Mayor is Down 286

By a Twist of Fate 292

The Grange Picnic 300

The Bridal Shower 310

Up in Flames 315

Epilogue 329

DEDICATION

This work is dedicated to the Baker County Library Staff, past and present, who have accumulated and maintained an outstanding collection of local and regional history.

Prologue

January 3, 1964

Dear Ellie,

    It was so nice to hear your voice when you called on New Year's Day. I do wish you had felt up to the trip out for Christmas. But, for heaven's sake, don't apologize for being under the weather. Taking an airplane trip in winter is not such a good plan anyway, especially in light of the crash at Montreal last Thanksgiving weekend. Even though I flew off and on for fifteen years or more, my knees came close to buckling every time I boarded.
    As I told you on the telephone, Carrie May is helping me move into a nursing home. We visited one in Salem just before Christmas and had a holiday dinner there. It was quite nice. It's true, I don't like finally giving up my home. Yet I'm just not up to doing anything that requires physical effort. Carrie says I'll eat better over there, and there will be someone to give me my medications as I need them. Carrie gives me so much of her time, but she is planning to go on up to Alaska in June, and she wants to make sure that I'm settled in and doing okay before she leaves.
    Carrie was digging early yesterday morning, she found Mother's old trunk in the attic. I guess she thought she was finding love letters or something because she says when she saw this huge pile of letters tied with a pink ribbon, she was ready to spend the day reading. When she found out they were from you, she promptly brought them to me.
    I had certainly put them out of my mind a long time ago. I first packed them up when I went to France, although I've come across them several times since. I pulled a few of them out and had her read them to me. When I drifted off, she kept on reading to herself. When I woke up, she began scolding me for never telling her this amazing story of your year in Copperfield.

We talked on and on about it. She would read a snippet; then we'd visit. It was dark before she went home. She says she'll be back tomorrow to finish the attic. Then on to the basement. When she gets that done, we'll have an estate sale.

My Lord, I hate to even think about it; but I am beyond rational thought anyway, so it doesn't really matter. Are you sure that you took everything you might want for Sandy Fern when you were here last August? If you think of anything, be sure to send a list right away. I do still have your Homer Winslow painting of "Prout's Neck, Maine," to say nothing of my crystal and silver. But I can certainly understand, and I can't blame you or Sandy for not wanting to pack my junk around.

I've decided to send your letters along for you to share with your family. Carrie says it's too bad I didn't get them out years ago and write a book. I told her, "fat chance." After all those years of working for the Journal, I couldn't have brought myself to sit still for a book. Besides how could I have written anything about that occasion without having to live it all over again? That's something I have never wanted to do. But I have to admit, your letters are quite entertaining. Strangely enough, there are a couple of letters in the packet that are from me to you.

Carrie May found one of them a treasure for asking questions. Was it cold when I went there? Was everyone jolly? Was anyone rude? Why do you suppose they gave up their weapons so easily? And on and on. She obviously doesn't understand the import of declaring martial law.

I'm becoming a little tired now, and I'm sure that Carrie has things to do besides listen to my old dictaphone and type letters. She does such a good job though. She says she'll come to the nursing home every day so we can go on with the letter writing and reading books. She started doing that almost ten years ago now. She's such an angel and very good friend. I don't suppose I'll get to see her blush while she types this. She says she doesn't blush at her age, but I don't believe her.

As I said, I hope you're feeling better than you did at Christmas time. And I hope that recalling Christmas, 1913, will be as entertaining to you as it has been for us. Please call or write. Maybe we should renew our pact of 1913 to write every week. Really, I would if I could make these old fingers fly over the keys like I did then.

Love from your cousin,

Charlotte Fern

P. S. Do you remember the poem you wrote after your visit to the canyon when Cord died in '56?. It was tied in with your letters. You might want to start with it just to set the mood. So here it is.

My Memories

The home of my youth is but an aching memory,
Of people vanquished like dew-drops in a timeless sea.
Echoes of my heartstrings, repeat their lonely song
Of love, laughter, and friends where I once belonged.

Dreams meander through my days in endless rhyme
Treasured thoughts swirl in the swollen sands of time,
Renewing the reason for my being, once thought so grand.
As I recall a fragment of history of this god-forsaken land,

Where cows pasture now, and deer graze in the evening sun.
I ponder the battles we so bravely fought and mostly won.
Goodness conquered the contentious evil harbored there
Then moved on to better things, though I know not where.

For I am but a frail prisoner of God's gift in time and space,
My thoughts are captive to such experience as they embrace.
I will release them now if my somber soul can but condone
The pain of giving meaning to what is mine and mine alone

—My memories!

PART I

September, 1913

Sunday	Monday	Tuesday	Wednesday	Thursday	Friday	Saturday
	1	2	3	4	5	6
7	8	9	10	11	12	13
14	15	16	17	18	19	20
21	22	23	24	25	26	27
28	29	30				

"... WE'LL BUILD A LITTLE NEST
WAY OUT IN THE WEST
AND LET THE REST OF
THE WORLD GO BY."
—J. Keirn Brennan

September 9, 1913

Dearest Lottie Fern,

At long last I am on my way to Western adventure. The train pulled out of Philadelphia Station just a few minutes ago at 4:30 p.m. If all goes well, we will reach Chicago in about 24 hours. We'll have a short lay over there, then on to The West. Am I ever thankful for the successes of the railroad builders. I have a very difficult time picturing myself on such a long walk. When I think of the pioneers who traveled by wagon across this great land, I just thank God for the good fortune of my being born to live in the 20th Century, instead of the 19th.

But it has still been hard. At times, these last three weeks, I've just sat in Father's chair and stared at the walls, wondering if I'm doing the right thing. And if I'm not, then what is the right thing? The lump in my throat and the hurt of leaving behind my twenty-three years of life with family and friends has been almost as painful as saying "Good-bye" to Father three months ago.

I still can't believe he is gone and that I'll never see him again. When Mother departed, it didn't seem so awful, I guess, because Father was there to comfort me. Besides, she had been ill for so many years. But for Father to keel over right in the courtroom and die before the day went by was just too severe.

In the weeks that followed, as I cleared his office and finally our home, I kept thinking he would walk through the door, put his arms around me and say, "Ellie Kathleen, what do you think you're doing? I'm going to need those things!" Well, it's done now. The law books are in the Courthouse library, and except for his favorite shirt, tie, and trousers and Winslow Homer's "Prout's Neck, Maine" from his office, which I shipped West with my trunks, everything else is gone. I wish I could have saved more of his collection of watercolors. But alas, it would be impossible to take good care of them. I donated them to a local art gallery instead.

As for my accommodations, my berth is quite comfortable, I think, though I have yet to sleep in it. The day coach is pretty well filled

---

It was 5:30 p.m. when we arrived in Chicago. We have almost four hours here. It is so hot, they are calling out warnings for us to stay indoors while we wait. There is a quaint little soda shop across the street; so I may wander over there for part of the time. Perhaps they will have cold sandwiches available. Otherwise, I will walk a few blocks to a real restaurant. We'll be boarding again at 9:00 p.m.

Hello, it's morning. The countryside looks quite different. Instead of small farms and villages all along the track, we're in the corn and hog country. The farmsteads are quite beautiful with large houses painted white and huge red barns that one can see both near and far. We should soon be reaching buffalo and Indian country that we Easterners find so fascinating.

This morning, many of the passengers are mesmerized as they watch the milepost markers go speeding by, one per minute. It is really something. We only slow or stop at the various depots along the way while they fling the mail on to the platform and pick up an outgoing bag. Or, perhaps, we come to a halt for a few minutes while someone boards or gets off the train.

I can always tell if someone is likely to get off. A team of dozing horses with harness tugs dropped from a buggy, a hack, or a wagon will be waiting patiently. Then there are the longer pauses in the middle of nowhere while we take on water for the steam engine, or we wait for an oncoming train to pass. I'm going to nap now for a time until dinner is served.

Hi Lottie. It's the next day. There just wasn't much I could add. I've been staring at the latest fashions according to my Vogue magazine. They are quite outrageous. The beachwear looks positively shocking. I can't wait to try some. Ha! Ha!

Occasionally, I can observe a herd of horses, but not much else. We are approaching the great Rocky Mountains. I can't believe that we will really cross such a great height. But it will happen. We are already making our way along trestles and through tunnels and coming in sight of what looks to be mammoth forests.

Clearing the forested areas, we are again in view of small settlements. I hadn't seen any for many, many miles, but now there are meadows and ranch buildings in the distance. Also we are crossing creeks and rivers much more frequently. Soon, we'll reach the Snake River. My heart is racing as I consider my teaching position on its banks.

We crossed over the Snake River during the night and came through the Paloose country. As we neared Pendleton, I could see what several of the passengers were talking about—the checkerboard. The fields are harvested, leaving the golden stubble to be plowed under. These fields are bordered on all sides by land that is already plowed and ready for fall wheat planting.

I'm quite surprised by the look of Pendleton. I thought that you told me it was one of the larger towns in Eastern Oregon. We have a wait here, and while it is hot, it's not as bad as Chicago. I can see a few blocks of stores, the courthouse and several livery stables. There are three saloons directly across the street. There are quite a few cowboys bustling about or just leaning up against the buildings. According to the lady I have been visiting with all morning, the ranchers come to places like this to hire help, or to buy and sell horses for their ranch operations.

I can also see the loading platforms where there is a steady stream of sixteen-horse teams pulling wagons up to the grain elevators. My friend tells me that some of the wheat will be loaded and shipped to Portland. But most will wait to be traded on the market and shipped east.

There is considerable conversation here at the depot about the Pendleton Round Up, now in its third year. They say that the Indians and cowboys come together for riding and roping contests. Since you told me that Governor West rode in this parade two years ago, I've been wondering if you've had any thought of coming over from Salem this year.

—

Well, here I am on the last leg of my long journey. I have seen both deer and elk when there is a clearing of any size. I also saw a coyote. At first, I thought maybe it might be a wolf; it was so large. But the gentleman sitting across the aisle at the time said wolves are not plentiful here, and besides they don't travel alone. So much for the legend of the lonely, but romantic life of the wandering Lobo.

We are now in the heart of the Blue Mountains with miles and miles and miles of forested country. Since I need to plan to get off the train in Baker City and spend the night there before going on to my new home, I'll seal this with my love and mail it to you from there.

My next letter will be all about my new home. The latest arrangements are that I will board with the general store owners. They have two children, both in school. I think the youngest is in the first grade and the older in fifth, or maybe it was sixth.

I can't wait to unpack my books and get copies of the children's textbooks to see what I'm facing. My salary will be $35.50 per month, except for December, when there will be only ten days of school instead of the usual twenty. That month, I will make $17.50 plus a $2.50 Christmas bonus. My room and board is rather reasonable at $10.00 per month.

Still, I just don't know what I will do with all that money. There's one thing I can be sure of. Father would laugh and say, "Ellie Kathleen, I am just going *to have to increase your allowance." Or, he would say, "If you would use your head, you would open an office of law where you can make at least $3.00 a day if you are any kind of a lawyer. Then who knows, maybe you can run for governor some day." Poor Father, he would never surrender and admit that "It's a man's world, after all."*

Please write as soon as possible. My address will be General Delivery in Copperfield, Oregon. I'll be looking every day for a letter because I'm sure I'll be quite lonely.

With love from your cousin,

Ellie Kathleen

A Troubled Cowboy

Pulling a curtain to one side, Cord Williams glanced out the window of the ZX Ranch headquarters, noting the storm-colored sky to the West. Looking down, he caught sight of the cook's twin daughters, who were busily strewing flowers along the walkway in preparation for the big event. The sunshine reflected brightly on their white pinafore dresses as they laughed and spun in circles.

In contrast to the children's enthusiasm, Cord's mood was as dark as the approaching storm. Hoping for a downpour that would utterly ruin Bonnie Jean's garden wedding, he almost jumped out of his skin when a friendly hand grasped his shoulder.

"Well, boy," Norm Barstow boomed. "I guess you and I never anticipated this turn of events, did we?"

"Not in a million years," Cord murmured.

"Come on. Have a drink with me. That's my little girl I'll be walking down the aisle, and I'm a mite nervous about the whole thing."

"Okay," Cord assented dully, turning toward the buffet to receive a shot of bourbon and water.

Before the two men could engage in conversation, the mother-of-the-bride, called plaintively, "Norm where are you? The guests are starting to arrive."

Taking his leave, Norm said, "You'd better pick your spot, Son. I have a feeling the place will be crawling with people before long."

Cord tossed down the rest of his drink and sauntered out to the veranda, then off the steps into the yard. For the next half-hour, he stood quietly, greeting men he had worked with on the ranch and tipping his hat to ladies who were looking his way. Then moving to a position in view of the wide front steps where the woman he had thought to marry would be descending, he waited in agony.

As the band struck up a prelude to the wedding march, he shifted his weight in an attempt to look unconcerned. Yet, no matter how or where he stood, he felt conspicuous and uncomfortable. Watching resolutely for Bonnie Jean and her father to emerge from the front door of the ranch headquarters, he sensed that other guests were staring just as intently as he.

When the bride stepped into the bright sunlight, Cord found her more strikingly beautiful than he could ever have imagined. Despite his preoccupation with her stately approach to the flower-bedecked archway where the preacher and wedding party waited, Cord became aware that people were looking in his direction instead of following the progress of the bride. Confusion mocked him and tightness constricted his throat. He could only think to himself, "What the hell am I doing here?"

His felt impelled to slip away once Bonnie walked past, mount his horse, and ride. But he had reluctantly agreed with Norm that he would stick around for the reception and say a proper good-bye to the new bride.

Bonnie Jean, now twenty-one, held out her hand to be received by another man, a scene Cord couldn't fully comprehend, even as he stared. Seven years ago on her 14th birthday, he had ridden up to the ZX to see if they were hiring any cowhands. He had been a mere kid, himself, at 21; and he looked back in amazement at how quickly a bond had formed between the two of them.

He knew now, to his chagrin, that he had taken that bond for granted far too long, and had assumed it would never be broken. The proof of his error lay in the fact that she would soon be Mrs. Al Mason, not Mrs. Cord Williams. Closing his eyes on that thought, he recalled events of the past couple of days.

—

Jumping from his horse and racing through the gate to gather her in his arms when he arrived on Friday, he was flabbergasted at her first words. "I don't remember inviting you to the wedding," she announced.

"What wedding?" he grunted dropping his arms to his side.

"My wedding, dearest," she replied acidly. "But you, my friend, are not a part of it."

Cord had thought he was going to choke. All the dry dust of the hot August trail welled up in his throat, and for the moment, all he could think of was getting a drink of water. Without a word, he spun on his heel and rushed off to the well. He gulped water at the pump, then yanked his hat from his sweating head and thoroughly doused his face and neck in the bubbling trough water.

Norm Barstow, the ranch foreman, drove up in his new Model A just as Cord pulled a spare neckerchief from his pocket to sop excess water from his hands and face. Glancing first at Bonnie Jean, he proceeded toward Cord with hand extended for a friendly shake.

Later that evening Bonnie invited him for a walk where she commenced to scold, "What did you expect, Cord Williams? You come riding in here after two years of nothing, no letter, not even a message by way of a drummer; and you think

I'll just come running so you can go on your merry way like you always do after a few months of hiding out here in the desert. Well, I've had enough of that.

"Besides, I've grown to love Al; and he certainly loves me," she said dreamily. "You should see the house he built for us. I can't tell you what that means to me. He didn't even propose until after he drove the last nail, and then he was so sweet and shy that I couldn't get mad at him for not letting me be a part of it."

Cord hardly heard the soft words she uttered. He was still back on the two years bit. Had it really been two years? "No, it wasn't two years," he declared. "I didn't even leave here until February because I especially waited through the fall to spend Christmas and Valentine's Day with you. No, it was just a year and a half ago. And I couldn't send you a message. Just as soon as I was able, I came back. Bonnie, honey," he took a step toward her to take her in his arms, "I came back so we could get married."

"Yes," Bonnie Jean responded sardonically as she pushed away from him. "And you expected me to just be sitting here waiting—waiting to run my fingers through your soft, shiny black hair, as velvety as a young colt's nose. And to look up to stare into your dreamy blue eyes, and to practically dangle in front of you while I stand on my tip toes to reach my arms around your neck. Well, guess what, Cord Williams, I've grown up. All that bully excitement that I thought I could die for two years ago is just that—stupid little girl excitement. I know that you and a lot of others think Al is too old for me at thirty-five. And he's not nearly as handsome as you, but he loves me—enough to be considerate of the things I want and the way I feel. Besides when would you have ever been able to offer me a home? If I did consent to marry you, we'd probably end up living in a damned bunkhouse or worse."

Cord grabbed her by the wrist, wanting to hold her and kiss her, but the cold look in her eyes stopped him. After a brief moment, he dropped his hands to his sides. Still, he couldn't quit clenching and unclenching his fists, desperately trying to control how he felt. Giving her one last look of longing, he turned and walked away.

He had planned to tell her about getting rolled on by a bucking horse last fall at the Pendleton Round Up and about spending two months in the hospital while his back healed. There were so many things he had wanted her to understand. One thing he had never really talked about with her was his mother and his childhood on the Indian Reservation. In fact, he wasn't sure she even knew he was half Indian—a half-breed. He had always been afraid that she might not love him if she knew.

—

Recovering from his reverie, Cord realized the wedding ceremony had concluded. People were lining up for the reception. Again, Cord yearned to leave, but he found himself drifting in line toward Bonnie Jean and her new husband. He managed a limp handshake with Mason. All the while his impulse was to gather Bonnie Jean in his arms and shout, "She's mine! She's mine!"

Instead he found himself leaning forward to kiss her gently on her cheek, while mumbling. "Bonnie, darling, you deserve all the happiness in the world. Make sure that's what you get."

Bonnie drew back, looking teary-eyed and more than a little surprised as she gazed up at him. Then she half whispered, "Thank you Cord. That means so much to me."

Cord moved on. He felt as if he were going to suffocate. Upon reaching the end of the line, he replaced his hat, pulling it so tight on his forehead that it hurt. As if in a dream, he kept on walking straight out the gate to the hitching rail. Untying his horse, Patches, he tightened the cinch on his saddle, mounted up and rode. He let his horse choose the direction when they came to the corner of First and Main Street in Drewsey.

Patches paused a moment at the intersection, then plodded southward to continue the journey they had begun a week earlier. The procrastinating thunderstorm struck with a vengeance within the hour. Chilly and disheartened, Cord spent the next two nights en route along the main road. Traveling east through the most desolate of Oregon's deserts he remained awake throughout most of the nights. The stops he made were merely to allow Patches to eat and rest. Then, instead of sleeping, he allowed his thoughts to turn to his recent sojourn with his mother on the Lapwai Indian Reservation in Idaho.

During the day, he stared with uncertainty at every road crossing trying to decide his future. Would it be mining or ranching, construction or railroading? There was plenty of opportunity for this kind of work in the southeast corner of Oregon in 1913. But he would rather break out of the mold he had been in since the age of 14 to find something new and interesting. After all, he wasn't looking to the future so much as he was trying to forget the past and Bonnie Jean.

Cord stayed the third night in the small town of Ontario, located near the Idaho border. The clouds and occasional showers of the past two days had passed. The temperatures rose that day into the high nineties. If he hadn't given himself permission to sleep in this morning until past ten o'clock, he could have probably made it all the way to Huntington.

Being as hot as it was, he decided to spend another day en route, staying that night in Weiser, Idaho. He put Patches in the livery stable where he ordered a good brushing and a fresh supply of hay for the night. For himself, he'd find a hotel, a hot meal, a steaming bath, and a good bed. Maybe, then, he could decide what he was going to do next.

After a fitful night in a stuffy hotel room on the second floor, Cord tiredly faced the day. Tugging the string open on his gold coin stash, he realized that his bankroll was quickly diminishing. His plan for that money had been to give it to Bonnie Jean to help set up housekeeping. So much for plans. He decided it would be a good idea to lighten his load. He'd discard his food provisions and cooking utensils. No matter what he concluded about his future, he would not be so far from civilization that he'd need a coffee kettle or a frying pan. He might keep his tin cup, though.

Another thing, he was positively ruling out any further cattle or horse wrangling, so he might as well find a taker for his chaps. An extra couple of bucks couldn't hurt. He'd look around for a second-hand store after breakfast.

His long, shiny, black hair was tickling the back of his neck as he walked and was contributing to sweat driveling down his back. While out on the range, he often wore a braid. But among settlers and townsfolk, he left it hanging loose. So he went to the barbershop operating out of the front of the hotel for a shave and a haircut.

Although the barber was a friendly sort, Cord felt no particular inclination to talk as he relaxed while being transformed from a longhaired saddle tramp into the look of a suave city slicker. His mind drifted to matters of concern for his future until he found himself listening to the conversation of the two fellows who were waiting for their turn at the chair.

"I don't know," said one. "From what I hear, the OR&N is probably not going ahead with that Homestead to Lewiston rail route anymore this summer, if ever."

"Is that so? That'll put a rather big hole in events down there on the River, won't it?" the second fellow asked.

"You could say that. Power company has given up on their big plans too. I've heard they're quitting with what they've got."

"How much is that?"

"About 600 kilowatts, according to the news report."

"Quite a ways from the 220,000 they were bragging about, wouldn't you say?"

"Yup, there's a little short fall, I'd say." The first speaker paused. "Still, as long as the ore doesn't play out, there's quite a bit of mining that will keep things going, I suspect."

"Be too bad if the town had to fold all right. I hear it's a real rip roarin', hell-raisin' place," the second fellow chuckled.

"Yup, it's wide open. People coming in a lot from the outside now. Poker games, roulette tables, dice, they've got it all. They've even changed the train schedule so it runs on Friday instead of Thursday. Then it runs again on Saturday. Hotel business is getting better by the day."

"I guess if you can't get a room in the hotel, there's a thriving business out back with quite a few beds."

"So I've heard," said the first fellow.

The barber finished and was brushing a sprinkling of Cord's hair from his clothes to the floor. Signaling him to get up from the chair, he remarked, "You fellows wouldn't be gossiping about Gomorrah on the Snake, now would you?"

"Yeah, just talking about a little place over on the River called Copperfield."

Cord flipped a couple of coins on to the counter and reached for his hat. "Sounds like my kind of place," he murmured. Checking his dwindling supply of money, he decided to have a breakfast of straight pancakes.

After a call at the second-hand store where he'd sold his chaps and trail gear he walked on over to the mercantile store to outfit himself. Underwear, socks, three new shirts, two pair of Levis, a soft black velveteen vest, and a replacement for his tall black hat. He chose a light gray Stetson, then picked up Patches to head out—perhaps to Copperfield. That place would more than likely give him an excuse to wear the fancy shirt he'd been drawn to at the merc.

"Regular gambler's shirt," the clerk had told him. "Why you can stuff a whole deck in these detachable cuffs if you know how." Gambling was not one of Cord's vices. He'd simply been enticed by the bright blue and red narrow vertical stripes decorating a white shirt, with wide cuffs, and a stiff collar.

Patches, too, felt renewed by the extra care in Weiser. He cantered into Huntington, Oregon, a little after noon that same day. Cord hitched his horse to the rail in front of the nearest restaurant, then lunched on a sandwich and beer. Then he mounted his horse and rode a few blocks further to the livery stable.

—

"Needin' a place for your horse?" a man of about thirty greeted him at the front of the building.

"Actually," Cord replied, "I'm thinking of finding a buyer for my horse and my outfit. Cord's the name," he informed the liveryman, reaching cross-armed over the saddle horn to shake hands.

The man did not respond or give his name. Instead he began looking the horse over. "Looks like a squaw pony," he said. "'Ja get him from an Injun?" He paused, circled the horse, then spat a stream of tobacco juice. Cord stared at him, watching his every move.

"Only good Injun's a dead 'un, I allyus say. How much ya want fer 'im?" The man continued by rubbing down Patches' front legs, picking up a foot to inspect the shoe.

Cord's face turned a deep red as anger sent his stomach churning. He'd like to take this bastard to task and leave him face down in the dirt. Yielding to temptation though would probably earn him a bullet in the back. So he held his tongue. Gritting his teeth, he replied, "I only said I was thinking on it."

He began to wheel his horse around when the stable hand said, "Well, I wouldn't buy him myself, ya understand. But there's an old boy named Clayton Locksley, from over Mormon Basin way. That's about twenty-five miles yonder," he indicated with a sweep of his hand to the west. "Well, he rode in on an old mare this morning. Said I could sell her to some kid for a plugged nickel as far as he was concerned. He said he'd walk afore he'd ride that stumblin' old nag again." The man laughed. "He was sportin' a pretty good limp. Guess the nag must 'a fell on him."

The man spat tobacco again as it became apparent Cord was pulling away. "Tell you what, if'n I see him again, I'll send him around. Where ya hangin' out?"

Cord hesitated. His opinion of the stable fellow hadn't changed any. But then again, he had been all set to rid himself of his cowboy ways including sitting in a saddle for a living. "I'll be over at the hotel across from the depot for a while. Tell your friend to ask for Williams if he's interested."

"Well he won't want your outfit. Got a better one of his own right there on the rack."

Cord rode to the hotel nearest the railroad depot. If, he was going to have to drag his saddle and bedroll pack along, the closer he got to the whistle stop, the better. The Copperfield schedule posted the departure time of today's train at 2:30—about an hour and a half away. A mixed train, Number 5, was setting on the siding, apparently readying for departure, even as Cord worried about being stalled here for several days. In fact he had no choice but to stay tonight since he still had Patches to worry about.

Gambler's Luck

On the other hand, he could just ride out, go on to Baker City and probably find a ready market for his horse. Removing his saddle and outfit, Cord shuffled through his pack for a currycomb and began currying Patches. He had just moved from the left to the right side of the horse when he heard steps echoing along the boardwalk.

"Hello," a voice called. "You must be the fella with a horse."

"Obviously," Cord grinned to himself; "I am a fellow with a horse." He ducked under Patches' neck to face a man in his early fifties. Blue cotton work shirt, red bandana around his neck. Gray hair peeked out from under a rather new looking white Stetson hat. The man extended his hand, "Locksley's the name. I guess Burt over at the livery stable told you I am in the market for a horse."

Cord nodded. "Heard you had some bad luck riding in."

Locksley squeezed past Cord and began mouthing Patches, checking his teeth for age. "Six years old, huh?" he questioned.

"'Bout that," Cord replied.

"Yeah, I should 'a never started out on the old mare this morning. She's probably 21, 22 years old. Eyesight's gone bad. She didn't fall in a badger hole just once, but three times coming in. Third time she pinned me, then had the gall to roll on my leg as she got up. If I'd 'a been carrying a gun, I'd have probably put her out of her misery right then." Locksley rubbed down all four legs on Patches, checking his hocks and feet.

Rising to stand up straight, Locksley continued, "She's been a good old horse though. Our daughter used to ride her to school all the time. Daughter's been married going on five years now. Old mare's been nothing but a feed bill for a long time. But," he paused, seeking understanding, "I rode her 'cuz I gimped up my good horse the other day rounding up cattle." Patting Patches on the rump, Locksley turned his full attention to Cord.

"Do any roping off this old boy? I see he ain't wearing a brand. Shows a strong resemblance to the horses those Agency fellows ride over Ironside way."

"Actually," Cord admitted, "he's from the Agency herd. The foreman gave him to me a couple of years back. We didn't brand him so I could sell him if I wanted to. He's used to wrangling and roping though."

"You know the foreman over at the Agency?" Locksley asked.

"Depends on which foreman." Cord had a feeling he was being checked out. "I worked for Norm Barstow, mainly between the Agency and Drewsey."

"Heard of him," Locksley said. "How much you asking?"

"Got any use for my outfit too?" Cord asked.

"Not really," Locksley replied. "I see you got a rifle there. I could use that if you're selling it."

Cord noticed a pair of cowboys coming along the boardwalk. "I guess a hundred ought to do it," he responded.

"Pretty hefty price for an untried Indian pony. Mind if I try him out?"

"Guess not," Cord hoisted his saddle and blanket to the horse's back. Tightening the cinch, he listened as the two men greeted Locksley.

"'S'matter Clayton?" one of them challenged, "Old mare won't take you home no more?"

"Not if I can help it," Clayton grinned. "You boys'll vouch for me while I take this pony around the block a couple of times, right?" He chuckled as he mounted Patches.

"Sure Clayton," said the first.

The men closed in on Cord. "This here's Pete, and I'm Gaylen," the taller of the two men said.

"Cord's the name," Cord responded, proffering his right hand.

Handshakes completed, Pete asked, "You a gambling man?"

"Can't say as I am," Cord replied.

"Heading out on the train?" Gaylen inquired.

Cord didn't appreciate the strangers' being so nosy. But being away from his home territory, he knew from experience, it didn't pay to antagonize people.

"Maybe," he replied. "I'd like to sell my saddle first."

"Yeah, we moseyed on over to look at it when we heard Locksley say he wasn't interested," Pete said. "Ain't got but a couple of bucks in my pocket right now, but I'd sure be behold'n if you'd play us a hand or two of poker. I'd like to see if I could win it."

Gaylen laughed. "If you're going to hang out in these parts, it'd be worth your while to learn some about the pasteboards. Me and Pete here could sure teach you."

"I'll think about it," Cord answered.

Locksley had returned. Stepping down, he patted Patches fondly on the neck. "Horse shows pretty good spirit all right," he said agreeably. "I'll go on over to the bank and get some money. You prefer a draft or gold coin?"

"Jeez," thought Cord, "How in the hell do I know?" Still he had a certain feeling that banks couldn't be trusted. "I'll take gold, I guess."

"Be back then in about 15 minutes," Clayton said as Gaylen and Pete fell in step with him to go on down Main Street.

Cord felt his gut churning, perhaps warning him that these guys might be setting him up in some way. But for the moment, he still had his outfit. Several people were starting to gather to take the train down river. Cord piled his rigging on the ground and untied one end of his bedroll to pull out the nosebag. Patches nickered, being clearly surprised at this gesture in the middle of the day, but he took to chomping eagerly on the remaining oats in the bag.

Cord relaxed a bit when Locksley approached again, alone.

When he received the five shiny $20 gold pieces, Cord felt relieved and a little giddy. "Tell you what," he said. "I'll throw in the nosebag, the curry comb, and the hackamore. Patches has never had a bridle before."

"That's good," Locksley said. "I'm not a bridle man myself unless there's no other way."

The deal completed, Locksley draped the nosebag with the currycomb over his arm, propped the rifle in the crook of his elbow, then snagged the hackamore lead and took possession of his new horse. Cord looked down at his saddle, kicked it with his toe, and wondered what he was going to do with it. He guessed he'd hang around until tomorrow to see if he could find a buyer. "Must be somebody wants a good Hamley," he muttered to himself. With that, he retied and securely fastened his bedroll and saddle blanket, slung the saddle over his shoulder and crossed the street to the hotel.

The clerk looked at him strangely as he stepped up to register. But when Cord flipped a shiny gold piece in front of him, the man inquired what he needed and for how long. The train to Copperfield whistled its departure as Cord picked up the pencil to sign his name on the register.

The clerk said, "Room 212, right two doors, top of the stairs." He jerked his head toward the stairway. "Tell you what though. I'll store your saddle out on the veranda. Don't want the smell in the room, you understand." Cord looked up to see if he was serious.

Twitching his nose slightly, Cord checked the odors floating around him. Stale kitchen smells of burned liver and onions, mixed with people odors of sweat and perfume, not altogether pleasant, and the odor of cigar smoke, sweetened by the smell of beer and liquor from the lounge permeated the air. It made him want to laugh at the absurdity. By comparison, his saddle merely smelled of horse and leather, both pleasant to him. Checking his mirth, he said, "Fine, for a few minutes. I'll just take my bedroll up to my room; then I'll come back for the saddle. I'll take it over to the stable and store it."

"All right," the clerk replied, while leaning over the counter to watch Cord undo saddle strings to remove his bedroll enveloped in a pair of army blankets. "You just getting in from a stint in the Camel Corp?" the clerk wanted to know.

"Nope," Cord answered, not volunteering any information about his army blankets.

After Cord finished chucking his gear and putting the saddle on the rack in the livery stable, he reluctantly thanked Burt for helping him sell his horse. Then he slowly ambled back down the boardwalk trying to figure how he could go about selling the saddle. By now, the Copperfield-Homestead train was whistling its departure from Blake's Junction at the entry to Snake River Canyon.

As he came abreast of one of the dozen or so saloons along the walk back to the hotel, he noticed Pete and Gaylen belly-up to the bar. "Must be relieving themselves of those last two bucks they said they were carrying." Inspired by the laughing good time the two cowboys were having, Cord decided to join them.

"So," greeted Pete, "Here comes our horseless cowboy. Wadja do with your saddle cowboy?"

"Stored it over at the livery stable," Cord answered cheerfully. He'd seen Locksley ride out of town a few minutes ago, so he felt he had nothing to gain by being deceptive or unfriendly.

"Think you want ta learn the game of poker?" Gaylen punched Pete's shoulder to signal his intent to pressure Cord.

"I've never played before. Where do you play?" Cord had no desire to hunker down outside in the hot afternoon sun to play cards. Then too, he knew that playing for money was illegal in Oregon. It wasn't something you could do out in the open.

Pete turned to the bartender. "Okay if we take our friend to the back room for a little game of poker?"

The bartender frowned, staring at first one, then the other of the cowpokes in front of him. He flipped his bar towel on a stool in passing, saying, "I guess. But you'd better be cleared out afore supper time."

Cord glanced around the poorly lit room, realizing for the first time that the three of them and the bartender were the only ones in the saloon. Again, he felt his skin crawl, wondering if he was being set up.

"We need a drink first," Gaylen announced. "What'll you have?" he turned to Cord.

"Just a sarsaparilla," Cord replied.

"How lucky can we get?" Pete muttered, "A plumb sober cowboy."

"Sure," said the barkeeper. After pouring the sarsaparilla drink, he shoved the filled glass and two more beers along the counter.

"Guess you boys can take your drinks with you." Pete and Gaylen quickly grabbed theirs and proceeded to a door in the rear of the saloon. Cord followed reluctantly.

Entering the gloom of the back room, he was surprised at the level of activity. Three men were playing slot machines along one wall. Another half dozen were placing their bets at a roulette table. Several other gaming tables and a large pool table occupied the middle of the room, just lying in wait for potential customers.

Toward the back of the room on the side opposite the slot machines, there were a few tables with chairs arranged around them. Each had a couple of decks of cards and player chips in evidence.

"Is this really your first time at the table?" Pete asked incredulously.

"It is," Cord replied.

"Well, here's the way of it, then," Gaylen informed him. "There's high stakes games and low stakes. We're definitely low stakes. That means you put ten bucks on the table."

Cord's hackles were still rising causing him to wonder what he was really getting into. Gaylen continued his monotone on the meaning of a full house, three of a kind, a royal flush, a straight, and two pair. By the time he finished, Cord realized he hadn't comprehended a thing that was said.

Pete, too, finally deciding that Cord really was a rank beginner. "Might not even know a heart from a spade," he thought. "Tell you what," he addressed the other two. "Me and my partner'll play a few hands, and you can watch."

Cord relaxed a little as he observed the betting process. After five or six hands, he said, "Okay, I guess I'm ready to play. But how about we don't actually buy the chips. Let's just use them for placing bets and settle the money issue when the game is over."

Gaylen and Pete, having downed quite a few beers over the course of the last few hours happily agreed. Then, too, if they didn't have to cover their bets up front, they'd have more money for drinks. At any rate, Pete said, "Sounds all right to me. Probably won't take long to rack up $10, you think?"

"Probably not, as long as it ain't my ten," Gaylen retorted.

The game began. By the time Cord had lost five dollars, Gaylen and Pete were taking turns leaving after every hand to relieve themselves or to get another beer. At this rate, Cord's $10 would be spent long before supper even if the drinks were only ten cents each. Fat chance of getting rid of his saddle.

About then, Cord's luck changed, or he began to understand the concept of bluffing a bit better. Or the other two were just too drunk to notice. In another hour, he had won the whole $30 in chips.

Gaylen and Pete had a brief conference on the rules of going from low stakes to high stakes, then decided the honorable thing to do was for each to pay up the $10 owed and start over. Cord agreed, pocketing two of the $5 gold coins Pete and Gaylen flipped on the table and left the other two to cover his future bets.

Strangely Pete and Gaylen stopped drinking. Even so, after another three hours, Cord had collected the chips several more times. The disgruntlement of his playing partners was getting pathetic. While they obviously had not been down to their last two dollars as claimed, they also hadn't planned on losing $50 apiece to Cord. "Probably was the sum total of their wages for at least two months," Cord thought.

For all that it had been fun, Cord was getting hungry, and he still had no real taste for gambling. He remembered a few years back when he'd ridden to Nevada to take three hundred cows for breeding stock to a new ranch the Agency had acquired. On his way back, he'd stopped in Winnemucca and lost all but two dollars on the wheel. He'd vowed then and there that he'd never tempt Lady Luck so seriously again. So in spite of his newfound skills, he had no intention of capitalizing on them, even if they were real. Somehow, he doubted that.

He rose from the table, produced $50 from his pocket and said, "Tell you what boys. You can pick up my Hamley saddle at the stable, and take half my winnings so you can find some other beginner who's not so lucky. In the meantime, we'll just pretend this afternoon never happened."

Pete looked at Gaylen in astonishment. Cord had long since decided they were just a pair of simple cowpokes with no ulterior motives after all. So he wasn't surprised when both tipped over their chairs in their rush to get to their feet to shake his hand.

"If that's the way you want it?" Pete exclaimed.

Gaylen said, "You sure you ain't never played poker afore?"

"I'm sure," said Cord as he finished scribbling a slip of paper to serve as a bill of sale for his saddle. Handing it to Pete, he was only too glad to turn and leave the room, which by now had become quite crowded, noisy, and smoke-filled, just the kind of place he didn't care for.

A Cowboy In Trouble

Cord slept in, remaining in a half-dream state until nearly 7:30 the next morning. Each time he turned in his bed, he tried to figure why he wasn't at the ZX and how much longer it would be before he would get there. Finally glimmers of the last few days began penetrating his sleep-drugged brain. At first, he just plumped his pillow, twisted on his back and tried to concentrate on his future.

He could not envision himself repeating any of the jobs he had held in the past, mainly doing ranch work with an occasional rodeo thrown in for excitement. Never again! He tried to imagine a job in construction, in a mine, in a sawmill. No sharp image would come into focus, so he buried his head under the pillow attempting to drift off again.

Turning and twisting but finding no comfort, he finally climbed wearily from the too-warm covers and pulled on his clothes. Remembering yesterday, he realized that the small pack of clothes along with the pair of army blankets his mother had insisted he take when he left Lapwai were the sum total of his earthly possessions. Cord dejectedly propped his head on his hand, lowering his elbow for support to his knee. Even the thinker's position did not lead him to a clear notion of where he was going or what he was going to do next.

Yesterday, he had come to the conclusion that Copperfield would be right, but this morning, he wondered why or if he really wanted to go into a hot dry canyon to live among gamblers in a dying town.

He knew that if he could go where he wished and do what he wanted, he'd go to Wallowa where the senior Chief Joseph of the Nez Perce was buried. His uncle, Bearclaws, had described to Cord an enchanted land richer than any other. It had supported a large band of Nez Perce and their horses for many years. That was before the white-man battles that forced the tribe to the Reservation at Lapwai thirty years ago.

Bearclaws told of the beautiful rippling waters in the cold streams and the lake with no beginning. The fish from it so tasty they were without equal. The tall grasses fed deer and elk so sleek and fat that in winter, their hides reflected gold in the morning sun. The wondrous canyons with rainbow colored walls were from the land of dreams. Early summer mornings were the best when riding through the warm mists was like gliding effortlessly in a canoe on a quiet river.

But both Bearclaws and his mother had sternly warned him never to go there unless in the company of a white man because the Indian's presence in that region was forbidden by white man's law. Yet it was his Garden of Eden, and he would reach it some day, if only to peer at the towering mountaintops and feel the freedom and peace of the land.

As a young boy, his friends and he would often hike to a rimrock overhang on the Reservation, throw themselves on their bellies and crawl along with their willow-stick bows and arrows pretending a take-over battle in the Wallowas. Whenever he now heard the song of the white man about their flag and heard the last words, "the home of the brave," he knew where the hearts of his brave childhood friends lived, even though it was no longer their home.

Cord recalled the times they appointed him to be the conquered white man in those battles. He also remembered the abuse the others heaped on him for his stupidity and greed. It was then that his thoughts would turn to his white father.

Cord didn't know if his most pleasant memory was of time spent with his industrious, talkative father, or if it might have been that with his quiet, shy, but always smiling mother. In either case, all such memories ceased to exist for him 20 years ago when he was just eight years old.

Although the details of his recollections were beginning to fade, he could still vividly recall his father's return from work, usually after dark. The senior Williams would pick up his small son and toss him high in the air, laughing at the child's shrieks and giggles. Putting Cord down, he would go to Redwing, whose name was different now. He would hold her close, tenderly caressing her arms and back. First she would lean against him, then turn her head upward for a kiss. She, too, would giggle, though Cord did not know why.

Grasping her husband's hand, she would lead him to the table he had built from small, halved logs, the bark still clinging to them under the tabletop. She would signal for him to sit on the bench made in the same style. Sometimes she would fall into his lap to kiss him again. Other times, she would tug hard to get him to release her hand, which he never seemed willing to do. Then she would dish up his supper from the kitchen range and set it before him. She loved to watch him eat, so she would seat herself on a smoothly cut block of wood that she often used for a stepping stool to reach the high kitchen shelves.

After a few bites, Tom Williams would declare that this food was pure ambrosia, the true food of the gods. He would chew happily, spearing bite after bite with his fork, while describing what had happened at the mine that day.

Cord also remembered his father teaching him to read—usually on a rainy day or on a very cold one when he didn't go to work. His mother would again draw up the block stool while Cord sat on an inverted set of deer antlers that were rigged with softly padded deer hide.

Later at Lapwai, Cord had the reputation of a whiz kid at the Christian school because he could read just about anything. Perhaps it was because he could show off and be rewarded by both the teacher and his fellow students, but he really liked to read. When he was eleven, the teacher taught him about poetry. Of course, it was white man's poetry, even though the teacher was Indian.

On one occasion, he asked his teacher if the Nez Perce had no poetry. The teacher explained to him that in order to live a happy life, he had to forget about Indian ways. He might have believed Mr. Griffin, the teacher, but his uncle Bearclaws had spent a great deal of time telling him the history and tales of the Nez Perce. While describing details of great battles the Nez Perce fought trying to hold their land, the old man was often reduced to tears. When he felt he needed to pick up the pace, he'd also recite moral tales featuring coyotes, rabbits, and eagles, all of which made a lot of sense to Cord.

Having spent considerable time at Lapwai while his back healed last fall, he knew that he would do whatever was necessary to survive without "getting along as an Indian" on a reservation. He knew he lacked his uncle's courage to adapt to such an idle existence. He also knew he would work hard every day of his life if that were necessary in order to avoid just sitting and waiting to die.

Sighing, Cord finished dressing, then rose to pick up his leather vest from the top of his pack. When he put it on, he felt the weight of the money in his pocket. Briefly, he considered going away to the mountains to live in solitude. Then he remembered, he didn't even have a horse.

Cord was just finishing his breakfast of pan-fried potatoes and scrambled eggs when a voice from the hotel lobby caught his attention.

"Yeah," the newly arrived man was saying, "the Carter boys found his body last night. He was lying in some brush about 150 feet from the dead horse."

The clerk's voice was not quite as loud, and Cord missed his part of the conversation.

The voice resumed, "Oh yeah, they definitely figure they know who did it. They said they met an Injun riding that same horse a week or ten days ago, up by the cemetery in Malheur City. The guy had black hair done up in a braid. He had his head covered with one of them stupid tall black hats, and he was wearing black woolly chaps. He was riding a fancy saddle, too good for an Injun, unless he stole it. Anyway the Carters figure the Injun had probably sold old Locksley the horse, then followed along to steal him back as soon as Clayton got off for a pee break. Locksley's rifle was lying right there on the ground no more than thirty feet away from him. He musta got in a gun battle with the Injun, or maybe the Injun was running off with the horse, and Locksley got off a shot and accidentally hit his own horse."

Cord listened intently as he rose to pay for his breakfast. Moving closer to the conversation, he heard the clerk asking, "How'd they know the horse was Locksley's and not the Indian's?"

"Hell, that's easy," the cowboy laughed. "The horse had Locksley's outfit on it. Old Clayton wouldn't steal anybody's horse, that's sure. Hell, he had money to pay for about anything he ever wanted. I know. I worked the harvest for him last fall."

"So what are they doing about Locksley now?" the clerk inquired.

"The Carter boys sent me on down to contact the Baker sheriff, which I did a while ago from the depot. They said they'd stay right by the body until he can get there. Sheriff'll probably come in on the morning train if he had time enough to catch it. Then, I suppose he'll get a horse from the stable, and go on up there. If he does, he should get there before dark. I dunno. I guess if the sheriff doesn't show, they'll take the body back to the ranch this evening."

Cord didn't think the hotel clerk, nor apparently anyone else in the lobby had any knowledge of yesterday's transactions. Yet he hoped Gaylen and Pete had left town early this morning like they said they would. If they had, that probably left only Burt, the stable hand, with any knowledge of the details. But, even those would be known to the sheriff within minutes after his arrival. At least, if he were the sheriff trying to back track a horse deal, the livery would be his first stop.

Cord's heart was thumping hard as he considered the ramifications of those jerks identifying him as Patches' previous owner. It was true, he had visited his father's grave in Malheur City as he rode through to Agency Valley last week, and they quite likely had seen him. With any luck though, his newly barbered hair, his blue eyes, and the fact that there was no trace of the woolly chaps would work sufficiently in his favor to throw suspicion elsewhere, at least for a while. Pulling his gray Stetson as low as he could, he walked quietly through the lobby escaping everyone's attention. All eyes and ears were thoroughly glued to the man telling everything he knew about Locksley, the Carters, the sheriff, and whatever other topic came up. For the moment, that guy was truly the man of the hour.

For a brief moment, Cord considered going to look for Gaylen and Pete to have them vouch for his innocence. Then he changed his mind. While they'd been perfectly happy yesterday evening, they might not be so charitable about losing so much money this morning, "especially," he thought bitterly, "to a half-breed."

Cord crossed the street to check on the train schedule. Right now, he'd take any destination just to get away. He'd even hop a freight if it were going east. The time table revealed that the next train would be from Baker City. If the sheriff were on it, he'd be here in another hour or so. While standing on one foot, then the other, wondering what his chances were of getting out of Huntington undetected, a man wearing blue bib overalls, a gray work shirt, and a straw hat approached him. "Must be a farmer," Cord concluded.

"Hey fellow," the man said, "How would you like to earn a couple of bucks?"

Cord tried hard to control his trembling hands. "Doing what?" he asked sullenly. Of all the times for somebody to want something!

"Loading a piano on my wagon."

Cord could feel the desire to look past the man, but he held his eyes in place to look squarely at the fellow. The man's hair was beginning to gray at the temples. He was in his late fifties or early sixties, stood just a little shorter than Cord, about six feet. And he was definitely a farmer.

"It's just down the street a ways. You see," the farmer launched into the story of his problem. "My mother-in-law died a few weeks ago. Now the house is sold, and she left her piano to my wife. But I've moved that monstrosity before, and it'll take several good men to get it loaded on my wagon to take it home."

On the one hand, Cord would have an excuse to get away from the depot unnoticed. Maybe he could jump a freight later on somewhere down the tracks. On the other hand, the fewer people he met, the better. "You said several men," Cord queried. "Where you getting the rest of your help?"

"I think the neighbors on either side may be at home, maybe even the people who bought the house. But I figure I'd better bring a little help with me, or neighbors'll think I'm crazy." At this point, he extended his hand, "Ed Miller's the name."

Cord supposed he had nothing to gain by being secretive about himself. "Cord Williams," he responded. "I guess I could help you out a bit. I've got some time on my hands until the next train anyway."

"That so?" Ed remarked.

As it turned out, there were no neighbors or new owners near the empty house when the two men pulled up in the wagon. But there were a couple of planks lying near the yard fence, which were useful in getting the piano loaded. In fact, when it came to lifting the instrument, Ed was impressed.

"You know, I think if you were able to get a grip on this boxcar," he announced, fondly patting the piano, "I'll bet you'd lift it all by yourself." Cord smiled in spite of himself. He had frequently impressed other men with his brute strength.

"Sure wish I had your help at the other end when I have to unload this thing though. I'm not sure my old lady can handle it."

"So where are you headed with it?"

"Down the river a ways. About fifteen miles. Got a little dairy setup there. Take me all day to get there, I'm afraid. Gotta make sure I don't tip this piano over or get it scratched up any on the way."

Cord's thoughts began spinning. Fifteen miles—all day in the opposite direction. No one in town at present really knew who he was or where he would be going. It just might work; but first he had to get his stuff back at the hotel, and he hadn't checked out earlier.

"You coming back this way before long?" Cord asked.

"Why? Where were you headed anyway?"

"Well if I left today, I was going to Nevada; but later on, who knows, maybe down Copperfield way," Cord replied.

"You either have to take a train or ride to get anywhere from here. I suppose you don't have a horse, or you wouldn't have been hanging around the depot. Tell you what though, there was a miner came through a few days ago, riding a mare. He left her with me saying he bought her from my brother at the livery in Copperfield. But he didn't have any place to take care of her at the mine. He wanted me to buy her, but I didn't have the price, so I agreed to keep her until somebody might be riding through and would be willing to buy her or at least take her back to my brother. Figured the guy could pick up his refund whenever he wandered over that way again."

Cord almost asked, "How much?" Then he decided it would be poor policy to circulate the money he had on him. The banker might know something about Locksley's gold if some of it got deposited from an unlikely source. But the proposition did sound good.

"Tell you what," Cord offered after a quick decision on how to handle things. "I'll go check out of the hotel, and I'll come help you with the piano job. I can probably work out something on the horse. Maybe I can locate the miner, maybe work for him a while and make him a deal." Cord paused, then added, "I'm kind of short on cash myself. I didn't really know how I was going to afford a ticket anyway," he added in order to further his image as a man down on his luck, not one who had just sold his horse and outfit in a lovelorn snit.

"Okay," Ed said, grinning from ear to ear. "I'll just drive on up the street there and get this wagon turned around in the right direction, then wait for you to get your things."

"Fine," Cord said. "I'll be back in a jiffy." Cord felt like sprinting to the hotel to hurry his departure, but he ambled along at a somewhat leisurely pace to keep from arousing anyone's suspicions.

—

The train whistle sounded repeatedly across the late summer morning as #7 came into view from the West. As the squealing wheels noisily brought the passenger train to a halt, a tall man, wearing his hat low on his forehead, stepped out of the caboose on to the platform. He was carrying a blanket and a pair of saddlebags. The train was still moving when he swung to the ground along side the track. Walking quickly in purposeful strides, he made his way forward. Entering the depot, he made a brief stop at the telegrapher's window.

Shoving a completed brief Western Union message to his office in Baker City across the window ledge, Sheriff Ted Yargo addressed the clerk. "Keep an eye on my belongings," he ordered. "Be back within the hour." Not waiting for a reply, he resumed his rapid progress to his planned destination across the street to the Depot Hotel.

—

The hotel clerk hardly glanced up when Cord returned the key after going to his room to pick up his pack.

"On your way, huh?" the clerk murmured while continuing to study several sheets of paper he had spread on the counter in front of him.

"Guess so," Cord responded.

"Stop in again when you're by this way," the clerk invited.

"Sure will," Cord replied in as cheerful a voice as he could muster.

—

While entering the hotel door, Sheriff Yargo was surprised to accidentally brush shoulders with a man of equal height, though more than a decade younger and a stoneweight lighter. The man was carrying a rather large, neatly compacted bundle tied with a length of lasso. The exterior of the bundle showed only the trappings of an Army blanket.

Observing the man's proud height, the sheriff concluded the fellow had probably just finished a stint with Uncle Sam. Tipping his hat politely, he murmured his apology for not looking where he was going. The hotel clerk noticed the encounter and called out, "Sheriff you're a fast one. I suspect you're here about the Locksley murder."

"That I am, Joe," said Yargo in a deep resonating voice. Moving forward, he queried, "You got anything for me?"

"Can't say as I have. Been beating my brain for the past hour and a half trying to remember if I saw any Indian types lurking around."

"Why Indian?"

"That was the report that Barnes fellow gave, the one who said he wired you."

"Oh, what exactly did he say?"

"Let's see if I can recall. He said he reported to you that Locksley was found dead at the Dixie Creek forks over toward Mormon Basin. Said the Carter boys are waiting for you before moving the body that they found late yesterday evening. Then he said the Carter brothers told him they figured from what they knew about the dead horse lying there, a long-haired Indian, wearing black woolly chaps rode through there about ten days ago. They thought the Indian had probably sold the pony to Locksley then followed along to steal him back and pocket the money."

"How'd they know Locksley owned the horse and not the Indian," Yargo wanted to know.

"The horse was wearing Locksley's outfit. But I sure ain't seen any Indians lurking around here."

"None sitting around on the sidewalk that you know of, huh?"

"Nope, not in front of this hotel, anyway."

"Well, let me see your register," Yargo commanded. "Maybe a guest will recall something that'll help."

The sheriff perused the register, noting six sign-ins the previous day. Unfortunately five were designated Mr. and Mrs. Further bad luck, four of them had already checked out. That left only one single. Yargo studied the signature, then requested, "Joe, how do you make this one out?"

Joe returned from pouring a cup of coffee and squinted at the signature from his side. "Looks like C. Wilson, maybe Wilcox. Can't say for sure. Looks like one of them doctor-type signatures. But I can tell you about the man. You just met him in the foyer there as you were coming in."

"Huhm!" grunted the sheriff. "I've warned you before, Joe, to make sure a signature is legible before you hand out a key."

"Sorry," Joe murmured. "Guess I was kinda busy."

Taking a few seconds longer with the register detail, Yargo added, "Looks like he checked in about 1:30 yesterday afternoon. Did he come in on the train, do you think?"

"Can't say. He registered, then was gone three or four hours, then came in, ordered a bath, ate his supper, and as far as I know, went to his room the rest of the night."

"Gives him a pretty good alibi for the night, I guess."

"That and the fact that his hair is cut short," added Joe. "Was one funny thing though. He came in here toting a saddle and tack. I don't know if he was looking for a horse or just got shuck of one. Anyway, he took it on over to the livery stable for Burt to look after. That's when he was gone for most of the afternoon."

"You know anything about this Barnes fellow, the one that reported the murder?"

"Nothing particular. Man of about 26 or 27 years old I'd say. I've seen him around a few times the last couple of years. Says he worked for Locksley about a year ago. All I know about this morning is he stood around reporting the murder for fifteen or twenty minutes, then hightailed it out of here, saying he was going back to rejoin the Carters."

"What about the Carters? Know them?"

"Not well," Joe responded. "They hail from down Nevada way. Been up in the Basin for a while though—probably a year or more. Can't say whether they might be mining over Malheur City way, or if they're cowboying for some rancher up there."

Flipping the register to a new page, Yargo pushed it toward Joe and said," Thanks anyway. Guess I'll go on over to see Burt at the livery stable. Have to get something to ride."

―

Cord was puffing lightly from his hurried trip to the hotel and back. He eagerly tossed his pack under the buckboard seat as he rejoined Ed Miller at the end of the street connecting to the road heading into Snake River canyon. Announcing, "I'm ready," he hopped up on the buckboard seat.

The conversation was sparse until they were well away from Huntington. Toward noon, Ed handed Cord the reins while he scrounged beneath his feet for a flour-sack wrapped around a pair of cheese sandwiches and a jar of sun-warmed milk.

He divided the booty with Cord, then for some reason began asking questions on a variety of subjects. Cord fielded them with some measure of truth. He even admitted to playing poker the day before, letting Ed think he had lost both his horse and saddle to a couple of cowpokes.

Later in the afternoon, a light sprinkle began. Having been tempted to play a few notes on the piano before loading it, Cord felt the need to do something to protect this beautiful instrument from the rain. It's wonderful rich tone was unlike any piano Cord had ever heard. It was much more like accompaniment for a heavenly choir than any of the dozens of player pianos he had listened to in the saloons he sometimes frequented.

"Look Ed," he said, "Let's stop and put my blankets around the piano."

Ed objected, "Aw this is just a squall. Probably be over before we could get the damned thing covered up."

"If your wife warned against scratching it as you say," Cord countered, "she sure won't be happy if it's damaged by the rain."

Ed sighed, drew the horses up, wrapped the reins around the brake stick, and began loosening the ropes used to hold the piano steady. In the meantime, Cord found his pack, undid the two army blankets, then retied his clothes inside the flour-sack pillow cover he had folded among his things.

The Sheriff Investigates

Drawing his hat down on his forehead, the sheriff set out in a stride that would have made a ten-year-old run full tilt to keep up.

Burt had no knowledge of the Locksley murder, but he was chockfull of information about the horse purchase. Yes Locksley had bought the horse the previous day because the mare he rode in on had stumbled and fallen on him one too many times. Paid $100 in gold he had told Burt when he collected his gear to start home. Locksley thought he'd made a good buy and was anxious to get home to show his wife and to get on with the grain harvest. No, Burt hadn't seen any Indians, much less a longhaired one. Yeah, he knew the name of the man who sold the horse, "Williams," he said. "Can't recall the first name though. Carl, maybe, or Kurt, something like that."

"You sure the last name wasn't Wilson or Wilcox?"

"Couldn't have been. He said to tell Locksley just to ask for Williams at the Depot Hotel."

"He must not have actually registered, then," observed Yargo.

"You sure?" Burt asked. "I could have sworn he came out of the Depot Hotel earlier this morning when I came back from having coffee."

"You don't say," remarked the sheriff. "Funny, he came out again a little while ago. Joe said he stored his saddle and tack here yesterday. Can I see it?"

"Sorry, can't oblige you there sheriff. Pete Ford and Gaylen Harrington from up Weatherby way came by the first thing this morning with a bill of sale from this Williams guy. They said they won the saddle fair and square in a poker game yesterday afternoon. Well, they didn't exactly win it. They 'fessed up that he gave it to them after they spent the afternoon teaching him the finer points of playing poker. They thought he was headed down Copperfield way and might need some skills along those lines."

"You got the bill of sale handy then?"

"Well, no, sheriff. Those fellows took it with 'em, but it was signed by Williams all right."

"Guess that's that then," the sheriff muttered almost as if he were talking to himself. "No long-haired Indians around, though, you're sure?"

"I reckon you could hang a braid or two on this Williams guy. A good barber can sure as hell remove 'em in a hurry. But he didn't strike me as the Indian-type. He spoke like an educated gent and seemed pretty mellow."

"Did you notice the color of his eyes?"

"Sure did. They were blue. Must be Irish, or maybe German."

"I thought so too," the sheriff added. "So what you got in the way of a horse I can use for a few days?"

Burt chuckled. "Got the mare Locksley left here. But I guess you wouldn't be wanting to ride her," Burt said quickly, seeing the scowl on Yargo's face. "Nah, I have a brown gelding out here. Bought him about a week, ten days ago from some cattle buyer out of Baker City. He was most anxious to take his sore butt back on the train after delivering several hundred head of long yearlings from ranchers hereabouts."

"Sounds okay. If you'll get him ready, check his feet and shoes, and put up a bag of oats, I'll be back in a half an hour or so. I'm going to check in to see if the barber collected any long black hair yesterday, then take a look at the other hotel registers up and down the street.

The sheriff rode out a while later, after securing the extra blanket and his saddlebags across the back of the saddle. Burt figured Yargo hadn't found any evidence of importance because all he said was. "If anybody asks, I'll be out in Mormon Basin country to see if I can get any leads. Should put up tonight at the Locksley Ranch. Maybe I can do something there to help out after we pack the body in."

Burt wondered about the "we" part, then speculated maybe the sheriff was deputizing somebody to go with him. Yet that wasn't Yargo's style. In his years as sheriff, he'd made quite a reputation for himself for bringing in the guilty. But his methods usually called for getting a fix on the criminal first, then calling out extra deputies or a posse to take the accused alive.

Yargo checked his watch at the north end of Main Street in Huntington, flipped a little notebook open, noted the time, and returned the notebook to his vest pocket. He planned to see how long it would take to reach Locksley's place of demise. Several things were not adding up in the picture he had put together so far.

As he rode north and climbed out of the Burnt River Canyon to the west, he tried to put events in order in his mind. So far, he knew from the message he received in Baker City that there were two brothers named Carter, who had come across Locksley yesterday evening. Then a fellow named Earl Barnes had contacted him, reporting the homicide and requesting he be on the lookout for an Indian with long black, braided hair, wearing black woolly chaps and a tall black hat when last seen. Barnes added that the Carters would be waiting at Dixie Creek Forks until he could get there if he could come this morning.

Yargo didn't know what to expect at the Forks. Maybe Carters were running a scam and they'd be long gone when he got there. Or maybe, they were just mistaken about who sold the horse to Locksley. Maybe Williams had bought the horse from an Indian, then changed his mind and sold it. As he topped the ridge out of the canyon, he noticed fresh horse prints in the rain-sprinkled road dust. "Must be the Barnes fellow returning to see what's going on," the sheriff noted.

Generally, Yargo didn't care to have help from the public in a manhunt before he knew the identity of the criminal. Fellows that got in on the action from the beginning tended to muddy the waters with their opinions. They were likely to exaggerate the facts more than necessary. But once a suspect was certain with or without a name, it was far easier to control deputies or posse people.

Regretfully, the sheriff considered that if he were a man exercising extreme caution, he'd probably have taken the time to locate Williams. Two things were in evidence for certain. One, Williams had sold Locksley the horse yesterday, and two, he couldn't have killed Locksley if the Carters and Barnes had any of their facts right. Williams couldn't be fifteen or twenty miles up Dixie Creek on the south side of Pedro Mountain and at the same time be playing poker in Huntington. Still it might have helped to find out just where Williams did acquire that horse. It probably would have cleared up the Indian thing once and for all.

As Yargo neared the lower reaches of Pedro Mountain in Mormon Basin, he began looking in the distance for signs of some activity and the possible site of the Locksley murder.

He rode for another half-hour before detecting one set of willows leading away to the north and another line developing somewhat to the south. "Must be the place," he thought. While he wasn't wearing spurs, the powerful kick of his heels against the horse's side worked just as well. The gelding broke into an easy lope heading downward the last mile to the Forks.

The three men spotted Yargo riding toward them several minutes before his actual arrival. They were standing in the open along the roadside as he approached.

"Afternoon fellows," he greeted the trio. Stepping down from his mount and swinging the reins and lead rope free of the horse's neck, he turned to the men and proceeded with a round of handshakes.

"Sometimes," he thought, "a nervous, not-so-firm, handshake could tell reams about a situation."

No such luck today though. Each man gave a warm firm hand into the sheriff's grip and introduced himself as well.

"Earl Barnes," the first man said. "I telegraphed you earlier this morning."

"Jeff Carter," the second man greeted Yargo. "My brother Ralph and I found the body when we were looking around for a place to bed down last night."

Ralph might have been a little on edge, Yargo thought. But maybe he was just the quiet type, being the youngest of the three assembled. His handshake was steady enough.

"I want to thank you fellows before I forget," Yargo launched the conversation. "It's always a pleasure to deal with people who take their civic duty seriously."

"That's okay Sheriff," Jeff observed. "Poor son-of-a-bitch is over here if you want to take a look." All three men walked ahead of the sheriff into a brushy area about 100 feet from the water's edge.

The grass and weeds were somewhat trampled down near the body, which had thoughtfully been covered with a saddle blanket to prevent flies and other wilderness creatures from full access.

The sheriff surveyed the immediate area determining that the body wasn't dragged to its present location. Still it could have been carried easily enough if more than one man was involved in the killing. He'd have to study the footprints he could see near the water's edge for any sign of weight differential in the imprints.

Barnes was folding back the blanket. Yargo kneeled on one knee to inspect the body, determine the direction of the fall if possible, and to see if the trajectory of the fatal bullet could be detected. Also, he checked for any other clues that might provide information on the cause and time of death.

Reaching in his vest pocket for his minuscule notebook and pencil stub, he wrote: Body oriented to northwest indicating shot from behind. Bullet entered back of neck, tearing away front of throat. Noting other apparent details before turning the man completely on his back, he began questioning the witnesses.

The brothers reported they had ridden in from the south and arrived close to dark. The sun had already set. They noticed the horse first. Seemed it hadn't been dead very long. It was still warm and bleeding. Then they spotted the man.

"Why didn't one of you ride on to the ranch last night?"

"Well, Sheriff," said Jeff, "it didn't take much imagination to figure this for murder. We could have taken him on to the ranch, or we could have ridden out last night to contact you. But we had been on the trail all day. Our horses were tired. There was a killer out there somewhere, and it is the dark of the moon.

"We talked it over and decided one of us would go for help first thing this morning. In fact we were just deciding on who'd go, Ralph or me, when Earl rode up. Even then, we had a tough time deciding if two should go, in case the Indian was somewhere along the way, or two should stay, for the same reason. But we finally decided we'd better hang in here and send Earl on by himself."

"Makes sense," the sheriff agreed. "Have you checked around for tracks?"

"Not much," Ralph replied when neither of the other men seemed inclined to answer. "Guess we can do that now if you want."

The sheriff rose saying, "I think the best thing to do now is get the body loaded on a horse and take it on to the ranch. Can't be more than another couple of miles."

"It's about three miles," Earl said quietly. The sheriff glanced in his direction, noting that he was looking rather green from having viewed the grisly throat of the dead man. "If you like," Earl added, "I can put him on Morris here and walk him in."

"Why don't you do that? Jeff can go along with you. Ralph can back me here while I look around a little more. Then we'll be along too. Probably get there about the same time you will."

Jeff looked at Ralph, whose head was lowered, his eyes trained on his boots. "Sure Sheriff. Whatever you say," he said pensively.

The four men carefully secured the body across the saddle of Earl's horse. Jeff led off a few minutes later, the reins of his horse wrapped loosely around his right hand. Earl followed, gingerly leading his horse into the late afternoon sun.

While the sheriff looked around for footprints leading away from the scene anywhere in the radius of a couple hundred yards, he noted that Ralph stayed put. Yargo didn't know why, but he really didn't think he'd find any moccasin prints, and strangely enough, he was pretty sure Ralph didn't think so either. On the other hand when he noted the location of the gun and began looking at it as a telltale sign, Ralph came to life.

"We never touched that gun, sheriff," he protested as he watched intently while the sheriff kneeled to study that object before touching it. "Kind of looks like it was thrown there, don't you think?" Ralph asked.

"One thing's sure," the sheriff responded, "Locksley never threw that gun over here after he was shot. He must have thrown or dropped it before he tried to outrun the bullet that got him. That would mean there was probably more than one shot. Maybe there's a cache of cartridges around here somewhere." With that, the sheriff rose to get the blanket from his pack. He realized there was probably very little point as far as evidence was concerned, but he'd try to wrap the gun to check it later for fingerprints.

Yargo tied the blanketed gun to his saddle, then looked the dead horse over for any additional information he might glean. He was pretty certain he had the picture of how things had happened. Locksley had dismounted his horse, planning to walk to the creek's edge. A shot rang out from the south hitting the horse between the eyes and stopping his forward progress within one or two steps. The horse fell on his right side. Locksley grabbed for his rifle, got it loose, probably in the midst of a barrage of bullets. Instead of dropping to the ground to use the dead horse as a shield, he started to run parallel to the creek. Maybe the horse was still thrashing around.

As Locksley entered the thicker brush, he may have tripped, or he may have been planning a belly flop for cover. At any rate, a bullet caught him in the neck, and in his forward momentum, the rifle may have flown out of his hand to its resting-place.

That scene made sense to the sheriff except for the detail of the rifle. It was located almost exactly behind Locksley. On top of that, its barrel was 180 degrees in the wrong direction if Locksley had dropped it as he ran. It really looked as though somebody had simply taken the rifle by the barrel and hurled it thirty feet in the direction of the shooter and away from the location of the body.

Well, he'd have to work on that for a while. Certain that he had the scene well in mind and was finished with recording a number of details in his notebook, Sheriff Yargo said, "C'mon, let's ride."

A meek Ralph Carter quietly obeyed.

The shower performed as predicted and was over after only a few oversized drops. Still, Cord wasn't apologetic for his insistence on placing his blankets around the piano, and he was pleasantly surprised later when Ed's wife, Pauline, rewarded him with the last piece of apple pie after dinner.

Then, too, his cause was not hurt by the fact that the Millers thought the army blankets originated during his service in the U. S. Cavalry. They assumed that he had served for quite some time and was reticent to talk about his past. Just how they came to that conclusion, Cord was not sure. It was just that when they got close to inquiring about the last six or seven years of his life, he managed to steer the conversation in a different direction.

Actually, he had never been comfortable explaining his relationship with his employer's daughter. It had been stormy and exciting and thought provoking, especially after her eighteenth birthday. She had become a full-grown beautiful woman. For the next year, Cord tried, at times, to get used to that fact. But to him, she was still a kid until she began demanding commitment. When she turned twenty in February, just before he left, he told her he wanted to go to see his mother over in Idaho, but when he returned, they'd get married. Truthfully, he was planning to build up a small saving so Norm Barstow wouldn't feel obligated to continue to take care of her. Yet to report that he had spent nearly six years wrangling cows on the ZX, a job he didn't even like, seemed without purpose.

"Hell," Ed said later when he and Polly were readying for bed downstairs, while Cord had retired in the loft with the Miller's two young sons, "He might have even served in the war."

"What war," Polly wanted to know. "Not the civil war, certainly."

"No, no," Ed replied. "You know, the insurrection in the Philippines against Spain."

"Good Lord, Ed, that was fifteen years ago. He's too young for that." Cord heard no further conversation, and he very willingly drifted off to sleep and to dream.

Friends on the trail

On Saturday morning Cord woke to the sound of a dog barking at yipping coyotes. He first thought it was Teddy, a dog he used to own. Then he realized he wasn't out on the range somewhere gathering cattle. He was snuggled in a real bed, but not for long.

A sense of urgency descended on Cord so pronounced that a heavy dose of adrenaline pulsed through his veins. So much for any temptation to pull the covers more tightly around himself and ignore the creeping dawn of the rising sun.

Flinging the covers back, he quickly pulled on his clothes, tied his bootstrings, donned his hat and quietly began descending the loft ladder. His attempt at making a noiseless exit was for naught because Pauline was already busily shaking the grate to remove the ashes so she could light the kitchen stove.

"Good morning," she called as she spied his feet, then his legs descending the ladder.

"Good morning," Cord returned. "I suppose Ed's out milking the cows already."

"He's gathering them up," Pauline replied. "I'm going out to help him as soon as I get this pesky fire going. It has already burned out once. Too many ashes on the grate."

"Is your bucket already out there? I guess I can take time to help him."

"What do you mean 'take time'? You ain't goin' no where, are you?"

"Yeah, Polly, I need to head out this morning. I've been lying around here too long now."

"Some lyin' around," Pauline laughed. "Well you go ahead to the barn. I'm running a little late. I'll get breakfast goin', then get the boys on their feet. They're sure gonna to miss you around here. A whole week now, they haven't had to get up and do morning chores. I kinda hate it too. With more milch cows coming into full production any day now, we're going to have too much milk again.

"Going to have to start shipping cream for real instead of just making it into butter for the hotel in Huntington. Much as I don't care for churning butter all day long, I don't relish hauling them cream cans around neither. You can mention to Ed that he's going to have to deliver the hotel butter and this five-gallon can of cream today. I've got over a gallon of new cream saved up in the next can already. Oh yeah, and you can tell him that breakfast is waiting for him to get through milking."

"Sure Polly," Cord muttered as he made his exit thinking all the while, "That woman can sure get up a head of steam when she starts talking."

—

Ed was just locking down the stanchions on three cows when Cord entered the overhang area built on to the east side of the barn. "Mornin'" he called. "I wasn't sure you'd be back for another session with Old Buttercup after she kicked you over last night," he laughed.

"She didn't hurt me any, only my pride. I'll be watching her this morning," Cord answered.

"Tell you what, you milk January, and I'll keep score with Buttercup. Damnedest cow, she gives the richest milk and a lot of it. Only dries up about five or six weeks out of the year. But she's a mean old biddy."

Both men settled down, seated on blocks of wood. Bracing their heads into the cows' flanks, they commenced their musical tug of war. Extracting streams of steaming warm milk, they began the process of filling their buckets. Rhythmically mesmerizing, the ping of each stream soon filled the bottoms of the pails. After that, each tug added milk that absorbed itself quietly into mounting layers of foam.

Rising shortly after Ed finished one cow and seated himself at the second, Cord announced, "Pauline says you have to take the butter in for the Depot Hotel today. She also has a can of cream ready to go."

"Oh hell, I was planning to get that fence repaired over by the creek bank today. Now that the water's barely knee high, these old biddies'll be climbing the bank on the far side and wandering off where they don't belong, 'specially since the flies are getting thicker every day." Ed paused. "But I guess it don't make a helluva lot of sense to set around here squeezin' out a supply of cream and butter, then letting it go bad so as it won't sell. What you planning today, Cord?"

"I guess I'll mosey on up to find that miner today, see about working a deal on that mare. It's either that or I'll have to go on back to Huntington and ride the rails out somewhere," Cord replied.

"God, Cord, that's going quite a bit out of your way. Why don't you just take that nag on back to the stable like we talked about the other day?"

"You don't think there'll be trouble if I do that?"

"Hell no. The miner and me agreed I'd do that first chance I got, anyway. That guy isn't wanting to build up a big feed bill here, that's for sure," said Ed. "Tell you what, Cord. Since you're bound and determined to be on your way, you take the mare and ride her on down to Copperfield. See what you think. Hell, maybe you'll decide to come back and spend the winter with us. Poll and I could sure use your help."

A hundred possibilities flitted through Cord's mind. Could he get down the river like he originally planned without further delay? The story about the miner wanting a refund probably wouldn't be too welcome in Copperfield. Still it wasn't logical to suppose the sheriff or his deputies would be looking for him there without his long black hair and woolly chaps. But what if somebody made something out of his showing up on another man's horse?

"Sure, Ed," he said after deciding he'd take the risk. "I can do that. You're sure you can trust me with that horse and your outfit? If that miner decides he's been robbed, he'll come after you first."

"If you ain't to be trusted man, I don't know nothin' about this world we're in. I'm damned near 60 years old, married to my third woman, raisin' my second family, and I think I got a pretty good idee who can be trusted and who can't." Pushing away from his second cow, Ed continued, "Here, Cord, you can take my bucket of milk along with yours on up to the house. I'll turn these Bessies out and close the gate. You tell Polly to get her fanny in gear and have that butter wrapped and packed. I'll be in for breakfast shortly."

Cord nodded, took the two buckets and headed back to the house.

—

The kitchen was a little smoky when Cord lifted the milk buckets to the counter area, but the aroma of coffee brewing and sausage frying made Cord's mouth water. "Could be there's something to be said for getting married and settling down, after all," he decided.

"So is Ed going to haul the cream and butter in?" Polly began.

"Sounded like it. He said for you to get the butter wrapped and packed," Cord informed her.

"And what are your plans anyway?" Polly wanted to know.

"I'm borrowing Bell, the miner's mare—going on down to Copperfield to see if I can get work," Cord answered.

Pauline turned away. He knew she was disappointed. But he was beginning to wonder just why. She didn't seem to mind being out around the ranch doing things. He could appreciate that milking the cows was not really woman's work. Polly had dainty hands, perfect for playing the piano as she had readily demonstrated on his second evening here. They had sat side by side on the piano bench, she, playing every song they could think of, and he, serenading in his rich baritone voice. Occasionally Ed and their two sons joined in on the chorus, but mostly they just sat back and enjoyed, applauding when appropriate.

Of course, Cord had been more than a little surprised to see Polly at the milking barn at all that first evening, much less getting half again as much milk as her husband, in the same amount of time. When he later remarked on her success, she laughed and said, "Buttercup likes me. She doesn't hold up on me like she does for Ed."

Ed came in, and the three of them sat down to breakfast. For once, Polly didn't pursue a hundred different topics of conversation. But she did refill everyone's coffee cup not once but twice. When she rose for the third time, Cord got up too, picked up his coat and hat from the pile by the door and muttered that he'd better get Bell saddled and be on his way before the sun got too hot.

Ed said, "I'll be along in a bit," then went on sipping his coffee.

—

Cord dipped into the wooden barrel, filling a small pan with oats, then coaxed Bell to come to him. She gratefully chomped on the oats while he slipped the hackamore noose around her nose and secured it over her ears.

He turned toward the barn to see Ed emerging with his own bridle outfit to catch his horse. While saddling their mounts, both men were silent, each wondering how to start their parting conversation. Ed finally said, "Well Buddy, it's sure been nice having you around the last few days. We must 'a done as much work this past week as the old lady and I would've done all winter. Sure you can't stay a while longer?"

"Thanks anyway," Cord returned. "But I need to think seriously about rounding up a little pocket money so I can put an outfit together for myself."

"How was it, again, you came to be without anything at all?"

"You know how it is," Cord hesitated. "When you go depending on Lady Luck at the table." Cord hadn't satisfied either Ed or Pauline's curiosity about his past. "Sometimes you win. Sometimes you lose."

"Threw your rig, your horse, and everything in the pot, huh?"

"Kind of like that," Cord replied.

"Must 'a been holding a helluva hand to bet it all like that," Ed pursued. "Sure wish I could keep you on." After a long pause, he continued, "but me and Pauline couldn't offer you no more'd 'n room and board, leastways not until the end of the year or so. Gotta save all we can to make the mortgage payment in November."

Cord finished tightening the lattigo, wishing things were different. He wouldn't mind settling in for the winter right here. But he knew as sure as anything, somebody would have a wagon break down, or a baby would arrive on the scene before it was expected. Polly would likely spend the night with some family or other in the area. Then it would only be a matter of time until the gossip mill passed on information about him to the wrong people.

Just yesterday, a rider had stopped to ask for a drink of water and had caught Ed and Polly up on the news of Locksley's murder. Ed had later remarked that Sheriff Yargo had quite a reputation for tracking his man. Cord had the feeling that the sheriff tracked more through gossip in the neighborhood, than by following actual tracks.

Cord smiled to himself thinking how Pauline would be telling everyone for months to come how this "dark angel," as she called Cord, had helped dig out the well for cleaner water—water that had been muddied up by runoff from the rain. She'd mention how he had almost single-handedly dug a new and bigger root cellar. And he could just hear her laughter as she'd tell about his being up on the roof making repairs while Ed stood by or skinnied up and down the ladder to supply shingles or nails. He had no doubt that her audience would take an extraordinary interest in his identity.

Having finished preparing their mounts, both men met in front of Bell. Cord reached to shake hands with Ed, then found himself being embraced by the older man. "We sure do wish you the best of luck, boy. And you just leave Old Bell at the Iron Dyke Livery in case you decide to go on up to 'Copia to the mines or something," Ed said, stepping back. "If you do leave Copperfield, you tell that brother of mine where you're goin' and tell him I'll be down there for a visit before winter sets in. I'll pick up my outfit then. And don't you worry none about the feed bill at John's. I reckon I can pick that up, for cryin' out loud, seein' all you done for us."

Cord turned, reaching for the hackamore lead on Bell when he noticed Pauline and their two boys hurrying toward them. She was carrying a white bundle along with his army blankets secured around his bedroll. Rushing up to him, she announced, "Just a few scraps to keep you goin'. There's a sandwich, some cold milk, and some cookies."

"Thanks," Cord smiled. "I was just coming back to the house to get this stuff." Pauline in handing him his belongings, impulsively wrapped her left arm around his neck and gave him a sisterly peck on the cheek. He returned her quick hug then swung his attention to the two boys, shaking their hands and bidding them good-bye.

Pauline looked at Ed, who seemed to be having some difficulty adjusting a button on his shirt, while Cord tied his pack securely in place. "You all come back now, as soon as you can," she issued to Cord's high swinging form as he drew himself securely into the saddle.

"Yes ma'am," he answered. "You enjoy that piano your mamma left you, Polly. Maybe we can have a song-fest again one of these days when I get around to coming back through."

Cord walked Bell as far as the gate at the end of the lane, a hundred or so yards away. The boys hurried along at the horse's flank. They opened and shut the gate for him. He told them "Thanks," and told them to mind their mamma and their manners.

"You bet," the boys replied.

Cord stared northward to face a daunting climb where the river narrowed and mountains closed in ahead. As he doubled back along the creek bed toward the main wagon road, he came within hearing distance of the Millers. He heard the ka-thump of a post being tossed from the stack by the side of the barn, and he heard Pauline say, "Sure going to miss him though. He certainly is a good singer."

Cord smiled, feeling good about having real friends someplace again. Then he heard Pauline call, "How much Indian do you think he is?"

"Don't know," Ed answered. "Maybe none at all. Blue eyes and wavy hair usually don't happen to Indians around here. 'Sides that, he did shave once while he was here."

Cord didn't hear Pauline's next remark if she made one, but after a bit, he heard Ed say, "I got a feeling he's runnin' from something." Again, Cord couldn't hear Pauline, but Ed continued. "If not the law, maybe just himself. Man like that'll never stay in one place for long."

Ridin' on Down the River

Cord thought about Ed's assessment for a long while. He had thought he was ready to settle down with Bonnie Jean, but the more miles that he put between them, the more he felt that he was the lucky one. He hadn't made the big mistake after all.

The morning passed pleasantly enough, Cord thought. There was an abundance of wild life, fluttering, singing, jumping from the underbrush, or just plain grazing along the river and stream banks. Often times, the rhythm of the mare's feet clicking against rocks and gravel along the roadbed furnished a kind of drumbeat for the echoing sounds of other activities between the canyon walls.

Eagles and hawks made graceful swoops to snare little creatures. Once in a while they swooped so close to the water that Cord supposed they were catching fish. Deer sometimes jumped up from their repose startling the mare into a rapid side step. Other times, if they were already grazing, they would raise their heads, stop chewing, and eye the passing rider as if to wonder about this strange animal with a stick protruding from its back. Such were the images and lyrics of nature's melody.

Then the orchestration would falter into a pianissimo as the walls narrowed, and horse and rider ascended along a high grade with no real riverbank below. Twice the rises were so sharp and thickly strewn with avalanches of shale-like rock along the faint route of the canyon trail that Cord felt compelled to walk, leading his horse.

Mostly the descent from such places occurred within the next half mile. Being just as rapid as the rise, travelers soon found themselves right back along the river enjoying the valley where dancing bubbling creeks gurgled merrily. But the mountain waters' freedom and joy was short-lived since they were all too soon swallowed up into the quiet bosom of the Snake. It was at these junctures that Cord would dismount to allow his horse to rest and to ready for the next exhausting climb.

Cord arrived at the town of Robinette about noon. He was surprised to see so much hustle and bustle in one place. It reminded him of Huntington although its rail shipping area was minuscule by comparison. It was evident, however, that Robinette had grown in importance as a shipping point for cattle, ore, lumber, and produce from the higher valleys even if the trains were scheduled for only three runs a week. In addition to the depot, Cord noted there was a post office, a hotel, and a tavern as well as a scattering of houses where the bosses of the commercial enterprises lived.

Having long since consumed the scraps Polly provided him, he decided it would be a good idea to stop for a drink and another sandwich or two. Bell would have liked to snatch a few bites of the tall grass as they turned along the approach to the village. But Cord pulled her head up and proceeded to the nearby tavern.

Although Ed had told him Copperfield was an approximate 20 miles beyond Robinette, he inquired anyway just to make conversation with the bartender. There were no other customers.

"It's 20 miles by rail. Takes two or three hours on horseback. Going to work in the mines, are you?"

"Don't know," Cord replied. "I'm just looking for work."

"Most of the construction is over. Railroad's planning to start up again at Homestead, I guess, but not this fall. Quite a few power company families been packing out in order to get settled before school starts, I hear. There's a sawmill up Pine Creek a mile or two if you like sliver picking. You look more the cowboy type to me, though," the bartender observed.

"I've served my days at that," Cord grinned. "I'd like to make a little better wage than a dollar a day."

"I know what you mean," the man laughed. "I guess you could try the saloons. You might want to know, I hear their having a little trouble down that way. A pair of fires broke out last month. Each guy thinks the other one lit the match. Burned one outfit to the ground. The other one wasn't hurt too much."

When Cord finished his drink, he called his "Thanks."

The bartender responded with a friendly invitation in his best imitation of a southern drawl. "Ya all come back, now ya hear."

Cord put on his hat, saying "Sure thing."

The ride on down the canyon was almost as uneventful as before. But he did meet a few people. He also caught up with and passed a buckboard loaded with several cream cans. Since they were headed away from the Robinette depot, Cord supposed the cans were empties ready for a refill at some nearby dairy establishment. After his experience with Buttercup at the Millers, Cord was pretty sure he wouldn't be asking for a job at a dairy.

There was always Cornucopia; but he had heard the winters were hard, with even more snow than he was used to seeing in Agency Valley. But he'd bet there was a lot less wind. The temperatures were about the same according to the hands who wandered through the countryside in search of adventure.

As the hot sun beat down this late summer afternoon here in the canyon, Cord had a hard time featuring the weather getting cold enough to snow within the next hundred years, much less the next hundred days. Bell was getting dripping wet with sweat, so Cord took another turn at walking. Just when he decided to mount up again, he heard a train in the distance. He decided to stop and watch it pass even though he couldn't be more than two or three miles from Copperfield. If his horse was fresh, he might have decided to race the train. Every cowboy bragged that his steed could outrun a locomotive. But Cord knew that 90% of them were exaggerating, and the rest didn't stay in the lead for long. The iron horse just had a lot more staying power, whether cowboys liked it or not.

As the train went by, the engineer and fireman waved to Cord, having spotted him leaning forward, his arms crossed over his saddle horn. Cord's attention was riveted on the two men in the engine so that he caught only a glimpse of the single passenger car in the midst of the mixed train. Still, he thought he might have seen a lady's hat sporting bright blue feathers as the sunshine glinted off one of the coach windows.

—

"Hey Billy, she's a comin' in on the train," shouted Ollie Parker as he burst through the swinging panels on to the sawdust floor of The Golden Star saloon.

"Whoa boy," Marty Kellner's thunderous voice and club-like left arm interrupted the forward progress of the nine-year-old boy. Just where do you thing you're going?" he demanded.

"I come to tell Billy, the school teacher's comin'," the wriggling, kicking boy puffed.

"But you can't come in here, you know," said the saloonkeeper. "The honorable mayor has said no minors without an adult to accompany 'em, no matter what the time of day. Now where's your pa?"

"He's at the mine, 'a course; and Ma's getting ready to meet the train 'long with the other ladies. And I come to tell Billy like he wanted me to," said the frustrated child as he was being lowered to the floor.

"Well suppose I take care of telling Billy," offered the bulky man. "You just scoot along out of here, now." Pushing the child, none too gently, through the same swinging doors he had just entered, Marty succeeded in disengaging the youngster's presence from the premises.

Turning back to his damp cloth and bar polishing, Marty's double chin folded in on itself, revealing the considerable disappointment he felt regarding Ollie's eager report of the eminent arrival of the new school ma'rm. Frowning, he thought about calling Billy so that he could meet the train. On second thought, he decided not to bother.

Marty had hoped against hope to continue to employ sixteen-year-old Billy Mitchell through the fall and winter of this second year of business in the boomtown of Copperfield. It was very difficult to hire anyone to do the grunt work in a saloon. They either wanted to make big money as hirelings in the mine, on the railroad, or for the electric company. Or if they wanted to spend time around a saloon, they wanted to drink, try their luck at gambling, or sleep with the "working girls."

But his plan began to look bad two weeks ago when the school board voted to hire a woman from back East for the teaching position. Hers was the only application they had received all summer; so after a brief discussion, they figured that she'd undoubtedly serve for at least a few months. They couldn't see letting their new schoolhouse stand empty the way it had since last March when the previous teacher caught the Saturday afternoon train out of town, never to return.

From Marty's point of view, as well as that of a number of youngsters in the area, good news would have been that the teacher changed her mind and decided to remain in Philadelphia, or that she caught the wrong train somewhere along the line and ended up in California.

Marty knew that Billy didn't share his opinion of teachers as being meddlers and busy bodies, who messed around in a man's business, especially if the man's business happened to be in the liquor trade. In fact, his young employee had become a very happy lad since learning that school would be in session, beginning on the 17th of September.

As he told Marty, this would be his last chance to get his hands on all those books that were stacked on the desks in the schoolhouse, just waiting to be used on a first-come, first-served basis.

"Hell, Billy," Marty had opined, "If it's books you want, I'll get 'em for you somehow. The County School Superintendent said when he was here in May that he'd ship down all the books we need."

But Billy persisted. "Nah, it's not just the books I want. What I really want is somebody to talk to who knows about the world, about the presidents, about wars and stuff like that. Someday, I want to ride, like the Rough Riders did with President Roosevelt, and I want to see those airplanes fly like they did at Kitty Hawk."

"Where?" asked Marty.

"At Kitty Hawk, you know in North Carolina where the Wright brothers convinced people that they could build an airplane that would fly. O'course, now they got real planes. But I want to find out about things like that when they happen, or at least hear about them from somebody who knows how they work."

So it was going to be a lost cause in the long run; but for today, the floors would be freshened; the tables cleaned, the drinking glasses washed and the wood piled for fire in the evening in case it got too cool for comfort. The guys just didn't spend half as much money if it got cold. Funny thing, men could crowd around, jostle each other on hot summer nights sweating like pigs; and they'd stay until the wee hours just to palaver and have fun. But let it cool off so they had to put on an extra shirt, and they were gone.

"Oh hell," Marty muttered, as he heard Mayor Sullivan from the Painted Angel approaching from down the street pounding on his marching drum. That meant "the band" would be meeting the train. He'd have to get out his horn and join in. Resigning himself to his civic duty, he yelled out, "Hey Billy, c'mon, we got a train to meet. Your school teacher's on it."

It was only seconds until Billy burst through the back door. "What did you say? Did you say the school teacher is here?" Bumping a stool as he raced to the bar, Billy managed to catch it in mid air, then tumble over it, knocking down two more stools before he landed face down on the floor.

"Hey clumsy, take it easy." As Billy righted the stools, Marty reminded him, "Go comb your hair and look at least half-way presentable if you have any intentions of actually going to school to this dame."

Marty untied his apron, hung it on a nail of one of the support logs and reached under the backside of the bar for his horn. He waited briefly for Billy to reappear from the back room. Together they went out of the dark saloon into the hot afternoon sunshine. About fifty people were making their way to the train platform. Two coronets, Marty's horn, Mayor Sullivan's drum, and Duane Wickert's clarinet began to get in sync as everyone came together in front of the small depot.

The engineer sounded three short blasts of the train whistle, and the screeching wheels made their final revolution. The band struck up strains of "School Days." They were about half way through their rendition when the conductor put the steps down from the passenger car, and a vision of beauty emerged.

Ellie was struck by the barrenness of her immediate surroundings when the train came to a halt beside the tiny Copperfield depot. While she had been watching the deepening canyon all the way from Huntington, she had occasionally seen a few trees along the hillsides, but here, she expected to see a little more greenery. Nothing appeared but the same scraggly trees and dried weeds and needle grass. The glaring brightness of the hot summer sun accosted her like heat from an open oven door on bake day. The crowd cheered wildly as the conductor steadied her arm and she stepped gracefully from the car to the platform.

Coming into full view, she was shocked to hear several wolf whistles and a loud, "Wow," erupt from along the outer perimeter of the gathering. "How rude," she thought, while a part of her wished she could yield to the temptation to smile and wave like the celebrity she seemed to be.

Trying to assess just what was eliciting such behavior, she quickly reviewed the high points of her appearance. Her honey blond hair was secured in the confines of a bright-blue feathered hat that matched the color of her eyes. The fine silvery net veil that reached as far as mid-cheek was almost invisible. Her full-length dark blue skirt brushed the tops of her arches, which were petitely encased in black patent leather, high-topped shoes. Finally the snowy ruffles of her silky white blouse fluttered like wings in the light breeze. Billy Mitchell thought she looked like a magnificent butterfly floating down into a field of clover. For that matter, her delicate features and natural beauty was not lost on anyone in the crowd assembled to meet her that day.

The strains of "School Days" faded as Miss Delaney stopped a few feet from the door of the depot. The mayor, handing his drumsticks to the player on his right, moved forward, and with a magnanimous gesture, removed his derby from his head. Bowing at the waist, he swept the ground in front of her with his hat's brim,

"Welcome to our fair city, Miss Ellen Kathleen Delaney," he pronounced with clarity. "We trust that you will find happiness and success in your endeavor to teach our children. I am Harvey Sullivan, mayor of our town, and you may come to me at any time with any problem that occurs." Pausing briefly, he looked around. His wife, Lucille, was moving forward from among the fifteen or twenty matronly looking women, and behind her was Clara, the wife of the general storekeeper.

Before reaching the mayor's side, Clara had emerged in front of her companion. Hurrying forward with arms open to embrace Miss Delaney, "Oh, you poor dear," she cried, "You've come such a long way. I'm Clara Hoffstetter, and you're making your home with us." Two children appeared from somewhere, whom Clara introduced as Jeffrey and Cecile.

Then in some unspoken language that included a wave of her arm, Clara seemed to be dispersing the crowd as she clutched Ellie's arm. "We'll be having a reception at the school on Monday evening," she announced to no one in particular. But Ellie soon learned that Clara didn't have to talk to anyone in particular. Whatever she proclaimed was almost as good as a royal command. By contrast, the mayor's wife seemed to shrink into invisibility; and a few in the crowd took Clara's announcement as their cue to depart. Ellie reflected on the strangeness of it all, as she hurried along the short distance with Clara from the depot to the general store.

"Don't worry about your things," Clara was saying breathlessly. "Your trunks have already arrived. My, my, you must have brought a ton of books with you. I hope you didn't bother to bring a very large wardrobe. While your room is quite adequate, the closet is rather small. Of course, if there's not enough space, we can always store some things in the attic. If you didn't carry a lunch on the train, I can set things up a little early for our afternoon tea. I'm sure I can find something for a sandwich if you are hungry. At least you can have a teacake with your cup of tea. I'm sure you need something after all that time on the train. Where did you say you got your degree? I understand it was a law degree. My, my, the world is changing so fast."

Ellie wondered if the lady was ever going to stop talking. But she was not anticipating a question buried in the middle of the chatter she had just been listening to, and she had to have the question repeated when she realized Clara was waiting for a reply.

"Oh, I attended classes at Penn State. My cousin Charlotte Fern Hobbs studied there also," she threw in lamely, then wondered what had made her declare that piece of information. Ellie was not the type to chat aimlessly. Her years with her father had taught her to stay on subject and to be succinct. Feeling almost dizzy in the hot summer sun, she concentrated, attempting to get back to what Clara was saying.

She didn't have more than a couple of seconds to worry about it since Clara was off and running about the weather, how the days were uncomfortably hot, but how the nights cooled the instant the sun went down. "The nights would be even colder, except the River water holds the heat close to the ground instead of allowing it to rise in the night," and on and on.

For the first time since the train had stopped, Ellie turned her attention to the River. It flowed only a few hundred feet to the east and its banks were rife with stacks of lumber. Wagons and tools were everywhere, and echoes of pounding mallets and hammers filled the air so that other sounds of the town were practically drowned out. All except those of the tinny player pianos issuing forth from the saloons that were interspersed among the business establishments. Glancing along the main thoroughfare, Ellie could see a bank, a mercantile, a hotel, a pharmacy, and, of course, the general store, where she and Clara were now entering the wide front door.

Settling In

As Ellie's welcoming ceremony was coming to a close, Cord arrived in Copperfield. Several men, holding music instruments, were still standing near the loading platform by the tiny railroad depot. Fifty or so other locals including women and children were crowded around.

Cord rode on by, not really able to see through the crowd to observe the new arrival and object of this gathering. He'd wager, though, that their attention was being given to a lady wearing a hat topped with bright blue feathers.

Copperfield, like Robinette, was a little more substantial than Cord anticipated. The storefronts, in his opinion, didn't have the same look of long-range stability that seemed prevalent in Robinette. The buildings in Copperfield looked to have sprung up overnight in the not too distant past. Very few were painted, although some bore traces of whitewash. There was a two-story hotel and a few other two-story jobs here and there. There were also a number of squat one-story buildings with false fronts common to mining towns. Cord noticed that at least fifty percent of the establishments were saloons, often flanked by boarding houses on either side. At the end of the street, just before the traverse of Pine Creek, he came to the Iron Dyke Livery Stable, John Miller, prop.

Approaching a young lad sitting atop the corral fence, Cord inquired, "Can you tell me where I can find John Miller?"

"He's gone to Halfway. He'll be back after a while. What did you want him for anyhow?"

"Well, I want to stable my horse. But I'd like for her to have a good rub-down, first."

"I can do that," the boy of about thirteen grinned. "But it'll cost you."

"Tell you what," Cord said. "You give her a rub-down and put her in a stall. I'll be back in a lttle while. I'll settle the cost then. Oh, and you can put my saddle some place safe so nothing happens to my pack." Cord handed the reins to the boy, and turned back along the route he had just come.

To his right, he noted a rather large two-story building with barred windows along one wall on the ground floor. If the whole building was devoted to being a jailhouse, there must be some truth to the lawlessness in this place. Although, he'd been told there was no law enforcement other than the county sheriff. Cord learned later the community meeting and dance hall occupied the top floor, mainly for use by people who didn't frequent the saloons.

As he walked along toward the now dispersing crowd, Cord could easily distinguish the houses of ill repute as they were euphemistically designated. These were generally facing the alley behind the saloons. Windows in these houses were open, and curtains were fluttering in the light breeze that blew through the canyon.

As a matter of curiosity, he continued along the boardwalk to its end. From here he could observe the train chugging away from the depot to disappear into a tunnel leading on down the River. Up from the corner where he stood and to his right, Cord could see another stable about a block away. Sounds of a hammer accosting an anvil rang out from the blacksmith shop located at the building's far corner. Accompanying this ear-splitting pounding was the timid gurgling of water spilling over the edge of a trough near the hitching rack. The water was delivered to the trough through a pipe from a ditch high above the street area behind the blacksmith shop and stable.

A dozen teams and wagons lined the rather wide boulevard in the area before the next saloon and the post office just ahead. Several people were gathered around the post office door where they were visiting.

Standing to get a view of the rest of the town, Cord's eyes swept a ways up the hill, also to his right. There, stood a school. Amazingly it was new, and it was painted a brilliant white. The afternoon sun reflected off two high windows above the front porch and from the whitewashed wall of one of the two outhouses close by. No other building in the town gleamed so brightly.

When Cord crossed the boulevard to enter the Golden Star saloon, he had to stand for a moment, allowing his eyes to adjust from the brightness of the day outside. Moments later, he could see the bar and the stools where he took a seat. He was glad he had chosen this bar rather than any of those further down the street where most of the men had gone after greeting the town's new arrival, whoever that might be.

Voices were audible from the rear of the saloon. The more mature voice was saying, "Billy, please put the glasses out on the shelves. Then, perhaps, you'd better skeedaddle. I think we have a customer." Shortly, a lanky, teen-aged boy appeared loaded down with a tray of glassware, which he began stacking on the counter behind the bar.

Then a rather heavy-set man, not more than 5'8" in height, sporting a thick mustache entered the serving area behind the bar. He waved Billy from the room, then turned to Cord.

"What'll you have, stranger?" he inquired in a booming voice.

"Something as cold as you've got," Cord replied.

"I think I can fill the bill," the man replied. "How about a red-eye sour?"

"Sounds good."

"Did you come in on the train?" the man wanted to know.

"No," Cord replied. "I rode in." Wondering how he had been spotted and designated so easily as a newcomer, he was also aware that more questions would be launched. He added, "From up river a ways."

"Oh, yeah? You looking for work?"

In his usual reserved manner, Cord was inclined to refrain from a discussion about himself. He lifted his drink to engage his mouth for a few seconds while he considered his next answer. He decided to play it safe, not revealing too much, yet garnering as much information as possible.

Slowly replacing his drink on the bar, he replied, "Could be."

"What did you have in mind?" the man queried.

"Something to make an honest dollar would be good," Cord replied.

"I'm looking for some help."

"I'm not much of a bartender," Cord remarked. "Usually not a drinker either. But it's a kind of a scorcher out there today."

"Sure is," the man agreed happily. Then he swiped his hand on his apron and reached across the bar, "Kellner's the name, Marty Kellner."

Cord obliged, "Cord Williams," he responded as he half rose to accept the handshake.

"Well Cord Williams," Kellner said, "I don't need a bar tender so much. I do most of that myself. As you can see, I'm just opening this place."

Cord had been aware of the pungent odor of freshly sawed timber, and of the sawdust on the floor that had the clean smell of green pine. Again he was glad he had chosen this saloon in spite of the lack of the usual décor such as paintings over the bar, or collections of wagon wheels and oxen yoke that were common in many saloons nowadays. He noticed that there was no performance stage or even a player piano and wondered how the man could make a living with nothing to offer but drinks. Turning his full attention to Marty Kellner, he said, "I guess that's apparent you're just opening. What's the job then?

"I hope I don't scare you off," Marty answered. "But a couple of months ago, my saloon burned to the ground. I opened for business in an empty building at the other end of town at the time, but the Town Council said I couldn't sell liquor at that location. So I rebuilt here as soon as I could. But the bad boys who run this town are threatening to shut me down some other way. They're sore because I bring in the best liquor around—no moonshine here, and I don't try to gouge the men for a whole week's pay in one night." Marty shrugged his shoulders. "So I have a lot of good customers, kind of the upper crust, if you know what I mean."

"And how does that apply to me as far as a job? I'm not a lawman either."

"I'm not looking for a lawman," Marty chuckled. "A good one wouldn't last five minutes in this town. These bastards carry a good supply of loaded guns. But they mostly use their fists when they fight," he added quickly. "I guess," he went on thoughtfully, "I'm looking for a roust-about, a bouncer if you will.

"I'm ordering in a player piano, but the stage isn't built yet. I do my own carpentering; but my wife, she's pregnant, just two months. Still I don't want her lifting like she's been doing, putting this place up." Marty eyed his customer to see how he was taking this information. He continued. "So if you can handle a team, haul a little lumber, then hang around of an evening to back me up just in case, I can pay $40 a week, and you can take your meals upstairs with Bridget and me if you're of a mind to," Marty concluded.

The blood in Cord's face made a slow drain when he heard the figure, $40 a week. That was more money than most working men could hope for, especially with groceries thrown in. "When you starting?" Cord tried hard to control his enthusiasm.

"Why right now, if you want," Marty grinned. "For today, you can just sit around, get the lay of the land, so to speak. Then tomorrow, we'll get a load of lumber and get going."

"Sounds good to me," Cord said. "Of course, this afternoon, I'll have to look into finding a room."

"There's a rooming house about four doors down the boardwalk there. Belongs to a widow who lost her husband to typhoid about a year ago," Marty offered.

Cord stood up and began reaching in his pocket for money to pay for his drink. Marty refused, saying, "It's on the house." It was worth the price of a drink he thought just to see the size of the man he had hired. Marty looked him up and down now. He had thought Cord was well built as he sat talking, but he hadn't realized the man was over six feet tall, probably more like 6'3". "Yeah," Marty thought, "he'll do nicely."

Continuing his conversation about the widow, Marty said, "I'd say the widow with the boarding house is about your age if you're looking."

"Not me," Cord grinned. "By the way, what was the big welcome all about a while ago?"

"New teacher," Marty replied. "Quite a looker. Her name is Ellen Delaney." He laughed. "I can imagine she'll be stirring things up around here, unless she's the retiring type, which I doubt. Or she wouldn't have wandered into a place like this. In my experience, even the quietest teachers make some kind of trouble before you know it."

As Cord left, he mulled over Kellner's comments. "Some good, some not so good," he decided. The one thing he noticed as he stepped on to the boardwalk again, there were no church steeples on the horizon. Even Drewsey had a church.

Cord did get a room at the designated rooming house. Returning to the livery stable, he rounded up his pack, spoke to John Miller to arrange for care of Ed's saddle and tack, then ponied up for a week's board for the mare. He flipped a two-dollar gold piece into the eager hands of the young stable hand. Giving the boy a wink, he sauntered away. He'd decide in a day or two if he had any real need for a saddle horse. If not, he'd ask John to sell her.

By five o'clock, he was ready to put in his first nightshift as a bouncer in the notorious town of Copperfield.

—

General Delivery
Copperfield, Oregon
September 15, 1913

Dear Lottie Fern,

    I am here, but I am still out of breath from my arrival day before yesterday. At 5:00 p.m. today, there will be an official community reception featuring the school board, as well as parents and students, who will be getting a preview of their new teacher. As you may suppose, I am working on my little speech. Actually, if I can think how to say it, I will tell them what I'm about to tell you. I feel as though I have fallen down the Rabbit Hole with Alice in Wonderland ever since the train started through the Snake River canyon.

    At Huntington, you'll remember the hills are rather unassuming compared to the tremendously overpowering mountains of the canyon walls in Burnt River canyon. They are just the nice little Sunday afternoon climbers much like the Adirondacks, but barren. In fact the whole area is a tawny yellow color, now. I remember you saying after completing your bar-exam consultations with Father, that they were a lush green color. Well, there's no green "carpeting" now, except for a few scrubby trees that the people around Huntington have planted near their homes.

    The big surprise came as we went down the canyon, which seems very much like up the canyon because the hills soon become mountains. Some are covered with nothing but small rock and hundreds of feet of rockslides. The railroad runs right next to the river most of the way. But there are places where one can almost reach out the car window and touch the sides of the mountains. That's especially true where the railroad actually ascends the mountainside to travel along it because there is no base for a road on the riverbank. To tell the truth, the mountain is the riverbank. Only a few small settlements are located through the many miles. You have probably encountered information about a place called Robinette. I was surprised that it also has a school, mainly because I didn't see evidence of enough people to populate one. I noticed a church there too.

    Anyway, after about four hours, out of Baker City, the train finally arrived at Copperfield. As I stepped down from the coach, there was a band playing "School Days". I later learned that the inestimable band members comprise the Town Council except for one fellow. They are also all saloonkeepers or workers in a saloon. In spite of the forward-looking construction of an electrical power plant and a railroad passage down river, saloon—keeping seems to be the major industry here. Oh yes, I should mention mining and sawmills.

    You'll be glad to learn that there is a physician, who doubles as the local veterinarian. And there is a jail with a community hall where the Town Council meets. Dances are also held in the hall every other weekend, as I understand it. There is a barbershop, a hotel, a pharmacy, a hardware store, and several boarding houses. There are two livery stables that do a thriving business. One operates a blacksmith shop out of a corner of the main building. The other provides free services for people who are visiting a local saloon or a house of prostitution. Oh yes, there are several of those. I'm not sure just how many. Conversation about them is strictly taboo—at least in the Hoffstetter household, where I have accommodations on the second floor.

The school is to the south and west end of town, visible when you first arrive from Huntington. It was constructed a little over a year ago, and is painted—one of the few buildings in town that is. Then there's the depot, the post office and one saloon, all before you come to the boardwalk along the main thoroughfare, dubbed Independence Avenue. Across the street, two doors down from where I live, there is a mercantile store. The Merc is somewhat in competition with the General Store that George and Clara Hoffstetter own and run. Although, it carries no groceries, and The Store carries no dry goods. So each business has its own niche. A two-story hotel, The Red Carpet, is just down the street from the Store.

I could be visiting some of these enterprises today, but I think I'll wait until after the reception so that Clara doesn't favor me with the history of each and every person she knows before I have a chance to meet them.

All in all, I could have ended up in worse conditions I suppose. After all, who would have thought a remote place like this would have running water piped into buildings, and all would have the benefit of electricity? It is a sight to see the beauty of the night sky. I walked a ways along the road back toward Robinette last evening just after sunset and was privileged to see the lights coming on as I came back.

The sound of player pianos is rather annoying at night until the air cools enough so I can close my window. It seems there are hundreds of single men, many of them foreigners, who work for the businesses I mentioned. Virtually all of them visit the saloons at least once a day. I guess until just last year, the saloons stayed open day and night. Thanks to the light and power available from the electric company, people were working around the clock, and the saloons stayed open in order to get all the business possible.

Now, however, there isn't a lot going on until later in the afternoon because most of the construction, railroad, and power jobs are finished. I'm sure I'll be spending my afternoons and early evening hours at school where the sound will surely be less vexatious.

My room here at the store is quite cozy. It's on the second floor. There is a four-poster brass bed, a roll-top desk, an organ, a blue upholstered chair, a wooden rocking chair, a small table and a nice sized closet. Since I arrived with three trunks plus my satchel, Clara was fearful that I wouldn't be able to store all my clothes in the closet. She was relieved to find that almost half of each trunk was filled with books. Then I brought Mother's checkerboard quilt and my embroidered bedspread, my favorite bedside lamp, and as I mentioned, Father's painting. I also brought my blue willow pitcher and bowl set.

The bowl set and the books caused a few problems because Clara had already equipped the room with her own pewter, plus towels and other linens. But she rather graciously surrendered and said I could use my own things if I preferred. As for the books, she instructed George to build a bookrack for me right away. In the meantime, the books are situated in one of the trunks, and my personal things are in another. My green steamer trunks tend to detract from the appearance of the room, being that it has white wallpaper with tiny blue violets in the pattern. And the linoleum floor covering is a smoky blue. But Clara says when the bookrack is in place, the trunks can be removed to the attic. Clara says she thinks she knows where she can get a nice highboy or at least a modest chest of drawers for my use.

Oh yes, there's a dressing table. I feel almost at home when I look over to see my hair brush, my jewelry box, and my box of dusting powder. As for bathing facilities, that is another matter. It seems as though I can choose either Friday night or Saturday night on the week-ends, plus any week-night I wish to use the bath-tub which is installed under the staircase in the storeroom downstairs. The children take baths on Sunday morning, and Mr. and Mrs. Hoffstetter will alternate their baths on the other weekend night.

There is a small trash burning stove just outside the bath area where there is one copper boiler and two large teakettles for heating water. But Clara says the water in the River is not all that cold, and the family often uses that source in the summer time in order to keep the Store cool. I can't help but think about how much I took for granted at home and then quite innocently assumed that everything here would be the same.

I do have a very good view from my second story window. By leaning out the window just a little, I can observe the comings and goings at the railroad depot, the school, and anything happening along the main street where there is steady traffic, even at this early hour of the morning.

Lottie Fern, it will be so nice to have you to talk to, even if it is by letter. Until I get better acquainted here, I must have a sounding board, and I don't think Clara will do. I thought as we came along the street the day of my arrival that she would never let up. She means well, I'm sure; but she changes the subject every two seconds, injects a question here and there, then keeps on talking as if she hadn't. Apparently she continues to talk until she runs out of breath, then waits for you to answer any questions she may have posed.

Clara is not like anyone I have met before. Even the way she looks is different. She is, I'd say, five foot, three inches, about the same as me. But she is very rotund. Getting behind the counter in the store is quite a challenge for her. She is gray haired, even though she can't be more than thirty-five. Her hair lies back in perfect *waves off her face. I think she must use a waving iron to put each tendril in place. She rolls the length of her hair in a bun high on the back of her head.*

She wears lace dickeys around her rather short neck. They make her look as if the lace is holding her head up. Then, even though it is very hot here, she wears long sleeves with lacey white cuffs. At least that has been the style of her clothing for the two days I've been here. She also wears high-top shoes, good for a lot of walking. I noticed the other matrons who were at the train were a little more relaxed in short-sleeved, button-up, open collar outfits and lower topped shoes. One lady's ankles were even visible. I gather that such exposure is often indicative of someone who plies a trade with the gentlemen, and that it's rather difficult sometimes to determine if a lady is actually someone's wife, or if she may be a prostitute.

I am certainly pleased though that the Hoffstetters have every appearance of being honest, hard-working, Christian folks. In fact, Clara promised that on most Sundays, we can rise early and go to Robinette for church services. I feel so lucky to find that there's a Methodist minister who travels from Huntington quite often for special services there. That will make the holidays seem a little less forbidding, I'm sure.

Now, Lottie Fern, I will expect a letter from you just as soon as you can get it here. I am so looking forward to the day when we can get together for a long, long visit. May it come soon.

My love,

Cousin Ellie K

Meeting the Community

Having completed her letter to her cousin and walked to the post office to mail it, Ellie returned to begin penning a few hundred notations for lessons that would begin on Wednesday. Then suffering the effects of the heat, she lay across her bed for a few minutes and nodded off to sleep. The next thing she knew, Clara was shaking her shoulder gently to awaken her.

"Miss Delaney, Miss Delaney. It's four-thirty. Perhaps you'd better freshen up a bit. People are beginning to arrive in town for the reception."

"Oh my," Ellie muttered sleepily, "I must have dozed off. What a waste of precious time. I have so much to do." With that Ellie was on her feet, reaching for the curtained window to let more light into the room. She glanced down to see wagons and buggies all around the store area on both sides of the street. Sound began to register through her dulled senses, and she could hear a steady drone of voices from downstairs. "What is happening?" she asked. "Is something wrong?"

"Oh no," Clara replied. "The farm wives are here to trade eggs and vegetables for groceries and other supplies. They also bring their needlework and sewing projects to show each other. So we have a small fair here several times a year.

"We can always anticipate a very busy afternoon when there is a social occasion in town. I just wish there were more of them," she added wistfully. "I'll see you downstairs," she said as she turned to go.

"I'll be right down," Ellie called as she began to unpin her hair. Sometimes she wished she dared to bob her hair the way some of the braver souls were doing back East. Yet again, she loved the way her hair tumbled heavily to her shoulders and below after being caged in a roll on top of her head for the day. Then brushing, one hundred strokes before bedtime, was a joy. She had inherited her mother's enamel brush with the stiff bristles that was at least twenty years old and would, no doubt, last another twenty years, perhaps long enough for Ellie to pass on to her own daughter.

"Where in the world did that thought come from?" Ellie stared into her vanity mirror in surprise. She put down the mirror and twisted her hair into a chignon at the back of her head. She didn't have enough time now to use the rat holder and place all the pins in a roll to keep it looking neat. Next she chose a white long-sleeved blouse, one with pearl buttons to the waist where a peplum was attached. Then she decided she also needed a freshly pressed skirt. Her new black velvet would do nicely. Now her attention reached the floor. She couldn't very well wear the brown high-tops she had on with a black skirt; so they too had to go. She quickly grabbed her black square-heeled, tie shoes and slipped them on her feet.

Checking the vanity mirror again, she decided to add her pearl necklace and bracelet to her ensemble, and to dab a little rouge on her cheeks. The hot sun had done some damage in just two days to her creamy white, smoothly textured cheeks and forehead. Digging among the items in the trunk for her box of face powder, she applied a sparse layer, then checked her appearance again. Finally she added a touch of cologne behind her ears and at the end of her blouse sleeves on her wrists, and she was ready.

"Oh my," she said aloud. "It's already a quarter to five." She had planned to finish the roast beef sandwich she had tucked into the cooler downstairs at lunchtime so that hunger wouldn't cause her stomach to rumble in its tightly corseted interior. But there was no time now. Grabbing her broomstick-lace shawl, she exited her room and made her way down the stairs to the store.

Clara was just buttoning a black bolero top under her chin. She looked rather somber all in black except for the floret design worked into the netting of her hat. "Oh Miss Delaney," she called, "You can't think to go out in the street without a hat. You can borrow my new white straw. It will fit nicely around your chignon."

Ellie glanced around the store at several ladies who were listening and observing this exchange. One whispered to another, who responded with an impish grin. Ellie noticed that all the ladies in the store were wearing poke bonnets, which readily hid their faces from view unless they tilted their heads upward to look around. "Oh well," Ellie sighed.

By this time, Clara was hurrying toward her, hat in hand. Without pausing, she placed it on Ellie's head, slipped behind her and shoved the hatpin in place. "There," she was saying, "That's much better. We must keep up appearances so there's no mistaking who is a lady and who is not. If you don't have appropriate hats and gloves, we will have to take care of that right away. I can't imagine though that you didn't wear a hat at finishing school. Oh, that's right, you attended Penn State. I suppose they are not so particular there. Well, come on, we're ready now. Children, let's go. It's getting late. Hurry along now, you'll be marching off to school soon enough. Let's get some practice."

As usual, in Clara's presence, Ellie didn't have to contribute anything to the conversation, as the group walked to the school two by two. Instead she let her mind drift to her speech. Only a few more minutes, and she'd be standing before a crowd of people. As many as twenty-five would be her students, whom she had yet to meet. She crossed her fingers of her ungloved hand to engage Lady Luck in keeping her from stammering, stuttering, forgetting, or otherwise presenting herself in any but a positive light.

Upon reaching the school porch, Clara began rounding up the mayor and the school board members. She then grabbed the pull rope on the school bell and allowed the bell to peal four times. "Children! Children!" she cried loudly as the last echoes died away. "You must be quiet now so we can all meet your new teacher. Mr. Sullivan, your kind attention please." With this remark, Clara maneuvered Ellie to the right of the mayor and a little forward toward the five men standing next to each other in the middle of the school porch.

Harvey Sullivan responded in a typically puffed up manner, appropriate to his political office. Placing his right hand with lightly closed fist on his watch chain, he withdrew his watch, glanced at it and announced, "Yes, yes, it is time." Turning toward Ellie, he said, "We are so joyed to be able to present you, Miss Ellen Kathleen Delaney to the school board members of District 68. Beginning on your left is Jack Griffin, newly elected member, Carson Swinyer, representing the area down river, Joe Halvorsen, who lives up Copper Creek, Henson Baldwin, our official poet and chorus leader, and finally our chairman, Abe Willoughby. Abe . . ."

Ellie was somewhat at a loss as she faced the crowd. She didn't know whether to turn to acknowledge each man, having her back to the audience or whether to go to each as he was introduced to offer her hand. As a compromise, she turned half around so she could see the gentlemen, yet her profile was visible to people in the schoolyard.

She was quite amused by the reactions of the school board members. Jack grinned with open friendliness. Joe stood, his legs spread, with his arms folded across his chest wearing a look that one might use when trading horses. Carson ducked his head, studiously observing the toes of his boots. Henson, however, doffed his hat and performed a deep bow, similar to that of the mayor's upon her arrival by train.

Abe approached her to shake hands. His grip was firm, and she determined immediately that this was a man of certainty, one who could be depended on.

"We're most happy to meet you Miss Delaney. We have a few rules of conduct posted inside the schoolhouse door that apply to both you and the children. If there are any questions regarding these, please don't hesitate to ask. Our primary interest here is educating our children in reading, writing, and arithmetic; and we find that they do best in a strongly structured environment. That means they don't leave the school grounds once they arrive until you release them. They are to keep strictly scheduled work and play times; and they do not engage in wrestling or other forms of physical contest. If there are supplies that you need, our school clerk, Mrs. Hunsaker, who is also the postmistress, and always available to you, is authorized for a certain level of expenditure between school board meetings. That is, if she deems your purposes are within the realm of good education. Otherwise, you will need to bring your requests and concerns to the board yourself.

"We also require high standards of conduct for our instructor, asking that you observe all rules of proper decorum. We desire that you set a good example whenever engaging in conversation in the presence of children. I'm sure your high level of education has prepared you well to meet this obligation. However, if you have questions, you can depend upon Mrs. Hoffstetter to enlighten you. Your being quite young and still single leads us to believe that her guidance might be needed. As I understand it, you have not attended a teacher's college, so perhaps your knowledge of how impressionable young minds are, may be somewhat limited."

Turning his attention more toward the gathering, he continued. "We meet when necessary and at the end of each six-week grading period." Swinging his attention back to Ellie, he said, "Now if you would like to say a few words, we will be most happy to listen. After that I believe the ladies have prepared a potluck for community members, and perhaps Henson will favor us with some entertainment, something we all find so enjoyable."

"Thank you, Mr. Willoughby," Ellie said softly. The welcoming speech, if you could call it that, had been almost like an attack. But she would proceed as planned. "I am most happy to be here," she said, clenching and twining her fingers together in front of her. "My trip West was very pleasant, and I have found nothing to detract from the enthusiasm I have for commencing teaching children in my own classroom. I am sure that your children will find the world of books as fascinating as I have always discovered them to be; and they will be very busy learning information of the greatest importance.

"The technology available to them now at their very doors, such as the railroad that was thought to be an impossibility less than fifty years ago, will surely necessitate harnessing their eagerness for learning about the past as well as the future. Again, I am very much looking forward to instructing them in all subjects of the curricula.

"As I have investigated, I find Oregon and, particularly, Copperfield very supportive in providing good learning tools. Your school is most impressive, and I am quite eager to meet everyone, especially the parents and the children. Please accept my gratitude for your finding me a worthy candidate to be your teacher. Thank you again."

"Whew, that's over," Ellie murmured to herself as the polite applause came close to drowning out the tinny music floating up from the town's saloons. She stepped down quickly to the bottom step greeting and shaking hands with parents and their very obedient children.

Only one parent stood out in her memory when the evening was over. She introduced herself as "Lillian Lawson," who truthfully declared, "This is my Jimmy, who can be quite a handful at times." Ellie wondered where Jimmy's father was since all other parents came forward with the father proclaiming that his children were models of good behavior, and if they weren't, he was standing by ready to "Whop 'em good."

While Abe Willoughby had been a little intimidating as he spoke so eloquently and so definitively, Ellie found no one else as impressive or as likely to have a superior education. She might find that fact to be an advantage, then again, maybe not.

With the introductions over, Ellie noticed Henson sitting on the bottom step, tuning a banjo. Seconds later, she heard Clara announce, "All right, everyone, supper is ready to be served."

Ellie had never seen so much food in once place before. The eight-foot table was piled high with breads, rolls, cakes, pies, salads of fruit and vegetable varieties, bean and potato casseroles, and at the far end, a barbecued mutton lay in wait. She suddenly recalled her roast beef sandwich and smiled because she had not eaten it.

Lillian Lawson prepared to serve a beverage from a huge bowl of punch that had been placed on a block of wood just beyond the meat-serving table. Abe Willoughby took his place ready to carve the mutton. Despite Ellie's reluctance to be at the head of the line, Clara pushed a plate into her hand along with silver service. "Hurry along now, Miss Delaney," she said. "You are the honored guest, you know."

Seating herself on a porch step with her filled plate in her lap, Ellie wondered, wryly, if other parents were as likely to treat her as just another child. Ellie finished eating long before the last person was served. Even though she found it a little difficult to breathe, she might have had another small portion of one or two of the salads. However, since proper decorum was an issue, she did not help herself to more of anything. She had taken three small samples of dessert as it was, one of chocolate cake, one of lemon pie, and one of a creamy fruit concoction that was probably inspired by a recipe for Waldorf salad since apples were the main ingredient. Of course, the men and older children had no such scruples, and before long, they had plied their plates with seconds and even thirds of their favorite dishes.

Again, Henson drew Ellie's attention from his seat on the bottom step at the far corner of the porch. Ellie felt impelled to edge nearer to watch him twanging away on his banjo. She stood, shyly looking down on the hunched man, who continued to adjust the tightening knobs on his banjo to tune it. Satisfied, he suddenly began strumming and singing in a high tenor voice. The selection was "Oh Susanna."

Children came pouring from all directions, and before long they were playing "Drop the Handkerchief," bouncing merrily to the music.

Henson commenced a medley of Stephen Foster's popular tunes, "Old Black Joe," "My Old Kentucky Home," and "Old Folks at Home." By the time he got to the third song, people crowded around to sing. Then Henson played "Waltzing Matilda," and the couples began dancing in the schoolyard.

The more he played, the more enthusiastic everyone became. "Skip to My Lou," and "Turkey in the Straw," brought men, women, and children to their feet, so that Ellie, being the only female wishing to participate without a partner, joined the circle dance with the children. At the end of one particularly strenuous rendition, Lillian observed, "Miss Delaney, you look so very graceful, I'm certain you will have a most enjoyable time at the local dances held in the community hall every other Saturday night. They are great fun and a fine way to become acquainted with the few young unmarried persons your own age."

Another matron, whose name Ellie couldn't remember, approached to say that the local Grange at Richland would be holding its booster night program shortly. "It is customary," she told Ellie, "for the teachers in the area to present some engaging item, either entertaining or informational. But please don't worry," she added. "I'll send some information with Emily that will assist you in choosing something suitable to go along with the annual theme."

Shortly after those brief encounters, and vigorous dancing, the ladies gathered their serving bowls, kettles, and dishes; and before she knew it, everyone vanished into the twilight. Those who had arrived by wagon and buggy planned to start their journey home before dark, although it really didn't matter because the teams of horses would find their way in daylight or darkness, with or without a driver.

Only Henson Baldwin remained as Clara and George replaced the few classroom chairs that had been taken outside for some of the older ladies' comfort. As he carefully replaced his banjo in its case, he called out, "Miss Delaney."

"Yes," Ellie answered.

"Will you be attending the community dance next Saturday night?"

"I will if it is proper and if the Hoffstetters accompany me," Ellie said in a subdued voice.

"Oh, I'm sure they will be there," Henson informed her. "I'll be there also. I'm looking forward to getting better acquainted."

Finding herself at a disadvantage since she felt obliged to avoid any personal interchange between herself and a member of the school board, Ellie blushed and turned away, murmuring, "Good night, Mr. Baldwin."

While walking back to the store a short time later, Ellie asked Clara, "What is the Grange, exactly. I've heard of it before, but I thought it was a secret fraternal organization for patrons of husbandry only."

Clara said, "That's true, but once a year, the Grange invites all but the itinerants and other profligates in the community to their Booster Night, in an effort to build support for issues concerning agriculture. In that way, they also feel free to offer their assistance in solving local problems. And they can request our support regarding their issues."

As Clara launched a lengthy discourse on who was who in the Grange, Ellie considered the irony of teaching school in the midst of a gambling, drinking, rowdy community that was surrounded by church-going, honest, and hard-working farm people. "I wonder," she remarked, "how many farm children there will be and how they will get along with the Copperfield children."

General Delivery
Copperfield, Oregon
September 17, 1913

Dear Lottie Fern,

    I just know that you will be writing soon, but I can't wait to fill you in on the particulars of my job. The reception on Monday evening was quite revealing. I think I may be getting some idea of the community as a whole. There is quite a dichotomy involved between the solid citizens and the not-so-solid citizens. Fortunately only the solid citizens seem to have children.

    I visited the inside of my school while walking yesterday. It is very well equipped. There are desks that bolt to the floor in four different gradations in size for a total of forty students. My desk is in the back of the room near the blackboard, which extends along one entire wall. There is a closet behind my desk that is large enough to hold my outer apparel and many school supplies including a good supply of chalk. In the middle of the back of the room, is a gigantic wood heater. It stands about three and half feet tall, up on legs that are at least six inches in height. It is about two and a half feet across and probably close to three and a half feet in depth. It is oval, and the wood is fed in by lifting about half the top area upward with a long rod handle.

    I find that it is all I can do to balance the lid open, then reach down to pick up a piece of wood to feed in. I guess the main idea is to be able to put a full day's fuel supply inside, then light it through a smaller opening at the bottom. That door serves a dual purpose, making it possible to withdraw the ashes that have fallen through the grate into a long box-like contraption. I'm sure we won't need any heat for quite a while, though, since the temperature here is uncomfortably warm well before nine o'clock in the morning.

    Anyway, there are windows all along the wall opposite the blackboard. They extend from about two feet off the floor to a height of about eight feet. Several small tables with chairs that seem hardly big enough for toddlers are located under the windows. There is a sizeable braided rug between the stove and the tables. The only other horizontal surface is a large library table that is at the front of the room. There are a half-dozen or so chairs placed around it. I was pleased to find it equipped with an up-to-date globe, a set of Britannica Encyclopedias, and a selection of the classics bound in attractive bindings.

    I had noticed boxes and boxes of textbooks in stacks along the blackboard area while in the room on Monday evening. They were just delivered last week from the County School Superintendent. It seems this is the year for all new textbooks. I have the duty of packing up the old books now stacked in the cloakroom and shipping them back to Baker City. They do have one unusual custom here. The school board actually buys the books for the students. So they have a stamped bookplate inside the front cover, warning, "*DO NOT REMOVE THIS BOOK from the classroom without your teacher's permission.*"

The cloakroom for the school is walled off along the front and side so it can be entered immediately upon coming through the front door. It has pegs for the children's coats, benches for their overshoes, and some small chairs where they can sit to tie shoes, etc. There is only one small window for this area, quite high up. Beside a big shelf along the front wall, there is a pitcher pump to get water to fill the four washing pans or to get drinking water. Clara says this arrangement is rather unusual because most of the schools in this area place their water pumps outside so the children don't make a mess. But this school board, rather bravely, put everything on the inside.

Of course, I wondered aloud why the school was not privileged with running water from the ditch above the town like everyone else. Clara laughed and told me to see how I could get it here using the force of gravity. It seems the ditch traverses from a ways up Pine Creek, along the hillside opposite the school and on down to the River. Clara told me that the water for town is piped down the hill and that there is no way to run it back up hill to the school, not yet anyway. She says they are thinking about building a water tower for storage the way some of the bigger cities do. Then everyone could depend on abundant water pressure for all locations.

After consulting my list of duties as posted inside the schoolhouse door, I find that in addition to maintaining the fire on school days, cleaning the floors as necessary, especially on week-ends, keeping the blackboard cleared of chalk dust, and otherwise maintaining a pleasant and organized environment, I do have one other responsibility. Out back are two latrines, one for the boys and one for the girls. I must check them morning and night, removing the lids, which are square boards, to see that the children haven't ditched papers or books into the hold. I also must keep a ready supply of catalog materials available for the children's use, and I am to make sure that the boys, especially, do not dawdle in the facility where they might print messages of an unsuitable nature on the walls. Both latrines are newly white washed inside and out, so I plan to set the rules and emphatically enforce them at all times. That, of course, will require a good deal of attention until I can find boy and girl monitors, whom I can fully trust.

I will also be assigning chores to others, including putting up and taking down the flag, carrying the fire-wood when heat is needed, sweeping and scrubbing the floors on Friday afternoon, and thoroughly cleaning the blackboard and erasers. There is an awful lot to think about that really doesn't have anything to do with teaching, don't you think? Or maybe, that's the real teaching, and students' learning from books is merely incidental to the children's needs as they go out into the world.

Outside, about four hundred feet down a gentle slope, there is a long shed, partially walled in, where the students tie their horses. Many of them ride several miles to school. But I have no responsibility for the barn or the horses. The people who live nearby make certain the horses are properly tethered each morning, and they observe the children as they pick up their mounts in the afternoons, tightening cinches for little ones if they don't have older brothers or sisters to assist them. I learned these details today when I asked how one little first grader could possibly pull herself up on a rather tall horse I had seen her dismount.

Upon reaching home yesterday, I inquired about how many students I would have. George, whom I have found to be a very knowledgeable man when it comes to the community, said, "There's no way to tell until school actually opens. Even then it may take a week for the stragglers to show up because they are still busy helping harvest the crops on the nearby ranches. When school closed last March, there were 34 students in all eight grades."

I haven't really told you about George, I think. I was astounded when I first saw him. He looks so much like one of my college professors, he could well be a twin. He is tall, about six feet. His hairline is receding. His brown hair is also beginning to gray a little. He is several years older than Clara, probably reaching forty. He is slender; his hands have the look of strength. They are broad with long capable fingers and spatulate nails. He wears gray work style shirts and black trousers most of the time. He also wears spectacles if he can locate them. He is forever laying them down, then searching for them when he realizes he isn't wearing them. When he relaxes in the evening at the kitchen table, his eyeglasses often fall forward on his nose, and if he looks up, he is peering at everyone over the top of his spectacles. That must be because his nose is rather narrow but otherwise nicely proportioned for a man. He smiles a good deal and is particularly cordial to any customers that come into the store. Cecile adores him, and I'd say Jeffrey thoroughly respects him. Clara, I think, just takes him for granted. Of one thing, I am certain, he is a man of principle.

Well, I must go now. Eighteen pupils began classes today, but it seemed that most of them knew of other children who will be reporting soon. I'll write again as soon as I hear from you.

My sincere best wishes,

Ellie K.

On the Job

Cord stirred sleepily in his bed at Winona's Boarding House. The smell of coffee and bacon brought him fully awake. He looked at the clock on the small dresser and delayed no further. Quickly donning his clothes, splashing his face, and brushing his hair back, he reached the street in about three minutes. He hadn't meant to sleep in. It was 7:35, and he was technically late for breakfast at the Golden Star.

Entering the side door near the back alley, Cord was surprised to see Bridget seated at the bar beside her husband, who was munching on a biscuit. She looked rather pale, and Cord's first thought that something was wrong. All week, Marty had carried a breakfast tray from upstairs, apologizing for Bridget's absence, all the while grinning like the cat that swallowed the canary.

Cord understood. Bridget being in a family way was experiencing morning sickness. But by lunch, she showed up carrying trays for both Marty and Cord. She was always genuinely perky, her red hair pinned neatly in place, and her clothes pressed and shiny, as if she were prepared to go someplace of importance. She and Marty were almost the same height, Marty being a scant inch or so taller.

"Well, sleepy head," Marty greeted. "I had just about given up on you for today. I guess that's what I get for paying your first week's wages last night. What did you do? Go down the street and celebrate?"

Cord slid on to the stool beside Marty, hurriedly arranged his napkin, and dug into a sumptuous serving of fried potatoes, gravy, venison steak with hot biscuits on the side. After taking a bite of each, he laid down his fork, and picked up the cup of coffee. For some reason its steaming aroma attacked his brain cells with a passion that he could no longer resist. Gulping the hot liquid, he vehemently denied any special activity the evening before. "Nope, I went home as usual. But it seemed a little noisier last night than it was earlier in the week. There must have been a humdinger of a brawl at The Painted Lady. I think I even heard bones cracking."

"Probably did. Lots of times, the saloons run out of the legitimate stuff that ships in on Saturdays, and the barkeeps go to serving moonshine. Brings out the beast in men. I don't do that myself. I guess that's why mine is a class-A bar.

"I know it galls the hell out of the Town Council members when they underestimate their order for the week. Sometimes they even resort to 'borrowing' a few kegs of beer and a barrel of whiskey to tide them over on a Friday night. But they must have thought they'd make it last night."

Bridget leaned into Marty's shoulder. "They really get annoyed at 'that damned trouble-making Irishman,' when they have to come begging," she added.

"Yeah," Cord nodded. "I was wondering last night why you closed so early. It sounded like there was plenty of business to be had."

"As I told you, mine is a Class-A establishment. Appeals to the ranchers, the crew foremen, and the town's businessmen. Since they pretty well keep away from the ladies of the night, they return home to their wives early in the evening. I just don't have any business after nine o'clock unless there's a special celebration. So," Marty shrugged, "I close. I wouldn't have it any other way."

"Well it's your business. But with your own player piano entertaining last night, I thought the fellows might stay a little longer. A few of them even joined in singing a couple of the Irish songs that are on there."

"I heard you belting out more than one yourself. Maybe we should get up a barber shop quartet or something."

"Might be interesting, but I didn't hear a bass in the crowd," Cord remarked.

"Speaking of the player piano, I think we should go get one more load of lumber this morning and extend that stage out another couple of feet. It'll keep the customers from putting their drinks on the piano or possibly tipping it over as they pass by."

"I'm ready when you are," Cord said, swiping his napkin across his mouth and rubbing it through his fingers to remove any traces of butter that had dripped from his biscuit.

Marty rose, as did Bridget. They stood face to face for a long moment. Then he pulled her to him, kissing her on the cheek. "Bye, baby. I'll be back by noon. Hope you're up to going dancing tonight like you thought. But if not, it's all right."

"I'll be waiting," Bridget murmured.

As the men walked out the door, Marty said, "How 'bout you Cord? Are you going?"

"Going where?" Cord replied.

"To the dance. By the way, Bridget said she met that school ma'rm yesterday. Said she'd bet that gal is a lot of fun, despite her school teacher ways."

Cord could feel the heat rising to his face. He was thankful for his rather darkly tanned skin. Little did Marty know that he had a yearning to meet this particular person for several days now. On Wednesday morning, he had seen her go tripping by the boarding house like a graceful young doe. Cord was actually almost to step out the door when she went by. On Thursday, he had peeked out his second floor window to note that she was on her way to school again at precisely the same time.

One of these days he'd be courageous enough to intercept her and strike up a conversation. But not too soon. He'd go to observe things at the dance tonight though, just to see if she could dance.

Marty was surprised at Cord's lack of response. "Well are you going," he asked again.

Cord replied, "I may go for a little while. Can't say that I know anybody though."

"Well you can bet the Hoffstetters will be there with their new houseguest." Marty offered. "I've been looking forward all week to seeing what'll take place," he added. "I wouldn't be too surprised if the young bucks around here get a little rowdy over that one."

"Might be worth it," Cord chortled. But inside his heart was doing a flip-flop, adding to the great feeling of excitement he had today.

General Delivery
Copperfield, Oregon
Sept. 20, 1913

Dear Lottie Fern,

I so loved your letter. I was so happy; I just had to cry when I finished reading it for the hundredth time. You asked about the town. I thought I had told you lots about it, but maybe you hadn't read my missive I mailed on Tuesday. Anyway, here's a sketch of the history, according to Clara.

Jake Vaughan owned the Copperfield site until 1908 when he sold it for $10,000 to the Eastern Oregon Investment Company out of Baker City. The price is very memorable around here because it far exceeded the going rate for a homestead, which is a $1.00 per acre up to a possible $5.00 if the farming potential is there. Vaughan definitely didn't have a producing farm, although there are a few fruit trees where he started an orchard along the banks of the Snake. The trees border private homes along the River in Copperfield now. There are also several garden spots that he may have tilled.

Anyway, the reason for the property being so valuable is that the railroad reached here that year. It was built to transport the copper ore from the Iron Dyke mine, which is a few miles further down Snake River. Also there is a U-shaped turn in the river here; and the drop in elevation from the upper part to the lower part is quite significant, probably more than a hundred feet. So the electric Power Company came in and proceeded to tunnel through that area, planning to divert the River through the tunnel to create hydroelectric power. They have just completed their project. I guess it didn't turn out as grandiose as they first planned, but at least we have electric power in a place that would otherwise quite likely have no amenities of civilization whatsoever.

In the same area, the railroad had already attempted to build a tunnel through about 4,000 feet of solid rock to extend their track on down the River where a plethora of resources awaits transportation. The River can't be used for shipping because in places, the fall is too great, making the water too swift, and in others, the undertow is too dangerous for any kind of water transportation. There are still many plans afoot for the railroad to continue on down the river to Lewiston, Idaho; but nothing of importance has been done since they completed their tunnel in 1910.

As for shopping, the General Store sells local produce from as far away as New Bridge and Richland, (about 35 miles). That produce is at its best right now, and the fresh fruits and vegetables are heavenly. Dry goods are received from wholesalers in Baker City from numerous places including some foreign markets; and there's a jewelry store located next to the pharmacy. I haven't had the opportunity to visit those establishments yet. Clara says the jewelry is appealing mainly to the "working girls." She says I wouldn't find anything that is satisfactory to wear in public, much less at school.

She does appreciate my brooches, but rings, she says, are only for the fourth finger on the left hand, and they are never worn unless one is engaged or married. Necklaces are out of the question. Furthermore, she says it's a matter of economics. One does not squander a teacher's pay for jewelry.

Thank goodness, there is mail delivery three times a week, Tuesday, Friday, and Saturday. I have my Sears catalog and will likely place an order any day now. I really do need a pair of shoes to wear between here and school that will withstand the mud, which, they say, gets quite deep where I have to cross the streets and the road beyond the boardwalk on the main street.

Copperfield has a dance pavilion, where they also hold occasional Baptist church services, or a Catholic service on Sunday. Ironic, isn't it? The unwashed, as Clara calls the work crews, are not allowed to attend the community dance on Saturday night, but they can go to church in the same place on Sunday morning. It is even more ironic that a corner of the ground floor of this building is devoted to jail cells.

Actually, the thinking is that Copperfield has climbed the ladder of success as far as it can. Other than mining interests, all that is left are small farms located on tributaries to the Snake. Pine Creek is the largest outflow that is nearby. It cascades from the high mountains to the Southwest. A couple of sawmills, powered by steam engines are operating along Pine Creek, but since the building boom is mostly over here, and the railroad is not likely to start again soon, they are talking of closing down. But that would necessitate hauling the logs they cut all the way up to the Halfway mills for processing.

Most of the several thousand workers who were here over the last few years lived in "Jungle Camp," which consists of a collection of tents located side by side below town on the banks of the Snake. It is an area where bathing in the River takes place at all hours of the day and night, and "ladies" just don't go there.

Others live up Pine Creek in work-shacks. Another place where "working girls" don't go is to the saloons. Their business takes place in their own abodes in the alley behind the saloons or along Pine Creek where they stay in "cribs." Just three years ago, they say there were fourteen saloons and thirteen red-light houses. Now there are seven saloons and only a couple of independently-run red-light houses.

Working girls don't venture out into the streets except to get their mail because of the many free-for-alls the town is noted for. The saloon owners decided the girls were too often the cause of them. In 1909, several women were injured in one all-out brawl between the railroad crews and the miners. Actually, the railroaders discontinued their tunnel digging in 1910, so there are only a handful of laborers left as compared to the good old days. George says that there isn't so much of that influence anymore. Rather, the saloon owners, themselves, have begun to fight.

As for violence, yes there is and has been lots. They mayor, they say, carries two .38 specials, except when he is representing the town at some official function. Rumor has it that he knows how to use them and can draw, fire, and replace the revolvers before anyone realizes what is happening.

So that's about it. Please tell me all about the social functions in Salem so that I can recall and look forward to life without tinny player pianos. The "Music in the Air" is the biggest drawback to living here.

I'm planning to make my debut into Copperfield society tonight when I will attend my first dance in the wild West. Since I have a great deal to do to prepare, I'll sign off until next time. Right now, I believe I will go to the kitchen to get a cup of coffee and, perhaps, a bowl of fruit or hot cereal.

Until next time, my love and good wishes,

Cousin Ellie K

A Hot Time in the Old Town

"Thank you, my dear, for serving the children's breakfast to them," Clara said as she bustled into the kitchen from the store. "I knew they must be quite hungry. My goodness it's ten o'clock already. Miss Delaney, I quite forgot to tell you that Saturday is laundry day at our house. That's because I must help George get our order for produce ready all day on Monday. It is such a hassle. Cecile, sweetheart, did you bring your laundry items down? Well, now Miss Delaney, what will you be doing today? It is such a beautiful day." Clara paused.

Ellie knew that she must respond. What was the question? Oh yes, what will I be doing today? "I, I . . ." Ellie wanted to say that she would be preparing for the dance tonight. She had been in a quandary all morning. She didn't know how to broach the subject. Clara and the Board chairman, Abe Willoughby, might think her too forward to even think of such a thing without first securing adequate chaperoning. She began again, "I have quite a few papers to correct."

Clara moved toward the door to return to the store. "Now hurry with your breakfast children. You have your chores to do, you know. Oh Miss Delaney, you will want to bring your linens down for laundry too. It is so nice to have a mechanical washing machine in place. Please get them now, and if you need to do your lingerie, you'll want to do it right away so it will be dry if you plan to go dancing tonight."

Ellie heaved a sigh of relief because she did, indeed, plan to go dancing tonight. She spent the rest of the day in a rush as she took her sheets, towels, and pillow tops down to the laundry room. While there, she located a small tub for hand washing. Refreshing her lingerie in very hot water, she succeeded in reddening her hands to match the color of the Indian paintbrush blooms that grew in beautiful clumps along the hillside near the school. Later as she set her hair with a curling iron, warmed over a kerosene lamp, she noticed her hands hadn't improved very much. She would have to see if Clara had any tincture of lemon to rub out the redness.

Clara warned Ellie against wearing anything but a pastel or a dark color while in public, lest she be mistaken for one of the other "ladies." That positively eliminated her red gown, and her blue dress needed some repairs. Reluctantly she selected her third and last choice, a pale yellow-cream two-piece dress with alternating peach and pink stripes. It was lightly trimmed with black velvet, laced with black beading. She hated that the peach velvet sleeves and yoke tended to wash out her light complexion. Holding it in front of herself for inspection, she decided she would have to wear extra rouge and face powder even though she rarely did so. That, too, might be offensive to Clara, but she'd just have to apply it at the last minute, so there would be no time for argument.

Supper came and went. Ellie helped Cecile and Jeffrey with the dishes giving Clara time for her bath. George stood before a picture-size mirror mounted on the doorframe nearest the kitchen. He stropped his razor skillfully, then filled the wash pan from one of the three teakettles whistling low on the trash burner. His face lathered, he began long strokes down his cheek and forward along his jawbone. Holding his mouth in a twist to one side, he turned to Jeffrey. "Son, remember to keep the door locked and make sure Cecile's light is turned off after she goes to sleep. Whatever you do, don't open the store for anyone while Mother and I are gone for a little while this evening."

Ellie returned to her room to begin dressing. Her heart was racing by the time she reached the top of the stairs. Tightening the velvet ribbon that held her cascading curls in place behind her head, she thought she couldn't do better in trying to achieve that pixie look her father so adored. Upon completing the final touches of getting ready, Ellie tried to relax while sitting in the overstuffed chair near her bed. But when her desk clock chimed nine times, Ellie began pacing the floor between sessions of sitting down to glance at her *Vogue* fashion magazine.

Though she told herself that this was surely not a momentous occasion, she was as nervous as a cat. Picking up her mirror one more time, she giggled as she compared tonight to the night of her coming out party a few years ago. What an affair that had been!

—

At long last, Clara called from downstairs, "Come along my dear, George and I are ready now."

It was only four blocks from the store to the dance hall above the jail. Ellie slowed to trail the Hoffstetters as they proceeded up the dimly lit stairway, wondering if she would be able to distinguish the tinny music blasting away from the saloon just across the street from the softer music echoing from above. Nearing the middle landing, her gown became entangled under the toe of her shoe, and she tripped. Bravely clutching her shawl, she almost cried out in pain from scraping her elbow on the stair wall as she fell forward to her knees.

Attempting to disengage her shoe before she tore her dress or embarrassed herself by having to raise the hem above her ankle, she was mortified to hear a melodious voice behind her uttering, "Whoa girl." She trembled as a hand closed over her arm to offer assistance.

Recovering her balance, she tilted her head to one side to peer from behind the flowered poke bonnet that Clara declared was her best match for Ellie's dress. Henson Baldwin favored her with a teasing smile. "May I," he asked, steadying her. Then he zealously tucked her wrist and forearm under his elbow and waited politely for her to proceed.

Ellie could feel her face turn hot and could imagine her blush glowing brightly in the dim light of the single bulb dangling from high above the stair case. She was thankful that George and Clara were well ahead of her. Being among the crowd assembled at the hat-check counter, neither was aware that she had fallen.

"Are you all right?" Henson leaned toward her to inquire.

"Uh, yes, yes I think so," Ellie stammered.

"Well then, Miss Delaney, I shall be most happy to escort you." With that he continued to guide her up the remaining steps and managed to squeeze both of them right next to the Hoffstetters at the counter so she could check her parasol, bonnet, and lace shawl.

"Oh, there you are dear," Clara began. "I think we're all set. George can go ahead and find seating for us while you have your things put away."

"That won't be necessary," Mr. Baldwin asserted. "At least not for Miss Delaney, you see, she'll be with me."

Clara raised her eyebrows at this turn of events, but observed the nod of assent from Ellie, so said, "Well all right then. Do take care."

Ellie wondered if she had made the right choice. On the other hand, after Henson had rescued her from a most embarrassing predicament, she could hardly turn him away.

George swung Clara on to the dance floor almost immediately. Doing his rather bouncy rendition of the two-step to the strains of "Hello ma Baby," he made Ellie wonder if the ballroom-style dance she was familiar with would serve her. But she had little time to worry. The band, composed of men playing stringed instruments along with the piano accompaniment of a rather heavy-set lady, commenced the song, "In the Good Old Summertime." Ellie found herself being swept on to the dance floor in a firm grip that didn't allow for error.

By the end of the song, Ellie found herself almost breathless. The appreciative stares of the audience on the sidelines were not lost on her. Several of the ladies clapped when the band finished. Ellie didn't know if it was for the dancers or for the enthusiastic beat of the band, but she was aware how Henson, in carefully measured step whirled her completely around the hall at least four times. Maneuvering her to the outside of others on the floor, she had been almost purposefully visible to everyone on the sidelines.

As they came to a stop, Henson bowed smoothly, one hand behind his back, and murmured, "Thank you dear lady. That was pure delight to dance with someone who can be so graceful and yet keep time with the music."

"You are quite welcome, Mr. Baldwin. I, too, am pleased to find such a fine dancer as you in this far country."

"Henson, old man," a voice rang out while approaching them from behind. "I didn't know you had it in you." The man laid a hand on Henson's shoulder then moved alongside. Bowing low, but not nearly so elegantly as Mr. Baldwin, he asked, "And who, may I ask, is this charming young lady? And where did you find her?"

"This, my friend," said Henson, "is Miss Ellen Delaney, our new school teacher. Miss Delaney, meet Wallace Carpenter. He is the foreman of the stamp mill at Cornucopia."

"I'm charmed," Wallace said as he reached for Ellie's dangling hand to press it to his lips. "Come," he said as he began tugging her hand. "You must meet my boys."

Though Ellie was hesitant, she allowed herself to be pulled along. Wallace whisked her toward the other side of the room where a half-dozen young gentlemen were gathered. All dropped their conversation to observe her and Wallace as they approached.

"Fellows this is Miss Ellen Delaney, the new school teacher here. I expect all of you to mind your manners and properly introduce yourselves before bothering her to dance. But just now," he almost shouted to be heard over the music, "This number is mine."

Leading her to the edge of the dance area, he wasn't amused to see Ellie looking over her shoulder toward someone leaning comfortably against the wall, somewhat isolated from the men they had just left.

Wallace took the liberty of pulling her a little closer than she cared for, obviously being more interested in the way he was holding her than in keeping step with the music. Ellie was shocked to detect the odor of liquor on his breath. Though she wasn't fearful of his antics, she did push him away with considerable force after he managed to step on her toes. As the band made its final flourish, Ellie requested Wallace take her back to Mr. Baldwin.

Murmuring, "Thank you, Miss Delaney," Wallace deposited her at Henson's side, then wove his way through the crowd back to his cronies.

Henson gathered her hand in his, looking quite contrite. "I'm very sorry, Miss Delaney. I should have kept that vermin away from you. He's tipsy, isn't he?"

"Maybe, just a little," Ellie replied quietly. "But it's not your fault."

When the music resumed, Henson turned to face her, bowing and said, "May have this dance, my lady."

Ellie couldn't help giggling. "I was beginning to wonder if any of you fellows around here ever actually asked permission to dance."

"Oh yes, we do if we aren't too tongue-tied or too fearful that we will be told 'No,'" Henson declared, whirling her on to the floor.

When the song, "Are We to Part Like This," came to a close, someone along the sidelines requested the "Virginia Reel." All of the married couples lined up for the "Reel," and several of Wallace's friends were able to find partners from among the young girls gathered in the back corner of the hall. They were most likely the daughters of families from surrounding ranches. Couples glided gleefully through upraised arms. With each change of partners, Ellie found herself saying, "I'm glad to meet you Eugene, or Adam, or Victor." Each of the Cornucopia crowd seized this occasion to introduce himself as ordered by his boss.

Victor was the first in line to request a dance when the next tune commenced. Ellie glanced at Henson, who seemed to be signaling, "It's up to you;" so she accepted, still working on Wallace's final tidbit of information. He had informed her that Henson was not known to accompany a lady to community dances.

Victor remained quiet, but was an accomplished dancer. Ellie wanted to ask him about his work, why their crew happened to come to Copperfield, which was quite a distance from Cornucopia, as she understood it. Also she wondered what kind of ore they were mining, but she stifled her curiosity, knowing that too much conversation would be interpreted as a personal interest in the man. When the dance was finished, Victor guided Ellie back to his group and completed introductions to Ronald, Frank, and a shorter Italian-looking man named Joe. Ronald stepped forward to claim Ellie for the next dance, then returned her to Henson's side at the end.

"How are you holding up, Miss Delaney?" Henson inquired, as he escorted her on the floor for the fifth time.

Ellie replied, "I'm fine. I'm truly enjoying myself." When they reached the opposite side of the room, Ellie drew closer to Henson to whisper, "Who is that man over there, the one in the white shirt with the wide cuffs and the black velvet vest?"

"I really don't know, my lady," Henson mused, pondering on why Miss Delaney seemed to take such an interest in this particular fellow, who had shown no apparent sign that he returned her curiosity. "I don't think I've seen him before. But now that you've pointed him out, he must have some credentials. Probably works for some rancher. The railroaders and miners aren't allowed to attend these dances anymore."

"Why is that?" Ellie asked.

"Too much opportunity for them to mix it up in a free-for-all fight, you know. After the one on the 4th of July last year, the mayor told their foremen to keep them away. He paused, then added, "Things would have been all right if they'd have taken their quarrels to the street. But chairs flying around the hall while people are trying to dance is a bit risky."

By this time, they were spinning past the mystery man again. As Ellie stared, Henson remarked, "He is a bit of a handsome devil, wouldn't you say? Probably carrying quite a lot of Indian blood to look so noble."

Another turn on the floor, and they were approaching the stamp mill crew when they heard one man loudly declare, "The next dance is mine."

"You think so," another responded.

"You want to make something of it?" the first voice snarled.

"Yeah, I think I do."

Ellie glanced nervously around the room. Wallace was nowhere to be seen. Timidly, she asked, "Do you think we ought to tell Mr. Carpenter?"

"I wouldn't dream of it," Henson laughed as they watched the entire mill crew head for the door. "Besides, I imagine he's across the street at the saloon by now."

A few moments later, one of Ellie's students burst into the hall, "Fight, fight," he yelled. Every man to the last one on the floor released his partner and made a mad rush to the door. Only Henson Baldwin came to a graceful stop next to the pianist. Along the sidelines, George Hoffstetter, Joe Halvorson and Abe Willoughby remained seated beside their wives while the yelling, cheering voices echoed from outside.

The next thing Ellie knew, she could hear bottles being broken and more thuds than that of only two men pummeling each other. She began to feel sick at her stomach when she realized she was the catalyst for the good time everyone was having outside.

Those remaining in the hall were debating on whether to just turn out the lights and go home. None noticed that Ellie had turned to run down the stairs. Even Henson, who was visiting with the pianist about a recent song he'd acquired, was too distracted to notice. But when he realized she had left his side, he broke into a run, yelling, "Miss Ellie, Miss Ellie, come back." He raced down the stairs, jumping two or three at a time, but still failed to catch her before she rushed out the door where she began screaming, "Stop, stop, I'll dance with all of you."

The melee continued in spite of her. So she reached to take hold of an arm bunched and ready to land a vicious left hook. Barely feeling her touch, Cord spun around to see who it was. Noting the danger she was in, he yelled a command.

"Get back inside, Miss Ellie. Go now!" Cord caught a blow to his right temple that resounded like a two by four hitting a stone wall. Still he hardly staggered. "I said, 'Go'" he spat between clenched teeth and paused long enough to give her a shove.

Then he continued to swing around, ducking another blow to his head. He managed to land a punch to the perpetrator's solar plexus that sent the brawler flying into the street.

By this time, Henson had reached Ellie's side, and for the second time tonight, was catching her before she could topple to the ground. "Come on," he ordered, "Let's get you out of here."

Ellie was aghast when Henson clamped his arm around her waist and picked her up, to run back toward the dance hall door, carrying her as if she were a disobedient child.

Puffing, he let her dangling feet touch the floor just inside the door. Then he helped her stand upright to face him. "What did you think you were doing?" he demanded. "Don't ever mix in men's business like that again!"

"I, I'm sorry," she sputtered. Then raising her arm to swipe the back of her hand across her forehead, she started up the steps to retrieve her shawl, bonnet, and parasol. At the landing, she met both Clara and George.

"Dear me," Clara began fussing. "Where did you go? You look just awful." Seeing that Ellie was quite distressed, George stepped forward to take her arm, saying, "Here are your things. I think we better go out the side door and bring ourselves home."

"Sounds good to me," Ellie returned, as she tried in vain to prevent tears. When Clara realized she was crying, she soothed, "Here dear." She produced a handkerchief from inside her sleeve. "Now come along and don't pay any mind to that brawl out there. I'm so sorry you had to see such a thing on your first Saturday night in Copperfield."

George continued to assist Ellie down the stairs, anxiously inquiring when they reached the street, "Are you all right?"

"Yes," Ellie sobbed, "I'm all right."

"Well, then, why are you so upset?" George wanted to know.

Ellie pulled away from George, to dab her eyes with Clara's handkerchief, then choked out, "He really isn't a very nice man is he?"

George paused, as he considered the possibilities of just which man she meant, then settled on remarking, "No, I think not. None of them are very nice, Miss Delaney. There now, it's okay," he comforted as he took his post again at her side.

Clara caught hold of Ellie's other arm saying, "Come along dear. I'll fix you a nice cup of hot tea."

"Jimmy is that you?" Lillian Lawson peered through the open doorway into pitch darkness. Her right arm was elevated heavenward. A lantern dangled from her fingertips shedding its feeble light a scant few feet into the moonless night. The narrow canyon walls permitted nothing to be seen but the brilliant stars above.

"Jimmy," Lillian called again, "Answer me if that's you." Her voice quavered a little as she reflected on the long night she had spent fretting about her fifteen-year-old son, who hadn't returned by the usual 4:30 hour this Friday night, the second week of school.

A cough and a snort from Ginger in the corral across the ravine from the house let Lillian know that her suspicions were correct. Someone was approaching on horseback. The horse's hooves were now scraping lightly on the gravel letting her know that the rider was very near.

Suddenly Mac's blazed face loomed out of the darkness to halt at the front steps of the farmhouse. Lillian screamed as a slumped body lurched sideways and fell from the saddle to the ground at the horse's front feet.

"Jimmy! Jimmy! Jimmy, what's wrong?" she screeched as she dropped the lantern quickly to the top step of the porch and raced to the side of the still figure now curled into a fetal position on the ground.

Squatting beside him, she gently raised his head to her bosom. The stench of whiskey and vomit assaulted her. "Ugh," she proclaimed as she dropped him abruptly back to the bare ground. "What in the name of heaven have you been up to?" she shrieked.

The figure stirred a couple of inches to one side, then rolled on its back, emitting a low groan and exhaling a deep breath.

"I said, what have you been up to, young man?" Lillian repeated loudly.

Somehow, like coming out of a fog, Jimmy collected himself enough to moan, "Aw, Ma, I'm all right. Just leave me alone. I wanna sleep."

"You'll not sleep," growled Lillian, "even if I have to get the broom."

With that threat, Jimmy raised himself to his knees. His head dangled downward along his arms as he attempted to crawl forward. He succeeded for a few inches, then tumbled nose first into the dust.

Lillian gave up any hope that this disgusting piece of humanity lying sprawled before her, the very flesh and blood that had once been a part of her, would get to his feet tonight. She rolled him on to his back, then positioning herself at his head, she leaned over to place her forearms firmly under each armpit. She almost giggled as his head lolled back and his cap rolled off to one side. But her anger surfaced again quickly. As she tugged and drug Jimmy's almost lifeless body up the four wooden steps and across the few feet of porch area to the front door, she puffed and spat words of anger with each inch of progress. Once inside the door, she dropped her burden and went back to retrieve the lantern. It was then that she realized the first fingers of dawn were beginning their certain crawl across the hilltops. The time was somewhere near 3:30 a.m.

"Damn," she muttered as she finished tugging Jimmy's one hundred twenty pounds to the middle of the room. Fortunately, it was a seasonally warm night of 60 degrees or more, so she pulled the throw cover off the easy chair and tossed it carelessly over the sleeping boy. Then she went to her bedroom to put on a flannel shirt and a pair of her husband's coveralls, pulling both over her knee-length nightdress. With buttons and buckles all in place, she went outside to take Mac to the barn to unsaddle and turn him loose.

Mac's soft nickering told Lillian how much he appreciated the removal of the paraphernalia that had been tightly attached since school closed the afternoon before. Lillian scuffed her untied shoe in the dirt path as she made her way back to the house. She wished she could really kick something to vent her frustration. Instead, she allowed a tear to trickle half way down her cheek before she swiped at it with roughened knuckles.

She wished Ben were here. It wasn't fair that she had to cope with Jimmy all by herself while Ben followed the wheat harvest through Umatilla County and sometimes as far as the Paloose country in Washington State then over into Montana, before returning to Union and Baker County in late September each year. With so much construction, mining, and other business enterprise in Copperfield the last few years, Lillian begged Ben to forget the wheat harvest and just take a job closer to home. But he'd have none of it.

This last summer when she pointed out to him what a hell-hole Copperfield was becoming and that Jimmy would have the whole summer with nothing but a few chores to occupy his time, he only laughed, chucked her under the chin and said, "Aw honey, it's only for three months. What can happen in three months?"

Indeed, what can happen? Just about everything. But up until this night, it hadn't really affected her or Jimmy. But now it had, and somebody had to do something to bring Copperfield's rowdiness to a halt before someone really got hurt. But where could she turn?

Placing the lantern on the wash stand inside her bedroom door, she levered the chimney upward and blew out the light. Then throwing her clothed body crossways on the double bed, her legs dangling over the edge, she could again feel tears trickling slowly down—this time dampening her ear.

Before she slept, she silently ticked off the names of neighbors she could count on to back her in a move to shut down the saloons and those slutty houses of ill repute in Copperfield. Undoubtedly Marge Wilson would. Her husband had returned home last payday with a dollar and some change from his $35.00 weekly salary. He said he'd lost it on the wheel. Jordan and Alberta Cox had just spent all last Sunday afternoon speculating about how many laws were being broken. And Jack Klegg had actually stopped in at the sheriff's office in Baker City to see if all the trafficking being conducted by rail was actually legal. That and the fact that dynamite and liquor were being hauled in quantity on the same train for delivery at Copperfield was surely against the law.

But whether all those concerns were meritorious or not, there was one thing that the sheriff couldn't deny. Children of fifteen, unaccompanied by an adult, should not be able to frequent the saloons or bawdyhouses, much less buy liquor. Just as Lillian resolved to wallop Jimmy good with his daddy's belt as soon as he was able to stand on his own two feet, she thought of the best ally of all—Miss Ellen Delaney. With that, she rolled her face toward the pillow she had plumped under her head. Then she drew her legs up to her stomach and curled her head forward to sleep like a baby.

General Delivery
Copperfield, Oregon
October 4, 1913

Dear Lottie Fern,

Tonight there is another dance. I just told Clara I don't want to go. She is rather put out with me. I told her I was very tired and that I'd prefer to stay at home with the children. Not that staying with them matters. They go to bed when their parents leave for the dance. I also told Clara, I have nothing appropriate to wear. I only brought three gowns with me. I've worn one.

Clara says I absolutely cannot wear my beautiful red ball gown. She thinks men will get the wrong idea. And my blue and gold brocade is rather too formal for a country-dance. Clara suggests that when I'm paid on the 15th, I go to the mercantile down the street and choose some nice cottons, then have her sister, Rebecca Daniels, make a couple of gowns for me.

Rebecca is a mousy little woman, the exact opposite of Clara. I met her here at the store earlier this week. She is ten years younger than Clara, so I can see why she could have been over-shadowed as a child.

Clara explained in her best motherly fashion that a dark color would be a good choice for gowns. That way, I could change accessories, and no one will be the wiser if I wear the same basic dress to work. Shades of Mother, lecturing me when I was 16, don't you agree?

Of course, there's another reason I don't want to go to the dance. I have been reluctant to tell you about it. But when I went two weeks ago, the occasion was anything but uneventful. In fact there was a brawl, almost a riot. The awful part about it is that I think the men who started the melee were fighting over who was going to dance with me next. I didn't appreciate that one little bit. But Clara assures me it's not likely to happen again. If I do bring myself to attend in the future, I'm not going to be so foolish as to dance with every stranger who comes along, even if it means sitting out most of the time.

The first two full weeks of school have ended fairly successfully, I think. Most of the children have settled nicely into the routine. The only ones who are giving me trouble are the Riley twins. There are six boys in that family. The twins are the oldest. The four younger boys are 10, 9, 7, and 5. They never get out of line, at least not so far.

But I discovered the other day that Kip and Kurt have divided their schoolwork between them. Since they dress alike, Kip always responds to the arithmetic exercise, and Kurt does the reading and grammar. I guess it's gotten to be a game with them to quietly switch seats if I turn my attention to the chalkboard. That way, I am not so likely to succeed in checking on both of them in any one lesson. I finally caught on when their five-year-old brother, Andrew, started giggling. I had called on Kurt, and Kip apparently responded.

Now, I have them seated on opposite ends of the row in assigned desks so that it's almost impossible to switch seats during recitals. The worst problem I'm having, however, is that they are continually challenging the bigger boys to combat. I suspect one day soon, the 8th graders are going to accommodate them, or even Jason, who is a very athletic 7th grader. The Riley twins are in the 6th grade.

One other problem has developed that I'm quite concerned about. Last week-end, one of the 8th graders, who is 15, drank so much at some saloon here in town that he got deathly sick. He claims he can't remember where he'd been or any of the details from the whole day last Friday, not even coming to school that morning. But he was there. In fact I kept him briefly during the afternoon recess to help him learn how to take notes from his history book. I am requiring the 8th graders to develop a journal of their history studies.

Anyway, he frightened his mother out of her wits. She came to see me on Tuesday to ask if I had any ideas about the saloon elements that allow such a thing to happen. I can't say that I blame her for worrying so much. It is simply intolerable that they would take advantage of a young boy that way. But all I can think to do is keep my eyes and ears open to see if it becomes apparent where he got the liquor, then contact the law.

I'm going to be observing Jimmy, that's his name, very carefully to see how he progresses. His mother thinks he'll be fine by the first of next week. That's also the time when his father will be returning from working the fall hay and grain harvests around Eastern Oregon. She is sure Jimmy won't be repeating his drinking behavior or missing any more school.

Lottie Fern, maybe you can help me out with my wish list. I know you personally subscribe to a daily newspaper from Portland. Is there a chance you could bundle the main news pages once a week and send them to me? There is so much going on now. The Panama Canal, women's suffrage, the work of the Anti-Saloon League, to name a few. And the new inventions are incredible. I feel I just must have newspaper coverage from more than one source to keep up. I'd ask the school board, but I doubt they'd be interested. So I am limited to my own subscription to an eight-page daily from Baker City. Our mail service being what it is, I get three papers in Tuesday's mail, and three on Friday.

I am already beginning to adopt a rather provincial attitude like so many of the people around here. At first, I was quite shocked at the limited topics of their conversations as they visit with one another at the store. But I have to admit that with the high walls of this canyon sheltering me, I am having increasing difficulty remembering there is a whole wide world out there.

I am so looking forward to your next letter.

My abiding love,

Cousin Ellie K.

Dancing the Night Away

When the first dance in October rolled around, Ellie was still smarting from the treatment she had received at the hands of Cord Williams and Henson Baldwin. In the last two weeks, she had learned what little there was to know about Cord. He was working for Marty Kellner doing the chores that her oldest and best student, Billy Mitchell, had been doing before school opened.

Billy was orphaned about two years ago. His mother died in childbirth in the spring; and a bucking bronco rolled on his father later that summer. Ellie's heart went out to him constantly. In her opinion, he was her smartest student and definitely destined for greatness.

A ranch family from Homestead gave Billy a home at the first. Then this last summer, he got a job with Marty Kellner rebuilding his saloon. Billy would have much preferred living at The Golden Star, especially since he admired Mrs. Kellner so much. But that was not to be.

The difficulty developed because of the continuing trouble between Kellner and the Town Council. Mayor Sullivan was "just holding his breath," according to Billy, to catch Marty in a violation of City Ordinances. So the Kellners couldn't take a chance by letting Billy stay around after they re-opened the saloon. Instead, Billy took a job working part time for the blacksmith, Tom Harkins. Mr. Harkins gave him a home as well.

More than once, Billy sighed and mentioned that "Miss Bridget is just about the nicest person I know." Every day at noon Billy gulped down his lunch, then ran as fast as he could over to The Golden Star. He'd go up the back stairs, visit for not more than ten minutes, then be back on the playground to help supervise the younger children. The first time he left, Ellie didn't notice his departure from the school ground. But she did notice his return at 12.30. The posted rules clearly stated that "Children must stay at school once they arrive unless the teacher releases them, or their parents arrive to take custody."

So when Ellie noticed Billy's exit at noon on Thursday the first week, she came close to keeping him after school to speak with him. Then she thought she found a way out. Billy was clearly an emancipated individual at 16, so did not fit the category of being a child.

By the third week of school, Ellie finally admitted her guilty knowledge to herself and to Billy when he arrived early on Tuesday morning to help her with the morning chores. "How are your friends, the Kellners?" she inquired.

"Oh, they're great, just great. They have finished the platform for the player piano, you know, and they've dug a hold in the floor to keep the extra supplies of liquor cool."

"Billy," she admonished, "You're not going into the saloon are you?"

"Oh no, Miss Delaney," he replied. "But every day, I can hear the piano playing downstairs while I visit with Miss Bridget." Continuing, he added, "They have this guy, Cord Williams, working for them now. He likes to keep the piano going, I think."

Ellie knew immediately that he had to be the one she had encountered in the fight at the first dance. She was also pretty certain she'd seen him coming out of Winona's Boarding house, quite frequently, just after she passed it on her way to school. She refused to give him the satisfaction of knowing that she knew he was there. So she would look straight ahead until she came abreast of the post office. Then she would turn her head slightly, just in time to see him pausing to cast a look in her direction before entering The Golden Star.

"Do you like piano music, Billy?" Ellie inquired as a way to keep the conversation going.

"You know I do, Miss Delaney," Billy returned. "If I could, I'd sit and play one all day long just like Mr. Williams does."

"Is that all he does?" Ellie queried.

"Oh, no, I didn't mean that. Mr. Kellner always finds plenty of work to do. He likes the place to be clean and neat both inside and out all the time. Did you know he already replaced the sawdust on the saloon floor? Says he likes the nice fresh smell of newly-cut sawdust." I bet the guys in the other saloons haven't swamped out their joints completely in the three or four years they've been operating. And here, Mr. Kellner has done it already in a little over a month.

"Really," Billy continued, "Mr. Williams is a hard-working guy. You have to stay on your toes to keep up with him. I know because I followed along while he and Mr. Kellner hauled in the last load of lumber to finish the platform on Saturday."

"I see," said Ellie. "So where does this Williams fellow come from."

"You know, I asked Miss Bridget that, and she said he didn't really say. I asked her too how old he is. He's so tall and everything. She said she didn't know that either. She thought he might be getting close to 30. She's 32, you know. Going to have her first baby. Mr. Kellner is kind of worried."

All the while Billy had been chatting away, he was washing down the chalkboard, stacking the erasers to take outdoors to pound, and replacing short pieces of chalk with nice long ones. Ellie observing his progress said, "The board looks very nice, Billy. Not at all streaked like it was last week. It will be much easier to read now."

Billy smiled, then picked up the erasers and went outside. Ellie turned her thoughts to the forthcoming Saturday night dance when Cecile and Jeffrey came galloping into the room.

Jeffrey had a bouquet of asters his mother had let him pick from her yard. Ellie handed him the vase from her desk and requested he go fill it with water from the pump. In a flash, she made her decision about attending dances again. She would go to the second dance in October. After all, most of the people she met so far, had been very nice. And Clara, herself, had said that the chances of another fight were quite remote.

"It only happens about once a year," Clara informed Ellie. "Besides, you have to get out and meet people, or they will think you're a recluse." That was her argument when Ellie declined to attend the dance a week and a half ago.

When Ellie had expressed her distaste for arousing male competitiveness that seemed to occur in her presence, Clara had told her to ignore the buffoons, even if she were more terrified than gratified by their attention.

"Ellie," she confided, "don't worry. You're perfectly safe. Men might tear each other limb from limb over you, but there won't be a one dare lay a hand on you, young and pretty as you are. If he did, he'd risk instant death from the other men. Of course," she added laughingly," the trick is to choose one who is tough enough to beat off the competition and yet be a gentleman when he is with you."

"I guess that's true," Ellie had replied. On the issue of tough, her thoughts flew to Cord Williams. She had heard rumors that he had cleaned up, so to speak, at that first dance, no questions asked. Tom Harkins informed George the next day that after Cord put the first fellow on the ground, several others came at him, only to receive a bitter lesson in the ways of tall timber, whatever that meant. But she did gather that Cord won, hands down.

But Ellie had no evidence of his being a gentleman. So she guessed it was high time to find out, even if she had to play the brazen hussy and ask him to dance in a Lady's Choice number. As it turned out, Ellie didn't have to be unduly forward.

As Saturday drew near, she briefly considered wearing her red gown. But she knew Clara wouldn't permit her to do so without a fuss. Still, she had only three gowns with her, and she certainly couldn't wear the same one she'd worn to the September dance.

So having to eliminate the red one, she settled for the two-piece blue and gold silk brocade that her father had told her matched perfectly the depths of her blue eyes. It really was beautiful and definitely too formal for a country-dance. But she had no choice.

Before another dance, she'd have to obtain a bolt or two of cotton and have Clara's sister fashion a gown similar to those that other ladies wore. Maybe, Rebecca Daniels could fashion one of the newer style gowns with an empire waist. Unfortunately there would not be time between her payday and the dance on Saturday night to have a gown made for this dance.

Thus, holding her ball gown up for inspection on the morning of the dance, she checked the seams for fraying. It had been four years since she had worn it. The fine netting of the yoke and neck were decorated with sequins. The high collar bore a single large pearl stitched at the vee of the neckline. The blush silk velvet trim broke the lines of ecru lace mid-bodice that continued under the arms to form the bodice in back. The same silk trim topped the lightly gathered skirt that flowed graciously to the floor. Ellie made one change to the original gown. She removed the fitted portion that extended from the elbow to the bottom of the puffed sleeves and stitched a gathering hem in its place. She found no need for further alterations.

As might have been expected by the local citizenry, Clara intercepted several invitations that were issued during the course of Saturday afternoon by potential escorts. Each suitor wished not only to take Ellie to the dance, but also to escort her home after. At closing time for the store, Clara climbed the stairs to Ellie's room to report.

Clara had, quite naturally, declined all such proposals without recourse and remarked to Ellie in disgust, "I just don't know what's the matter with those animals. They know, or they are certainly going to learn, that a decent woman doesn't go traipsing all over the place with the likes of them without a chaperone."

Ellie was speechless and ready to ask that she be allowed to reject all such requests in the future. But before she could say anything, Clara spat a single word, "Men," and turned to go. Looking back over her shoulder, she said, "George and I will be attending the dance. We'll be leaving about nine o'clock."

"Thank you," Ellie murmured.

Ellie barely had time to sit down beside Clara at the dance before Henson Baldwin was whirling her on to the dance floor. About half way around the room, he pulled her closer to say, "You're very beautiful tonight, Miss Delaney."

"Why thank you Mr. Baldwin," she pulled back from his tight embrace to look up at him. "You make me think it's the first time you noticed," she said impishly.

"Oh no," he said, leading her in a step that was new to her. "I noticed right away when you got off the train. In fact, I said to my neighbor, 'Wow, what did

Copperfield ever do to deserve this?'" His eyes twinkled as he twirled her away, then back into his arms closer than before.

It was at this moment that Cord entered the dance hall. His expression turned rather dark when he caught sight of Ellie and Henson. Ellie did not appreciate the message he conveyed. Still she smiled.

Clara was fanning herself as if it were hot when Ellie resumed her seat at the end of the dance. She leaned forward, covering her face behind her fan, then whispered to Ellie, "There's that awful man who was in the midst of that brawl last month."

The color rose to Ellie's cheeks in full flame. While she had no proof that the man was, indeed, not awful, she knew he was strong and courageous. Because her thoughts were spinning out of control to think of some way to defend him, Ellie was relentlessly staring at Cord, not thinking of the message she might be sending until she realized he was staring back.

She ducked her head and pretended to reach down to adjust her shoe lace. But contact had been made, and now she would have to live with the consequences, particularly those with Clara. She had hoped to gather a little more information before having to deal with her "keeper" as she had secretly begun to think of Clara. Even before she actually saw Cord making his way toward her, she knew he would be requesting a dance at the first opportunity.

Thankfully when the music resumed, it was a waltz. She had not seen Cord on the dance floor, so she had no idea how awkward or graceful he might be. As it turned out, after the first few seconds, she quite forgot about the dance and became engrossed in conversation.

Cord's opening sally was, "I suppose I should introduce myself," he paused, "Or do you know who I am?"

Feeling giddy and silly, she replied, "More importantly, do you know who I am?"

"Well, let me see. The way I remember it, we became residents of this town on the same day, and somebody just happened to mention your being the new school teacher, a Miss Ellen Delaney, I believe."

"Is that so?" she laughed. "Well, it just so happens that within days of your arrival, a little bird told me your name is Cord Williams. In fact, I think you pushed me out of the middle of a brawl outside these very doors last month."

"Aw, I remember it well," he said. "If I would have had a choice, I think I would rather have danced with you."

"Oh, me too," Ellie said eagerly. Then she realized that her remark had been a bit forward. "Well, too darned bad," she thought. "It is the truth."

"But I didn't know if you could really dance," she added, "or just bounce around like a boxing man. I've never put on boxing gloves, you know."

"Hmmm," Cord murmured, "I find that hard to believe."

"Oh really," Ellie retorted. "Do I look like a boxer?"

Cord gently pulled her closer as he amiably whispered, "You look like an angel. You dance like an angel, and you feel like an angel."

Ellie pulled back even though her body said, "Move a little closer."

"Flattery will get you nowhere," she challenged.

"It's not flattery," he said offering a full smile.

His teeth are so white, Ellie noticed. Then she began to catalog his other attributes. He was tall, but not overpowering in spite of the difference in their height. His arms were muscular, but she already knew that. He was graceful. For the first time, just as the song came to an end, Ellie noticed that they had been dancing as if they were one the whole time. He might not be a Henson Baldwin. But he was good enough for her. And if the waltz was his only skill, she thought defensively, so be it.

"Do you wish to be seated again?" Cord asked her. He leaned his head toward her face in order to hear her reply over the noise of the conversation around.

"Not really," she said stretching upward. "But I can't very well stand here with you."

"Fine," he said, as the music started up. "Let's dance. It was the heel and toe polka. As couples circled the outer boundaries of the hall, Ellie noticed George pulling Clara on to the floor just ahead of them. Clara glared at her without pause.

"Well to the devil with her," Ellie decided and turned her attention to Cord to continue the kind of banter they had enjoyed through the first waltz.

Again Cord did not drop her hand between dances. Most of the married women were staring openly at them by now. "Well let them stare," Ellie thought defiantly. But two dances later, she began to worry. "Cord," she stretched on tiptoes so he could hear. "Please return me to my chair."

"Are you all right?"

He gazed at her in surprise, which gave her the opportunity to say, "Oh, yes, but my feet are getting a little tired."

"That's a lie, if you ever told one," Ellie scolded herself. If there was one thing she knew she could do, it was dance all night with Cord.

She no more than took her seat, when Henson dashed up to ask her for the next waltz. He actually managed to get her to her feet before Clara could begin chiding her for her behavior. But once there, Ellie didn't feel that she would be able to give the effort it took to make their dance look like a work of art, as they had done before.

Still Henson didn't seem to mind. When they reached the other side of the hall, he said, "Hadn't you better slow up with that new fellow? Mrs. Hoffstetter is close to having apoplexy, I think."

"She is?" Ellie attempted to act surprised. But seeing Henson was not taken in by her little act, she said, "Yes, I suppose she is." Feeling anger at the restrictions being imposed on her first by Clara and then indirectly by Henson, she asked, "What do you suggest I do about it?"

"I suggest," he replied, "that you get your things and let me take you home, now." He felt her body stiffen, then added, "That should dampen your new friend's spirit a little."

Ellie didn't like the emphasis she heard in Henson's voice to say nothing of his suggestion. "He's not my 'new friend,'" she snarled. "His name is Cord Williams."

Henson reacted to her anger, "I know who he is. He's a bouncer for a saloon, and not just any saloon, but for The Golden Star, whose owner has been in hot water with the mayor ever since he set up for business."

"I don't suppose it could be the other way around," she retorted.

"What other way around?" Henson wanted to know.

"That the mayor is in trouble with him. From what I can gather, he isn't the one who permits prostitution or gambling, or lets youngsters buy drinks." Ellie had still not recovered from the shock of the Jimmy Lawson incident, though she had no idea which merchant had plied the liquor.

"But he isn't established government, either," Henson replied quietly.

Ellie wanted to accuse Baldwin of apathy in the face of the town's problems, particularly those in connection with children drinking, also the fires that had happened over the summer. But she decided against it. He was a member of the school board, so was more directly her employer than even the Hoffstetters who were beginning to engage in conflict between themselves over the Town Council and its actions.

Clara was not what you could call apathetic, but she didn't want to upset the status quo, which she felt had been good for business. George on the other hand, said he was getting sick of the whole thing and was ready to go to the authorities himself.

Having finished the dance, Henson was escorting her back to Clara's side, apparently with the attitude that he was no longer interested in rescuing her from her indiscretions.

He thanked her for the dance, and she politely thanked him for offering to escort her home. She added, "I don't believe I'm quite ready to go yet. After all, the dance will be continuing for at least another two hours."

Overall, the people at the dance seemed more relaxed tonight. Perhaps there were more married couples than the last time. At any rate the din of conversation was much louder. People gathered in small groups all around the room, both men and women, to visit.

As a result, Clara apparently didn't think she should shout over the crowd to bring Ellie in line. When Ellie looked at her though, she could detect the seething anger that Clara usually reserved for lashing out at some drunk she found sleeping off his latest spree in front of The General Store.

Ellie's own temper was beginning to fray to the point that she felt she had to escape somehow. So she leaned close to Clara and said, "Excuse me, I'll be back in a bit."

With that said, she rose and walked out of the hall, collecting her wrap before going downstairs. By the time she reached the ground floor, Cord was right behind her. Seeing that she had every intention of going on outside, he reached around her to push the door open.

Startled, she turned to face him.

"Are you all right?" he asked with great concern.

"Yes, I'm fine," she replied. "I just need some fresh air." She was perplexed by his presence. Her intention had been to walk a ways, maybe toward the Iron Dyke stable and back, but now she supposed she'd have to stay put just outside the door.

"Do you want to go for a walk?" Cord asked as if reading her mind.

"Yes, I guess so," she said uncertainly. Then throwing caution to the wind, she said, "Will you accompany me?"

Cord gallantly offered his arm. It seemed so comical to Ellie that she giggled. Suddenly her spirits were lifted, and she was floating along by his side, losing all concern for tomorrow, or even for the rest of tonight.

They had only gone a short distance until their conversation turned on themselves. "How did you come to decide to teach school?" "Where do your parents live?" "Do you have brothers and sisters?" "Have you always been a bouncer?" "Do you prefer ragtime or the blues?"

Before they knew it, they arrived at the other end of the town at the school. Cord asked if she'd like to sit a little while before returning. Ellie said, "Yes." And they went on talking.

Eventually, Ellie thought they should go back to the dance. She had been drawn as if to a magnet by Cord's deep voice and ready answers to her questions, even though, at the moment, she couldn't exactly fill in his life story. Maybe she'd been too busy relating her own, since Cord was the first person in Copperfield to show interest in her as a person, not as "the school teacher."

At any rate, Ellie wanted badly to feel his arms around her, but he made no move to oblige. So the only solution was to return to the dance.

Nearing the hall, they could see people exiting.

"Oh, oh," Cord declared. "Looks as though we're a little late."

"It would seem so. Perhaps you should see me home quickly."

Thus they turned to cross the street, hurrying toward the exterior stairway of The General Store. Ellie told Cord to continue on down the walk before Clara and George would see them together because she felt her "keeper" was going to be totally unforgiving for her two-hour absence from the dance. If she were lucky, she might make it to her room and be able to pretend sleep before the Hoffstetters would reach home.

Cord not only continued on without argument as Ellie quietly ascended the stairs, he went across the street and around the corner out of sight before Clara and George came into view. He knew his weren't the actions of a totally honorable man, but he also knew he had no right to put Ellie in a compromising situation.

Ellie did make it to her room. She even managed to remove her dress in the darkness. But hearing George and Clara coming in, she dived under the covers before finishing preparations for bed.

As they entered the front door of the store, Clara declared angrily, though with lowered voice, "Well if she's not in her room, George, you'll just have to go look for her like I asked you an hour ago. After all, we don't know that man at all."

George answered with equal fervor. "Clara, I've told you before, Ellie is a grown woman. She's capable of taking care of herself. I'm not going out of here like an angry father to run her down."

"Oh!" she heard Clara shriek. "You make me so mad." A few moments later, Ellie's door swung open. The hallway light shown directly on her dress now draped across the over-stuffed chair opposite the door.

Ellie was so upset by Clara's anger and potential interference she decided not to fake sleep. She started to rise to face the ogre, but the door flew shut before she could get to her feet.

"Oh well," she thought. "Tomorrow is another day." Although she couldn't understand their words, she could hear the Hoffstetters continuing their conversation for quite a while.

If she just hadn't implied to Clara that she would be returning to the dance, it was possible she could wiggle out of having to answer for her early departure, especially with George's support. But she supposed she couldn't be that lucky.

General Delivery
Copperfield, Oregon
October 22, 1913

Dear Lottie Fern,

You know Clara gave me some advice a few weeks ago. She said in order to avoid embarrassment and men fighting over me, I needed to find a man who would be strong enough to protect me and yet be a gentleman. Well, I think I have found the one man who can do exactly that.

His name is Cord Williams. He's 28 and ever so handsome. He has wavy black hair and very blue eyes. He's over six feet tall and has all the right muscles in all the right places. Besides that, he is a divine dancer. He doesn't say much, but when he does, it is to the point. So I must tell you all about last night.

The Hoffstetters accompanied me to the dance even though there were fellows all afternoon who dropped by the store to inquire if they could escort me. Clara and George kept telling them that in light of my experience at the first dance I attended, I had specifically requested that they accompany me.

The dance was even more crowded than last month—and loud. The community ladies were serving sandwiches and punch, which was spiked by ten o'clock, of course. But that's another story.

Henson appeared to be in wait ready to ask me to dance the moment I sat down next to Clara. He is really an accomplished dancer, and he puts his heart into it. We had barely gotten on the floor when Cord came through the door. I was rather embarrassed to hear clapping from the ladies on the sidelines when our dance ended. Clara was beaming, then she said something harsh about Cord, and before I knew it, I was staring at him. He was looking at me too, so I ducked my head. But I was too late.

He came over immediately and asked me to dance. I've never had such a good time in my life. We danced almost constantly for the next hour. I didn't even sit down between dances. Then when I did, Henson was there again.

Henson, too, made some disparaging remark about Cord, about him being just a bouncer in a saloon and that I should nip our friendship in the bud. I was so angry that I decided to go outside for a short walk. To my surprise, Cord came right behind me. In fact he opened the door into the street for me.

So I invited him to take me for a walk. He did, and we walked and talked and talked and talked. When we finally decided to go back to the dance, it was just breaking up, so I hurried up to my room and pretended to be asleep when the Hoffstetters reached home. I hate thinking that I'm a grown woman, yet I feel compelled to act much younger in order to avoid a confrontation with that woman, Clara, that is.

I was certainly expecting her to scold me thoroughly this morning when I went downstairs. But she didn't say anything, just sniffed from time to time like the whole thing had insulted her. By noon, she got her voice back and was talking about other things. So maybe George convinced her that she has no right to interfere. I don't know, but I can't believe I've heard the last of it.

Now don't go getting all frowny, dear cousin. I know Father would not approve because I suppose he'd figure Cord is a man without prospects. Still that seems to be the case for everyone around here—unless they are already married and have six children.

It's true; Cord is a bouncer at Marty Kellner's saloon. Marty, though, is running a straight place with no connections to gambling or prostitution. All other saloons are involved with one or the other or both. Clara told me that Marty is having a great deal of trouble with the Town Council. They don't plan to renew his liquor license for some reason. She says they are just jealous and are trying to force him out of business. His saloon is only a little ways from the train depot, and it is the one that the train people always recommend.

The married men, who want to avoid trouble with their wives, go there for refreshment. I've met Marty's wife, Bridget. She is really nice—a little hot-tempered, they say. She has red hair and is charming and witty. She and I are planning to start taking walks after school each day. She is expecting a baby in March.

Bridget has invited me over any time I'd like to come to use her kitchen to make some of the pastries I complain about missing. I'm looking forward to doing that soon. Maybe that way, Cord and I can become better acquainted from time to time.

After my walk this morning, I spent the rest of the day getting tests ready so I can determine what to put on the progress reports for my students. I didn't know time could fly so fast. Here it is at the end of the first grading period already.

Now Lottie Fern, please don't worry; and don't fuss at me about Cord. If he shows any inclination of being other than I think he is, I'll run away quickly. I didn't travel this far just to settle for a board shack in the wilderness and a dozen kids. Also, I promise I'll remember Father's advice when he said, "Ellie, be happy above all else." That means I won't take any great risk with my future just because a man is tempting me.

My love,

Your cousin, Ellie K

P. S. So you really enjoy your work as secretary to Governor West, or are you just saying that because you don't believe you'd get any clients if you were the first lady lawyer to have her own office? Maybe I should come join you, and we could set up a law office together. You could handle the business cases, and I'd take the divorce cases! There are getting to be a lot of those, nowadays, you know! Write soon.

The Second Fire

Cord rolled restlessly on the hard mattress that was flopped across an old set of bedsprings in the corner room on the second floor of Winona's Boarding House. "What an awful dream," he was thinking to himself. It was as if he had died and gone to Hell. There was screaming. Somebody yelled, "Get down, get down." Then he heard a very clear word, "Fire."

Coming fully awake, Cord was never totally sure of the next sequence of events, but he must have grabbed for his pants, probably putting both feet in the legs at once. Then rearing to his feet, catching one suspender over his shoulder, he began stomping his feet into his boots. Registering somewhere in the back of his mind was the thought that he ought to put on a shirt, and gloves would be good. But there was no time. He ran for the stairs. Grabbing the banister, he practically jumped to the landing, then skipping more stairs, he leaped completely past the bottom three.

Hitting the street at a dead run, he was only momentarily forced to pause to seek the direction of voices. Sure enough, a glow to the south end of town, about two blocks away, spelled fire. "My God," he yelled at the top of his voice, "its Marty's!" He had no bucket, but he knew he had to have water. Uttering a half-prayer, half-curse, he just hoped there would be a bucket at the horse trough by the blacksmith shop. Racing around the first corner, he practically flattened Billy Mitchell. Billy recovered and shouted, "Here!"

It was a miracle. Cord had a bucket of water in his hand. "Gimme another one," he yelled. Somebody did. With a bucket sloshing wildly in each hand, he ran like the wind. Seconds later, he was throwing his pitiful seven or eight gallons of water into the flames near the front of the building.

People were pouring into the streets from every building in town. Ladies in their nightgowns and some ladies still in their work clothes, which looked very much like nightwear, were gathering across the street from Marty's. Men were calling to each other to get buckets and shovels. A bucket brigade was almost in place.

Cord couldn't think what to do; maybe Marty and Bridget were still on the second floor where they slept. Maybe they hadn't made it out. Cord sprinted for the side door. Bridget stood near the whiskey cart just to the left of the stairs that led to the second story entrance.

"Cord," Bridget screamed. "You have to do something. He's in there."

"In where?" Cord yelled.

"In there, trying to get the liquor into the hold. You gotta do something," Bridget screeched back.

Cord gave the door a shove. It was locked. He hit it with his shoulder with all his strength. The cross board in the middle wouldn't give way until his third whammy. Then it cracked, and the nails were disengaging at the top of the diagonal. Cord grabbed with both hands, tearing his fingers as he desperately pried. It finally loosened bringing a vertical board part way with it. But the two by four at the bottom wouldn't budge. Cord reached inside to see if he could get the bolt lock undone. As he strained into the four-inch gap, his arm buried to his elbow, he felt a hand under his where the bolt should be.

"Cord is that you?" Marty's voice was gravelly, and he was choking and coughing when Cord yanked his arm back out of the door, then reached to catch the man who was stumbling into the night air.

"What the hell are you doing? Trying to kill yourself?"

"Cord," Marty choked. "I got some of it—most of the stuff behind the bar. But you gotta get those kegs down in the hold. If you don't this damned fire will get so hot, it'll burn the whole goddammed town."

Cord raced through the billowing smoke. Flames were spurting out the front through broken windows. The threat was there that the back of the saloon would ignite at any second.

Moments later, Cord began jamming the whiskey kegs, beer kegs, and whatever else through the small door behind the bar to the six-foot hold close by. The trap door to the hold was already raised, so there wasn't much effort involved in shoving the kegs off the edge. As they tumbled the four to six feet down into the hold, he could hear the kegs sloshing and creaking. He hoped the tops wouldn't give way, but down in the hold it didn't matter so much. As soon as he could lower the trap door, they'd never catch fire.

On his second dash to the liquor room, he lost control of trying to hold his breath and began to cough. He really wished now that he had his shirt. Then he felt a bar towel draped over one of the kegs. He hoped its dampness was mainly from water and not alcohol. Pushing it to his nose, he groped around, but to his surprise found only three more kegs. Today was Friday; there should still have been twenty or more kegs in here. At his best, he couldn't have rolled more than ten out of the little room just a moment ago.

Now kicking the last three barrels into the hold, he grabbed the trap door and sealed the flammable liquid beneath the boards. Then he lowered himself to his knees and began to crawl toward the side door. As he went, liquor droppings already in the sawdust began to ignite all around him. Crawling as fast as he could, he almost made the door when a beam in the middle of the building began, creaking and breaking.

Somebody outside was yelling, "Stand back, it's giving way. The whole front and probably that side wall are going to fall."

Then he heard a woman shrieking above the rest of the commotion. "Cord's in there. Somebody get him out." Was that Ellie's voice he wondered. But there was no way to identify the woman's high-pitched scream.

Cord reached the log railing that served to anchor the building. The log had been carefully peeled and it felt good to his touch, but he had no idea now where the door would be. Was it left? Was it right? The fire was flaming so brightly behind him and was getting so hot, he couldn't seem to open his eyes wide enough to see through the tears. Then he felt the slivery remains of the board he had cracked earlier. Pulling with all his strength, he got himself into the doorway just before he lost consciousness.

The next thing he knew, he was rolling on the ground, or trying to. As he willed himself to open his burning eyes, he found himself looking at the stars in the black night sky. Ellie was there, trying to cradle his head on her lap while holding a cool cloth to his cheek and shoulder. But she wasn't rubbing with it. Others were standing almost in a full circle around them. In trying to get control of the searing pain in his lungs, Cord was sucking in his coughing as best he could. Still his body was heaving and thrashing uncontrollably.

Once or twice, Cord realized that his upper left arm was in terrible pain. There was a burning that exceeded the pain in his chest if that was possible. When the spasms of coughing subsided a little, he reached with his right hand, but Ellie, with surprising force, pushed his hand back just as he touched a smear of blood. It felt like his skin had come too.

Ellie muttered something, then she lifted her chin upward. "I said is the doctor coming? Cord shouldn't move until the doctor sees him. And I can't keep him from touching the burn on his shoulder."

While Cord tried to comprehend what was going on, Doc Hunsaker pushed through the crowd. "Let me through, let me see," he ordered. As he dropped to his knees beside Ellie, he said, "Somebody get a knife and get those pants off. How's his back?" he questioned Ellie.

"I think it's all right," she replied as she fought to control her voice through tears.

A pair of knives ripped up each side of Cord's legs. No real damage here, Doc," a man's voice said. "Not here either," echoed another.

"Fine," said Doc. "Somebody got a blanket? As soon as I get this shoulder covered with a poultice, we can move him. If he wouldn't have had this suspender on, he might not have lost any skin, even here. But, we'll get him in cold water in a few minutes, and it'll all grow back in a month or two. That cloth on his face sure helped, Miss Delaney. It's good to know some people know what to do."

The two men who had removed ninety per cent of Cord's clothing turned their attention to the crowd of onlookers urging them to back away and let the doctor and Ellie take care of their patient. "Give them some air," one of them commanded.

Then a lady came forward with a blanket and a white sheet. The men rolled Cord half way up on his right shoulder while Ellie pushed the sheet almost totally under him. Then the men picked him up, hammock style, and put him on the blanket while the doctor steadied him in place and held the poultice to his bleeding shoulder. Once the blanket was under Cord a half dozen men came forward to gently raise him and carry him like a baby to the doctor's loft over the post office.

Ellie rose to her feet and looked down at her water and blood-soaked nightclothes. They weren't a pretty sight. She had taken the half slip from some lady of the night who had quickly soaked it in water before handing it to her when Marty, Bridget and she began realizing how badly the flesh on Cord's shoulder was burned. But Ellie knew she shouldn't douse the wound—only keep it cool. So she flopped her own gown over the area to keep it dry while she maneuvered the wet slip into place along the side of his face and neck.

Numb from activities of the past few minutes, Ellie stood, not knowing what to do. Another resident from the Painted Angel saloon came to her with a blanket, wrapping it gently around her shoulders. "It's all right honey," she murmured. "Everybody is concerned about Cord and the fire. They won't remember anything else about this night, comes morning." Ellie wondered what else they were supposed to remember. While her wet clothing was clinging to her body, she was certainly covered decently enough. For a brief moment, she wanted to giggle. What if she had been wearing her new Lady Godiva bloomers instead of her regular nightwear?

The rest of the population was engaging in staring at the fire, which had begun to die down. Twenty minutes, and The Golden Star was converted from the two proud stories of a well-constructed building to rubble. Only the corner posts and part of the crossbeams were still intact. Even they were smoldering, in spite of the ton of water men had managed to fling in their midst.

Ellie wanted to follow the doctor and Cord. But she hesitated in her misery of muddy, wet clothes. Doc Hunsaker was just turning in to the doorway of the post office to head upstairs with his patient. The best she could do, she supposed, was go home, clean up, and try to get some more sleep before dawn. Besides, even though her face was hot, partly from the fire, and partly from embarrassment, she was beginning to shiver.

As she turned her attention to getting back to the store, she saw Clara bustling up the street toward her. She anticipated the soon-to-be-aired barrage of questions. "What happened? My goodness, a lady shouldn't be out in the middle of all this ruckus. What were you thinking? I just don't know what I'm going to do with you. Are you all right? Here let me pull this blanket tighter. I know just what you need. You need a good hot cup of tea. How did you get all wet? I absolutely don't know what the world is coming to when young women go out in the night to put out fires. Was anyone hurt?"

"It could be," Ellie thought, "that Clara really did want to know if anyone was hurt." The fact that it was Cord who was the only person injured caused Ellie to burst into tears. Despite the fact that both women had carefully avoided any conversation for the whole week about Ellie leaving the dance Saturday night, and they certainly hadn't cleared their feelings on the issue, Ellie fell sobbing into Clara's waiting arms.

General Delivery
Copperfield, Oregon
October 27, 1913

Dear Lottie Fern,

 I just don't know if I'm cut out for life in the wild West. You are probably reading about the fire that happened last night here in Copperfield, and you'll definitely know about it before you get my letter. In either case, it was just terrible.
 You know my friend I told you about in my last letter, Cord Williams. He was the only person to get hurt. It was the Kellner's place that burned for the second time in less than six months. Anyway, Marty, Cord's employer, tried to get the liquor out of the way of the fire. He was almost overcome by smoke, so he sent Cord in to get more of it put below the floor.
 The fire was so bad and so hot. When I heard people yelling, "Fire," I grabbed my robe and ran out to see if I could help. I found Bridget, Marty's wife crying. She was probably in shock. She wasn't wearing a very warm gown, so I gave her the robe I was wearing. Most of the other women gathering around had less clothing on than I, or perhaps one of them might have helped her.
 I was only there moments before the roof started caving in, and the walls were giving way. Bridget started screaming that Cord was still inside. So several men ran around to the side door. They found him lying unconscious just inside the door. He has second degree burns on his face and neck. They are worse on his shoulder and arm. His skin was scorched, and he was bleeding. The doctor came, and they took Cord back to his place.
 I'd like to go see him this morning, but I can't because I suppose it would be "inappropriate." I did go to find Bridget. She and Marty are staying with friends across town. They are both pretty bummed out. He doesn't know how he can afford to re-build again so soon. He had just gone to Baker City on Tuesday to insure his property and borrow enough money to finish paying his construction expenses. The liquor didn't burn, thanks to Cord. But the bar and fixtures and the player piano went up. So did all their personal belongings. As they said, because of the previous fire, those didn't amount to much.
 Marty is talking of going back to Nevada. Bridget doesn't see how they can get there, get set up in business, and make ends meet, all before it's time for the baby to arrive. I just don't know. She offered my robe back, but I asked her to please keep it. I hope I won't be needing it for street wear any time soon.
 Marty does say he's going to the sheriff this time to get him to investigate. He went to the District Attorney last time to show him a lantern that had probably been used to start that fire. The D.A. came and looked around, asked questions for an hour or so, then said there wasn't enough evidence to prosecute. He said

that since another saloon had burned that same night, it might be the work of some community people who were attempting to reduce the number of saloons doing business here. He had heard rumors about youngsters in the immediate area being able to buy liquor, but he didn't investigate that problem, I guess.

Marty figures the Town Council is out to get him and that the reason the other saloon burned last summer was accidental. Anyway, the other fellow took the proceeds from his insurance and bought the hotel. There is even some speculation among Marty's friends that the other man may have burned his own place to get money to invest.

"Nobody, but nobody, in their right mind," says Marty, "would be crazy enough to invest in a saloon in Copperfield now, when the railroad crew is almost gone, and the power company men will all move on shortly. So it would make sense that Duane Wickert, that's the man's name, would buy a hotel instead."

When he said that, Bridget jumped in to ask why he'd even think of rebuilding if he thought that way. His reply was that he "just wants to be here when the rest of those *   *   * are six feet under."

I didn't like to hear him being so bitter and so determined to get revenge, but some men are that way. Marty's planning to ride to Baker City on Monday. He'll see his lawyer on Tuesday, then try to get the sheriff over here.

School is fine. I put the grades out for the first marking period, and everyone has shown progress in the academic subjects. I'm planning a poetry, watercolor project for part of the humanities during the coming six weeks. There are some very talented youngsters whose work I'm truly looking forward to. I always thought I would enjoy teaching. I really had no idea how much. It must be a blessing of sorts that Father didn't live to see this day and my wasted law degree.

By the way, thank you for the newspaper shipments. The postmistress, who is the school clerk as well as the doctor's wife, was gushing to everyone about how nice it is that you are doing such a wonderful thing for our school. She is quite a lady.

It would be nice to see you face to face for a long visit, Lottie Fern. But I know that's next to impossible for the time being. Please keep writing often. Your life sounds so very interesting. It almost makes me want to look into politics, and believe me, I would if it weren't that I'm have such a good time with my students.

Love,

Cousin Ellie K

The Sheriff Calls on Copperfield

Dusk crept into the misty corners of daylight as a cold rain continued falling from low-lying black clouds on Monday in Baker City, Oregon. Deputy Gregory Allen pulled his Mackinaw tightly to button the top loop. He walked from the Courthouse foyer, descending twenty-two steps to the mucky pathway below. He sloshed along the muddy pathway past the hitching rails and made his way through the deserted streets to the back room of the Geiser Grand Hotel. He wondered what Sheriff Yargo would do about the complaint he was about to report.

Several years had passed since the old boys of the back room had engaged their ideas to install a bit of organized vice in the remotest corner of the county, actually the remotest corner of the State. Problems of a serious nature had never surfaced until lately; it was little wonder that the citizens of Copperfield were beginning to demand that something be done. They wanted to halt the progressive development of gambling, prostitution, and other forms of unseemly sin.

As Greg reached to open the alley door of The Geiser, he tipped his hat and quietly greeted Mrs. Johnson, the Methodist minister's wife. She was hurrying toward the Post Office to mail some letters before closing. Pulling the door shut behind him, Greg took a moment to remove his gloves, unfasten his coat at the neck and let his eyes adjust to the dimly lit room. A single gasoline lantern sat on the round table in the far corner. It was the primary source of light. There was also a hint of light from around the edges of the door on the pot-bellied stove in the opposite corner.

Between these two points, four men were seated at a large table. District Attorney, C. R. Deschinger, one of the town bankers, Arthur Baxter, the County Sheriff, Ted Yargo and the hotel's manager, Caleb Wilson paused in their card game. Ted pushed his chair back to greet Greg. "You look like a man with a mission, Deputy. What's up?"

"Oh, a little excitement, Ted, down in Copperfield. It seems that their esteemed mayor and his competition are at it again. You heard about the fire yesterday. Well Harvey says he wants you to get Kellner off his back 'before he has to kill the son-of-a-bitch.' You know they got in a row over renewing Kellner's liquor license recently."

"You'd think Sullivan could handle something like that on his own," grumbled Yargo.

"Yeah," Arthur Baxter put in. "He sure as hell told us he'd have no problem managing things after he held that Saturday night special election in his saloon. Ain't that right, C. R.?"

Deschinger crafted his answer carefully, even though he was sure he had no enemies at this location, political or otherwise. Tugging lightly on his left shirtsleeve to release the binding effect on his shoulder and readjusting the wrist area where his hand used to be, he replied. "It seems to me he agreed that there'd be no need for any law enforcement from the County. But I guess he must be finding 'Sin City' a little more difficult to control than he first thought."

"Maybe we should all pay Mr. Sullivan a visit before things get completely out of hand," Baxter remarked.

C. R. jumped in quickly, "Nah, Arthur, Kellner is a newcomer. If he and Sullivan are getting bad blood stirred up, we need to leave the matter to the law, right Ted?"

Yargo hunkered down a little from his full 6'3" height as he mumbled close to his chest. "Sure, C. R., It's nothing I can't handle. I'll ride over there tomorrow and see what Sullivan is really up to. I can't imagine him thinking he needs protection from a saloon bum out of Nevada. Must be something more complicated than that."

Rising from his chair, Ted tossed his hand of cards to the table and turned to his deputy. "Come on Greg, I'm going to have to pull the black's front shoes and reset them before I take on a sixty-mile ride into the brush country."

As the sheriff donned his hat, pulling it low over his forehead, obscuring his dark blonde wavy hair, Greg said in some surprise. "You're going to ride over there? How come you don't take the Studebaker?"

"You know the condition of those roads this time of year!" Yargo countered. "Hell, I'd be stuck half the time. If I tried going to Halfway and down, I'd never get past Keating the way it's been raining. If I'd go the other way, I'd have to go over into Idaho to get there. That damned grade is so narrow and steep, I'd probably end up in the Snake River. I'd rather depend on a sure thing—like a horse."

"There's always the train," Greg observed.

"Yeah! Big choice! I can either be in Copperfield for an hour between the train run to Homestead and back, or I can stay three days between runs from Huntington. No thanks. I can't think of a damned thing I ever lost in Copperfield." With that, Greg and the sheriff closed the door as they departed.

C. R. muttered, "He's right, you know. I just made that jaunt by train myself when Kellner was bitchin' about being burned to the ground last summer."

Baxter extracted a toothpick from his pocket, leaned back in his chair, entwining his feet around the chair's legs and inquired. "By the way, what did you make of that business, anyhow?"

"Hell I don't know. I guess the son-of-a-bitch was burned out all right, but I couldn't make sense of it. He didn't have any proof on who did it. He's always got a bevy of kids hanging out there. I was kinda worried if I got to digging too deep, I'd find some self-righteous Christian brother at the bottom of the heap."

"So what did you do about it?"

"I told Kellner to come up with some evidence other than a kerosene lantern, and I'd look into it." C. R. chuckled. "Then I told Harvey he might want to refuse to renew Kellner's liquor license whenever he's ready to open up again."

Baxter exploded. "Now you tell me! I just approved a loan for that bastard a couple of days ago. Gave him two grand to pay off the repair crew and re-stock his liquor."

"Well shit! Arthur, you could have asked. But then I don't suppose he listed me as a credit reference," C. R. remarked.

"Hell no, but he did have a letter of recommendation from his previous bank in Nevada where he hails from. Seems to be a pretty good risk from what I could tell," said Baxter.

Caleb Wilson muttered, "I'll be damned. Nevada you say? Is he mixed up with the importation of that madame and her ladies they brought in from Nevada about a year ago?"

C.R. shook his head, indicating the negative. "I don't think so. Loretta and her crew were doing business a bit outside the law down there. Seems they had a lucrative little blackmail scheme going on the side. One of them happened to foul up with a State senator from Reno though, and Loretta was requested to leave or else. In fact, I guess the Senator was wavering on deciding to launch a full investigation when Loretta up and loaded her wagon, her ladies, and their clothes, hitched up the mules and left town one fine fall morning about 4 a.m."

"But no," C. R. continued, "Loretta came in from Elko way. Kellner had opened for business in Winnemucca when he first came over from Ireland about 20 years ago."

"Huh," Wilson grunted. "Wonder why he left Winnemucca."

Baxter supplied, "He told me it was the weather. Nevada is mostly what you'd call high and dry, cold and hot, and always windy. Gets snow sometimes from October to May. You have to admit, down there on the Snake, the weather is a hell of a lot nicer. No snow, no wind to speak of, although it gets pretty damned hot."

"Evidently in more ways than one, nowadays," C. R. cut in. "But you know, come to think of it, old Kellner did arrive there about the same time as Loretta and her girls. You suppose any of them are from Ireland? I hear there are several flaming red heads!"

"Wouldn't that be the cat's meow!" Wilson tossed out.

"What's that?" asked Deschinger.

"Well, if Loretta and her crew turned out being in cahoots with Kellner, and all the time, she's sleeping in Harvey's crib."

All three men chuckled. Wilson came back with "Beats the hell out of me though, why you fellas decided to invest in a place so damned far from anywhere."

"Think about it," C. R. said earnestly, adjusting his armless sleeve and leaning forward on the table. "You have to understand the times. We had a bastard of a Prohibitionist candidate thinking about running for governor in '10. He was openly declaring death to all saloons. It looked for a while like we might not only have to close down the saloons, we'd have to empty the wine cellars to boot. That, of course, was the negative impetus. Then there was and is a helluva lot of money to be made. Wouldn't you agree, Arthur?"

"I should hope to say," Baxter concurred happily. "We couldn't have planned it better if the angels had given us a road map on a silver platter. Where else, that is where else close at hand, could you find a couple of thousand men working without benefit of family around? Making good money, with jobs that'll last another ten years, probably." Baxter paused. "Although, there are signs of slowing some now because of the completion of the tracks and the turn-a-round at Homestead. But they'll be going hell-bent for leather again as soon as the OR & N makes its big push to Lewiston, Idaho. Most likely they'll get going on that next year."

Deschinger added, "Yup, as long as the train runs, people will make trips both ways up and down the River to Copperfield to spend their money. You didn't mention that mining will be around there for decades—especially if they ever locate the main source of that copper vein. It has to be there someplace."

"If it's such a money maker," Wilson jabbed, "How come you fellas didn't hang in down there?"

"Well," Deschinger winked at Baxter. "We couldn't very well pick up, give up our businesses and go live there; and besides we were just interested in keeping some part of the country wide open and away from the Temperance ladies and our esteemed governor!"

"That's a good one," Wilson remarked. "Since when can you find a spot where there's no Temperance ladies? The minute a man gets married, his old lady becomes a believer, even if she isn't a joiner. That's especially true if the old man gets drunk more than once or twice a year—or if their union is blessed with any off-spring." Caleb paused a moment to consider what he'd just said. "You don't mean to tell me that nobody in Copperfield is married."

"Oh, no," Baxter answered. "There's quite a few good citizens right there in town and another forty or fifty who get their mail and send their kids to school there, but live out a ways. But don't you see, that's the beauty of it. While there are no churches, there is that element of stability."

"Yeah, they cry 'Wolf,' every so often. Now that the women have the vote, their wolf howls are getting twice as loud," C. R. put in.

"Course, the main complaints have been about moonshine being served whenever a saloon happens to go dry. Gives some of the heavier drinkers back-door trots or at least a bad headache. Then," Deschinger added, "they're not quite sure what the legal drinking age is down there. Speaking of women voters, I kind of worry about that woman whose 15-year-old kid came riding home on old Dobbin so drunk and sick he couldn't stand up."

"I guess he almost died. I think we probably haven't heard the last of that." Deschinger paused. "Well gentlemen," he said, hoisting himself by levering his good arm on the table, "I think I'd best be getting home for the night. Mother will be getting worried." Reaching for his hat on the peg on the wall by the heater, he said, "And so I bid you a pleasant good evening."

"Good night," Wilson murmured.

"I guess I better be doing likewise," Baxter added. "Thanks for the hospitality. I see by the size of the chip stacks, the house did all right tonight. I presume you'll stash my chips in the drawer for next time, right?"

Wilson rose to see Baxter out, closed and chained the door, turned down the damper on the heater, and stored the remaining chips for each of the players in a small side-table drawer. He turned out the lantern and made his way to the lounge where a few of the hotel's guests were dawdling over cocktails before dinner.

—

Sheriff Ted Yargo rode out at daybreak on Tuesday, his mackinaw snugly buttoned all the way from his chin. A stocking cap peeked from under the rim of his wide-brimmed hat. The rain was not helping his lousy mood.

He just wished he'd been able to catch that damned Indian a few weeks ago before the man had apparently skittered over the Malheur County line. As it was, he'd collected his deputy badges back from the Carter boys and told them they were no longer duly sworn officers of the law. They had replied that they were bound to get that "murdering redskin," anyway. They planned to ride on toward Nevada. They maintained they had seen the Indian skulking around the Malheur City area when they first came from Nevada two years ago. They thought he might be a Paiute.

Yargo had lost a full week's time riding through sagebrush and juniper trees, spotting nothing but deer and jackrabbits, trying to find a trail. Then he went back to Huntington to follow up on his investigation and return the livery horse. He knew all during the time he spent out of his jurisdiction that he wouldn't have been able to do a damned thing if he found the man. The Carters assured him, though, that if the Indian turned up in Malheur County, they would lure him back into Baker County, probably by offering him a horse or something. But the Indian wasn't there, or any place else in the Mormon Basin region for that matter.

The sheriff also berated himself for not detaining the Williams fellow to see what he might know about the Indian that the Carters so clearly described. But as far as anyone seemed to know, Williams had disappeared into thin air, as well.

Yargo wasn't able to find out anything new when he re-checked with the saloon keepers. They were all so damned nervous that he was going to start enforcing the letter of the law on them after that fiasco a year ago. That was when an over-zealous preacher had taken it upon himself to close down the saloons for selling liquor on Sunday, for promoting prostitution, and for several forms of gambling. But the preacher was still living there in Huntington despite attempts by the saloon patrons to burn his church and run him out of town. So the bartenders "heard nothing, saw nothing," and would "say nothing."

It was too bad, in Yargo's opinion, that the religious folk were always poking their noses where they didn't belong. Without their interference, a lawman could ride in, belly up to the bar, and get a line on a criminal just by asking the barkeep a few questions. But when some hell-fire preaching reverend somebody or other got into the act, accusing regular businessmen of all kinds of stuff from petty larceny to treason, a law officer didn't stand a chance of getting at the truth. "Leaves a bad taste in your mouth," Yargo was thinking.

That along with the Anti-Saloon League prohibitionists constituted the main reason Ted had little interest in going big-time in law enforcement. He thought about the several opportunities offered him to move over toward the coast. He knew those offers were made because of his well-deserved reputation for "getting his man." And he had done everything he could to protect that reputation until this Locksley incident had come along. In most cases, that murderer would have been swinging from a rope in the Courthouse square by now.

Well, he didn't have to contend with any such problems where he was headed today in spite of the fact that this Copperfield thing was beginning to give him an itch. He'd never heard of saloon men quarreling among themselves like this. They mostly let the law of supply and demand govern their issues. When the demand dried up, they moved on or changed their occupation. As Caleb Wilson had observed when he had to dispose of his little hotel on Fourth Street in Baker City, "No use beating a dead horse." So he had sold out and moved on to manage the Geiser Grand.

Ted dismounted at the stage stop at the lower end of Powder Valley. He checked his horse's feet to see if his after-dark farrier job was holding up. Then he went inside for an early lunch, having skipped breakfast except for a cup of coffee. Visiting with a ranch hand who was also drinking coffee, he learned to his dismay that Kellner had ridden through late yesterday on his way to Baker.

The hand said Kellner was pretty het up about getting the law involved. His saloon, he reported, had been burned to the ground for the second time in less than six months.

"Damn," Yargo muttered. "It'll be pretty hard to do a decent investigation with the main complainer out of town."

"Don't know about that," the hand remarked. "He was going to see his lawyer, then planned to roust you out and see to it you went back with him. Wouldn't be surprised if he beats you back, he was so excited."

Ted finished his lunch and made his way to pay the owner. "Well he'd better have a fast horse if he's going to do that. My mount is pretty hard to catch on a day-in, day-out basis."

From there Ted made steady progress over the Sparta grade to New Bridge. At Richland, he took a coffee break in mid afternoon. Continuing on to the Snake River, he turned north, arriving in Copperfield just after dark. He thought about going to the hotel right away. It had rained most of the day. His clothes were damp through, and he smelled like a sweaty horse blanket. Worse yet, his feet felt like they were slogging in warm pee. Nor had he come up with one single thought on this trip to improve his mood.

Instead, he decided he'd put in an appearance with Mayor Sullivan to see if he could begin to make any sense of the whole mess. "It's typical," he thought wryly. "Two goons get themselves into difficulty, and they holler for the law to come and referee."

After stabling his horse, Yargo went to The Painted Lady. The mayor greeted him warmly and invited him to the back room to hang his coat by the stove to dry. Ted found it pleasant to stand near the potbelly stove, turning his hands palm-down to warm them. His fingers felt tingly in spite of the fact he'd been wearing gloves.

"So what's going on?" he asked when Sullivan returned from the bar with a drink in hand.

"Here, you'd better have this. It'll help get your circulation going again. Must have been a damned hard ride for you to get here already. I thought maybe you'd come in on the train earlier today." The mayor walked to the opposite side of the stove to face the sheriff while they talked.

"Nah, I decided I'd come down and stick around a day or so, see if I can figure what the real trouble is."

"That Kellner bastard is the real trouble," Sullivan responded. "He can't get it out of his head the Duane Wickert is trying to run him out of town."

"Well, is he?" the sheriff asked after a short pause.

"Hell no," Sullivan retorted. "Wickert wouldn't do anything like that. He's a businessman for God's sake. Runs the hotel right across the street from here. Got a position on the Town Council. He wouldn't be playing arsonist, or having it done, for that matter."

"I know about Wickert being on the Town Council," the sheriff growled skeptically. "Sounds like you're lining up pretty solid on Wickert's side. So what's really going on? The D. A. told me Kellner's an Irishmen, just likes to row."

"That's pretty much it," Sullivan agreed. "Only thing is, he's causing a lot of trouble while he's at it."

"How's that?"

"Well when he burned out in July, he collected his insurance, of course. So first he goes down by the River at the edge of town where Carmelita has her establishment, and stocks up on supplies, orders a bar in, and starts selling within a week or ten days. We're kind of particular to keep the liquor trade up here on Independence Avenue. Don't want the ladies getting involved or hurt in a barroom brawl or anything. So we tell him he can't sell liquor at that end of town. The son-of-a-bitch gets mouthy and says he's got a license, and he'll sell liquor anywhere he pleases. Then because his trade is mostly with ranchers and the crew foremen around, he guarantees us there'll be no problem. He'll even hire a bouncer if that'll satisfy us. 'There'll be no brawls,' he says." The mayor paused.

"So then, what happened?"

"So we tell him, his license was issued for only one year, and it runs out the 15th of October. That's how long he's been here, since last October. And if he doesn't get his ass back where it belongs, we're not going to renew."

"Well he closes up his operation, hires a kid and calls on some of the ranchers and the sawmill foreman up Pine Creek way and gets his saloon rebuilt on the old spot. In the meantime, maybe because that kid, Billy Mitchell's his name, is kind of a ring leader, the next thing we know, we got a woman by name of Lilly Lawson in here screaming her head off that somebody tried to kill her boy by selling him liquor. So I point her in Kellner's direction because I figure the two boys, who are about the same age, got together and got into the liquor supply one Friday night after school.

"Well this Billy kid says, 'No way.' Kellner believes him and gets all sympathetic with the Lawson woman. He promises he'll personally patrol the town to see that the out-of-town kids go home right after school at night. So that's what he does. He goes down to the school barn a couple of times, spots out the kids' horses and evidently watches to see that they ride out every day after school.

"Now he's ingratiated himself even more with his line of customers who are beginning to take it in their heads that our town is too rough for ordinary folk. We tell 'em, 'maybe the ought to be building a church or something to entertain their kids.' Then they won 't be hanging around our saloons unsupervised.

"Next thing you know, Kellner hires himself a bouncer, a real tough. He cleaned up on a half dozen guys in a brawl at a dance the first week he was in town.

"Is he part of the problem then?" Yargo wanted to know.

"Oh no," Sullivan chuckled. "He's got his own problems. He's a pretty good-looking guy, pretty well built. I heard he took up with the new school ma'rm last Saturday night. Shook old lady Hoffstetter up to the core. The teacher boards there at The General Store with the Hoffstetters, you know.

"Anyway, Kellner shows up at our weekly Council meeting first week in October and demands we renew his license. By this time, Duane Wickert has gotten pretty well fed up with Kellner for bad-mouthing him about that damned fire last summer, and says he and his bartender, who is also on the Council, ain't voting to renew. Kellner is costing him business, which is most likely true. While Kellner was closed down, the ranchers and their hands went on over to the hotel when they were in town. Now they've returned to the Star.

"When we took the vote on the license business, Frank Lawrence and Charlie Thatcher decided to back Wickert, so Alan Greene and I were outnumbered."

Ted was beginning to tire. The effects of the drink on his empty stomach were taking their toll. Handing his glass back to the mayor, he pulled a chair up closer to the stove and sat down. The warm fire was making him sleepy, although his clothes were still damp, and he smelled worse than ever.

The mayor moved another chair beside the sheriff, placed one foot on the seat to lean on his knee, making eye level contact with Yargo as he continued to talk.

"Kellner waited a week or so, then came to the Council meeting last week and brought his goon with him. We were kind of afraid there'd be trouble, but we knew Charlie could handle himself pretty well if anything started, so we went ahead with the meeting. Kellner just asked if we would reconsider his license renewal, and Duane says, 'Hell no.' So he jumps up and says, 'You fellas'll be hearing from my lawyer.' Then the two of them up and left."

"You think now that he's burned out again, and has no license, maybe he'll pull up stakes?" the sheriff interrupted.

"Oh, hell no," the mayor laughed. "He's really out to show us up now. I heard he rode out yesterday to fetch you, as a matter of fact."

"Yeah, I heard." Ted replied, rising from his chair. "You could have mentioned that when you wired my office yesterday."

"Sorry, Ted," Sullivan murmured. "I didn't think nothing about it. Or if I had," he chuckled, "I might not have told you anyway. Each little word on those wires costs money you know."

"Huh!" Ted retorted. "Do you think you've pretty much given me the picture now Harvey? Or will I have to talk to Wickert and Thatcher?"

The mayor shrugged. "You can talk to anybody you want to," he said in a quieter voice. "You going to see Kellner?"

"If he gets back before I decide to leave. I guess he wants me to investigate the fire, but I imagine the rains from last night and today have pretty well destroyed any sign of evidence. It'd take a pretty big kerosene spill to still be showing on the ground now. If the arsonist used pre-soaked kindling, it would be damned near impossible to determine even if there hadn't been any rain—especially if the fire was very hot."

"I should hope to tell you it was hot," the mayor said, half grinning. "Burned that bouncer character pretty bad I understand."

"Oh, where is he?"

"They took him on over to Doc Hunsaker's that night, from what I heard. I don't know if he's still there or not."

Yargo stood and turned toward the saloon lounge, "I'm going to call it a night for now. I'll be back to talk to you tomorrow to let you know what I find out."

"Fine, fine!" Harvey said as he escorted Yargo through the saloon toward the street. They had almost reached the door when Marty came bursting in. Spotting the tall man beside Sullivan, he stopped in his tracks. Then he propelled himself forward, saying, "You must be the sheriff. I meant to catch you before this."

"I'll bet you did," Sullivan laughed.

Marty scowled at the mayor, then addressed the sheriff. "Let's go somewhere we can talk in private," he requested.

Yargo, putting two and two together and noting Marty's wet clothes and muddy shoes, replied, "Not tonight, Mr. Kellner. I'm tired; I've had a long ride, and I understand you've been at it for two days. We can start fresh in the morning."

Anger dropped like a rock over Marty. "I might have known," he exploded. He turned sharply to leave the saloon.

"I'll be at the hotel at seven in the morning," Yargo called after him, then remarked to Sullivan, "Hot tempered bastard, huh?"

The mayor grinned from ear to ear. "Now you can see what we put up with," he said. Yargo continued out the door and across the street to the hotel. He noticed Kellner leading his tired horse up the street and around the corner.

General Delivery
Copperfield, Oregon
November 1, 1913

Dear Lottie Fern,

 So much has happened since my last letter. Cord stayed with Dr. Hunsaker for several days. The doctor wanted to make certain that the second degree burns on his arm and shoulder and at the base of his neck would not get infected. He wanted to be able to check about every two hours, even at night. I didn't see Cord until Wednesday.
 The sheriff talked to Marty the first thing that morning. Then he went to Doctor Hunsaker's. He wanted to know Cord's opinion of whether or not there was arson. Then as I was walking by a little before 7:30 to go to school, Sheriff Yargo stopped me to ask what I could tell him.
 I don't know why he thought I could tell him anything. According to Clara, I was close to being insane when I went out in the middle of the night in a state of semi-undress.
 "Heaven's sake," she said, "I don't know what people are to make of you. There you were in the mud and water holding that creature on your lap. At least that's what they're saying. I just can't figure you out. After George ran out, I went to your room only to find you gone. By the time I made myself presentable to go out in public, there you were looking like a rag mop, standing in the middle of the street all by yourself.
 "Miss Delaney," she continued to scold, "You must consider your reputation. How do folks know, how do I know," she interposed, her hands flying upward on each side of her head as she pulled her shoulders back sharply, "that you were even in your bed and not in somebody else's that night? Why you weren't even wearing your kimono."
 I felt my face burning, and I started to rise from in front of my vanity. But she came from behind me and put her hands on my shoulders. Then she leaned down to laid her cheek on mine and said, "I'm sorry child. I'm just trying to protect you from yourself."
 I suppose she may have made that move out of compassion, and she really does have a heart under that calculating exterior. But I have the feeling that the thing that is uppermost in her mind is for everyone to perform to her specifications.
 I did tell the sheriff about giving Bridget my kimono, then filled him in on the fellows who ran to the back stairs and found Cord collapsed inside the door.
 Yargo wanted to know if I had been able to smell kerosene, or, if while I was running from the Hoffstetters, I had been able to determine where the fire started. He asked which part seemed to be burning brighter. I told him the front was the worst. Then he wanted to know why I thought the men came to the front of the

building where the door was locked to throw water on instead of going to the side of the building where Cord was.

He seemed to have some doubt about Cord being in there by himself. I told him Marty sent him in as far as I knew. There were other questions as well. I can't even remember all of them now.

Marty told me later that the sheriff was trying to determine the veracity of his accusations that the men who were helping in the bucket brigade were probably the same ones who set the fire in the first place. "Hell," Marty said, "They weren't even trying to control the fire. If they would have had kerosene in those buckets instead of water, they would have thrown it on instead, I do believe."

I thought that was carrying things a bit too far. When I got there, every man in sight was working as fast as he could to douse the fire. But Marty does have a point that the fire was definitely started at the front of the building, probably with kerosene, because when he came downstairs from their living quarters, the front door was so engulfed in flame, he didn't dare go near it. After he yelled for Bridget to go down the outside stairs, he decided to try to get the liquor into the hold. He said he thought the men would be able to control the fire since the lumber in the walls was still new and not completely dried.

In the end, I don't think I helped the sheriff discover anything new. I did tell him about the bad feelings between Marty and the Town Council. Then I asked him to go see Lillian Lawson about Jimmy.

When I saw Cord after school that day, his face and neck were so awful looking. Dr. Hunsaker had removed all the bandages about an hour before when he applied a layer of ointment of some kind to keep the blistering under control. The burn is a very deep red from the base of Cord's throat all the way up the left side of his jaw to his hairline on the back of his neck. His eyebrow and lashes on that side and some of his hairline are completely singed away. The top of his ear is actually blistered in spite of the doctor's efforts.

This morning Cord went to apply for work at the sawmill located a ways up Pine Creek. He says if Marty decides to rebuild, they'll need lumber, and he intends to earn money to buy supplies until such time as Marty's insurance comes in. Now, beginning tonight and until enough lumber is sawed and delivered, Cord will be staying in a tent with several other workers at the mill. If he tried to return to his room at the boarding house, he'd have to walk at least three miles a day—in the dark. He has to be at work at 5:00 a.m., and finishes after 6 p.m. in the evening.

I'm so disappointed. Just when it seemed we might be able to find a little time to spend together, he'll be away six days a week. Cord met me outside his boarding house yesterday. He wanted to walk me to school, but I declined. I can just hear what Clara would say. But I agreed to come visit at the Carpenters after school where Bridget and Marty are staying. I presume their presence as chaperones will be adequate to satisfy Clara.

Cord and I did go for a long walk on the Saturday before the fire. We went toward Robinette and were gone for about three hours. But as far as I can tell, Clara is none the wiser. She thought I was at school.

It was so pleasant just to walk hand in hand and talk. Cord told me a little about his childhood. His mother is Potairatomi Indian from Oklahoma, and his father was of German descent. His mother lives on the Lapwai Indian Reservation in Idaho. His father was killed in a mining explosion near Malheur City, which is on the Baker County boundary about a hundred miles from here. He looked so sad as he was telling me, I couldn't ply him with more questions.

He was eight when his father was killed, so he spent time as a child on the Reservation. But he hadn't been back there for years until very lately when he went to stay with his mother for a time.

I remarked that we are somewhat kindred souls in that we are practically alone in the world. I was able to tell him about Mother, but I began to tear up when I related the circumstances of Father's death. He put his arms around me then and held me so tenderly.

Oh, Lottie, I'm beginning to want to cry again. I don't know if it's about Father or about Cord, but my handkerchief is positively sodden. So I will quit and get this posted this morning. That way, it will go out in today's mail.

I've told you before, how nice it is to be in touch with you to tell you all my troubles, or in this case write them. Please write soon. I want to know every detail about your jaunt to Portland with Governor West for the commerce convention.

My love,

Cousin Ellie K

Meanwhile Back at the Courthouse

Late on Halloween afternoon, Sheriff Yargo called on the district attorney.

"Well, hello, Sheriff," Deschinger called when Yargo opened the door. "I was beginning to think you had taken up residence down on the River."

"Fat chance," Yargo retorted.

"Have a seat. You must have come across something pretty interesting to be there for three days."

Yargo pulled up a client chair and sat. Pushing his hat high on his head, and leaning back in his chair with his long legs stretched toward the DA's desk, he replied. "Actually, I wasn't there the whole time. I rode out as far as Robinette on Wednesday, then to Huntington on Thursday to see if I could get any further leads on the Locksley murder."

"That case has really gotten to you, huh, Ted. Don't you know you win some, lose some in this business?"

"I haven't lost yet," Yargo grumbled. "One of these days I'll get it all put together. I did run across that Williams guy down in Copperfield, the guy that sold Locksley the horse."

"So what did he have to say?"

"To tell the truth, I didn't ask. He's the one that got burned in that saloon fire last Saturday night. He looked like he was in so much pain every time he opened his mouth to speak, I cut the palaver short as possible. His neck and face were all bandaged up, but I was still afraid his face might fall off, so I just asked a couple of questions about the fire.

"But now that I know where he is, I can follow up any time I want to. I'll probably yank him up before a Grand Jury if I can ever get a line on the murderer. I've been thinking it over, and it doesn't matter much if he did sell Locksley that horse. The Carters may be able to identify the Indian if he ever shows up, but there's no way in hell they can swear the Indian was riding Williams' horse the week before. When the Carters talked me into riding over to Agency Valley last month, we saw at least ten other Paint horses there. They looked almost identical to Locksley's horse. Even the Carter boys agreed on that point."

"Well, I wish you luck, Sheriff. But that trail is getting pretty cold. Now tell me, what did you make of the Copperfield uproar?"

"Not much," Yargo replied. "I can't tell if that Kellner fellow is just a crackpot seeing spirits walk every time he rounds a corner or not. I am pretty sure that Sullivan and his cronies are making things tough for Kellner. But I can't put a finger on anything they're doing that's illegal. Hell, they got the power of the vote not to let Kellner stay in business if they don't want him to."

"What about the Williams guy? He add anything to the mix?"

"I only asked him a few questions, specifically whether he could corroborate Kellner's claim about being sent into the burning saloon to put the liquor in the hold. He said yes. Then I asked him when he found out about the fire. Later when I went back to The Painted Lady, a couple of guys vouched for William's story that he came running out of Winona's Boarding House hell bent for leather after somebody on the street started yelling 'Fire.'"

"So that was it?" Deschinger inquired.

"I also asked Williams if he smelled kerosene or had any reason to suppose the fire had been set. He said he'd been in too much pain to think much about it. But at that moment, he couldn't remember anything except for his short visit in Hades. He said if anything came to him, he'd get in touch. I can't make up my mind if he is being totally forthcoming and was slow and deliberate with his answers because of the pain. Or is it possible he didn't really want to talk to me.

"So I went to catch the school ma'rm Williams mentioned being there when he came to after they drug him out of the burning building."

"What did she say?"

"Nothing I didn't hear from other sources. I'll put it all in my report. Well I take that back. She didn't add anything about the fire, but she did start harping on kids' buying liquor in downtown Copperfield. She told me to talk to a Lillian Lawson, lives up toward Robinette. That's how I came to decide to go on to Huntington."

"Lawson. Isn't that the one claimed her kid almost died from whiskey poisoning or rot gut or something?"

"The same," Yargo replied.

"What did she have to say?"

"Well the teacher, uh Miss Delaney, had told the Lawson dame to go talk to all the saloon owners, not just the bartenders. The women figured to make them so nervous, they'd order their barkeepers to be more careful next time."

"Was that the size of it?"

"No. One way or the other, Mrs. Lawson figures she got to the bottom of the whole thing. But she can't prove it because Jimmy, that's her kid, can't remember a thing about the whole affair."

"So what did she decide happened?" Deschinger prodded.

"It seems Davy Wickert had his 13th birthday that day, and he invited Jimmy over after school to see a new rifle he got for a present. His dad is the hotel owner, you know."

"Yes, yes, I'm aware of that. Go on."

"Being kids, they took a few rounds of ammunition and went down along the river bank to shoot anything that moved if it wasn't wearing pants. I gather it was a pretty hot day, so when the boys got back, Davy invited Jimmy into the hotel lounge for a cold drink. I don't know what of, but Jimmy had a chunk of cash on him. His mother figures he may have paid for several drinks being that they were celebrating Davy's birthday. Then it seems the Wickert kid had to go on up to the family apartment on the second floor.

"But by now, Jimmy may have been feeling his oats. He went back out on the street according to what Mrs. Lawson could put together and struck up a conversation with some doll a little older than any of the schoolgirls. That's all she's sure of until he got home about three in the morning, so drunk she had to drag him in the house. Oh yeah, she had notes she took on what each person told her. She read off the list in case I wanted to check out her story. Funny thing was, she never mentioned Kellner or that Mitchell kid that works for him."

"Well, what did Sullivan and Wickert have to say about the situation?" Deschinger wanted to know.

"You mean about the drinking? I didn't talk to them about Lawson. Sullivan just happened to mention that Kellner had kids hanging around there all summer, particularly Billy Mitchell. Harvey thinks that he was probably the source of the liquor the Lawson kid got into."

"I take it Mrs. Lawson doesn't agree."

"Not for a minute," the sheriff replied. "Her husband was working in the harvest over here at the time, and she found out later that the old man had sent Jimmy a $20 gold piece for his birthday, which was on the following Sunday. Jimmy got the twenty in the Friday mail, she said, because she found the opened envelope in his pants pocket when she went to do his laundry."

"Musta been flashing the gold or at least hinting at it to the shady lady that picked him up," Deschinger remarked.

"That's how I figure it," Yargo concurred.

"Well boys will be boys," Deschinger shook his head. "Damned kids shouldn't be allowed to pick up the mail. If he wouldn't have had money, the drinking spree wouldn't have happened." The district attorney adjusted his sleeve over his prosthetic arm. "Sounds like you don't have too much to go on."

"I suppose I could go raise a little hell about selling liquor to minors. But that's pretty much old news by now. Also, I kind of hate to stir up a commotion about the girls down there. Those poor bastards working twelve, fourteen-hour days at the mill or in the mines have to have some outlet. Otherwise they'd probably kill one another."

"My sentiments exactly," Deschinger nodded.

"As for the fire," Yargo continued, "who the hell knows?"

"Probably nobody," the D. A. agreed. "But I can see where bad blood might be building up even more now between Wickert and Kellner over this Lawson business. Wickert's probably the one planted the idea in Sullivan's mind about Kellner and the Mitchell kid, especially if he found out it was his own kid who got the ball rolling. It'd be interesting to know if a barkeeper was on duty at the hotel at the time."

"Uh, do you want me to hop a train and go back down there to follow through?"

"Nah, let's let sleeping dogs lie on that one." Deschinger shoved a copy of a letter from the Oregon governor's office across his desk for Yargo to read. "We've probably got more than we can handle right here for the time being."

"What's that?" Yargo asked in surprise at Deschinger's comment, even as he began to read. When he finished, all he said was, "Oh shit!" Shoving his hat tight on his head, he got up and went out the door.

The following week, the story was headlined in the daily paper, "LOCAL OFFICIALS WARNED TO ENFORCE LAWS AGAINST VICE." The kicker read, "Baker City and Outlying Towns Fail to Enforce Laws Against Prostitution, Selling Liquor on Sunday, Selling Liquor to Minors, and Gambling."

Booster Night

Classes for the next week were uneventful except for the children's excitement to participate in preparing an exhibit of watercolor paintings for the Grange booster night. Their work was to depict the lesson each painter had learned from his or her chosen poem. Ellie's favorites were those of:

Laura Gentry, a portrayal of a bee at work. It was based on "The Song of the Busy Bee" by Marian Douglas, and Laura rightly concluded that it provided a lesson against idleness.

Jeffrey Hoffstetter's sprawling, gigantic oak tree, inspired by a poem entitled, "Little by Little," comparing the growth of an acorn and its ultimate immensity to the growth of wisdom in a boy.

Sharon Dickenson's black, white, and gray painting of the "Spider and the Fly," by Mary Howitt, spoke of the lesson in flattery.

Andy Raley's depiction of "The Little Kittens," poet unknown, pictured two fighting kittens soaked to the core with snow and ice. The kittens ultimately determined it was better to get along than to get in trouble and be thrown out of the house into a storm.

Wade Swinyer's painting elaborated on a beautiful mystical sprite inspired by the poet, Gaspard. He depicted the lines "First she pouted, then she wept, then she laughed."

Ellie believed that Wade's painting captured the essence of the symbol of death, perhaps, more eloquently than the poem itself. "Such a result possibly came about because of the translation from the French," she mused.

When each child held up his or her painting on Friday and explained it after reading the chosen poem to the class, only Wade encountered argument from the other children. Older students demanded to know why he considered death beautiful and where he got the idea that the sprite represented death in the first place.

He told them quietly, "I didn't, the poet did."

"Perhaps," Ellie thought, "hers was not a good decision to include this poem as one students could select."

Cecile Hoffstetter, during the afternoon recess remarked that she still didn't believe that pretty lady was a symbol of death.

Then children spent a hectic afternoon on Friday making sure they correctly identified their paintings on the back. Ellie directed the older students to see that those in the primary grades had accurately and legibly copied their poems, then fastened them to the front of their paintings. Every student also had to check the exhibit of another classmate for accuracy and correct identification. The Raley twins were still copying their poems when Ellie announced an early release after recess.

Even after the paintings were stacked neatly to be carried to the store, Ellie still had a ton of organizing to do. Mrs. Cox, the Grange lecturer, had agreed to request the Grange master, chaplain, and gatekeeper to judge the paintings by age groups, and not necessarily by the student's grade in school. Also, Clara and she decided on appropriate ribbons and prizes for each participant so that all the children would be rewarded for their efforts. Very little differentiation would be made between the chosen winners and their peers.

Ellie was pleasantly surprised. Clara having interposed herself in the conversation got a little carried away and generously offered to discount the prizes to the Grange by 50%. Then having become involved, she said to Ellie, "Now you just don't worry about a thing, I'll be delivering the prizes on Monday myself, and I'll notify Abe to be there to present them."

It was ten o'clock that night, long after her normal bedtime, when Ellie climbed into the Hoffstetter surrey and tucked a blanket securely around Cecile and herself for the homeward trip from the Booster Night program. Jeffrey was seated between his parents in the front.

Her mind was abuzz with the events of the evening. Ellie had been more than a little nervous as she launched her mini-lecture on life's lessons learned from poetry. But with the humor of Mark Twain and Lewis Carroll, and a bit of bathos regarding the "Gingham Dog and the Calico Cat" by Eugene Field, her efforts were well received.

One thing was certain. She had no desire to participate in the Hoffstetter conversation. The rather dramatic developments at the meeting's close had set the two of them at loggerheads. Instead, she let her head loll forward and her thoughts turn to a more pleasing topic, Cord Williams.

She attempted to re-live the Saturday afternoon before the fire. She ached to have him sitting beside her right now. Remembering the feel of his face, the rippling muscles in his shoulders and the soft touch of his hands, she yearned to trace her fingers along his lips and, especially, his nose. It was so unusual in its perfection. Where most mature men tended to have flared nostrils, his were narrow, almost petite. She remembered Henson's remark about the look of nobility; rather he had said "noble look" of someone with Indian blood.

She recalled her stolen glances that she spent marveling on how perfectly symmetrical his facial features appeared. She had practically memorized each arching line of his forehead as he sang. Yet, she knew in her heart that it was his blue, blue eyes that caused her knees to weaken and her heart to flutter. She fervently hoped his ear and neck would heal without leaving scars and that the next time they met she would be able to caress his wounded places. Given the slightest opportunity, she had every intention of running her fingers through his wavy, jet-black hair that rose softly up and back from his forehead.

"Fortunately," she thought, "on Saturday she had been able to reach the security of her room, remove her shoes, coat, and hat, which may have somehow revealed her outdoor adventures of the day." Thus, Cecile had found her relaxing when she came to call Ellie to supper.

That she could be so lucky a second time was highly unlikely. Clara had just interrupted Ellie's pleasant reverie by shouting about how the Grange people could have been a little more patient. Not being able to return to the warmth of her feelings and memories of Cord, she squirmed uncomfortably and spent the rest of the two-hour ride back to Copperfield, sleeping and thinking about her next letter to Lottie Fern.

General Delivery
Copperfield, Oregon
November 8, 1913

Dearest Lottie Fern,

As the proverbial saying goes, "All hell broke loose," last night at the Grange Booster night. At first everything was light and pleasant throughout the potluck dinner and the planned program for the guests. But at the close of their meeting when the Grange Master said something about the good of the order, Ben Lawon got up and said, "What are we going to do about conditions in Copperfield? We cannot let this lawlessness go on, or somebody is going to be badly hurt. It's just a matter of circumstance that it was one of their own bunch that suffered in last week's fire, but the man who got burned could easily have been any one of us."

You can imagine how I felt about him putting Cord down like that. But I didn't say anything.

After a good hour of discussing and reporting things that have been happening in Copperfield, including Jimmy's getting drunk, they decided that their only recourse was to contact the Governor. I, somewhat reluctantly, suggested if they wanted action sooner rather than later, they would want to petition him instead of writing a letter. I sort of let the cat out of the bag by suggesting that the Governor was already aware of a lot that had been happening in Copperfield.

The Master suggested that they retain a lawyer to get a properly worded petition. Then Clara jumped up to inform them that I had earned my degree in law. The "Ohs and Ahs" in the room were quite rewarding, and before I knew it, I was preparing a petition for them to sign.

We did agree that I'd have it checked out with a "real lawyer," before submitting it. I neglected to tell them that you would be the lawyer. So, Lottie Fern, here is the rough copy of the first page for you to check. Please, please, for your younger cousin, please. If you find anything wrong, we might have to meet again to re-do the whole thing. Everyone who signed it swore they were registered to vote. Isn't it neat that Oregon women can vote? It's the first time I have come to really appreciate that fact.

Since I am exhausted from being up until 2:30 a.m., I am going to sign off for today. I did sleep a little while on the ride home. But I wasn't nearly so comfortable as I was in my berth on the train.

I kept thinking of the story of a local couple who tried to cuddle and sleep on their way home after a dance one night. Their comfort was rather rudely interrupted when they found themselves unceremoniously tossed to the ground. Their team of horses, it seems, had sidestepped a cow that was resting in the middle of the road. One horse went to the left, the other to the right. I can just imagine the couple's surprise when the cow rose up underneath their buckboard.

For now, I'm going to seal this letter and send Jeffrey to see that its gets posted and mailed out on the train today.

Love,

Cousin Ellie K

P. S. We have fifty signatures including mine. Marty and Bridget signed just this morning. I guess we could have had more, but many of the women from the ranches haven't registered yet. This issue has them quite concerned, so it may be that Governor West will be able to count on their votes in favor of his platform for the next election. Wouldn't that be a hoot if Copperfield voted to go dry?

Draft of petition from Copperfield:

"To his Excellency, Oswald West, Governor of the State of Oregon. We the undersigned citizens, taxpayers, and residents of the town of Copperfield . . . Do most respectfully call your attention to these facts: That the town of Copperfield is an incorporated town . . . That for several years past the officials of the town have been chosen members of a certain clique, who from year to year dominate not only the government of town affairs, but any citizen who refuses to sanction their official or unofficial action. That because of this state of affairs, the town has become disrupted and an undesirable place to reside in, our families we feel are unsafe and that our property is in constant danger of destruction by incendiary fires and possible loss of life; that the situation is deplorable and serious and we appeal to your Excellency for relief and pray that you may take whatever action you deem necessary to relieve the distressed community of the most deplorable state of affairs. We most respectfully invite an inspection of the official conditions of the present administration of the town of Copperfield, by the state authorities. And your petitioners will ever pray."*

*fn. The above is the wording of the petition as it is recorded in the Circuit Court proceedings of 1915 in Baker County in the case of Steward and Warner v. Oswald West, B. K. Lawson, et al.

A Sunday Stroll

Answering the knock at the door on Sunday morning, Marty boomed, "Hey fellow, what are you up to?" Come on in, have a seat," he said, directing Cord to the living room. "You're out pretty early on a Sunday for being a working man, aren't you?"

"Oh, I don't know," Cord replied, sinking down on to the flower-patterned couch near the door.

Esther Carpenter poked her head through the door from the kitchen, "Hello Cord. Would you like a cup of coffee?"

"Sure would," Cord half rose in greeting. "It's a little nippy out there this morning." Esther quickly returned to the kitchen without answering.

"Like I said, Cord, what are you up too?" Marty persisted.

"In general, not much. Doc Hunsaker ordered me to come by to check me over today for one thing."

"And somebody named Ellen Delaney is another thing," Marty teased.

"That too, that too," Cord looked a little discomfited as Mrs. Carpenter placed a silver tray on the end of the coffee table containing cream and sugar, then handed him coffee. Not seeing or hearing Bridget in evidence, Cord inquired, "Where's your wife and how's she doing?"

"She's doing all right, she says, now that I've settled down a little. She gave up on morning sickness, thank God. She just wants to sleep all the time. That's what she's doing now, sleeping."

"So how did she manage to get you to settle down?" Cord inquired.

"Actually, she didn't. I got to reading this article here a couple of days ago." Plucking a magazine off the coffee table and flipping the pages to the appropriate place, Marty handed it to Cord. He went on, "I've been doing some thinking. Maybe got an idea on how to get out of this mess in the liquor trade."

"Oh, how's that?" Cord noted that the article was about soda fountain equipment.

"Well, when we re-build, we will just equip the new saloon with a soda fountain, at least for a while. Maybe if things get back to normal and I get my license back, I'll re-open the bar. Marty reached to retrieve the magazine. "Says here," he reported, "They're really cleaning up in this trade. The outfit that manufactures this equipment came in for over a million bucks just this last year."

"You gotta be joking." Cord interjected.

"No sir, they can sell ice cream and all kinds of cold drinks. This fountain's got this carbonated beverage container. Makes sodas. You ever had one?"

"Yes, I was treated to one at the Pendleton Round-Up last year. Didn't give it much thought except to wonder that they still had ice around in September, which brings up a point. How are you going to manage ice in this hell-hole when it's so damned hot in summer?"

"That's the beauty of it, you working at the sawmill and all. We'll get The Golden Star up on its foundation again, and we'll build us an icehouse right there in the hillside like a root cellar. Probably have everything ready to go in a month or so. Then when Pine Creek gets a good covering of ice a few miles up the draw, maybe even before Christmas, we can chop it, haul it in, pack it in sawdust, and by golly, we'll have ice until next Christmas," Marty enthused.

"Hmm," Cord murmured. "Sounds all right to me, except for one thing. How are you going to raise the money? I realize you can come by the building and the ice easy enough, but how about this soda fountain contraption? I'll bet it costs a pretty penny."

"Did I ever tell you I got a brother in the banking business?"

"Can't say as you ever got around to that," Cord laughed.

"Well I do, in a little place back East, called Chicago, Illinois. Right in the same town with this Bishop, Babcock, and Becker outfit they're writing about in this magazine. I'm going to wire him tomorrow to get on over there and look into the investment possibilities. Then I'm going to sit down, maybe this afternoon, and write him a letter of request he can't refuse."

"Sounds like you got it all neatly thought out," Cord observed.

"Yup, I was explaining it to Bridget just last night. By the time I was through, she was tickled pink. She said she'd been worrying a lot about the baby. A saloon's no place to raise a kid, you know. What's more, those sons-a-bitches might just leave me be and not be trying to burn me out all the time if I run an ice cream shop.

"Besides, we can probably have our business up and running by February. Then," Marty shrugged his shoulders, "if things go plumb to hell around here, there'll still be the kids and most of my usual customers. Ain't a one of them I can think of wouldn't enjoy a dish of ice cream. I'll have fresh fruit from Eagle Valley in the summer. I'll work up some chocolate or caramel sauce, maybe some butterscotch. I think it'll work out just fine. The ranchers can even bring their wives and kids with 'em, not just their hired hands."

Cord was itching a little around his collar. He knew part of it was from his burns that were in the healing process. But he figured that part of it was because of Marty's plan. He could feel a knot forming in his stomach. An ice cream parlor, even in Copperfield, wouldn't have much need for a bouncer. After a month or so, whenever Marty got through building, Cord's job would be at an end after all. But he didn't say anything to dampen Marty's spirits.

Twisting on the couch and turning his head slightly, he did notice Bridget going from the hallway into the kitchen. He decided she was probably wearing Ellie's kimono as he stared at the flowing garment that scarcely reached mid calf on the back of her bare legs. Bridget was a good four inches taller than Ellie.

He reluctantly turned his attention back to Marty when Bridget saw him. She rushed to greet him. "Cord!" she exclaimed. "I didn't know you were here. My goodness, it's ten o'clock already. Ellie promised to go walking with me at 10:30. You can come with us," she invited, then coyly retracted, "unless you want to go by yourselves." Her eyelids fluttered, and she winked at Marty.

"I'd prefer to leave that up to Ellie and what she wants to do. I was just wondering how I'd be able to get her out of the house under Clara's watchful eye," Cord said ruefully.

"Well now, you just leave that to me," Bridget said. "I'll go get dressed and just go on up there and get her right now."

"Don't you need to have breakfast first?" Cord worried.

"Oh heaven's no," Bridget replied. "I wouldn't dream of bothering my hostess for a late breakfast. Marty's been bringing me a tray every morning since we've been here. He's such a darling," she said, reaching to pinch her husband's cheek. Rushing down the hall and up the stairs, she returned fully dressed a few minutes later. Then she practically galloped out the front door on her way to get Ellie.

"Well," murmured Cord. "I'm so glad to see the Kellner family in such good spirits." Marty resumed chattering about his plans for the new business, branching out into how he was going to start right away this week, building a crib, tables, and chairs, and other furnishings and into how he was going to build their living quarters entirely on the ground floor this time.

"Bridget don't need stairs to climb in her condition, anyway. Then if I'm lucky," he continued, "the weather will cooperate by not snowing in the upper valley yet, and I can get some help from the ranchers putting up the walls and throwing a roof over them right after Thanksgiving. Do you think there'll be enough lumber on hand by then?"

Cord answered in the affirmative, then rose to take his cup to the kitchen. Ellie and Bridget entered the front door as he was returning to the living room. Bridget evidently hadn't told Ellie of Cord's presence, because on seeing him, her face lit up like a star in the night sky. She dashed past Bridget and flew into him, wrapping her arms around his waist, burying her cheek against his chest and squealing, "Oh, Cord, I'm so glad to see you."

"Me too," Cord murmured in embarrassment as he lightly embraced her, then pushed her away. Placing his hands gently on her shoulders, he pushed her in front of him as he said, "Let me look at you." Solemnly, he teased, "According to what I can see, you haven't changed much in the hundred years since I last saw you last."

"Well you look a hundred years older, at least," she countered, then hugged him again. This time, still feeling awkward, he didn't put his arms around her. Not only were Marty and Bridget staring at them with wide-mouthed grins, Esther Carpenter had come into the room to greet her new guest.

Marty saw the uncomfortable look on their hostess's face and said, "Okay you two, it's time to unclench."

This time, it was Ellie's turn to be embarrassed. But she took it in good humor saying, "Oh I'm sorry Mrs. Carpenter. But I haven't seen Cord since Wednesday evening, and I've been so worried."

Mrs. Carpenter offered coffee again, but was refused by everyone except Bridget, who returned to the kitchen with her.

Cord and Ellie were still standing when Bridget came back, her cup of coffee in hand. She realized that they were quietly, but earnestly, conferring about their plans for a walk. So she offered gaily, "You two go ahead. I'm afraid your walks are a bit too long for me anyway. I'll just have Old Funny Face here take me out for a while this afternoon." Bridget rumpled Marty' slightly balding pate, then sat down beside him on the flowered couch. She noticed the magazine he had clutched in his right hand, the same way he'd had it all day yesterday.

"Got things figured out yet, hon?" she asked, leaning closely on his shoulder to peer down at the magazine.

"Just about, just about," Marty trumpeted.

"Well, if you don't mind, Bridget, I'll walk with you first thing after school tomorrow," Ellie announced.

"That's just fine," Bridget replied. "You two go on now, shoo," she waved them away with her hand.

Cord reached for his hat and cheerily said, "We'll see you in a while then." He held the door, and Ellie stepped out into the cordial sunshine. "Quite a lot brighter," she thought, "than it was a few minutes ago."

Leaving the Carpenter house, Cord and Ellie, hand in hand, headed toward the Iron Dyke livery stable, then west on the Pine Creek road. Strolling slowly, they saw only a half dozen people in evidence along the boardwalk of the main street. The shriek of children's laughter could be heard behind them, but none were to be seen along the streets.

Thrilled to be here keeping stride with Cord, Ellie's heart was pounding. Her cheeks were bright but grew brighter in the crisp fall air. Her thoughts, however, were mostly dark. She worried about facing Clara, but dammit she was not going to allow that woman to dominate her life. She had to admit that Clara hadn't been at all interfering in her career. She had in fact been supportive in instances when she had accosted Abe Willoughby on behalf of acquiring more play items for the children's use at recess time. As a result, they now had baseball bats and balls as well as jump ropes and some board games for use indoors when the rains came.

Ellie's other concern was Cord. He was so quiet that she had to carry the burden of their conversation. He was so polite that she considered twisting her ankle or tripping some way in order to establish closer contact than just his hand over hers. So it wasn't long until Ellie simply ran out of things to say. The Pine Creek wagon road was rather steep, and ruts were several inches deep where the run-off from the latest rain had deepened the natural wheel tracks. Cord and Ellie either had to straddle one of the ruts or walk to one side as they climbed. When they reached a grassy area close to the roadway, they paused. Ellie was puffing lightly, but she launched all the topics she could think of. She had already asked about his job and whether he like it, where and how he took his meals, whether he would consent to let her do his laundry, now that Bridget was dislocated. She also inquired about how long he would be keeping the job that she assumed he didn't particularly care for.

His replies could be summed up in a hundred words or less. "I don't mind the job. It's something to do. There's a cook shack for single men. Breakfast is at 4:00 a.m., lunch is staggered, dinner is at 6:30 p.m. I'll be keeping the job long enough to fill Marty's order, about a month. No. I'm not bringing you my laundry. I can do it myself on my noon break a couple of times a week."

In frustration and a desire to turn their conversation to more intimate topics, Ellie started to hum. Like her mother, she resorted to music to see her past the rough spots in her life. Before she reached the chorus while humming "Redwing," Cord joined her in his deep baritone voice singing out the words. Ellie drew up in astonishment, then sang with him, even though she was certain his voice drowned hers out entirely. When they finished, Cord dropped her hand, and put his arm around her shoulders, pulling her close.

"You have a wonderful voice," she tipped her head upward to address him.

"You're not so bad yourself," Cord laughed. "My mother hates that song."

"Oh, why's that?"

"It's sort of a long story," Cord replied.

Ellie pulled back, grasping both his hands in hers. "We have time," she declared. "Tell me." She dropped herself to the ground and pulled him down to sit beside her.

"Mainly," Cord began, "I'm sure she started hating it when my dad died. He used to play a banjo and would sing to us quite a bit. If his friends came over with violins or sometimes a guitar, they'd play late into the night. 'Redwing' was one of his favorites, but he always reserved it to the last song. He'd play it through a time or two, then he'd stand up and sing. When he'd finish, he'd say, 'Well, Redwing, I'm not dead yet.'

"They'd hug each other and if they didn't have company, they'd send me to bed, pick up the lamp and go to their bedroom." Cord grew quiet, then said. "I guess it's just too painful for her. When we got to Lapwai that fall, she wouldn't let anybody call her Redwing anymore, not even the people who thought that was really her name. When the whites registered her in the Indian territories, they named her La Wanna, so that's what she goes by now."

As usual, Cord had a withdrawn expression of pain as he talked about his parents. Ellie was sorry she had forced him into this change of mood. She said quietly, "Your father must have been very romantic."

"That's probably true. At least, he was with my mother," Cord smiled.

Ellie reached to take his hand again. "How about 'Daisy Bell,' do you know that one?"

"Sure," he answered, then launched into "There is a flower within my heart . . ."

Ellie could imagine their voices echoing from the hills around. Laughing merrily at the end of the song, she said breathlessly, "How about 'Down by the Old Mill Stream?'" They resumed walking and another half dozen songs later, she was presented a rare treat when Cord took both her hands in his and sang, 'Let Me Call you Sweetheart.' Ellie didn't join in this song. She was content just to look up at him and listen.

The look of longing in her eye spurred Cord into action at long last. He embraced her gently then pulled her chin upward and bent to kiss her. One kiss led to another, then another, until Ellie thought her insides would boil over.

Cord held her tenderly at first, then began caressing her back and hips. She, in the meantime, had clasped her hands along the back of his neck until she felt him flinch and remembered his burns. She drew back sharply, letting her hands drop. "I think we'd better start walking again," she breathed.

Cord laughed, saying, "I think you're right." From that moment on, Ellie was so supremely happy and giddy that she no longer worried about a topic of conversation. All she remembered later was laughing and singing, drifting into the lumber camp, dropping by the cook shack where they picked up a supply of apples for their lunch, then meandering, half dancing back to Copperfield.

Although she tried to adopt a calm demeanor as they stole quietly toward The General Store, where Cord delivered her at the bottom of the outside stairway, she knew that the first person to see her would notice the glow of radiant happiness she was exuding. It grew even brighter after the warm hug and kiss Cord gave her before leaving.

"Same time, same place, next Sunday, sweetheart," he said huskily as he traced the tip of her nose with his finger.

Ellie wanted to firm up a commitment for the Saturday night dance, but she knew Cord was still hurting from the burns on his face, neck, and shoulder. At least, he probably had no interest in being among a lot of people who would stare at him. It wasn't until she joined the Hoffstetters, who were still arguing over the petition to Governor West that she realized she hadn't said a word to Cord about Booster Night and her role in their request for action.

General Delivery
Copperfield, Oregon
November 15, 1913

Dear Lottie Fern,

    Things are going well here I believe. Sort of quiet considering. Marty thinks the Town Council has learned about the petition. At least there's some indication among the gossipmongers that the mayor is spending valuable time away from his own business to call on other businessmen. Maybe he's just shoring up his political banks. It's likely he'll be running for mayor again next year.
    Another detail that may be giving them pause, which I'm sure you know all about, is the newspaper coverage about Governor West serving notice on Baker City. I'm sending you a clipping from the 'Herald' that I read just today. You'll be able to compare this coverage to your other sources.
    Cord continues to work at the lumber mill. They estimate they can have all of Marty's lumber cut in dimension lengths by the 10th of December. If Marty had used the same building plan he had in August, they could have shaved almost a week off the cutting time. That would have been good news. I don't like Cord's being away from town. But I guess I'll survive. We're not planning to go to the dance tonight. Cord isn't terribly enthused about it. He hates for people to stare at his burned face and neck, but I'm just so happy that it's healing okay, I could care less what other people think.
    I got my paycheck yesterday. So I went shopping for fabric. The mercantile, fortunately, still had several summer prints to choose from. Clara says they should make up fine for wearing to the dance. I ordered a piece of Emerald green velveteen to make a special Christmas gown. I'll see how well Clara's sister is able to sew and fit me, I think, before I hand the velveteen over. It would be very time consuming for me to make a gown by hand. But I suppose I could if worse comes to worse.
    Back to the Governor's actions. If our Town Council is worried, they're not showing it. Clara was telling me that Wickert's bartender, Charlie Thatcher, who also serves on the council, was spouting the other day about what he'll personally do if enforcement people come to close down operations here in Copperfield.
    Clara and George are still quarrelling over the right approach to solve the problem. It gets rather comical at times the way she stamps her foot and says, "Well, I just won't have it George. We're not going to get involved and take a chance on losing our business."
    He tells her that the Hoffstetters will take a stand when the time comes, and if half the customers take their business elsewhere, so be it. He says that half will be moving on anyway, and the store will not have alienated any of the good people still living here.

The thing he's most concerned about is that nobody gets hurt. So Clara tells him that nobody has been shot so far, and he says, "There's always a first time." Then before you know it, they're not speaking to each other, sometimes for hours at a time even though they are working side by side in the store.

Clara huffs around the store cleaning and straightening, and unless there are customers, George sits at his desk making entries in his ledger. It's rather hard on the kids. Cecile looks so wide-eyed, as if she might burst into tears at any moment, and Jeffrey leaves unless he's in the middle of some chore or other. I really feel sorry for them, but I believe they are probably the only youngsters among my students who are aware that anything is going on.

At school, I'm beginning to line up a program for Christmas. I've been scanning skits and one-act plays that we might use for the occasion. I have invited Mr. Baldwin to accompany the children with his guitar or his banjo. He has a rather nice tenor voice that blends well with their voices. I'm looking forward to that, but there have been too many other things, the fire, Cord getting hurt, the sheriff's visit, Booster Night, and the petition to name a few. I just don't believe I'll be as eager about the Christmas program as I was about the poetry-painting contest we worked on for several weeks before Booster night.

Maybe the children will be able to infect me with some of their boisterousness. Maybe too, it's just the thought of facing Christmas without Father and the benefit of church services, ringing bells, and falling snow.

They say snow is unlikely here, but if I really want to see some, I can ride over to Jim Town, or better yet Cornucopia. They claim it gets ten feet deep there. I don't know if that's an exaggeration or if it is true.

Well enough of melancholy! I'd better get this signed, sealed, and in the mail. Cord and I plan to go walking again tomorrow. I'm not quite sure how I'll get past Clara, but "where there's a will, there's a way."

Love from

Cousin Ellie K

Meeting in the Back Room

"Do you think all the boys will make it tonight, C. R.?" Caleb Wilson asked as he pumped a pair of gas lamps into full force in the back room at the Geiser Grand.

"I don't know," the district attorney replied, advancing from the doorway to the large round table in the middle of the room. "I'm just afraid if they don't all make it, they're likely to misinterpret what they see in the press." C. R. Deschinger set his drink on the table, then seated himself.

"I suppose you're right. How's Ted handling the situation?"

"I'd say he's pretty shook up. Ted's a good man when it comes to catching criminals, but he'd rather take a beating than get out there in the trenches telling men how to run their businesses. Damned law enforcement is getting to be more about parking spaces and who's using them than it is about wiping out robbery and murder."

"Ain't that the truth!"

The street door swung open and Baker City's mayor walked in accompanied by four of the town's saloon owners. Within minutes three more men arrived. While everyone was greeting the district attorney, the hotel manager, and each other, two more fellows came in. Caleb had one of his bartenders take orders for drinks all around. Shortly, four more came from the lounge area carrying their drinks with them.

The sixteen men seated themselves around the table, enlarging the circle as necessary to be included. Some men placed their drinks at arm's length on the table. Others sipped theirs, continued to hold them, or placed them on the floor between the chairs. Deschinger stood to address the assembly.

"Gentlemen, I trust all of you have either been contacted by the sheriff or his deputy with notification from the governor to discontinue a number of vices as he calls some of our business practices here in Baker City. He says this is necessary in the name of operating within the limits of the law."

One of the men growled contentiously, saying, "Yeah, I don't know where the bastard gets off. I got a business to run not a social agency for wayward girls. How the hell does he know what I'm doing in my own establishment."

Murmurs of agreements echoed among the assembly.

"Calm down, gentlemen," the D. A. commanded. "I'll tell you how he got a line on what's going on. He's got a spy among us. Greg and Ted are out right now asking questions to see if they can get a line on him."

"Oh is that so? Well a little tar and feathers ought to solve that problem if we can finger the son-of-a-bitch," declared one of saloon owners.

"Possibly, possibly," Deschinger chuckled. "But more to the point is whether there is anything illegal going on."

On that remark, the tavern owners visibly shrank down in their chairs, and previously belligerent voices fell to a low murmur.

The mayor came to life at that point. "Spy or no spy. I'm out there every day looking into the actions of my chief of police. Now, believe you me, he and his boys are keeping a lid on things. What the hell I want to know is why the damned governor is over here poking his nose in our business anyway! We haven't had any criminal activity to speak of, especially in the outlying towns that he's accusing. Shoot, we're just an oversized cow town with a few unruly cowboys who occasionally raise a little hell on a Saturday night. The same for any of the other small towns like Huntington or Sumpter for that matter. How he can drift right on past Pendleton, for instance, and land in the middle of our main street is more than I can understand."

"That's a good point, Sam," the D. A. said. "Could be because he rode in the big parade at the Round-Up there a couple of years ago. Why don't you take your views up with him?"

"Well, by God, I will," the mayor replied.

"In the meantime, the rest of you fellows, if any of you have even one pair of dice lying around your place, you're going to have to store them until this thing blows over."

"How the hell long is that going to be?" grumbled another tavern owner. "I got a payroll to meet for three bar-keeps, a pair of bouncers, a cook and a dishwasher. That's seven families who are depending on my establishment to make a profit. That's multiplied by what, about 25 times in our city if you factor in the hotel lounges. Those of us maintaining a few game tables are depending more on the profits from our games than from the liquor we sell."

A second owner chimed in. "If we're going to make up our losses by selling liquor only, we'll sure be hiking the moonshine income in this county. I thought that our esteemed governor's plan was to cut down on the drain in revenue caused by illegal liquor traffic. This will only make it worse."

"Hell, Jim, all you really have to do is water down your drinks by half. That's a lot better than taking a big chance on most of that rot gut you get from the moonshiners anyway," offered a third saloon owner.

Deschinger interrupted, "You're not saying your serving shine are you, Jim?"

"No, no," Jim quickly replied. "But you can bet your bottom dollar, the towns around are going to be having a helluva time getting enough supplies in if we suddenly increase our sale here by 30% or more."

"It'll just put them and some of us out of business, that's all," an older voice proclaimed.

"That may be," Deschinger agreed. "But we can't openly go against the law. Our only chance is to get out the vote, next election, and start getting the law changed."

"Fat chance," Jim grumbled. "The sob sisters are pushing for outright prohibition, not a loosening of current laws."

"You're right about that," the D. A. remarked. "All the more reason why we've got to make the necessary adjustments to look like we're 100% legal."

"Yeah, well what about our girls?" came a question from a man who had not yet spoken.

"They may have to take up dress-making for a while," Deschinger chuckled. Seeing no one was sharing his humor, he said, "C'mon guys. The governor is all the way down there in Salem. As soon as Ted and Greg get a line on the snitch, and we take the necessary steps to eliminate him, things will die down, and we'll get back to normal."

Another man, who hadn't said much, asked, "Can't we create a diversion to get the governor off our back that way? I hear there's quite a bit of contention over there in Copperfield. Isn't that so?"

"You mean throw a smaller town or two to the wolves, so to speak?" Jim inquired.

"Might work," Deschinger said. "But the town won't be Copperfield. Those fellows are armed to the teeth. Ted and I have both been down there, and that's one hot bed of controversy. None of those fellows will be cleaning up their act, in spite of a call on them from the sheriff. What we need now, Gentlemen, though, is a plan. I've been thinking about what's come to light here tonight.

"I like the mayor's approach," he continued." Point out the holes in the governor's harassment and run a public propaganda campaign on them. Secondly, we need to stash any evidence of illegal activities around here indefinitely. And third, we'll use any out-of-town publicity to our advantage to downplay whispers here. Then finally, we need to, as we said, ferret out the governor's conduit and send him packing.

"Now is there anything else we can do to make sure we're not going to be caught short?"

"I don't suppose we can create some good public relations by pointing out our need to be able to operate our businesses without government interference," Jim remarked.

"Not if there's anything illegal going on," Deschinger laughed. "And on the four points the governor is listing, selling liquor to minors, selling liquor on Sunday, allowing prostitution, and gambling, there aren't too many voters out there who are ready to legalize any of those activities."

The door opened quietly from the lounge. The county's tall sheriff stepped through the door, pushing his hat back from his forehead.

"Ted," Deschinger greeted, "Glad you could make it. We've been having a little chat about our problems here. You got anything for us?"

The sheriff made his way across the room to the district attorney's side. He nodded politely to each man as he passed.

"C. R., mayor, gentlemen," he addressed them formally. "I've just had a long talk with Doug Milaney. You'll be glad to know that he's wiring Salem tonight to resign his position on the governor's task force."

There was an audible gasp as several men half rose from their seats. "Doug is the spy?" the mayor raged.

"Yes sir," Yargo replied. Noting the hostility among the men, Yargo said quietly. "Now gentlemen before you get all steamed up, realize this is the man with the evidence. Furthermore, the evidence has already been turned over to the State Attorney General. So any measures any of us would take in retaliation would just make matters worse. In my talk with him, I pointed out to Mr. Milaney that his work is done here. In his zeal to name names, dates, and places, he has compromised himself and will not be able to add anything to what he's already presented.

"I don't expect any of you will be throwing a going away party for the man, but I've personally guaranteed him a safe departure if he makes it soon. This will be after he goes to the press and announces his resignation along with a statement that he wishes to move on. What's more, he won't be passing on any of his discoveries to the press, nor will the State's attorney general, if we just quietly put a lid on everything and proceed with business as usual."

"Does that mean, Ted, that we can get back to business as usual?" Jim asked.

"No, Jim," the sheriff replied. "My hand has been played. I've notified all of you to clear out evidence of gambling and prostitution, and to keep regular business hours with customers who are of age as required. It's my duty now to see that you do, and you'd better believe it."

A stunned silence fell momentarily. Then the men began rising to leave as Deschinger quickly dismissed the meeting. All were grumbling about the snake, Doug Milaney, and his cohort, the governor of the State.

"So Doug hired on with the governor," Deschinger remarked to Yargo when the room was cleared of all but Caleb Wilson. "Sure as hell can't tell who your friends are anymore. How'd you come to figure him anyhow, Ted?"

"Something he said to Greg a couple of days ago when we were making the rounds. He was standing in the Stockman's Exchange when Greg walked past him to post the governor's letter. Milaney announced that things were soon going to be different all over our town. Greg started wondering how he came to that conclusion since he's always hanging around one bar or another. We talked it over, then went to ask him."

"I'll be damned," Deschinger said wonderingly.

"By the way, C. R., I'm taking the train first thing in the morning to check out a rumor from over Weiser way."

"Yeah, what's that?"

"The town marshal in Weiser heard that I'm looking for a long-haired Indian in connection with the Locksley murder. He got to talking to one of the barbers there about a hank of black hair dangling on a rack in his shop. Then, he sent word to me that the barber had cut it off some guy, two, maybe three months ago."

Deschinger shook his head. "You just don't give up, do you boy?" Adjusting his arm, the district attorney rose to get his hat.

The two men bid Caleb Wilson good night and left by way of the alley door.

"And so another town hall meeting concludes without benefit of the press," Caleb remarked to himself. He began stacking empty glasses to put them on a tray bound for the kitchen.

General Delivery
Copperfield, Oregon
November 29, 1913

Dear Lottie Fern,

  I appreciated your nice chatty letter of November 17. I'm sorry last Saturday slipped by somehow. There was a dance that night, and I was busy most of the day getting the finishing touches on my newest gown. Clara's sister, Rebecca Daniels, has stitched three of them for me. They are cotton, and I think I can convert them easily to full service for work, just by removing the ribbons and some of the more sophisticated trim. Hopefully, I won't raise any eyebrows when I do that. I do know the children will appreciate the brighter colors.
  The one that Rebecca finished yesterday is a pale lavender with tiny purple flowers, each with a smidgen of green stem. All three are prints that are quite dainty. One is light blue, and the other is pastel pink. All are certainly more appropriate for dancing than my dark blue, black or brown wools. Most of the ranch women wear cotton frocks, as they call them, to the dance. So I'm surely not going to look out of place.
  Cord said he really likes the blue gown because he feels so much more at ease. I'm sure he'll like the lavender even more. He says I don't have that princess look that I had when I wore my brocade. I don't know if I approve of his comment or not, but he does seem much happier. Then maybe that is because his burns are finally healing, and he doesn't have to keep his shirt collar (or my hands, tee hee) from irritating his neck. The whole burn area is now a bright pink, and he thinks he looks gruesome. I tell him he just looks handsome.
  Anyway, then Thursday was Thanksgiving. I was impressed with the over-flowing tables at Booster Night, but Thanksgiving was a veritable feast. We traveled all the way to New Bridge, which is about eight miles the other side of Richland. The two Grange groups joined for the occasion. Everything those ladies served was home grown, home cured, home canned, or had something to do with home.
  Clara took Boston baked beans. I think she was out to provide something that was not designated as being from "home". They were delicious too. I spent Wednesday evening at Bridget's preparing lemon bars. You remember those, don't you? They were Father's favorites. I can't tell whether Cord is impressed or not. How can you tell when every utterance from the man's mouth is dripping with honey? I know now why Father always referred to conversations between sweethearts as "sweet nothings, whispered in the ear."
  After gorging ourselves when the meal was served around two o'clock, Cord and I and four other couples, all married, went for a walk. It was almost as if we were in a wilderness when we reached the edge of the settlement. The grass,

although withered, is knee-high. The stream we were walking along is also running quite high. One couple decided to cross it for some reason. She balked on getting wet, so he picked her up and carried her across. They made it fine going over, but as he was climbing the bank on our side coming back, he stumbled and dropped her. The other three couples were standing on the bank cheering them on as they crossed, so one of the men was right there to catch her, but not before she was soaked.

As a consequence, our group was minus that couple for the rest of the walk. Both husband and wife rushed to their house in New Bridge, just ahead of us. She was outdistancing him at every step. He almost had to run to keep up with her. I don't think she was very happy.

It was a wonderful walk. The sun was shining. There were wild birds galore along the water way, mostly ducks and geese, but we scared up some ground birds, quail, I think. There are so small and cute with their little topknots. We also spotted a herd of deer out in a meadow-like area. They are absolutely the most beautiful creatures I have seen in the wild.

As the sun began to dip in the late afternoon, it got rather nippy, so we made a hasty retreat back to the Grange Hall. George and Clara were playing cards with neighbors from Copperfield. They were all but finished, so I gathered the children from outside and we were soon homeward bound.

I wish Bridget had felt well enough to come. Cord and I could have ridden with them. As it was, Cord rode with the Carpenters, who are the good friends of Marty and Bridget. Under the circumstances, Clara, at least, was happy. I can always tell when she purses her lips and tightens her jaw, she is aching to tell me what I can and can't do. She was smiling though, all the way home, and chattering with George, repeating all the gossip she could remember.

You are right, I didn't really fill you in on the particulars of the Booster Night program. I was very happy with the reception I got for my contribution to the program when I finished. But that feeling was pretty well demolished when the conversation settled on Copperfield. Anyway, only one of the paintings that I favored was chosen. That was Wade Swinyer's. It was the only one that the judges agreed on unanimously. The others were chosen more for content than for artistic talent. So Lucille Carpenter's "Jabberwocky," which was, of course, a complete figment of her imagination won the eight to ten-year-old competition. "Auguries of Innocence," by William Blake, was their choice for eleven to thirteen. "On the Bridge," by Kate Greenaway captured their attention for the primary group. I hated to see Eugene Field lose out though, or for that matter, Alfred Lord Tennyson, or Christina Rossetti.

I know, I know, I can just hear you say it. "Ellie K., you're such a romantic," at least according to one Charlotte Fern Hobbs. But I just can't wait to do this again next year. I'm going to devote twice as much time to it. There's so much to learn from poetry.

I was pleased that the prizes Clara chose for presentation to the children on Monday differed only in color, not in quality or quantity. The children were all so happy about Wade's being named champion artist. I couldn't believe how gracious they were. Even the Riley twins said something nice to him. I was quite surprised because they've been heckling him all fall to see if they can make him angry. That seems almost impossible, by the way. He is always as serene as he can be. Well, what else would a gifted artist be? Some of them anyway!

The best news to come from all the poetry lessons is that Cord has promised he will spend some evenings this winter reading with me. I can't wait to hear his deep voice, reciting, "How do I love thee, Let me count the ways." Maybe we'll have a duo reading, similar to our singing. Oh, Lottie, I would never have believed I could be this happy.

I'm waiting to hear what develops between you and your new friend. Please tell me, and don't give me that routine that you're planning never to marry? What's the advantage to that, huh?

My Love,

Cousin Ellie K.

Slipping on Ice

True to his plan, Marty completed building the needed household furniture for the Kellner's new home before beginning construction of The Star. The kitchen range was delivered right after Thanksgiving. Bridget spent the short November days bent over Mrs. Carpenter's sewing machine stitching shirts and dresses for Marty and herself. She also hemmed diapers and used scraps of material that Rebecca Daniels gave her to make crib quilts, rugs, and potholders.

By the first of December, Cord began delivering a load of lumber each night to The Golden Star. Marty commenced laying out the foundation area and was hopeful, in spite of the short days and frequent rainstorms, that he would be able to move Bridget back home before Christmas. As it was, he feared that she'd catch her death of pneumonia as she staunchly accompanied him each day. He wouldn't let her do much. But she did hand him tools and nails and she sat on pieces of lumber on the sawhorse while he sawed, or she held one end of a board steady while he nailed.

Ellie came by as soon as she finished after school each day. But by that hour, it was getting dark. While Marty wished he could continue by lantern light, he felt he had to quit in order to get the "girls" inside before the evening chill began to set in. So his routine became one of starting to work at daybreak, returning to the Carpenters close to mid-morning for breakfast when Bridget joined him. Then it was back to work until past noon. After a quick sandwich, he and Bridget resumed sawing, nailing, and fitting the foundation into place. About 5:30 he would see Bridget and Ellie home, grab a light supper, then race back to the site to help Cord unload lumber and take care of the team at the livery stable.

At the end of the first week, the afternoon routine was interrupted by Cord's steady delivery, amounting to three wagonloads a day from Thursday to Saturday. In the meantime, Ellie decided the process needed a shot in the arm if the Christmas deadline were to be met. On Tuesday, she began a lesson in civics with the 6th, 7th, and 8th grades that soon involved the entire school.

"Most of you have been to Sunday School," she announced, "But who knows the story where someone says to God, 'Am I my brother's keeper?'" Several hands shot upward.

"Martha," Ellie called. "What story is that from?" Martha Jones dutifully recited the details of Cain and Abel, and the subsequent conversation between God and Cain. After skillful questioning and guidance, a consensus was achieved in which the older students agreed that ours would be a better world if everyone were his or her brother's keeper. Out of the blue, the youngest of the Gentry children, a fourth grader, wondered, "What if you don't have a brother?" she asked.

"That's silly," pronounced Evie Franklin, who had no brothers. She was an only child. "It means sisters, too," she argued. Other students giggled.

"No, now," said Ellie. "That's a very good question. What if you have no brothers or sisters, do you have any obligation to anyone?"

Billy Mitchell quickly responded. "Of course, you do. Your obligation is to the whole community or the whole country, or for that matter, the whole world."

"Very good," Ellie commended Billy. "Now if it's the people in your own community, how to you 'keep' them?" In other words, what does it mean to be a keeper?"

"It means to take care of them or help them if they're in trouble like we are supposed to do in our own families," Mickey Riley offered.

"That's good, and that's right. We all remember that Jesus said if you fail to feed the hungry or give drink to those who thirst, you are failing to care for Him, didn't He? Now for your homework for tonight. When you get home today, think of someone you know who needs your help in some way so that you can practice being your brother's keeper."

"I know, I know," Aliesha eagerly waved her hand.

"No, no," said Ellie. "You bring your ideas to class tomorrow."

It was no time at all on Wednesday before Ellie, with Billy Mitchell's ardent assistance, was able to guide the students into a help mode for Marty and Bridget Kellner whose home had burned to the ground with all their belongings, not once, but twice, since the last school year. By noon, the older students had carefully printed an announcement of a house raising at the site of The Golden Star on the following Saturday. The men were to bring hammers, and the ladies, a pot-luck dish for the noon meal. All would gather by 10:00 a.m. As a reward, the Copperfield band would furnish music for singing and dancing inside the new building once the walls and roof were in place.

When school let out, each of the children took a finished poster, which was augmented with the primary students' colorful artwork. Several were posted throughout Copperfield. Students who lived up Pine Creek were able to relay two of their posters on to Jim Town and Halfway. Those living up the River found ways to have their posters placed in Richland and New Bridge.

By four o'clock in the afternoon the following Saturday, music filled the air. Ragtime tunes and old-fashioned favorites rang through the open doors of the Golden Star. By six o'clock, the ranchers were loading their tools in their wagons to depart. The day workers from the local mills and mines went in search of their usual Saturday night entertainment, and the townsfolk returned home to care for their families. The dance at the community hall was not very well attended that night. Cord and Ellie left early, walked and talked, and spooned for a time, then took to their separate living arrangements by half-past ten.

Cord and Marty decided Sunday morning that they would move the household furniture from its storage place at the jail to the new residence. On Monday, the electric wiring would be strung in place, and the interior walls would be ready for finishing. Within the week, the house would be ready for occupancy, if not completely finished.

For the second time in a month, Marty and Bridget rode the train out on Tuesday to shop for household goods to be shipped to Copperfield on Friday. Marty enlisted Ellie's help once again for creating and distributing an announcement inviting help to haul ice from several miles up Pine Creek the next Saturday.

The newly dug root cellar behind The Golden Star was almost ready for use. Cord spent most of Monday shoring up the cave walls and ceiling and adding a door. On Tuesday evening, he proudly exhibited the ice house interior to Ellie, who remarked, "It's every bit as nice as the new house, don't you think?"

"Hmm," Cord replied. "Maybe we should just forget about the ice, and move in."

"I don't think so," Ellie laughed.

"Why not?" Cord whined with mock disappointment.

"Because, my dear," Ellie said sarcastically, "I need windows with curtains, and cupboards, and closets, and lots of rooms for children to play."

"My, my," Cord taunted, "You don't settle for just a little bit!"

Ellie twisted in his arms to look up at him, "No, I don't," she said softly. "And I just hope you'll remember that."

"You can count on that, my darling," Cord whispered, pulling her close and brushing his lips against her hair.

It was hard for Ellie to pry herself away, knowing that in their present location, no one was likely to intrude on their privacy. But she thought they had better seek a more populated environment before Cord would feel impelled to deeds that both knew were improper.

As for invitations to join in hauling ice on Saturday, Ellie prepared and posted several around the town herself. She felt that enough people would show up to accomplish this job, especially since everyone had such a good time at the house raising. There would be no need to contact the outlying areas.

Besides, they couldn't load down the three wagons that Cord had managed to rent or borrow with too many helpers. Else, there would be no room for the ice they intended to haul.

The temperatures dropped sharply by the middle of the week, and on Thursday, six inches of new snow blanketed the town. The children were ecstatic, and if it hadn't been for their ongoing enthusiasm for preparing their Christmas program, all attempts at keeping them organized at school may well have been impossible.

On Friday, Tom Harkins called on Cord to help him at the blacksmith shop to shoe the teams of horses in preparation for Saturday's haul. The clouds lifted later in the afternoon, and Saturday broke with the thermometer sinking into the teens. All this was good news for a day on Pine Creek, cutting and hauling ice. But Ellie was only one of four women who felt inclined to venture out into the wintery weather. Henson Baldwin was among the fifteen or twenty fellows who went along for the ride, now that the mill had closed for the season.

Bridget wanted to go in the worst way, but Marty insisted she stay home, informing her he would tie her to their bed, if he had to. She surrendered, deciding she would try out her new sewing machine and make curtains while he was away.

By mid-afternoon, two of the wagons were loaded and ready for the return trip, each carrying a good 500 to a 1,000 pounds of ice. The ladies, after clearing and repacking luncheon items, dipped water from the creek where the ice had been removed. They added it to the remaining supply of milk one of the ranchers had provided in a five-gallon can. Heating it over the campfire, they added sugar and chocolate shavings, then called a halt to the men at work. They invited all to join them for cookies and a cup of hot chocolate.

Everyone was enjoying the break from their backbreaking labor when Henson came to the realization that Ellie wasn't among the ladies present. He quickly rose from where he was sitting on a log and went to Dorothy Morgan who was laughing as she dipped the last of the hot chocolate from the milk-can for refills.

"Have you seen Ellie?" he asked a trifle anxiously.

"Oh yes," Dorothy answered. "She and Cord left to take a walk just when we started building up the fire.

Henson reluctantly returned to his seat to finish his beverage.

"Son of a bitch," Henson murmured under his breath.

"What?" inquired the man next to him.

"Oh, nothing," he muttered.

"Must be something," the man returned.

"It's that Williams guy. He's off courting the schoolteacher while the rest of us are still here chopping and toting."

The fellow laughed. "Maybe he figured after loading most of the first wagon and more than half of the second all by himself, he needed a rest." The men soon rose and went back to their work. They quickly finished chunking the ice pieces loose and were ready to use the ice tongs and ropes to load the balance of the haul on the third wagon. Another half an hour, and they would be ready to head home.

At about that time, several became aware of a voice shouting from the nearby mountainside. They paused to listen.

"Ellie, Ellie, where are you? Ellie, Ellie, answer me."

This time, Henson didn't mutter. Jumping to the bank from a block of ice still in the creek he yelled, "Come on. That son-of-a-bitch has lost the school teacher."

Marty, sensing more than one crisis shaping up, dashed ahead of everyone else, except Henson, to locate Cord. Racing upwards from the creek along a pathway most likely created by deer and elk as they sought water at the creek's edge, he pushed pine and juniper branches aside to hurry on.

Within minutes, a dozen men descended on Cord, who was standing in a small clearing on a tree stump. As he circled slowly, he called "Ellie," then stopped to listen. He jumped down when he saw the approaching men.

Marty could see the desperation and worry in his eyes. "What happened?" he called as the men gathered around.

Cord was at once embarrassed and chagrined. "Well she, she," he stammered, "she wanted a few minutes to herself. She went into that brushy area back there. I, . . . I waited for at least ten minutes, maybe fifteen, and I started calling and pushing my way through where I thought she went. I was able to follow her as far as that tree over there. Then she must have come out in this clearing and gone the wrong way or something."

"Maybe she doubled back," Henson offered.

"I just don't know. She must have fallen and is hurt. She's not answering," Cord sounded ready to cry.

"Well, come on men," Marty ordered. "Scatter out around the perimeter of this clearing and look for tracks. I know the snow cover under the trees isn't very dependable for showing tracks, but if we're careful we can find them. Every man cover the ground in a clockwise direction from where you start. That tree Cord mentioned is 12 o'clock. Cord you take three o'clock. If she got mixed up and went in the absolute opposite direction, that would be it.

"Henson you take nine o'clock. That's probably about where she'd go if she tried to get back to the teams. I'll take six o'clock. That's down hill, and she might have thought she'd find the creek and follow it. If you find her, and she's not hurt, just give a yell. If you need help, use your gun if you have one. If not, try to get the attention of somebody around you. Now don't panic. Oh yeah, when you hear someone call, count to ten before you yell, so we can hear her if she answers."

The men scattered as ordered and began calling "Miss Delaney." Several voices, at once, rang out, followed by a short interval of silence. Now that Cord could leave the clearing where he thought she might return, he ran for the trees to the right. He didn't know if it was pure luck or the work of the devil, but he found a distinctive path at almost exactly the three o'clock point.

Cord's heart began to pound as he sprang forward into a full run. A couple of minutes later he was headed down hill as he proceeded toward a rather steep ravine. Not knowing what he might find, he jumped over debris from fallen tree branches and hardly felt the sting of overgrown brush and low hanging branches attacking him as he passed.

He did not stop to call because he soon spotted her footprints wherever the fresh snow lay exposed on the ground. Suddenly he broke into another small clearing that closely resembled the first. And there she was sitting on a fallen log with her back toward him, her chin resting on her palms, propped by her elbows on her knees.

"Ellie," he shouted.

She rose quickly to face him.

By the time he reached her, she was smiling and greeting him. "Cord, I knew you'd find me."

"Are you all right?" he cried, breathlessly, as he reached her side.

"Of course, I'm all right," she squealed as he hugged her, then swung her into the air and around as if she were a little child.

"Oh God," he moaned, as he stood her on her feet again, "You scared me so bad. How'd you get way over here?"

"I guess I walked," she replied solemnly.

"But why? Why didn't you stay where you were? Especially once you came out of the brush."

"I did!" she proclaimed. "I came out of the brush right over there." She pointed to a tree very similar to the one in the other clearing.

"No you didn't, you silly goose." Cord laughed. "You're nearly a half a mile from where you were."

"I am?" she asked in surprise. "I thought I took a trail that led me in a circle. So I sat down to wait. My father told me if I was ever lost to just sit down and wait."

"Were you?"

"Was I what?"

"Were you lost?" Cord was holding her at arm's length staring at her as if he couldn't get enough of knowing she was really there.

"No," she answered. "Never before. But I guess I was this time."

"I'd say so," Cord sighed. "Anyway, we've got to get back to tell the others you're safe." He took her hand and began tugging her along.

"Others, what others?" she asked anxiously.

"The men. They heard me calling and came running."

"Oh my," Ellie groaned. "I feel so silly."

Cord stopped briefly. He pulled her in front of him and cupped her face in his hands. "But you look so wonderful." He bent slowly forward to kiss her lips and breathe a prayer of thanks that he had found her so easily. Then he began yelling, "Marty, Henson, Everybody. I found her. She's okay."

He waited five seconds then yelled again. "Can you hear me? I found Miss Delaney."

The couple moved forward another hundred yards, and Cord repeated his call. Still, there was no answer. On his fourth call, however, a voice called back, "You need help?"

"We're okay," Cord yelled. Then he called again. "I found Miss Delaney. She's okay. You can come back." Similar to his previous calls, the words echoed across the canyon and back, 'come back, come back, come back . . .''

As they pushed their way slowly past brush and branches, they could hear the rest of the men calling one another, "Come back, come back, come back."

When they reached the first clearing, most of the men were already there. Probably those who had been headed toward the ice-hauling site had gone back to work. As for the others, none had run as far or as fast as Cord; so they were standing around, arms folded, talking quietly and waiting for the couple to join them.

Having come near enough for everyone to hear her, Ellie announced loudly, "I'm so sorry. I didn't mean to be so much trouble."

The men began to laugh in relief at the sight of her. Then they proceeded back down the hill to their work. Cord and Ellie followed slowly. At one point, Ellie told him to go on ahead, she was just a little tired.

"Are you joking?" he exploded. "If I were to show up without you now, they'd string me to the nearest tree. And I wouldn't blame them."

Ellie slowed, even more.

Cord turned to her with concern. "Are you all right? I can carry you."

"Oh, heaven's no," she sputtered. "I'm just so terribly embarrassed now. Everyone will be snickering and laughing at me."

Cord stopped to take her in his arms. "It'll be okay," he soothed.

"No, it won't." Ellie sobbed.

Cord was almost beside himself. He fell to his knees in front of her. Holding both her hands in his, he said sternly. "It will be all right. If a guy dares giggle, I'll flatten him. And I don't think the ladies will laugh because they know any one of them could have been in your place. Ellie . . ."

Ellie began pulling away realizing she was making Cord miserable because he didn't know what to do.

He stood, pulling her close again, "Ellie," he said huskily, "I love you. I won't let them hurt you."

"Oh, Cord, I'm so, so . . ."

He stopped again to tilt her face upward and to give her a long and tender kiss. Suddenly it hit him. He had to do the manly thing and take the blame.

"Besides, it's my fault," he groaned. "I shouldn't have let you leave the path. I should have walked on down the hill and waited for you. You never would have gotten lost. Oh, Ellie, I'm so sorry." He kissed her again. Then he laughed. "On the other hand," he announced, "I may just let you get lost more often."

Ellie began laughing too, then broke away and started to run back to the others. Cord caught up with her just as they were rounding a curve to come into full view of the departing wagons. Henson glared at them as if they had personally affronted him. Two other couples were seated on the back of Marty's wagon. Marty stopped the team for Cord and Ellie to hop on, then broke into loud singing as they resumed their journey. "Buffalo gals, won't you come out tonight, come out tonight, . . ."

Roberta Marlow

General Delivery
Copperfield, Oregon
December 21, 1913

Dear Lottie Fern,

 First I want to mention that The Golden Star is once again standing and almost ready for business. It was really a great challenge for Marty to keep everyone organized last week to get the walls and roof in place. But he did it!
 The living quarters have two bedrooms, a nursery, a dining area that's just off the kitchen, a living room, and another small room for sewing or whatever. The parlor, as he has begun calling the business part, has about half of its space for a work area and a bar or counter with the traditional stools in front. Then there's a rather large area for individual tables as you enter the front door. The rest of the space is just one big room in the event he decides to go back into the saloon business. There is a ladder opening for reaching the loft that he built over the business part of the building. Marty plans to install a regular walled-in staircase with a door to prevent the baby from climbing the stairs and falling.
 He says the loft is really for Cord or Billy if either of them decides to stay there by any chance. Cord is still staying at Winona's Boarding House for the time being. He says he wouldn't dream of having Bridget cook for him in her condition. She is really beginning to show now.
 We had one other occasion yesterday. Now, Lottie, don't fuss at me. I was perfectly safe the whole time. I couldn't believe it that everyone got so excited. Well I figured Cord would, but the others?
 It happened when we went to haul ice to fill Marty's icehouse. He'll use it in the business in the new ice cream parlor he's planning. Since he has never been able to get a renewal of his liquor license, he has decided that opening an ice cream parlor is definitely the way to go.
 Anyway there were about a dozen and a half men and three of their wives. We went up on Pine Creek to chop and haul ice. Cord was sitting down, taking a break when they finished loading the second of three wagons. It was cold, but the snow wasn't really as deep as it is right now in Copperfield.
 I decided to ask Cord to take me for a walk on up a rather wide pathway. We were coming back when I needed to find a place of privacy. So Cord told me to go off the edge of the pathway, and he'd wait right where we were. So I did. Then I guess I got mixed up. I was in some pretty heavy brush. When I found my way out, I knew I wasn't on the path, but I thought I would soon find my way back. Fifteen minutes or so later, I came to a place that looked just like where I had been. As it turned out, it wasn't, but I figured I might be lost, so I sat down to wait for Cord to find me. In the meantime, the whole crew of men came running to help when they heard Cord calling me over and over. I didn't hear him, but they did?

It wasn't very long at all until Cord did find me. It was so comical. Cord was so frightened. Need I tell you when Clara found out about it from one of the ladies today after church services, she was totally beside herself. Some of what she said does not bear repeating.

The Christmas dance was just dreamy last night. I wish you could see the emerald green gown Clara's sister stitched for me. I've heard that the Town Council is planning an especially rowdy celebration this Christmas. Oh well, I have promised to go caroling with the children who can be here on Christmas Eve. I hope Cord will come too. I enjoy hearing him sing so much.

You said in your last letter that the governor is definitely making plans to get Copperfield under control. There was another big fight last night, and some fellow got his eye badly injured. I heard that another has a broken arm. I'm waiting anxiously to find out how the governor is going to proceed.

I've sent a memento for you by mail early last week. I think you'll enjoy it. I surely hope it reaches you intact. As it says, "Do not open until Christmas."

Write soon,

Cousin Ellie K

The Town Council Meets

"Good afternoon, Alice," Clara Hoffstetter greeted the post-mistress. "How are you today?"

"Oh, Clara," said a frantic Alice Hunsaker. "Am I glad to see you. I'm just in an awful fret. You see there's this special delivery letter from Governor West that's addressed to Mayor Harvey Sullivan and the members of the Town Council. And I just don't know what to do. I can't close the post office, 'specially when the mail just got in with all the holiday greetings to everyone."

"So why do you have to do anything about the letter at all?" asked Clara.

"Well because, the mayor has to sign for it before I can release it."

"Oh, so why don't you just wait until he comes in?"

Alice was a tall, thin woman. Her salt and pepper gray hair was pulled back tightly into a bun behind her head. The most noticeable characteristic about this shy, rather retiring woman was her long fingers and capable looking hands. She had been a nurse before marrying Doc Hunsaker. When she developed a chronic cough four or five years ago, they thought it might result in tuberculosis. They decided that for the benefit of her health, they'd move to Copperfield. They had worried that the doctor's income might not be adequate in a small place like this. So she applied for and succeeded in becoming the post-mistress. Perhaps it was her nurse's training and the confidential nature of the medical trade that kept her from getting involved in gossip or community affairs in general. Thus, Clara was flabbergasted to find the woman in such a state. But she was all ears to find out why.

Alice was holding the letter up to the light, "You see, it's marked 'Urgent,' and maybe he should be doing something about it before the train makes its turnaround from Homestead."

"Oh I see. I guess he could always use the telegraph if he has to provide an immediate reply. But," said Clara, eager to be of assistance, "If Mohammed can't come to the mountain, I guess we can bring the mountain to Mohammed." Clara spun around to her son Jeffrey, who was standing in the doorway.

"Jeffrey," she ordered, "run over to the Painted Lady, and tell whomever you see there that the mayor has important mail he must sign for. Then stay there by the door until you bring Mr. Sullivan back here, or at least until you know he has received the message."

As Jeffrey dashed from the post office, Clara again addressed Alice. "What do you think it's all about?"

Alice leaned over the counter so her voice wouldn't carry if anyone else came in the door. "I think," she almost whispered, "it's something to do with that petition. In fact, it's so thick, I think it might have a copy of that petition—you know the one with the names and everything. I can see a list through the envelope. The list is typed, of course, but I can make out a lot of the names."

"Oh, oh my," Clara was shocked. "I'd be sorry if the mayor finds out about everyone who signed. George and I didn't sign for just that reason. 'George,' I said, 'George, we just can't afford to get mixed up in this kind of thing.'" Clara leaned closer in the window to announce, "But Miss Delaney did. That could cost her her job, you know. Oh my, I've got to talk to George right away. Uh, Jeffrey will bring Mr. Sullivan. Don't you worry." Clara quickly gathered the stack of newspapers and other mail to bustle from the post office. As she hurried toward The General Store, Clara saw Jeffrey emerging from The Painted Lady alongside the mayor.

Things moved at lightning speed after that. The mayor signed for the letter, sent Jeffrey to the other three saloons with the message that he was convening an emergency council meeting at 4:45 and that every member had to be there.

After Jeffrey left his first two messages, he was into his third 40-yard dash, just passing The General Store when his father stepped out of the door into the boy's path, "Hey there, son, what's going on?"

"I'm doing an errand for the mayor," Jeffrey puffed. "He's calling an emergency Council meeting."

"Oh, what about?"

"I don't know Dad. Let me go tell Mr. Wickert and Mr. Thatcher at the Red Carpet Hotel and I'll be right back."

"Okay, son you do that."

Jeffrey continued running as Clara came out of the store to pursue a previous conversation with George. "Here comes Miss Delaney now," Clara said, "I just don't know how we're going to tell her of the trouble she's stirred up for herself."

"What do you mean, 'tell her?' You don't have the foggiest idea concerning what's happening. You just take care of your own business for once. I've regretted not signing that petition ever since you talked me out of it at that Grange meeting." His eyes glinted sharply at his wife when he paused. "If there's one place I'd like to be, it's right in the middle of that make-shift city hall when our esteemed mayor and his cronies get theirs."

"George, you don't mean that," Clara exclaimed.

"Your damned right I do. If I'd had any idea that a bunch of hoodlums would be running this town, do you think I'd have opened for business here five years ago?" George demanded, indignantly.

"Now shush," said Clara, "Here comes Jeffrey."

Jeffrey and Ellie arrived at almost the same moment, though from opposite directions. Jeffrey quivered with excitement being eager to talk to his parents. Still he stopped politely while his father held the door open for the two ladies to enter. Clara first, then Ellie. Then he dived under his father's arm and into the store.

Jeffrey glanced questioningly at his father, seeking permission to speak while Miss Delaney was present. George gave his consent as he questioned, "Well, son?"

"I suppose Mother told you that Mayor Sullivan signed for that letter," he began, still puffing to get a full breath. "And then he stood right there in the Post Office and ripped it open. He looked at it for a few seconds, and then he says, 'Oh shit,' Uh, pardon me Mother, Miss Delaney," he paused to cast a glance in their direction.

"'I beg your pardon, ma'am,' he says to Mrs. Hunsaker. 'I am very sorry, but now we'll just see about this.' That's when he flipped me this silver dollar, and he says, 'See how fast you can get to the Eagle's Nest, the Bailey Saloon, and the Red Carpet to tell Mr. Lawrence, Mr. Greene, Mr. Thatcher and Mr. Wickert that we're having an emergency Council meeting at 4:45 at the city hall today. And they have to be there. You make sure that each of these gentlemen hears you good and loud, do you understand?'"

"So I says, 'Yes sir,' and I just ran as fast as I could. And here I am," he grinned as he flipped the shiny silver dollar high into the air.

"Miss Ellie," Clara began. "I don't know what this is all about for sure, but I think you should know . . ."

Ellie cut her off with, "Yes, Clara, I know it's serious. I have a letter here from my cousin, Lottie Fern. I'm sure I've told you she works for the governor. I was glancing at it walking home, and I saw something about a letter from Governor West to the mayor." Ellie was moving through the aisles toward the back room to the stairs. "So I think I'll go read it carefully now. I'll be ready to share what information I have at dinner. She left both George and Clara gaping as she made her way.

Removing her outer wrap, Ellie went to sit in the chair by the window and began to read:

My dearest Ellie K,

I thought I'd let you know that Governor West was very pleased with your petition and the signatures that have now been cleared as being legal. He is happy that the whole thing was done so well. He plans to move right along starting today. Now I know you'll want to be aware of the contents of the special delivery letter Governor West has mailed this day to Mayor Sullivan.

Basically after initial greetings addressing the mayor and each of his councilmen and the city recorder, the Governor goes on to say that he has had "numerous complaints from the area," that the citizens in the town of Copperfield believe their very lives and property are being endangered, and that he has this day given notice to Sheriff Yargo of Baker County to issue closure of all saloon establishments in Copperfield until such time as their "utter disregard" for the laws of the State of Oregon and the County of Baker is corrected. This correction includes but is not limited to the illegal sale of liquor to minors, the exercise of various gambling pursuits, the promotion of prostitution, both within and near the boundaries of Copperfield, and the practice of various pursuits that result in divesting laborers in the area of their legal wages to the detriment of their families.

Mr. Yargo has been given until Christmas Day to accomplish his commission, after which the County's District Attorney, C. R. Deschinger, will be held accountable for indictment and prosecution of all parties for which he has now, or for which he may have evidence in the future of any of the above violations.

Now Ellie, I want you to be especially careful. Apparently there are not only thieves in your midst, but also murderers . . .

Ellie was just in the process of turning to the next page of the letter when a soft knock sounded on her door.

"Miss Ellie," Clara was saying as she cautiously pushed the door open. "Mr. Hoffstetter is visiting with Mr. Kellner downstairs, and they want to know if you have any desire to pop in on the mayor's meeting since you have as much at stake as any of the rest of us."

Ellie jumped up, "I'd love to," she gleefully responded. Hurriedly, she crossed the room to her dressing table. Tidying her hair by relocating the large comb holding her rat in place and adding a few pins, she reached for her bonnet and shawl.

"Oh, Miss Ellie," Clara groaned. "I just don't know what the world is coming to when fine young ladies like yourself are getting involved in politics. I almost wish Miss Anthony had married and raised a nice family instead of working so steadfastly for women's suffrage. Pretty soon young women like you will be ruining their reputations to say nothing of ignoring their duties to husbands and children, to go off campaigning for some fool thing or another."

"Dearest Clara," Ellie commented, "Don't you worry about young ladies and their reputations. Why you were one of the many who made your way West without benefit of proper escort or even family here to receive you. What do you think history will say of women like you who were simply seeking adventure, just like the men?"

Clara was so taken aback that she did not answer, but just stared at Ellie, who was dabbing a spot of perfume behind each ear and on the handkerchief which she stuffed in the top of her dress. She impulsively tucked Clara's arm in hers and led her from the room.

"Mr. Kellner, I'm so glad to see you haven't been intimidated," Ellie called as she and Clara came into the store.

Marty beamed at her, as he said, "Good day, Miss Ellie. With you to champion my cause, how could I be intimidated? Besides, I clearly have very little left to lose as opposed to George here, who has a bona fide business to run."

Don't worry about my losses, Marty," George said in a melancholy tone. "I came into this world with nothing, and I'll leave with nothing. The same probably holds true of my venture here in Copperfield. I certainly came with very little. So if we're going to make that meeting, we'd better head on over there."

"Yes," observed Clara. "It's 4:50 already."

The trio departed from the store, and minutes later, they were pushing their way into the dimly lit dance hall.

Ellie was not surprised to see the five men sitting at the table near the podium. But she noted how Alan Greene blanched when he looked up from his notebook where he was recording the minutes of the meeting. Further, she smiled when Mayor Sullivan caught sight of her and broke mid-sentence to mutter, "What the hell?"

Recovering his political attitude in moments, he went on. "So according to the letter, we can expect a visit from the sheriff in the next few days. I want all the city records, and for that matter, your own ledgers open and on display for inspection should the sheriff have any questions about the legality of our operations."

"Humpf!" Duane Wickert guffawed, "If we don't have to look for any more trouble than C. R. or Ted will be giving us, I don't see why we are getting all excited like this. Hell, we got that letter almost a month ago from C. R. ordering removal of the slot machines. I didn't see Ted or him, either one, down here inspectin' things to see whether we complied or not." Turning to the mayor, he added, "For that matter, Harvey, I didn't see you go around to see that every single slot was taken out." Swinging around, he winked at Thatcher. "Did you Charlie? I just don't think we have anything to worry about here."

"Well, maybe not," the mayor agreed. "But just to be on the safe side, I'm going to notify the other saloon owners, then go out to Baker and check things out with our lawyer."

"Yeah, Harvey," said Frank Lawrence, the Eagle's Nest owner, "See if we can do anything about these petitioners while you're at it. Aren't they guilty of slander or liable or something like that with their wild accusations?"

"I'll be checking on that too, Frank. In the meantime, I see that we have an audience. Welcome to you Miss Delaney, Mr. Hoffstetter, and Mr. Kellner. I see only two of you signed the governor's petition. Perhaps you have some other business to bring to our attention," Sullivan said pleasantly, then smiled, showing his yellowed teeth. Wickert was also grinning like the "cat that swallowed the canary."

"No, no," said Marty. "We're just a little curious about a certain special delivery letter from our state's governor to our honorable mayor."

"Oh, is that it?" the mayor snickered. "So, here it is." He plucked it from in front of Alan Greene, then waved it gaily. "It will be posted for all to see along with the other official documents of the City. You can view it at the post office in that glass-covered lock-box in the lobby. It'll be there the first thing tomorrow morning.

"If we'd known you had an interest in the way people's feelings and opinions are shaping up regarding our dealings with Governor West, we would likely have invited some of our friends to occupy the other side of the aisle at this meeting."

"That's funny," chortled Wickert. "Maybe Miss Delaney and Mr. Williams could favor us with a proper marriage ceremony in the near future, thus melding our interests on both sides of the aisle."

"Mr. Williams has no interest in the feud that's going on here," Marty almost shouted.

"Obviously, Mr. Kellner, you don't either. I would think an end to this matter would meet with your approval." Sullivan remarked sarcastically.

Marty rose from his seat, his face flushed with anger, "Oh, I'd like to end it all right," he yelled. "Maybe now is as good a time as any."

"If that's what you really want," the mayor was challenging as Alan Greene rose, tipping his chair over, "Here, here," he commanded in an attempt to halt the mayor's response.

Ellie had also risen to place her hand on Marty's arm. She could feel the rippling flesh of his flexing muscles. As she began to apply pressure, praying he wouldn't turn on her, she caught movement out of the corner of her eye. Following the gaping stares of several of the Councilmen, she looked toward the hall door. Then she burst out, "Cord, Cord, you have to make them stop."

Cord strode into the room and was instantly by her side. Noting Kellner's flushed appearance and what looked to be some sort of conflict among Ellie, Marty and George, who was also attempting to restrain Marty by holding his other arm, Cord simply pulled Marty from them by grabbing both his wrists.

Now Marty focused his anger on Cord, who returned his glare in full measure, until he heard Alan Greene say, "Mr. Sullivan, this is not the time or the place. This is not at all appropriate—a brawl at a City Council meeting."

Sullivan turned his attention back to the council. "You're right, m'boy. Yes you are certainly right," he said grinning from ear to ear and carrying out a typical about-face in attitude as only he could do.

Hearing that the conflict was probably not between George and Marty, Cord released his grip. Marty continued to glare at Cord, obviously ready to strike out at anybody who happened to be within reach. Then he began rubbing his wrists and adjusting his rumpled sleeve, while saying, "You are so right, Mr. Greene. My suit against Mr. Sullivan and the rest of you would likely suffer a sudden death if we were to settle the matter in, shall-we-say, a somewhat more violent manner. Gentlemen," he announced, "I will see you in court."

Kellner grabbed his cap and promptly left the room. George was wide-eyed with embarrassment over the whole encounter. He felt that he was more than a little responsible for placing Miss Delaney in such an awkward situation. "I'm so sorry, Cord. I shouldn't have encouraged her to accompany us."

"What's this all about?" Cord asked as he stood, feet spread, still poised for action, his arms akimbo, and his face contorted in an effort to restrain a smile.

"Well, the mayor got a letter," George began.

"It's all right, Mr. Hoffstetter," Ellie broke in softly. "I'll explain to Cord. You go along now before Clara gets worried when she notices the meeting is breaking up."

"Yes, yes, you're right," George replied. "She'll be watching, that's certain." Retrieving his hat from its place on the chair to his left, he placed it on his head and edged past Ellie and Cord to leave. "Good night then," he mumbled. Cord and Ellie both noted the uncharacteristic slump of his shoulders. His steely gray eyes that usually reflected his firm stubbornness in almost any adverse encounter were downcast, and there was no hint of his normally cheerful smile.

Cord still had not changed his position since letting go of Kellner's arms. But he seemed ready and willing to listen as Ellie said, "Let's go somewhere we can talk."

"And where would that be?" he grinned.

"I don't know, maybe over by the pond near the tunnel. I'd say to Bridget's, but I imagine she's busy trying to get Marty to cool off right now."

"You can bet on that," Cord laughed. Taking her hand, he said, "Okay, let's go."

The couple made their way down the stairs just ahead of the council members, who were adding a few more colorful remarks about Marty Kellner and his hot temper.

Then out of the blue, they heard Wickert declare, "Furthermore, we're going to have to deal with that Williams bastard sooner or later."

PART II

January, 1914

Sunday	Monday	Tuesday	Wednesday	Thursday	Friday	Saturday
				1	2	3
4	5	6	7	8	9	10
11	12	13	14	15	16	17
18	19	20	21	22	23	24
25	26	27	28	29	30	31

"... THE DISTRICT ATTORNEY AND THE SHERIFF OF THE COUNTY HAVE REPORTED TO ME THAT THEY THEY CANNOT DO IT ... WE SHALL SEE WHAT A WOMAN CAN DO."
—GOVERNOR OSWALD WEST, DECEMBER 30, 1913

General Delivery
Copperfield, Oregon
January 1, 1914

Dear Lottie Fern,

I have been reading your letter of December 26 over and over for the past two days. I just cannot find enough comfort in it to prevent me from writing to beg you to change your mind about coming to Copperfield. I believe that Governor West is plainly out of his mind to ask you to come here.

I have been listening to the Hoffstetters bicker about this situation for most of two months now, and at this last hour, I have to conclude that Clara may be right. As rough as this town is, anyone who comes here to interfere in a serious way is in mortal danger. Her point is that if something were to happen to you, God forbid, it would simply be the end of the town for everyone. Not that I care about that, I'm just frightened to death for your sake.

The streets, beginning on Christmas Eve have been over-run with loud-mouthed, drunken braggarts, who have their mind set on doing bodily harm to anyone who dares to interfere. I know, and you have probably read, that they are planning to decorate the streets and have a big hurrah in welcoming you tomorrow. But when things get ugly, and I cannot see how they won't, it will be ever so dangerous.

Please wire Governor West and tell him you have found the situation intolerable, and if he wants to declare martial law, he should come do it. After all, he can bring a whole division of the National Guard in if he so chooses. Even if that's what he decides, Cord wants you to let me know so we can find a safe vantage point when the bullets begin to fly.

Clara has prevailed upon George to ride to Baker City this morning on horseback so he can meet you at the Geiser Grand this evening. He hopes to convince you that there has to be a better way. I am asking him to deliver this letter, though I doubt you will read it before he talks to you. In the meantime, I will pray that you listen to the man.

Your very worried cousin,

Ellie K.

Ribbons, Bunting, and Martial Law

Ellie burrowed more deeply under the covers as she listened to the morning sounds. It was the last day of the Christmas break, except of course, for the weekend coming up tomorrow. There seemed to be a great deal of noise in the streets. Men were shouting greetings to each other, "What do you think? Do you think she'll show?"

"Hell yes, she'll show! The governor wouldn't say she's coming if she wasn't'. Sure one hell of a coward though—hiding behind the skirts of a woman."

Ellie came fully awake. Lottie Fern was arriving on the train today. That is, she would be if George wasn't able to convince her not to continue her mission. How could that detail have slipped her mind? She flew to the window. Horses were tethered practically on top of each other at the hitching rails. "There must be a hundred or more," Ellie decided glancing up and down the streets. Men were scurrying up and down ladders like tree squirrels, tacking bunting to store fronts and tying pink and lavender ribbons to everything in sight—saddles, horses, hitching rails, buggy wheels and door knobs.

"You're not putting that on our store," she suddenly recognized Clara's shrill voice. "I don't care what the mayor ordered."

A deep voice answered, "We'll just see about that." Ellie could hear his spurs jingling as he apparently decided to depart.

Ellie hurried to get dressed. She took a moment to decide, then yanked on her black wool skirt. She grabbed and began buttoning her white, long-sleeved, satin blouse. She had to look presentable. Whatever else transpired, she was planning to get together with Lottie Fern.

In her mirror, she could see that her door was gently being pushed open. She was pretty sure she hadn't heard a knock in spite of the loud street noises, but she wasn't surprised to see Cecile pushing her way in, timid as a little mouse. She was still in her soft flannel nightie wearing her nightcap, but her eyes were wide with fright.

"Oh Miss Delaney," she sobbed as she ran to Ellie's arms. "I'm scared."

"There, it's all right, Sissy." Ellie resorted to Cecile's nickname. "There's nothing to be afraid of."

"But a man said a little bit ago if the governor declares martial law, everyone will have to turn in their guns, and another man said, 'I'd like to see 'em try to get mine. I'll guarantee you if they do, they'll burn their hands on the barrel 'cause it'll be blazing hot, I'll tell you.'" After a bit, Cecile let up on her sobbing. "I'm so afraid for your cousin."

Sissy moved closer to bury her face in the folds of the frill down the front of Ellie's blouse. "Now don't you worry," Ellie soothed. "Miss Hobbs won't be taking any guns. Remember our talk yesterday. There must be some soldiers present to enforce martial law before people have to give up their guns." With that she took Cecile's hand, pulling her toward the window. Lifting her up, they both stared at the scene below.

The light mist that was falling didn't seem to hamper anyone in spite of the fact that Ellie's own breath was fogging the window glass. "It must be chilly out there," she thought. Noting that the men were all wearing mackinaws, buttoned closely around their throats, she knew her opinion was correct.

"Look," she said to Sissy. "Do you see any soldiers under any of those hats and caps out there? You know I told you that soldiers wear special clothes, and you can always recognize them. Come on," she continued, "Let's get your clothes on and go see if we can find some breakfast."

Ellie gently pushed Cecile to one side, then opened her vanity drawer to extract a handkerchief. She squatted down to dry the little girl's tears.

Emerging a few minutes later into the kitchen area, downstairs, they could hear Clara yelling, "Jeffrey, Jeffrey, you come back here."

"But Ma," Jeffrey whined.

"Don't you 'but Ma' me. I said you're not going out into those streets, and I mean it. I'll lock you up until your father gets back on that train today if I have to. There was a telegraph message a while ago. That woman is coming in spite of what we tried to do for her, so you can just stay in here."

Again Jeffrey whined, "But Ma, all the other kids are out there, Billy and Jason and York. Even some of the ranch kids are around."

"I don't care if the good Lord himself is walking those streets, you're not going out there. It's too dangerous." Ellie heard the door slam, then Clara was flouncing into the kitchen. Jeffrey was about two steps behind.

Spying Ellie and Cecile in the kitchen, Clara groused, "Am I going to have to put my foot down with you, too?"

"No, mamma," Cecile whimpered. Though Ellie's back was turned because she was slicing some bread for toast, she was pretty sure the question was directed more toward her than to Cecile.

When Ellie swung around, she could see Clara's pursed lips and her air of disapproval of the whole thing. Clara recovered saying, "There's hot cereal on the back of the range, and the cream is in the pitcher out on the porch." With that, she spun back toward the store. She was still venting her anger when she slammed the door between the two parts of the building. The street sounds overpowered whatever else Clara was doing.

"Jeffrey, would you get a couple of sticks of wood from the porch. I'm going to make some toast, and I don't want the fire to die down too much. Have you had your breakfast?" Ellie was handing Cecile three bowls to place on the table.

"No ma'am," Jeffrey replied, then headed for the porch where he lingered to listen for a full minute before returning with the wood.

Sliding his legs across the bench to sit at the table while Ellie spooned the cereal from the kettle, he said wistfully, "I wish I was older."

"Were older," Ellie corrected. "I don't know about that," she continued. "But I think if I were you, I'd just go back to my room and watch everything happen. As you told me the day I arrived, you can hear the train five miles away. And you can surely see it as well as hear it when it stops."

"Can I come to?" Sissy asked eagerly.

"May I," Ellie corrected again. "Surely, we'll all go. Then after the train gets here, we can go to my room to watch. If they go to the City Hall the way Miss Hobbs says, we'll be able to see even better than if we were out there in the cold in the middle of that noisy crowd."

When the children finished eating, Jeffrey was off like a shot, and Cecile raced up the stairs after him. Ellie gathered the dirty dishes. She placed the washing and rinsing pans on the counter, used all the water from the tea-kettle, refilled it, then began washing the small collection of dishes, drinking glasses, and the cereal pan which she had emptied into her own bowl, to the detriment of her appetite. She felt uncomfortably full.

She took the cream pitcher to the porch, emptied it back into the cream jar, which doubled for a butter churn if the cream supply went unused for several days. She thought about how lucky she was to be boarding with the Hoffstetters. They took almost daily delivery of milk or cream from some nearby farm. Not all city dwellers, even in the metropolitan areas, could afford the luxury of fresh butter, cottage cheese, whipped cream, and tasty cold milk. Still she had to be careful not to over-indulge, especially where cream was concerned.

"With all the goings on in the streets today," Ellie mused, "I won't be going for a walk, at least not until quite late." She thought about going up to the school to get a head start on the weeks ahead. In that way, she might be able to unobtrusively join the crowd when Lottie Fern arrived. But she crossed that thought off her list of possibilities. She'd have to purely sneak past Clara for one, and for another, she had promised Jeffrey and Cecile a view from her bedroom window.

So placing the tea towel on its hangar, she went to her room instead. She spied several of Lottie Fern's letters and yesterday's cryptic wire on the top shelf of her bookracks. She reached for them to review the contents one more time.

The wire said quite simply 'Arriving early Friday afternoon. Have resignation papers. Will return same day. C.F." The letter, on the other hand, filled in some of the details.

—

Dear Ellie K.,

Here are a few of the details of how we see things happening by the end of the week. Governor West just returned from spending the Christmas holiday at his retreat near Seaside. But he was already aware of the Baker City officials' response to his order. He said he had thought as much.

He read letters from both Ted Yargo and the District Attorney, in which they attempted to explain away the Copperfield complaints as the work of "old women who run to the governor with the slightest complaint." They also state that their findings have been that no one has been hurt, and it's only a few saloonkeepers fighting each other in a dwindling market.

Nevertheless, he has asked me to be prepared on New Year's Day with a request for the resignation of the officials in Copperfield. If they will consent to sign the resignation forms, so much the better. But if not, I will present his proclamation of martial law when I meet at the Town Hall, dance hall, or whatever.

The men with me include Governor West's good friend, B. K. Lawson, who is a Lieutenant Colonel in the Oregon Guard, and Frank Snodgrass, the State penitentiary superintendent. They will immediately enforce martial law after the proclamation is read. The governor has clearly warned Copperfield through the press and through his communiqués with the Baker City officials for the last month that this day would come. Governor West is somewhat concerned that it may boil down to taking on Baker City as well as Copperfield, Huntington, and a few others. He is absolutely certain, however, that Colonel Lawson can handle the challenge.

I know they think, on that side of the State, that no one man can do such a thing. But they have never stared into the cold hard eyes of Colonel Lawson. Nor do they know how easily he can persuade others of the error in their ways.

Now Ellie K., don't you worry about me! I'm not looking forward to this occasion. I kept hoping against hope that Baker County would act responsibly. But I will do this for Governor West now that it has become necessary. I don't believe I'll be in any danger. It would be pure suicide for any man to lay hands on me, or threaten me in any way.

As for you, please stay off the street when I arrive. I hope you can make arrangements to have someone escort you to my coach car on the train so we can have a short visit at least. As I understand it, the train continues on past Copperfield for some few miles to Homestead, then returns.

As a precautionary move, in case there is violence, the governor has issued a request for the engineer to hold the train in Copperfield and to proceed only after I am safely on board. Unless something unforeseen occurs in the street, you could board at any time while I am holding the meeting with the Town Council.

So I will see you in just six days in Copperfield.

My love and good wishes,

Lottie Fern

Having finished reading the letter, Ellie decided to straighten her bed and her vanity. She then seated herself on her bed, leaned back, propping her head against the pillows at the head. Lifting her feet with shoes still tied, she crossed her ankles on top of the spread. She began reading the latest letter again, ignoring the shouts and speculations from the streets. But she paused when she heard one very loud voice spouting, "If old Ozzie thinks for one minute he can come in here and take over, I, for one have a big surprise for him."

"Hell," another responded. "All we need to do is send that little ol' gal on her way. Then when the governor shows up here with his militia, we'll be ready for 'em, one and all."

As Ellie shuffled the pages of Lottie's letter reading it through for the third time, she drifted off, wondering to herself about what Marty, Bridget, and Cord were doing. All three had declared they planned to be a long way back when the order came, as it surely would, to "hand over your weapons."

The next sound that Ellie heard through a couple of fitful dreams, in which she and Cord were disagreeing about something, was the train's whistle. She jumped up to rush to the window. Seeing the huge crowd surging toward the depot, some running, and hearing dogs barking and horses whinnying, she shivered as she observed the whole world gone mad.

Still she wanted a better view, so she went to Jeffrey's room to watch. The children weren't there after all. "Clara must have called them to lunch," Ellie decided. She had no more than pulled a stool to the window and perched herself for a clearer view of the train now drawing to a halt, when Clara and the children hastened to her side.

"Oh my," Clara said breathlessly, indicating that she had rushed up the stairs, "You missed your lunch, Miss Delaney. Perhaps you want to go have a bowl of chicken soup. The kettle is still on the range."

"No, no thank you," Ellie murmured as she watched the conductor placing the step for the passengers to emerge. Her heart skipped a beat as she continued to stare down.

There she was, Miss Fern Hobbs, as she was formally known, holding her skirt with her left hand, grappling a portfolio and an umbrella in her right while precariously balancing herself, ready to step into her moment in history. The five foot, three inch, one-hundred-and-four pound secretary of the Governor of the State of Oregon would be admired, praised, or damned over the next few weeks depending on the source. She would be described as petite and dainty, modest, yet firm, and in all cases a lady.

She was reserved, yet in the limelight, she was definitely in command. *The New York Times* wrote a few days later, "We like everything about Miss Hobbs from her name up and down. She sounds delightfully feminine in the best and most luscious western style, and that she acts with true dispatch, the citizens of Copperfield, Oregon, can testify."

At the moment the citizens of Copperfield were laughing, jabbing one another in the ribs, and anticipating the show of their lives. The politicians were preparing to scrape and bow, showing what fine gentlemen lived in these parts. The lumbermen, miners, and cowboys were flexing their muscles, awaiting action, perhaps a good free-for-all, after the cowed lady left town.

Lottie Fern was being gently handed downward, the gentleman behind her holding lightly to her elbow while the conductor reached to steady her descent. As she disengaged herself from her helpers, she pulled the top of her long black coat a little more snugly at the neck. Her jaunty black hat sat primly atop her head. She seemed to be asking directions or making a comment of some kind.

Ellie was caught up in the moment of how attractive her cousin always appeared. Her auburn brown hair was always perfectly placed. None straggled along her cheek, as Ellie's often did. She wore glasses that confirmed her pretty brown eyes, and when she smiled, everyone had the feeling that all was right with the world. The most noticeable feature was her perfect figure. It was incredible that she had determined to forego any opportunity for marriage and family. She had begun at age 25 to announce that she had no intention of surrendering her precious independence.

The crowd stood at a respectful distance, although they were noisy while the mayor went forward in his usual grand style to offer his arm. Lottie Fern apparently stared him down, then began walking rapidly from the depot to the boardwalk, making a beeline straight toward the city's center. It was little wonder she knew exactly where she was going, given the content of the many letters the two cousins had exchanged.

Ellie hopped down from her perch, and hastily made way to her room because the object of her attention had become obscured by the crowd. Clara and the children were by her side. The children climbed up to stand on Ellie's steamer trunk, and Clara stood to the opposite side. All four gathered to press their faces to Ellie's window. Below them was a sight to behold.

Lottie Fern, still proceeding in the manner of a major general at the head of the troops, headed right past Winona's Boarding House, The Painted Lady, Cliff's Cigar store, and the Gorman Pharmacy, marching straight to the entry of the jail. The men of Copperfield plus every curious on-looker for miles around were almost running to keep up with her. Reaching her destination, Lottie Fern did halt for a moment to await Duane Wickert, who had outdistanced Mayor Sullivan, to hold the door open for her.

As she continued inside, the street was suddenly swept bare of the entire crowd that had been in evidence there only moments before. It was as though they had been swept up in a whirlwind never to be seen again, though Ellie imagined she could still hear the echoes of their thundering boots climbing the stairs into the dance hall. The sound from the tinny player pianos, banging away at full volume in the saloons, drowned out any further noise from the crowd.

Ellie could feel the lump in her throat. She wanted so badly to bolt. Her breath was coming in quick gasps, and her heart was pounding madly. Clara and the children made a dash for Sissy's room where they'd be better able to see what might happen next.

Then, as if in answer to her prayers, Ellie spied Cord and Marty coming from The Golden Star. But it was only seconds until they too disappeared into the gaping maw of the open jailhouse entryway.

When they met at Bridget and Marty's later that evening, Ellie begged Cord to tell her every little detail about the meeting in the town hall.

Cord related how he and Marty had barely been able to push inside the interior of the dance hall. They had the devil's own time squeezing around the edge of the crowd so they were able to see Lottie Fern up on the band platform. She was standing at the podium rapping its top with a gavel that she must have found there. "Order," she called over the loud voices, "Order."

Her tone was a little high-pitched. "Nerves," undoubtedly, Cord reported.

"Will Mr. Harvey Sullivan, Mr. Duane Wickert, Mr. Charles Thatcher, Mr. Franklin Lawrence, and Mr. Alan Greene please come forward." Glancing downward, she directed, "Perhaps you gentlemen would lift that table up here." The several men she addressed did so immediately, placing it slightly to the left of the speaker podium.

"Mr. Sullivan," she spoke to the man nearest her on the platform, "'are there chairs? I'd like each of you gentlemen to take a seat at the table." The mayor and the others obeyed, smirking and grinning as they pulled chairs from behind the curtain at the rear of the platform.

When the five were seated, Lottie Fern banged her gavel again and waited for quiet. Just before she started speaking, Marty poked Cord in the ribs and whispered, "I bet that's him," pointing to a husky man to the right of the platform.

"Who," I asked.

"'The Colonel Ellie told us about."

Some guy beside Cord said, "Shhhh!" At that point a silence settled over the crowd. A pin dropping to the floor could have been heard.

"So this is Copperfield," Lottie Fern began. "Seems like a nice enough place, but you shouldn't have bothered. I won't be here long enough to enjoy your party decorations." Some in the crowd commenced clapping until she banged the gavel again. "I have come only to read the following communiqué from the honorable Governor Oswald West."

Lottie Fern paused briefly, turning her head slightly in the direction of the Town Council. "To whom it may concern," she paused. "In light of certain activities that have occurred or are now occurring in the incorporated city of Copperfield, I am compelled on this 2nd day of January, nineteen hundred fourteen, to respectfully request the resignations of all members of its government; namely, Mayor Harvey Sullivan, Mr. Duane Wickert, Mr. Charlie Thatcher, Mr. Franklin Lawrence, and the city's clerk, Mr. Alan Greene."

"Gentlemen, in order to expedite this procedure in an orderly manner, I just happen to have resignation requests fully prepared and ready for your signatures." She stepped away from the podium, and very much like a schoolteacher, she handed each man a piece of paper from the stack she had in her hand. "I do hope I have all the names spelled correctly," she said. It was unbelievable that she could give each man the right paper. But she must have because nobody made a move to switch forms.

Some guy at the back of the hall was getting restless while everyone waited for the officials to read the papers they'd been given. Cord glanced around to see who it was. That's when he spotted a man on each side of the exit door. Each stood ramrod straight, staring at the crowd. A bayonet rifle rested lightly in the crook of each man's right elbow.

"If I'd ever had any doubt about this being serious business, such thoughts flew out the window at that point. I was beginning to wish I'd never gone up there," Cord interrupted his report.

It seemed like an eternity when Mayor Sullivan finally said, "I want to commend you Miss Hobbs on the fine job you've done in carrying out your duties to Governor West, but my friends and I respectfully," he almost spat the word, "do hereby decline your invitation to resign on advice of Counsel."

A low murmur and shuffling feet started to swell in the hall, but Lottie Fern just stood there. Then she banged the gavel again and said, "So be it! In that event, I have one more document to read to you from the governor." She withdrew a single piece of paper and read it from beginning to end. As you can imagine it was filled with whereases and therefores. When she finished, she said, "Colonel Lawson, you may proceed."

Lawson stepped to the podium, and the crowd reluctantlysettled again to see what would happen next. "Gentlemen," he said, "I am here to enforce martial law." Then he basically went through the details of the Governor's proclamation explaining its contents. "As you heard I am authorized by the governor to impose and enforce such regulations regarding local government as in my judgement may be necessary to maintain the peace and dignity of the community and as will cause all the law violators in the future a wholesome respect for the criminal laws of the State."

He went on to explain the provision in Oregon's constitution, saying martial law becomes pertinent and enforceable when the highest official deems that officers in a lesser arm of government, in this case The Town Council of Copperfield, are failing to execute the law of the land in an orderly and constitutional fashion. "The only point to concern most of you here today is that you are herewith ordered to lay down your weapons. For the time being, that includes any you may have on your person. Please place them in the custody of the two gentlemen at the door."

Lawson continued as though he had announced a Sunday School picnic. "As for the five persons at the table here beside me, I now pronounce each of you is under arrest."

There was an audible intake of breath on the part of the crowd. But when Miss Hobbs stepped down from the platform, the men silently made a passageway for her to exit.

"When I saw she was going to leave, I stepped up to one of the soldiers, declared I had no weapon, and I was allowed to leave," Cord reported. Marty waited for Lottie, then followed her out.

As she reached the staircase, I approached her, "I'm Cord." She stopped. The frozen look on her face evaporated. She smiled the smile of an angel "I'm so glad to meet you," she said, extending her gloved hand.

"So now, my dearest Ellie you know. The rest is history," Cord squeezed her shoulders with his arm that had been resting there.

—

"Yes," said Ellie, "You and Marty escorted her to the train, and you saw that the saloon doors were nailed shut with notices, 'Do not enter' tacked on the doors. And you must have noticed that the tinny music had been shut off. There were five guardsmen pacing the street. Each was holding a rifle to his shoulder. I wonder what the man nearest Marty's thought when he found out it was an ice cream parlor," Ellie giggled.

"He had no way of knowing that until later. Then Marty had to take him in and serve him a chocolate sundae before he was entirely convinced," Cord said.

Ellie leaned her head on Cord's shoulder as he sat beside her on Bridget and Marty's new couch. "I was so nervous, yet so happy when you came to get me to put me on the train to go to Homestead and back.

"Lottie Fern was a little weepy at first. She had hoped I was going to go to Baker City with her and ride the train back here tomorrow. I explained that I had no time to ready myself for an overnight stay. I was sorry we hadn't thought of it a lot sooner. She told me not to worry."

"What else did you talk about?" Cord asked.

Ellie smiled up at him. "We talked some about you, how blue your eyes are, and how strong you are, and what kind of person you are." Ellie paused. "She was quite impressed, you know. She said you are just the kind of man to have around if I insist in living in a God-forsaken place like this."

Cord blushed. Ellie was certain since she was sitting so close, but she doubted if Marty and Bridget could tell, thanks to his ruddy complexion and the dim light overhead. So she added, "and here we are in Bridget's living room listening to the sounds of a very quiet and subdued town on a Friday night, the 2nd of January, 1914. No tinny piano music, no free-for-alls, no yelling or cursing, just plain old peace and quiet," she sighed.

"Thanks to your very brave cousin," Cord replied. "What do you think she'll do now?"

"What do you mean, what will she do now? She'll go back to the governor's office and continue her duties, just like I will go back to school on Monday, to appear before 31 excited little faces, each one being an authority on what happened today.

"And on what didn't happen," Cord said tiredly. He rose, pulling Ellie on her feet, then grasping her hand. "Come on," he said, "You've had enough excitement for one day. I'm taking you home."

PROCLAMATION

WHEREAS, a large number of law abiding residents of Copperfield, Oregon, and surrounding country have notified this office that there is an entire lack of law-enforcement in the said city; and

WHEREAS, it appears that there have been many breaches of the peace and that there is imminent danger of others; and

WHEREAS, the sheriff and district attorney of Baker County appear to be either unable or unwilling to enforce the law and thus give due protection to the residents of said city; and

WHEREAS, I deem it necessary in order that the laws of the State be faithfully executed, to call to my assistance, and in such manner as provided by the constitution and the laws, the military forces of this state;

NOW, THEREFORE, I, Oswald West, Governor of the State of Oregon, as Commander in chief of the military forces of the said state, do hereby proclaim martial law within the boundaries of the said city of Copperfield, Oregon, same to become effective on and after the second day of January, 1914 until such time as it can be re-organized and in a manner which will insure a decent respect for the laws of this state and a due regard for the rights of its citizens, All saloons and other places where intoxicating liquors are sold, except drugstores where liquors are sold for medical purposes upon prescriptions as provided by law, shall close forthwith and remain closed until further notice. The proprietors of said saloons and other places hereby ordered closed shall be given until four o'clock P.M. of January third, 1914, to remove their supply of liquors, together with all bar fixtures, from the said city of Copperfield, provided, however, that the placing of such liquor and equipment in the hands of the railroad company for shipment out of the said city on the first train out will be considered a compliance with this order.

Lieutenant Colonel B. K. Lawson, Coast Artillery, Oregon National Guard, is charged with the enforcement of this order and he is hereby fully authorized and directed to impose and enforce such regulations regarding local government as in his judgement may be necessary to maintain the peace and dignity of the community and as will cause all the law violators to have in the future a wholesome respect for the criminal laws of the State.

IN WITNESS WHEREOF, I have hereunto set my hand this thirty-first day of December, 1913.

(Sgd.) OSWALD WEST
Commander-in-chief of
The Military forces
of the
State of Oregon

The foregoing is as said proclamation appears in a certified copy of the answer in the case of Wiegand vs. West, et al. filed in the Circuit Court of the State of Oregon for Baker County.

The Party's Over

Ellie spent the day, on Saturday, fidgeting. She couldn't stay in her room, and when she went into the store on several occasions, she found the Hoffstetters weren't speaking to each other. Nothing new there.

Except for the loud and continuous activity being carried out by the militia as they moved liquor, gaming tables, and other paraphernalia into the streets, there was really nothing happening. Ellie had spent almost all of her Christmas vacation in anticipation of Lottie Fern's arrival yesterday. But aside from the short jaunt on the train to Homestead and back, it had all been much ado about nothing as far as she was concerned. Once Lottie Fern's safety was assured, she felt a rush of relief, and, believe it or not, quite a letdown.

Yet among the few people she did see today, she could detect shock and disbelief that the town was now under martial law. And if they happened to look in her direction, they either stared right through her, or their gaze imparted blame. "If that's really what they are thinking," she murmured, "It is certain that opening school again is going to be a very unpleasant experience."

She almost wished that if she were to blame, someone would step forward and say, "It's all your fault. You got us into this mess, now get us out." She knew in her heart that getting out of this immediate imbroglio would be much more difficult than getting in had been.

Finally in the late afternoon, she grabbed her shoulder wrap and announced that she was going out. She was mystified when Clara didn't pounce, yelling for her to be back by dark, or demanding to know where on earth she thought she was going at this time of day.

Once in the street, Ellie was pleasantly surprised by the warmth of the winter sun. Her spirits lifted further when she noticed a flight of geese, circling over the River. While watching and listening to the incessant honking of the wild birds, the full force of her mood suddenly slammed home to remind her that she was all alone in her predicament.

Yes, Lottie Fern had greeted her warmly, and they had embraced several times before they sat down to visit in the railroad car. But when Ellie mentioned one or two of her uppermost concerns, particularly what would happen next in Copperfield, her cousin shrugged her shoulders and remarked, "I'm sure I don't know. I've done as I was asked, and I'll be only too glad to be on my way home to Salem before this day is done. If everything goes right, I'll change trains in Huntington and go straight through to Portland. What a relief that will be," she sighed, dabbing her eyes with her handkerchief.

Ellie felt guilty knowing that Lottie Fern was undoubtedly experiencing painful emotions after the roller coaster of dread she must have felt for several days now. At the same time, she knew that the special bond that existed between them had grown thin since five years ago when Lottie came East to prepare for her bar exams, consulting on the finer points with Ellie's father. For her part, she remembered the two of them becoming quite close, almost like sisters. Lottie Fern often laughed at Ellie's feeble efforts to earn her bachelor degree.

Ellie shivered visibly, then decided to call on Bridget to see how she was getting along. She knew Bridget was trying to finish more than a dozen projects before the baby's arrival in March, less than ten weeks away.

Ellie was not surprised to find Cord and Marty seated on the living room couch, each silently engaged in reading or looking at a magazine. Bridget left her rocking chair where she was knitting baby articles to answer the door. "Ellie," she greeted happily when she opened the door. "Come in, talk to me. It's so quiet in here."

Cord stood as she entered the room, and Marty rose to give her his place on the couch. "You'd better enjoy the quiet now, little woman," he addressed Bridget, "because it won't be that way much longer." He pulled a chair from the dining area and returned with it to sit near his wife. "Quite some goings on out there in the street," he announced.

"Certainly is," Ellie answered. "What do you think is going to happen next?"

"I wouldn't want to try to guess," Marty declared. "All I've heard so far is how the Council is going to seek an injunction against the Governor, and they're planning to sue for interference with their business.

"If those guardsmen actually load out that liquor and the gambling tables on Tuesday, there'll probably be hell to pay. That stuff is private property, so the Council may very well have a case against the governor for illegal search and seizure."

Ellie wanted to discuss the fine points of the law in the matter, so she began by saying, "I don't see how that could be; they are the law breakers here." Surprised when she felt Cord's hand gripping her arm more tightly, she added quickly, "But I wouldn't know in view of the fact that they're presumed innocent until proved guilty."

"That's just my point," Marty beamed. "Cord, here, thinks that's not true. He says if you're accused, you're as good as convicted unless you can prove your innocence beyond the shadow of a doubt."

Ellie turned to look at Cord. She was chagrined to see the measure of disapproval in his eyes. After a few more minutes of meaningless chit chat with Bridget about what she was knitting, how long it would take, and how it would look in the nursery, Ellie rose pulling her shawl around herself, and asked to be excused. All three looked up, but no one questioned her departure. Cord thought she was planning a visit to Mrs. Jones' place out back.

But Bridget rose to peak out the kitchen window, then turned to Cord and said, "Where's she going?"

"What do you mean?" Cord inquired.

"Well she's walking toward the depot or maybe on up the hill."

Cord rose, "I suppose I'd better go see." Shrugging into his coat and plopping his hat on his head, he continued. "She seems pretty much on edge today. Like she's expecting trouble of some kind."

"As if we don't have trouble enough," Marty drawled. "That's funny!"

"You go ahead, Cord. I'll have supper ready in about an hour," Bridget announced.

"Okay," Cord replied. Once outside, he strode briskly up the hill, wondering what had gotten into Ellie. He had intended to ask her why it took her almost all day to show up at the Kellner's.

Cord watched her as she made her way into the schoolhouse door. By the time he caught up with her, she was seated at her desk. She raised her head to look at him, but continued to rest her upper body weight on her arms, folded atop her desk.

Cord approached slowly, then squatted beside her. "What's the matter, darling?" he asked gently.

Ellie drew a heavy sigh and after expelling the excessive air, she whimpered, "I don't know. I guess I just feel the whole world has turned upside down, and somehow it's all my fault."

"Well of all the," Cord started to say, "stupid things," but he switched to "reasons to be upset, that takes the cake. How can you think to take any blame?" Cord rose to his feet, pulling Ellie into his arms as he went.

"I don't know," she whined tiredly, pulling away to wipe tears from her eyes. Cord produced his handkerchief, which she gratefully accepted. Her mouth was still quivering as she smiled up at him.

Cord stopped that symptom with a kiss. Then pulling her along, he said, "C'mon. It's chilly in here. It's warmer outside." Just before opening the door to go outside, Cord pulled her to him again and planted another kiss. This time, Ellie responded with warmth. "There," Cord said, "that's better."

Stepping into the sunlight, now beginning to fade along the base of the mountains, Ellie asked, "Where now?"

Cord faced her, "I don't know. Where do you want to go?"

"Home," Ellie murmured. "I want to go home."

"Back to the Store?" Cord asked in surprise.

"No, no. I think I'm homesick for the sounds of the city. I want to go shopping. I want to go to church. I want to take long walks along the waterway in the park."

Cord felt the chill of a giant tug at his heartstrings. Ellie's outburst mirrored and exaggerated his own restlessness and uncertainty. A wave of regret swept over him, and he knew he could no longer ignore the problems hammering away in the back of his mind.

The couple sank down to sit on the schoolhouse porch steps where they had first become friends a scant two months ago. Cord thought back to that night that seemed so long ago. He should have avoided that encounter no matter how right it had seemed at the time. Now he was faced with trampling on an already badly shaken heart of the woman he loved. He could no longer defer the overpowering urge to get this over with. Squirming to sit sideways on his hip and face her, he moaned, "Ellie."

Ellie stared into his blue eyes and felt her spirits soar. Her handsome prince would come to her rescue. With a promise from him, she could face anything. "Just the two of us against the world," she was thinking, as she breathed, "Yes, Cord."

"Oh Ellie," he sounded incredibly sad. "This is so hard."

Any other time, Ellie would have pulled his head into her lap to commiserate with him, saying something like, "Oh, Cord, dearest. Nothing can be that bad." But as her spirits plummeted from Heaven to Earth, she turned away to hide her own fright. Then mustering her courage, she faced him again. "What is it you have to say?" she asked, desperation dripping from each word.

Without further delay, Cord blurted, "I'm going away for a while." He expected her to jump up, hands on hips, eyes blazing, perhaps even shouting, "and just where do you think you're going?" But she did just the opposite. She stared at him steadily while tears welled up, and at last cried, "When?"

Cord ducked his head. Grabbing for a small twig lying on the ground, he began tracing a figure eight in the soft, moist dirt between his feet.

"Tomorrow, or the next day."

"Why so soon?" she asked dully.

"Because, because," he said in an almost whisper. "Because I have no job, and I have something to clear up. I figure this is the time to take care of both problems. You know," he continued, "kill two birds with one stone."

"And just where are you planning to do the killing?" Ellie was getting past her melancholy into the field of anger.

"I thought I'd go back to Agency Valley to see if there might be a ranch job for the next few months." He turned his attention away from twig doodling to look at her. "I'll be back by the time school is out, I promise."

Ellie, too, remembered the steps where they were sitting and the night that seemed a lifetime ago. Especially, she remembered Cord telling her that when he came to Copperfield, he had just departed from his intended's wedding."

"You're going to see if Bonnie Jean is missing you," she hissed, all the while the green-eyed monster was pumping her veins full of adrenaline. Her capacity to keep herself calm vanished.

As she made a move to rise, Cord jumped to his feet, grasping both her upper arms in a deadly clamp. "Is that what you think?" he demanded.

"Yes, that's what I think" she spat. "Every time I think I'm getting close to you, and that something might come of it, you draw back, hiding in the shadows like some kind of coward."

Cord dropped his hands to his side. Disheartened, he couldn't blame her for her suspicions. They had been skirting the issue of marriage every time they'd been together for the past two weeks, ever since the ice haul.

But he still couldn't break through the barrier and tell her he was a wanted man and could easily be framed for murder by two over-zealous citizens who had seen him riding the Paint horse he later sold to Locksley. Two bounty-hunting witnesses and a sheriff, who was known for "getting his man," made him wonder, bitterly, how many men had been convicted for crimes they had not committed. Shaking his head, he returned his gaze to Ellie.

"Ellie, darling. I've never lied to you, and I'm not lying now. I love you. You mean more to me than anything or anybody in the whole world." He moved toward her to pull her to him. But she turned away.

Spinning toward him once more, she faced him crying, "You call that love? Damn you, Cord Williams, you're holding something back. It's like you're imprisoned in your past, and you won't tell me about it. Until you do," she gasped, "I have nothing more to say to you." She spun on her heel and rushed away toward the main street and The General Store.

Cord stood rigidly, flexing his hands into tightened fists. "I can't Ellie. I can't," he called loudly. Then he sank back to the porch steps letting his head fall into his hands. Trying to get a grip on his thoughts, he concluded that there was no way out but to follow his plan.

He would find the witnesses and challenge them, plead with them, beat them senseless, if necessary, until they agreed to change their story. Above all, he'd prove to them he wasn't there when shots were fired. He would, that is, if the sheriff would stay out of it.

"Once that's settled, Ellie darling" he said to himself. "I'll be back to claim you forever and ever, sweetheart, I swear."

*General Delivery
Copperfield, Oregon
January 4, 1914.*

Dear Lottie Fern,

    I didn't think I'd be writing so soon. Someone told Marty that you received word from the Governor to tidy up some paper work in Baker City. So I suppose my letter may arrive in Salem before you do.
    First I want to tell you that I've worried about your getting home all right since the day you left. Somehow you didn't seem in the best of spirits, as I had hoped you would be once your call on Copperfield was completed. You were so brave!
    Also thank you for your many compliments regarding Cord—that he's handsome, polite, and strong. But Cord is what I have to write about. He didn't make any effort to see me all day on Saturday, which I couldn't figure out. So I finally went to the Kellner's, and there he was, sitting around with Bridget and Marty, doing nothing.
    Then when I got into a difference of opinion discussing the Copperfield situation, Cord wanted me to be quiet. Being angry and disappointed I left to go to school. A few minutes later, he came along to find me.
    Oh, he was all smiles and support. I told him I felt like people were blaming me, and he scolded me royally, saying none of it was my fault. Then he got a look in his eye like he wanted to say something important. And I, the fool that I am, was ready to fall into his arms, agreeing to anything, running away, getting married, living with him in some secret hideaway, you name it.
    But guess what, his big important announcement was that he's leaving to go to Agency Valley to get his old job back as a ranch hand. We had talked a little about what he was going to do a week or so ago. I thought we agreed that he would try to find work in Pine or Eagle Valley or even in Baker Valley. That way, he could come see me occasionally.
    We realized, of course, that there aren't any jobs around here with the sawmill closed until spring. The other jobs in construction have already shut down. And the mines are much less active during cold weather. Even then, he mentioned Agency Valley several times. So yesterday, I told him what I thought, that he's going back to check on his ex-fiancé to see if she is still happily married. He didn't seem particularly surprised that I would think that, although he scolded and told me how much he loved me.
    In the end, I said to him that until he can tell me what's bothering him about his past, I don't want to talk to him. Now I just feel empty and lonely and ready to pray with all my heart that he doesn't leave.

Maybe Clara is the only one who blames me, and me only, for those soldiers patrolling the streets out there. But I have a feeling that there are others who think that way, because, of course, the rumor mill eventually got around to reporting that I not only signed the petition, I prepared it. Just what they expected to happen concerning their children's safety, I don't know.

Whatever it is, I feel so alone and helpless to do anything about it. Marty says the Council members are seeking an injunction against Governor West and that he heard their lawyer will be filing suit against the governor, you, the guards, and heaven knows who else. I'm so worried. I just pray I can keep the school children under control for their sake. They are doing so well.

Their parents were so proud of their performance at the Christmas program. I couldn't have been more proud myself. Their comportment was perfect. Not a single child forgot lines or where to be when it came time to perform.

I also enjoyed Christmas Eve. Cord went with us to go caroling. I don't think Henson Baldwin was too happy about his presence, but that's just too bad! Anyway just as soon as the children went home after caroling the whole town erupted with noise, drunkenness, and obscenities. They kept it up all night and all day on Christmas just to prove to Governor West that he was powerless to do anything about it. I guess they found out he isn't so powerless.

I'm beginning to get a little panicky about next year. If something positive doesn't develop here, I can imagine that the school may not open again. I don't think I'll want to go East. As much as I've missed being there over the holidays, I know there's really nothing there for me. Even if I got a teaching position, I'd just be another working woman, as you say, in search of a husband as far as the opinions of others go.

Then, as far as practicing law is concerned, it's no use. It's apparent you've learned that. Even if one of Father's friends would give me a position, I'd be nothing more than a glorified secretary. Even the lowliest law clerk, being male, would be of more importance to the firm than I. Most of all, I don't really want to study for the bar exam. After what you went through, all I have to say is, "No thanks."

Sorry for all the negativity. I hope that with the Copperfield challenge on hold, at least for the time being, you can get back to normal. Please write soon.

Yours sincerely,

Cousin Ellie K

On the Road Again

Cord walked on past The Golden Star straight to Winona's even though Bridget was expecting him for dinner. Oh well, she'd just think he was with Ellie. As he sat on the edge of his bed in his room, removing his boots and socks, he thought again about his choices for the immediate future.

Earlier this morning Marty and Bridget had asked him, in fact almost begged him, to move into the spare room Marty had built behind the main lounge where a soda fountain was being fully installed.

The room was intended for a storage area for liquor and extra furnishings in the event that The Star would again become a saloon. "But for now," he told Cord, cheerfully, "and until the militia leaves town, we haven't the slightest use for it."

It was a spacious room, about 15 feet square, Cord figured. It was the one part of the living quarters that was built entirely of fitted logs with no finished walls in the interior. The flooring was especially nice, being made from twelve-inch cut white pine.

Bridget had braided a large rug from spare clothing, mainly men's shirts, that people of the community had contributed after the fire. She planned to use the rug in the nursery to keep the floor warm, but when she and Marty decided to wall in a walk-in closet, the nursery space was too small to handle the rug she had worked for weeks to create. She laid it in the storage room instead.

The rug, along with starched white curtains that covered the two shuttered windows resulted in the room being quite pleasant. "If this is a store room, how come you put in windows?" Cord queried.

"Because, ma' boy. I don't ever intend to live in a building with only one or even two exits again." He proudly demonstrated his ability to rapidly raise one of the windows, which was anchored by a cotton cord in the window casing. Flipping a simple hook from its eye, he flung open the shutter, creating a space large enough for a man to crawl through in seconds.

"That's pretty nifty," Cord agreed.

"Yup, with a window in the middle of each outside wall, I figure it'll be a nice sewing or reading room for Bridget and the baby a little later on, especially if I need her to keep an eye on business for any reason. The afternoon and evening breeze coming down the canyon should keep the place cool."

"Well then, you don't want me cluttering it up." Cord said.

"Of course, we do," Marty countered emphatically. "We'd be obliged to you if you'd come stay with us. I feel like hell that I can't offer you the job you had, but that just isn't in the cards. What's more, I'm just a little spooked about all this militia business anyway. I guess it'll be all right as long as the guard is in town; but when those men leave, an extra pair of ears, particularly your ears, would be right welcome. You know, I don't buy that idea that Bridget or I must have dropped hot candle wax and started a fire in my sawdust floor the way that Wickert fellow would have people believe."

"Jiminy, man, you're making me feel guilty. But I can't stay here doing nothing for three or four months until some work opens up again. You know there are no jobs to be had at present. As for you and Bridget, you're going to have a hard enough time making ends meet, getting a new business started and all. You don't need me around to leech off you."

"Don't you even say that," Marty scolded. "You worked a whole damned month at that sawmill, and Bridget and I owe you a debt of gratitude even if I was able to pay you when the insurance money came in. Without you there, we'd still be huddling with the Carpenters, and you know it." Seeing the look of quiet desperation in Cord's eyes, Marty finally backed off, adding, "But if you have other things to take care of, we understand. Just remember that there'll always be a place for you at our table and a pillow for your head when you need it."

Cord had looked wistfully at his friend, saying, "Thanks Marty. I'm grateful."

Now that he thought back on it, he knew he made the right decision. Marty and Bridget didn't need him hanging around. With the militia in town, he was sure they were safe. Whoever lit the match the last two times would have to be an outright idiot to try again. Besides now that those engaged in illegal activities were on notice with the governor, they wouldn't dare try anything further with Kellners. The community in general had been outstanding with their sympathy and support, perhaps because Bridget was pregnant. Cord was sure that anyone who tried something from now on just might risk being run out of town on a rail.

Flopping himself on the bed after removing his belt and undoing the top buttons of his shirt, Cord fell into a fitful sleep. Within the hour, he found himself tossing and turning. Then he began dreaming. At first everything was very pleasant. He and Ellie were walking along a roadway. He wasn't sure where. They stopped; he put his arms around her to give her a kiss. Her hands strayed up the front of his chest then around the back of his neck where she began tenderly caressing him. Then suddenly her fingertips were burning like fire. She was scratching him with all her strength. His skin felt like it was scorching, just like at the fire. Then Ellie was biting his cheek and laughing at his misery.

The searing pain of her attack woke him, and he sat up with a jerk. His neck felt hot to touch. As he began massaging the scarred area, he noticed that his shirt collar felt very uncomfortable and scratchy. Cord decided to strip his outer clothes and crawl under the covers like he should have done in the first place. Yet when he tried to get back to sleep, he found himself wondering why he would dream such an awful thing about Ellie. He knew that she couldn't hurt him, that she wouldn't try; but when he wondered if she might not love him as much as she professed, his heart began to pound.

It was strange; he'd never had a moment's doubt that Bonnie Jean loved him. Somehow, he couldn't be that sure of Ellie. Then again, he'd had no particular reason to be so sure of Bonnie Jean.

As the night wore on, Cord grew chilly. He thought about getting up to check the closet for another blanket, but instead, he pulled the covers over his head, deciding to tough it out. Sometime after midnight, he dozed for a while.

By four o'clock in the morning, he felt as though he had taken a beating. Every joint in his body was stiff and sore. He had never put in such a night in his life. He finally crawled out of bed, yawned, put his clothes on and crept quietly down the stairs. He planned to get his horse from the livery, then pack his stuff and get an early start.

Winona said she'd keep his room in wait for his return. She said she could see his need to have a place for his things. Over the last few months, at $40 a week, he had built up quite a collection while shopping from time to time at the Mercantile Store. There was a framed picture, a wall clock, a small chest of drawers for tools, pencils, and paper, and cuff links among other things. "Funny what a man will spend money for," he thought, "if he has money to spend."

Although his stomach was growling from hunger, Cord planned to ride to Robinette before eating breakfast. He couldn't help but stare up at Ellie's window in the General Store when he rode past. He hoped she had been sincere when she said she didn't want to talk to him. Still, it hurt not to say a proper goodbye.

Cord consumed a big breakfast of pancakes, bacon and eggs, with fried potatoes, then rode on to Huntington before considering a need to eat again. In Huntington, he stabled his horse, rented a room, then bathed before his evening meal. He had thought about stopping to visit with Ed and Pauline Miller as he rode by, but decided against it because he was sure they'd make it extremely difficult for him to go on to Huntington without spending the night. Then, too, without a complete explanation, they wouldn't want to believe he had urgent business elsewhere in the first place.

Lord, how he hoped he'd luck out and run into those two gambling cowboys again. He figured to sound them out to see what they knew of the Locksley murder by now. If he failed to locate them, he intended to go on to Agency Valley, at least by day after tomorrow.

Cord spent the evening making the rounds through Huntington's saloons, inquiring about the two men he remembered only as Pete and Gaylen. After three hours of hanging out, talking to all the bartenders and visiting with any likely customers, Cord gave up his search.

Discouraged and heartsick, he returned for a night's sleep, then rode out on a cold, windy Monday morning. It wasn't so bad going up the canyons into Mormon Basin, but Cord felt the need to get off his horse and walk once he reached the summit. Holding the lead very short, he was able to use the horse to protect his face a little better. He was wearing a stocking cap under his hat. While his ears were well covered, the cap did nothing for his nose, which felt as if it might fall off at any moment.

He took a short break at Malheur City to visit his father's grave for the second time in less than six months. While there, he got out the sandwich and the apple he had purchased at the hotel for today's lunch. If the weather had been more pleasant, Cord may have continued for the full 70 miles from Huntington to Agency Valley. But upon reaching Ironside, he put in for the night at the Ironside Hotel.

Taking a break waiting for the weather to warm up somewhat the next morning, he delayed getting started. Still, he managed to ride into the Agency Valley ZX holdings a little after noon on Tuesday. Norm was overjoyed to see him, but as the afternoon wore on, Cord became aware of Barstow's anxiety regarding the reason for the younger man's visit.

When Cord got around to asking if Norm would hire him on for some kind of winter work, he was shocked by Barstow's forthrightness. "I don't think so," he answered, "I surely wouldn't want to hire you even if there was work, which there isn't."

Not knowing what to say, Cord drew a deep breath and waited.

"Look son," Norm finally continued. "I've been waiting ever since you got here for you to bring up the subject. Since you haven't, I don't know what your game is, but hell, Cord, you must know you're a wanted man."

"God, all Friday, Norm," Cord exclaimed. "How'd you find out about that?"

"It could be because the Baker County sheriff and a couple of bounty hunters came riding in here three, four months ago. They were telling me something about a horse, one that looked just like those Paints in that far pasture. They said you sold one like that to a fellow who was murdered the very same day over in the Mormon Basin. What do you know about that?"

"Did you say it was the Baker County sheriff?"

"Yeah," said Norm tiredly. "He said he knew he didn't have jurisdiction. He was just trying to get information in view of what the Carter brothers had told him."

"What did you tell him?" Cord worried.

"I asked you first," Norm demanded. "What in the hell took place?"

Cord didn't know what to make of Norm's testiness. The man had been like a father to him for years. That relationship might be hanging in the balance now as Cord began his explanation. Relating his state of mind and his reasons for selling the horse that Norm had given him as a Christmas gift four years earlier, Cord was apologetic for having made the sale.

"Hell, man, I don't hold that against you," Norm growled. "You're not supposed to marry a horse, only a woman. What I want to know is where were you when that man was shot?"

It was almost as if Norm thought he could be guilty of such a treacherous murder. Cord found that hard to comprehend. Nevertheless, he went on to tell him about playing poker with the two cowhands, then slipping out of Huntington the next morning, right after he found out about the murder.

Norm fairly exploded when Cord finished. "You mean you have an iron-clad alibi, and you haven't gone to the authorities? I'd have thought you were a better man than that. If you knew you were wanted, you should have turned yourself in. You know that!"

Cord's eyes flashed in anger as he shot back, "Nobody told me I was wanted in the first place. In the second place, I would go to the authorities at the drop of a hat, if I could get a line on those two cowboys. As a matter of fact, I spent hours just night before last combing every bar in Huntington to get a line on them. But I couldn't. Everybody looked at me like I'd lost my mind. The only guy who remembered them at all was the barkeep in that gaming saloon."

"It isn't your job to find those two toads. That's what you have a sheriff for," Norm retorted.

"Yeah, and what do I do in the meantime? Rot in jail while he looks around in his spare time? Hell, he can't even seem to find me, and I've seen him twice already, talked to him once."

Norm laughed. "Maybe you're right. But there are some guys you haven't talked to. That's those two bounty hunters who are looking for you."

"You keep calling them bounty hunters. There's no reward out for me as far as I know,' Cord complained.

"Well those two aren't exactly looking for money as a reward. They're just swearing that they are good law-abiding citizens wanting to catch the murderin' Redskin who did in their friend. I didn't think much of them though. I especially wouldn't trust the older one as far as I could throw a bull by the tail. So that's why I think that if you want to keep your scalp intact, you'll head on out of this part of the country. Or else you can take your chances with the authorities." Norm paused, then queried, "Don't you think you could rely on that hotel clerk and the bartender where you played cards to prove your innocence. If that bartender recalled the cowboys, he undoubtedly remembers you being there.

"I don't know," Cord answered in despair. "I just wish I'd have been here to have you advise me. I guess I've been afraid to stir the waters so I could furnish that damned sheriff with the truth."

"When the Carters left here, they went on down Nevada way," Norm remarked. "I don't know that they ever came back. But as vicious as they are, I'd have thought they would have found you by now if they had come back to Baker County. All I know is that I don't think you should hang around here in case they do return. Could lead to another killing, or maybe two," he ended under his breath.

"I suppose, under the circumstances, I'd better head on back to Lapwai and wait for spring planting in the Paloose. That'll start in another month or six weeks."

"If you think that's best." Norm said. "Say by the way, a fellow over Ironside way was telling me all about Copperfield yesterday. Guess he read it in the papers. Is it true a little ol' gal came in there and shut down the whole damned town?"

"That's just about the size of it," Cord grinned.

"I'll be damned," Norm sputtered, shaking his head. Withdrawing his foot from the corral fence railing where he had been leaning for an hour or more, he added, "Well c'mon up to the house. We'll see what's setting on the back of the stove. Iris took the buggy this morning, went on over to Bonnie Jean's. Bonnie Jean got herself pregnant first thing. So she and her mother have been keeping company every other day or so, working on baby clothes and things. Iris is planning to stay the night tonight, she said."

For some reason, the news triggered Cord's laughter. "So you're going to be a grandpa, huh?" he chortled.

"What's so funny about that?" Norm flared.

"Oh nothing, I guess. Congratulate Bonnie Jean for me when you get the chance."

Cord rode out the next morning heading east and north toward Idaho. The weather had chilled to around zero, but would probably warm to about thirty degrees today. At least the wind from yesterday had died down. Norm insisted Cord take an extra horse to carry his pack and a good supply of oats, "in case you have to spend a night or two out in the weather somewhere along the way."

Cord didn't think he'd have to. He'd taken seven days to get here last fall and he'd found no need to stay on the trail overnight. This time, he'd undoubtedly make it in five, especially since he had an extra horse. But you never knew.

No matter which way he went, he did have to go over a range of snow-covered mountains for at least twenty miles. Even some of his people got caught out in wintertime over that stretch.

—

The frosted door of Attorney Nelson's inner office flew open. The squat balding man sitting behind the huge desk near the corner window was so startled that he nearly toppled his chair as he popped his head upward to see what was happening.

"C. R." he choked, "You could give a man a heart attack!"

"Sorry Floyd. Your secretary wasn't in to announce me." Continuing his forward momentum, the district attorney plopped his briefcase on a bench placed along the wall by the door. He removed his suit jacket and hat, placing them on the coat stand, and swung toward the row of client chairs arranged along the solid wall away from the bookcase. He tugged one of the chairs to the front corner of Nelson's desk. Adjusting his prosthetic arm so that it bent at the elbow, he flung himself into the chair, then leaned forward with the eagerness of a performing poodle. "You needed to see me?" he asked.

Floyd rose to return some papers to an open file behind him, then scooted his chair closer to his desk as he sat down again. Steepling his fingers together, he brought his hands to rest in the middle of his barrel-like chest. He crossed his legs at the ankles and shifted his weight to the back of his chair.

Considering what he would say for a moment, Nelson responded. "Ughmm," he noised, clearing his throat. "You said to check back with you on Friday for any developments you might have concerning the hearing tomorrow. Uh, today's Friday."

"I don't know if there's anything to tell you that you don't already know. Ted's been down on the River and at Huntington for two days now working with that Lawson fellow. The mayor down there rolled over and told Lawson to do whatever he wanted to. He said the Huntington Council would cooperate fully. That cleared the way for Lawson's men to gather up all the gaming tables and slot machines to ship them along with the Copperfield collection here to Baker City," Deschinger informed his former law partner.

Nelson scowled, took a pencil in his hand as if to write, then bemoaned the Huntington mayor's action. "That sure doesn't help us any," he stated.

"What doesn't?" C. R. queried.

"The Huntington mayor, lining up without a fight," Nelson answered.

"I don't see how it makes any major difference, Floyd. I told you before, the gaming tables are not something we want to make an issue of. They may be private property, bought and paid for. But their use is illegal. Now the liquor, that's another matter. That's where you can draw the line. It's legal. It's legal to sell if the seller has a license."

"Yeah," Nelson murmured, "providing it was legally bought." Leaning sharply forward, his eyes narrowed and focused in a deliberate stare at Deschinger, he said in a confidential manner. "Just how much of that liquor do you suppose is legal, and how much of it is moonshine, do you think?"

"It doesn't make any difference," Deschinger responded. "All of it that was confiscated is in barrels or in commercially labeled bottles. So how could you know?"

"I guess you couldn't," Nelson swung back. "What I need to know, C. R., is how are you going to come down on this? You know, when it comes right down to cases, you and I are going to be duking it out on this thing."

The D. A. lifted his weight off his false arm and reached to loosen his necktie. "Nah," he said, "that's the beauty of it Floyd. We're both going to be on the side of the law for all intents and purposes. We just aren't in favor of the governor's methods of enforcement. You keep those headlines coming the way they have been. Hell, you're the people's champion in this matter according to the press."

"Hmm. If that's a fact, it's too bad my law clerk got carried away and gave that story to the *Oregonian* about the posse idea. I was rather surprised though when Yargo didn't follow through on confronting that damned militia outfit in Copperfield. I thought there had been all sorts of talk of standing up to Governor West if he dared come here with force."

"Ted's a good man," Deschinger observed. "But he's just a little ticklish about doing anything that might be considered unlawful. Anyway you can't win them all. I sure liked that headline the other day when they called West on his communiqué to Lawson to disobey any order of the Court no matter what it was. Then when Lawson tore up the injunction you had served, he walked right into our everlasting arms, as far as I can see."

"Headlines, schmedlines," Nelson grumbled. "I have a bad feeling about all this. We may be running a pretty good show for this part of the country, but over in the valley, the picture is, undoubtedly, quite different, I think. Take the flowers incident. I spent a fortune, to say nothing of a whole afternoon of my secretary's time, getting flowers sent over to that hellhole. The plan was for those birds to put them out in the saloons for the joke that the whole incident was supposed to be on Saturday. So what does our sniveling governor do but grab the publicity with his smart mouth, saying, 'Flowers usually are in order when last sad rites are to be performed. I have no objections to the saloons of Copperfield being appropriately decorated for the occasion.'

"I don't think I'll ever forgive him for that. Then to top it all off, his hand-picked hooligans locked the doors on the saloons while the owners were being arrested, and nobody even saw the damned flowers."

Deschinger chuckled lightly, "You have to admit though that those flowers must have added to the atmosphere in Wickert's hotel lounge where the governor's men were so shocked to find those pictures." His laughter grew as he imagined how "those men" must have reacted. Seeing Nelson staring sourly at the ceiling, as if he were off in his own little world, Deschinger grew serious again. "Come on Floyd. We've got this one in the bag, hands down."

"I wish I were as confident as you, C. R.," Nelson grumbled.

"Well, why the hell aren't you?" Deschinger demanded. "Do you have that demurrer ready to file at the end of the hearing arguments tomorrow? That so-called representative, that Collier guy, may just pull a rabbit out of the hat and make it sound as if the governor is right. You should have that demurer ready to put on the table immediately." Before Nelson could answer, he went on, "I can tell you, this Collier character can make you see blue where the color is clearly red if he puts his mind to it."

"Yes, I've heard that about him. By the way what are you doing about your own gravy train? According to the paper on Wednesday, old Oz is plainly out to get you, and probably Yargo too."

"You could say that," Deschinger said, drawing a deep breath. "I wish I'd been in town that day. The *Herald* editor has become something of a thorn in my side repeating every whisper of prostitution taking place anywhere in the county. But he's usually fair about printing both sides of a question. At least," he sighed, "I got my reply of innocence into print the next day. Our foxy governor may think he knows what's going on. Hell, he may even really know what's going on, but he sure as hell can't prove what I do and do not know. I can honestly say I've never set foot in a house of ill repute, so how can he prove I have any knowledge of their existence, I ask you."

"You not only got your reply to West in, I was really surprised when they put Lawson's remarks in about the posse story being false. I know that Lawson sure as hell believed it was true to start with, or he wouldn't have sent for fifty more militia men to protect him from going to jail in case Yargo went after him for ripping up our Court injunction."

"We'll have our day in court yet," Deschinger said revealing the bitterness he felt. "All those little details will be sorted out in front of a judge in the long run. To tell the truth, I think Ted had a lot to do with that disclaimer. He's pretty good at calming the waters. Somehow, Lawson also just happened to mention that the story about your number one client, Duane Wickert and his bartender buddy, Charlie Thatcher, was not true. But we know it was."

"Well it sure as hell wouldn't have done our case any good if those two clowns had made it down to Ballard's Landing and crossed into Idaho in the middle of the night," Nelson observed. "The press would have had a field day with that. I don't know what got into them, trying to sneak out of Copperfield on a railroad handcar after dark like that. I suppose they figured those militiamen would all be sleeping and none would be the wiser. Must have been a sight to behold when that soldier snatched them off that car with a lasso, kerthump!

"You know either one of those two bastards will look you right in the eye and agree to cooperate fully, then they'll go right ahead with plans to do just the opposite. If it weren't for the principle of the thing with the governor doing his dirty work the way he did, I'd be tempted to throw that pair to the wolves."

"You wouldn't do that to Harvey would you?" Deschinger asked in alarm.

"Hell no," Nelson was quick to state. "For a guy who succeeds in politics as well as he does, old Harvey's heart must be in the right place. He may weasel a little on the side, but up front, he's pretty honest about most things."

"Not to change the subject," Deschinger remarked, "but speaking of the press, I've gotten three or four calls a day from newspapers outside the area. This morning, The *New York Tribune* reporter wanted more information about that Hobbs woman. I told him I didn't know anything about her and that I wasn't her press agent. He practically called me a liar. He said he had it on good authority that she lived here in Baker City a few years ago and worked for a lawyer. He added that he wouldn't be surprised to find out that lawyer was I.

"I told him he was way off base and slammed the phone in his ear. Still it will be a hell of a note if you have to go up against her in court. She's the whole world's darling now, you know. But to have it come out that she's practically one of our own doesn't exactly make us look good."

"No, I suppose not," Nelson assented.

Deschinger rose to go. "Well, you've just got to win this case Floyd, because if you don't, we're going to look like a bunch of stupid assholes. It won't matter that West is probably going to drop out of the governor's race according to the press in Salem. We still have to be able to hold our heads up and win elections around here." The district attorney, in his usual whirlwind fashion, grabbed his hat, threw his jacket over his mechanical arm, dangled his brief case from the ends of his fingers and popped out the door.

Nelson's mouth rose at one corner in a lop-sided grin although he could see nothing funny in what was said. If he were still a youngster in knee-high britches, he probably would just put his head down and cry. Sometimes he wished he had never joined in a law partnership with C. R. Deschinger. He'd thought to be free of the man and his connections when C. R. became the district attorney, but if anything, the situation had gotten worse instead of better.

Glancing at the grandfather clock next to the coat stand on the far side of the room, he noticed it was 11:30 already. He decided he might as well go on over to The Grand for a bite to eat. Nancy, his secretary, would be back after lunch from her visit to the dentist. Then maybe he could get some work done instead of sitting around stewing about Copperfield and its complexities.

General Delivery
Copperfield, Oregon
January 10, 1914

Dear Lottie Fern,

    Here it is, the day of the hearing against Lawson for tearing up the injunction that the Copperfield Seven lawyer had the deputy sheriff serve him the other day. I don't understand how they tied that incident together in the same complaint with their contention that declaring martial law here was illegal. But I guess you know more about all that than I do.
    I'm so sorry you didn't get to go home on Friday as you planned. It must have been a shock to get that telegram from Governor West when you reached Baker City, asking you to stay over. I just keep remembering how weary you looked when you left here. I know you profess to love your job, but don't you think sometimes that the governor takes horrible advantage of you?
    If you had stayed the whole week in Baker City, I was planning to come on the train yesterday for another short visit. I'm so lonely without Cord.
    That rat left Sunday morning, a fact I didn't know until after I had posted my letter to you last week. I've not heard a word from him, and I can hardly stand it, especially if I start thinking about him.
    I don't know if it's the militia thing or what, but I've noticed my students are very unenthusiasic most of the time. Maybe it's my rotten attitude that's rubbing off on them. Overall, it's pretty dreary around here, even on days when the sun shines.
    I keep thinking, Lottie. Did we have any other way to go? I understand that before it's all said and done, the governor may take out the sheriff as well as the district attorney for failure to perform their duties. As much as I am wishing things were under control here in Copperfield, I hope he doesn't do that.
    I was so shocked the other day when I heard Colonel Lawson wired for more militiamen because the sheriff might be bringing a posse to arrest him. Clara was so upset. I could tell she was clearly frightened.
    I think this has been the longest week of my life. I thought maybe things would get better when they shipped those awful gambling machines and all that liquor out on Tuesday, but every time I venture into the store, either Clara or George are shouting about the right or wrong of it all.
    I did teach the children a little about martial law last Monday. I explained to them it is only temporary until the townsfolk can get a new group of people in place to be the Town Council and uphold the law.
    Stan Galleon's little girl announced that her daddy may be appointed the new temporary mayor, and that everything will be under control soon. I surely hope so.

I know dear cousin that you're just too busy for anything right now, but I hope you can write soon. Your letters always cheer me no matter how down I am feeling. That's true even if you fill them with news that I don't want to hear. It's so important for me to know you are there and you care enough to talk to me.

Looking forward to a brighter future,

Your cousin,

Ellie K

The Injunction and its Aftermath

My dearest Ellie,

    It's been almost two weeks since I left you. I hope you haven't dwelt too much on not hearing from me. I was so sorry we didn't part on better terms, and I felt very bad about leaving that Sunday morning without telling you goodbye. I do hope you'll have it in your heart to forgive me.

    I didn't get a job in Agency Valley, although I went there. I had no great appreciation for my Bell mare when I bought her after I came to Copperfield, but I found out on my trip that she's a honey of a walker. She couldn't believe it, I don't think, when I got off to walk the day after I left Copperfield. It was cold and windy, especially on top of the ridge going into Mormon Basin. But I didn't walk for long. Bell kept nudging me with her nose as if she were in a hurry. So I climbed back in the saddle and rode to the cemetery at Malheur City.

    I stopped there to eat my lunch and visit my dad's grave. I was wishing I had a shovel to clean around the gravesite. Every passing year makes it a little harder to find. If I hadn't made a point to visit and clean it two or three times a year most years, I suspect it would be sunken out of sight by now. My mother thinks I'm crazy to worry about it. That's not the Indian way. Nevertheless, I tend to draw strength from my visits, and I always feel a little more at peace with the world when I leave there.

    Speaking of my mother, I'm here in Lapwai now visiting until the spring-wheat planting begins. You can't imagine how surprised my mother was to see me again so soon. I hadn't written because she would have had someone read my letter to her, and I didn't feel like revealing my cancelled marriage plans to anyone else.

As I was saying about Bell, we made really good time on the ride here, but I encountered a bad snowstorm as I rode down from the Blue Mountains. I got pretty wet and cold, and I caught a cold. But a few days on my mother's diet of broth and herbs, and I'm okay again. While I was recuperating after my cough became more controlled, my mother brought me Papa's Shakespeare plays and asked that I read them to her. When I finished that first day, she took my hand and said, "You sound just like your father." She had tears in her eyes, and I even got a little choked up. After that, she visited with me more about the past than ever before in my whole life.

I remembered that Mother and I were not on particularly good terms when I was eight and we went to Lapwai after Papa was killed. Because she was so sad all the time, I took up with Uncle Bearclaws, whom I later learned was not really related because my mother is not a Nez Perce.

She had joined the tribe illegally when the government returned the Nez Perce from the Indian Territories in Oklahoma. They were on the trail for two days before Papa found out. He obviously was very surprised when she told him she had fallen in love with him, and that she just couldn't face life without him.

You should have seen her Ellie. In telling me how she and Papa got together, she started laughing and crying at the same time. She was particularly mirthful when she told how my father had sneaked to be with her on the train. Anyway, the crux came when he decided to leave her in Huntington while he finished his military assignment in Lapwai. He was able to find friends in Huntington and a place for her to stay. He told her that if he took her on to Lapwai he'd have to register her there. Then they'd have the choice of his staying on the Reservation with her or they would likely never see each other again. Well, he came back to her within the moon, she said, and they took up residence in Malheur City.

She did not laugh though when she told about coming to the Reservation after Papa was killed in the mine explosion. She said she didn't feel like a true member of the tribe, so she didn't talk to anyone, not even me. She always felt that the other women were fearful of her who "had no man." They also resented that she had a small sack of gold. The gold ran out, she told me, before I left the reservation.

"Maybe," she admitted, "it was my poverty that made me so hard on you even though I knew you were not yet a man. While I was doing everything possible to find a service I could offer others so I could obtain decent food and clothing for us, I felt that you could probably do better on your own." I asked her about the government dole. She said that it helped, but it wasn't enough to live on clean and comfortably.

"Why didn't you tell me that you needed money then?" I asked her.

"What good would it have done? You couldn't be coming and going from the reservation, especially at that time. As it is, you have your father's bearing and handsome good looks; so I knew you could make it in the white man's world. So I sent you away to work for the white man."

"Dammit, you have good looks too," I told her. "You didn't have any trouble when Papa was alive."

"No," she replied. "But I knew in my heart I was not Spanish as he told everyone."

"Then why didn't you go back to your own people instead," I wanted to know.

"Are you crazy?" she retorted. "After I ran away to be with a white man. At least here at Lapwai, your Uncle Bearclaws knew my plight. Besides I knew that if anything would happen to me, you would never be an orphan among the Nez Perce."

You can't imagine, Ellie, how bad I felt for her. I spent years resenting and blaming her for not even trying to "stay on the outside." But she had my best interests at heart the whole time. As she said, I'd been blessed with my father's looks. Except for my high cheekbones and my black hair, there would be no one who would take me for a half-breed, although I suspect that most people think I may be part Indian.

Even while she worried about my safety, she wanted to be off the Reservation too. But if she were with me, she'd be the mark of my heritage. Since she didn't want that for me, she surrendered her freedom. It is nice to get a glimmering of what she was thinking. That's when I remembered our little talk about commitment and security for raising a family.

Ellie, darling, I wish I could put your mind at ease now by presenting some definite plan for the future. But I can't. These things I've written about my mother and me may go a little way to explain my past that you accuse me of not sharing. Still, I have a few other matters to clear up. I hope you'll try to understand and trust me. I love you with all my heart, and I know we can and will work everything out eventually. I will be able to take care of you my darling, I promise.

Your loving friend,

Cord

Ellie read and re-read Cord's letter, weeping a little harder each time she finished.

—

Floyd Nelson gently pushed the door and poked his head to the inside. "You got a minute, C. R." he called. Then he finished opening the door wide in order to get his bulky body into the district attorney's office.

Deschinger looked up. Laying his pen that he had been using to sign some court documents to one side, he pushed back in his chair and said, "Sure Floyd, what can I do for you?"

"I just wanted to go over a couple of things with you to see where we're going next," Nelson paused.

"Such as what?" Deschinger prompted.

"For instance, if the judge comes down against the declaration of martial law, what do you think I should do first?"

"Sue the son-of-a-bitch! What else?" C. R. retorted.

Nelson knew without asking that Deschinger meant to sue the governor. The suit idea was already in the works on the one hand. On the other hand, Nelson wanted to know, "How? Should it be a class action suit for all saloon owners in Copperfield, or only for the ones who requested a predetermined amount. Then, too, do you think there's a leg to stand on where the gambling equipment is concerned regarding illegal seizure?"

"That, I would presume, would be up to your clients," Deschinger replied. "While it might give them some degree of satisfaction to get another bank deposit or two as a result of their investment in gaming tables and slot machines, the equipment itself will only be confiscated again anyway if they try to reinstall it."

"I take it you don't have much faith that those fellows are going to get back to business as usual very soon?"

"Not that kind of business," Deschinger admitted. "At least not until we get another governor. My advice would be to lie low on that issue. I'm sure there is not one of your clients complaining about all the money he made with those machines. So I figure they can take the loss. But shutting down their businesses entirely, that's a different matter. As West's mouthpiece pointed out, the two issues being considered are completely unrelated. The declaration of martial law is one thing; confiscating property and shutting down businesses is another."

"If the judge rules against your demurrer and says the governor didn't break any laws by sending in his troops," Deschinger continued, "West can still be held culpable for interfering in legal business practices."

"Possibly," Nelson commented. "If they can keep the mud off their shoes regarding the prostitution issue."

"You're not representing anybody in that business, are you? I thought all the houses down there were ostensibly being run by the working girls themselves."

"I guess they maintain that. But I don't think the claim would hold up very well if a full investigation were to occur. The bank records would probably tell a whole different story," Nelson opined.

"You'd better advise your clients to get those girls packed up and sent back to Nevada where they came from if they don't want to lose everything in the heat of this battle. Some say our esteemed governor is even tougher on prostitution than he is on the liquor trade. Still, I haven't heard of him saying the girls should be shot, but rumor has it that he has uttered those sentiments about bartenders."

"Speaking of what the governor says," Nelson inquired. "What are you going to do about the charity issue?"

"You mean, the governor's referring to my being elected district attorney as being an act of charity. As a matter of fact, I was just finishing my letter of reply that I will be sending to him and to the press as well." Deschinger leaned back in his chair. "Personally, I cannot conceive of any person with any degree of manhood taking a position of twitting a fellow being for the loss of a bodily member. So I'll challenge him to explain himself. Maybe he'll finally manage to crawl out on a limb and fall off in the eyes of the public on that side of the State." Shaking his head, he resumed his position close to his desk, then resorted to picking up a pencil to tap on the desktop in order to calm his frayed nerves.

"We can hope so," Nelson replied. "But to get back to the issue at hand, I learned that Collier is attempting to get those pictures from Wickert's hotel lounge to put before the grand jury when they meet. But if he doesn't present them here, he's threatening to take them to the feds."

"I know. That's not so good. Just how bad are those pictures anyway? Or do you know?" Deschinger asked.

"Well, I suppose it depends on which side of the church door you find yourself on Sunday morning. Some of our more liberal colleagues call them art. But I believe this jury would call them pornography. The ladies are most definitely nude."

"To bad," Deschinger said, clicking his tongue in sympathy. "Would you suspect just a hint of manipulation on the governor's part? I mean getting those pictures to the judge while he's still making up his mind on your demurrer? Then somehow getting the whole thing reported in the local papers? Collier is probably trying to create a little fear in the judge's mind that he might not get re-elected if he offends the sensibilities of too many of the gentler sex, now that they have the right to vote." Deschinger clenched his jaw tight, "Thanks to one Governor Oswald West."

Nelson felt that he had brought up one too many sensitive issues and should probably leave before the district attorney became so agitated that he wouldn't be able to think straight. So he rose, saying, "Well then, it appears that however the judge rules on Monday, I need to be prepared to appeal right away if necessary. And I'll get on with a suit for damages regardless of how many of the Copperfield saloon owners want to engage the Courts.

"I just wish they'd all get on board at the same time. But some of them are planning to pull up stakes and move on, especially if the militia hangs around much longer. They're saying the working men are grousing their heads off and planning to draw their pay to hit the road by the first of the month if this mess isn't straightened out."

"Damn," Deschinger swore.

Nelson pondered as he was leaving the room on why C. R. was particularly affronted by that news. Did he have some residual financial interest at stake? Mentally shrugging his shoulders, he thought to himself, "It's possible. Hell anything is possible." Such arrangements between the "businessmen" and local law enforcement officials were not all that uncommon in this neck of the woods, especially considering the business involved.

—

On the following Monday, the judge produced his 8,000-word proclamation in which he declared the Governor of the State of Oregon had broken no law by sending in the militia and deposing the local authorities in Copperfield. He carefully delineated between the issues of the militiamen's handling of closing down the saloons and confiscating the liquor and the governor's action in declaring martial law. So the door was wide open for bringing suit against Governor Oswald West, Fern Hobbs, B. K. Lawson, et al with regard to interfering in Copperfield business practices.

Three weeks later, Baker City officials destroyed the gambling paraphernalia. Coincidentally, on the same day, Nelson filed suit for two of his clients, Harvey Sullivan and Duane Wickert. They sued for $8,000, a buck a piece for each of the judge's words of repudiation against them in his decision on the injunction.

Later in the month, the governor ordered that Mayor Sullivan and his partner in the saloon business reclaim their liquor, which was stored in a warehouse in Baker City. The partner refused on the grounds that the governor took it, he could return it. Or better yet, he could pay retail prices for every drop of it at the conclusion of the suit hanging over his head in the Baker District Court.

—

Ted Yargo ambled into the district attorney's office, pulling up one of the client chairs. Settling into it, he pushed his hat back on his head and grasped the chair's arm rests. It was the first day of his return to duty in Baker City in two and a half weeks.

Deschinger had his back toward the sheriff while shuffling some papers. He turned around, adjusting his arm, and peered at Yargo as if to examine him on the witness stand. "How's it going?" he greeted.

"I was about to ask you that very question," Yargo returned.

"I suppose you could say the governor won round one." Deschinger replied.

"That's about what the papers are saying."

"I can't quite understand it myself," Deschinger shook his head. "Floyd had every proof in the land laid out. Even Frank Collier, the governor's advocate, says he did an outstanding job." Eyeing Yargo, he went on, "It looks as if you are home free from the wrath of His Highness, the governor, now that you've impressed his right-hand man, that Lawson fellow."

"It looks that way, C. R. How about yourself? You and the governor have been having quite a tussle lately, I'd say."

"Can't tell for sure," Deschinger said laconically. "If you can keep the lid on the restricted area here in town for a while until these Court sessions are finished, I suppose it will all die down.

"What I can't figure out, though, is how that man, West, can command such loyalty. Here's Colonel Lawson ready to fight and die for him. And that secretary, why she was ready to make a complete fool of herself . . ."

"She didn't turn out to be such a fool in light of what's happening," Yargo concluded.

"No, but she could have," Deschinger retorted. "I just wish I could command that kind of loyalty." Seeing the pinched look on Yargo's face, he changed course quickly. "Now Ted, that wasn't aimed at you. I know where you're coming from at all times, and I have no complaints. In fact, it's your dedication to checking the legalities of things before acting, that has probably saved my neck several times over."

Yargo accepted the D. A.'s subtle apology, at least noticeably. "What I'd like to know, on the other hand, is what the judge was thinking when he overruled his own injunction."

"Damned if I know what he was thinking," Deschinger replied. "I do think this piece in the *Morning Oregonian* from January 20, pretty well sums up the course he took. He began to read aloud.

"It says:

According to the facts alleged and stipulated, the defendant, Oswald West, acting in the capacity of Governor of the State, declared by proclamation that it was his belief that the laws in the town of Copperfield were being violated and the observance thereof not enforced and that residents of the place were subjected to danger of violence, lawlessness and even wanton destruction of property by incendiaries. No proof of these allegations have been made in court nor is the truth or falsity thereof in any manner a subject for judicial determination in this proceeding. The only question with which the court can on this feature concern itself is the authority vested in the chief executive and whether or not his discretion exercised in the acts complained of are subject to judicial restraint by means of preventive process.

Section 3848 provides: "The Governor shall have power in case of invasion, insurrection, forcible obstruction to the execution of the laws, or reasonable apprehension thereof, breach of peace, tumult or riot, or imminent danger thereof, to order into the service of the state any of the companies, batteries, etc."

Thus it will be seen that whenever an armed force is called out in response to a request from local civil authorities, the military is under direct and strict control of those authorities; but nowhere is it even intimated that the chief executive must wait for such request before he can act in his own discretion in carrying into effect the duties and powers reposed in him as head of the executive department of the Government. Were this so, some of the provisions of section 3848 would become useless and futile in all cases when, if for any reason, the local authorities fail to issue such request for military aid, whether needed or not.

If then in a proceeding of the nature where the preventive remedy by injunction is sought it is not within the province of the judicial department to undertake to judge and determine the wisdom or expediency of the acts complained of or to grant the relief prayed for, what then becomes of the constitutional provision which provides that "no person shall be deprived of life, liberty or property without due process of law; and that the right to trial by jury shall remain inviolate."

In assuming military control of the town of Copperfield, the members of the militia acting under orders of their superior assumed the position temporarily of peace officers and cannot lawfully go beyond the bounds of reasonable necessity; and if, as has been urged, the necessity did not in fact exist for such drastic measures invoked, and if thereby wrongs were committed as alleged, the commander-in-chief and those of his subordinates who participated would be answerable in a court of justice, either civil or criminal as the case may be, and thereby the provisions of the constitution that those accused shall have the right to face accusers and a guarantee of trial by jury applies, as this court views it, with equal cogency to and may be invoked by the executive and those acting under him as well as by the plaintiff.

It follows from the foregoing consideration that the demurrer must be overruled.

"The next article states that the governor's stand is for the militia to remain on duty in Copperfield until the elected members of the Town Council resign or until he is no longer Governor. I'd say that about sums it up, wouldn't you?"

"So there was no evidence offered on the issues or reasons for closing the town down, according to that," Ted remarked.

"Not in this go-round. For the time being, the issue is that the Council members are refusing to resign."

"How in the hell does that come into the law?" Ted questioned.

"Hmmmp!" grunted Deschinger. "That's a good question. What it comes down to is answering the complaints of that petition signed by the town's citizens."

"I don't see how in the hell that petition can stand up. There aren't more than fifty registered voters in that town. And, sure as hell, they didn't all sign it," Ted protested.

"Ah," breathed Deschinger, "but you forget the outlying community, whose preference it is to do business there."

"Screw the outlying community. They can go to Robinette, or Richland, or Halfway. We surely don't have to answer to every old woman with a bellyache who wants some medication from a nearby pharmacy, do we?"

"But, Ted, my boy," C. R. said in a less contentious fashion, "You forget they do have to get their mail in Copperfield." Leaning back in his chair and pushing the fingers of his good hand through his hair and to the back of his head, he went on. "Furthermore, I surmise we do have to contend with answering even the old women if we want to be re-elected."

Comprehending what Deschinger was saying, Yargo calmed down considerably to ask, "So where do we go from here?"

"Now, it is up to me and the grand jury to put on the table the pertinent evidence. The reason I called you over here this morning is to begin a complete investigation of the accusations of people who signed that petition. I think we can keep the business of "undesirable," probably meaning gambling and prostitution out of our presentation if you know what I mean. Being that I had notified the Council in November to discontinue all such activities, and I have the mayor's letter of compliance saying that they did so, that leaves the fires. We already have on record that there was insufficient evidence to prosecute for criminal activity.

"There still remains, however, the liquor issues—particularly that of selling to minors. We're going to have to go ahead on that one unless we find some way evident to squelch the pertinent testimony. According to what you were saying in November, there does seem to be some evidence that the Lawson woman may be able to substantiate. Hopefully, that won't be too serious."

"So you want me to head out again to investigate?" Yargo asked.

"That's about the size of it," Deschinger replied.

General Delivery
Copperfield, Oregon
January 24, 1914

Dear Lottie Fern,

 I want to apologize to you, first for being so brash, and second for causing you to have any doubts about your actions in coming to Copperfield. Of course, I realize that, as you said, "No girl likes to be that conspicuous." I know you weren't here to grandstand. And I can certainly appreciate your sentiments as stated in the newspaper that you did it for Governor West, and you wouldn't do it again, even for him. I can only repeat that I am truly sorry. Please forgive me.
 I received a letter from Cord last week. It was sweet. He's in Lapwai staying with his mother until spring-wheat planting begins. I try to empathize with him; he told me a lot of the sad details of his childhood. At the same time, if that's all that's bothering him, I can't see the relevance. I very much doubt that that is the entirety of his problems.
 I was visiting with Bridget the other day; and she told me how she and Marty begged and cajoled all day Saturday trying to get him to move in to a spare room they have. But he wouldn't hear of it. He said he had to get a job.
 Money is a very sore subject with him. His pride won't let him think about being dependent on someone else even for a minute. So you can imagine his reception when it comes to speaking of falling back on my trust fund for little extras in the event we marry. He positively will not hear of it.
 They're starting the dances again next week. They cancelled the one on the 3rd of course, since everything and everybody was in such an uproar. Then last week, they hoped the Court hearing would settle the matter of the injunction and lift martial law. But when the judge put his decision off until Monday, they cancelled again.
 I guess, now, they figure the militia is here to stay, so they might as well get their lives back to normal. The people who live away from Copperfield have been particularly disgruntled about the cancellations according to Alice Hunsaker. They can't see how it affects them if the saloons are closed. That just assures them of having a good time without the interference of fist fights or flying bottles on the dance floor.
 I brought up the subject of the dances because Clara came bounding into my room a little while ago to tell me that Mr. Baldwin mentioned how pleased he would be to escort me to the dance. I couldn't believe it. I thought she was going to suffer apoplexy, she was so excited. Apparently, I have her permission to have a social life as long as it doesn't include Cord. I have to wonder why she harbors such animosity toward him. As far as I know, they've never spoken a word to each other.

I don't know whether to tell Cord about Mr. Baldwin's invitation or not. I did tell Clara that if Henson Baldwin wishes to invite me anyplace, he needs to speak with me, personally. In the meantime, I'm not interested. Clara looked crestfallen. She pursed her lips and said, "Well if that's the way you want it. I just thought maybe you'd enjoy getting out and about once again."

I am not looking forward to the next two weeks. I have to make good on my promise to the parents to present an assembly open to the community. I have decided its theme will be centered on Oregon's birthday, and I'll present it the evening of the 13th.

I truly hope you're getting back to a more routine existence. I'm with you, wishing you didn't have to go gallivanting around the country, serving notice on corruption and vice. Now that Governor West has won on the issue of declaring martial law here, perhaps others will take heed when he gives them fair warning.

Write soon.

All my love,

Cousin Ellie K.

Be My Valentine

It was Friday night, quite after dark, when Ellie tugged the string on the light cord hanging from the ceiling in the school foyer. Closing the school's front door behind her and checking to see that it was secure, she turned toward the pathway through the snow-covered yard to hurry home. Locking her hands over her wrists inside the fur muff that had come as an accessory with her heavy winter coat, she hoped to warm herself as she clipped rapidly along the dirt pathway.

Although the coat, a heavy wool, topped with a fur collar, provided adequate protection against the cold, Ellie had become chilled as she let the fire die down in the schoolroom. That was hours ago, she thought, as she leaned into a brisk northeast wind. She hadn't intended to stay so long, but the Oregon Birthday assembly program still required a plan. For the life of her, she couldn't think of a way to move smoothly between the children's choices of performance items. Just one week away, and so much practicing to do!

Ellie would have dropped the idea of the assembly if she hadn't made overtures to the parents at the Christmas program, promising them a mid-winter assembly that would be open to the public. She was a little panicky, too, about the fact that last week's dance had greater attendance than ever. Folks were just itching for some social outlet where they could get together as a community. The frequent card parties and birthday celebrations they held at each other's homes just weren't enough. Especially, she supposed that was true among the men who lived at the job site without benefit of family.

Ellie felt a drop of moisture trickling down along her cheek. "If only Cord were here," she sighed. She had just reached the boardwalk and was cheered by the sound of her heels clipping along at an invigorating pace when a man stepped from the shadowy doorway of the first darkened saloon. He was directly in her path so that she had no choice but to draw up sharply. Before she had time to become frightened, she realized it was Henson Baldwin.

"Good evening, Miss Delaney," he said, tipping his hat.

"Hello, Mr. Baldwin," she said with some reservation. "You startled me."

"Oh, I'm sorry. Perhaps I should see you home so that no one else will do the same."

Ellie glanced furtively along the distance remaining between them and The General Store. Laughing softly, she said, "Well, perhaps." But she felt a shiver of apprehension ripple through her as Baldwin fell into step beside her.

Recalling the dangling dance invitation that she had so far managed to stave off, she was aware that Henson was about to make a renewed effort. She was not ignorant of the fact that he had been circling for several months trying to establish an intimacy in which she did not care to participate.

"How have things been going for you in light of our reformed ways here in Copperfield," Baldwin inquired with humor.

"Oh fine," she lied blithely. "I'm certainly sleeping much sounder now that the tinny music has halted. Do you miss it?" she asked in an effort to keep the conversation going until they could reach the store.

Henson laughed. "Not really. When it comes to music, I generally make my own. But I do enjoy a good band," he hastened to add. "Which brings me to the point," he continued cheerily, "Will you be attending the dance next week? It will be rather special, I think, being the Valentine's Day Cotillion, and all."

"Oh no," Ellie wanted to blurt, her thoughts whirling like a dust devil in July. Frantically, searching for a way out, she stammered, "Uh, I hadn't made any plans to." Reaching for some logical excuse, she said, "You see I'm rather bogged down right now trying to get my Oregon Birthday assembly ready for presentation.

"Say," she said, an idea having popped into her head. "How about you coming and appearing in my assembly. Then maybe I'll make the next dance. I'll even go with you if you'll come help me out," she chattered merrily.

Henson stopped short, so that Ellie, taken by surprise, had to turn back to see what was the matter. The light from the doorway of the Painted Lady shone dimly into the street. Since the mayor, or ex-mayor as the case may be, used the premises as his office, the light was a signal to his cronies that he was in, and it frequently sent its beams into the otherwise totally dark street far into the night. Ellie had often thought, "Old habits are hard to break." But tonight she was both grateful and chagrined to be able to see Henson's face by the gleam.

He stared at her darkly, his brown eyes wide with anger.

"Oh, I'm sorry," Ellie blustered. "I didn't mean it to sound like that. I just meant that once this program is over, and I have time to relax, I can get organized and have a new gown made, or order one. I just don't have anything to wear right now," she finished lamely.

Henson gave her the benefit of the doubt since he was well aware of the cheap cottons she had substituted for the stunning gowns she had brought with her from the East. But he was not entirely mollified.

"Look Miss Delaney," he groused, "I'll be happy to appear in your program. I have plenty of time right now, but don't assume I'm doing it so you'll go to the dance with me. I'm not in the habit of purchasing favors," he paused, "from ladies," he paused again "of any kind," he spat.

"I know that," Ellie pulled her gloved hand from her muff and coyly tucked it in his arm at the elbow. "I said I'm sorry. If I weren't so tired and distraught over this assembly, I certainly wouldn't have let my tongue err so."

"There," she thought, "that should be poetic enough to calm the troubled waters."

The couple had reached the entryway of the store. George was putting out lights and preparing to lock the front door. Ellie turned to Baldwin and said quickly, "I do hope you forgive me Mr. Baldwin, and thank you so very much for escorting me."

"I'll forgive you if you'll drop the Mister and call me Henson," he agreed, still growling.

Ellie recoiled slightly as she withdrew her hand, "All right, Henson," she murmured meekly. "Perhaps you can come by the school on Monday afternoon so we can discuss the program."

Henson wanted to delay her by asking, "What's wrong with tomorrow?" But she had literally vanished through the open door that George was holding for them.

"Good evening, Henson," he greeted. "Did you need something?"

"Good evening, George. No I was just seeing Miss Delaney home," he replied with a hint of satisfaction in his voice.

"Oh, well good night then," said George, gently closing the door and pulling the cord to extinguish the last light.

Henson turned to walk slowly back along the boardwalk toward the livery stable where he would pick up his horse to return home. He was still feeling hot under the collar about Ellie's bargain. "Who does she think she is?" he muttered.

Then he brightened a little. At least she had consented to go to the dance with him, without his having to beg like some pauper. He hadn't foreseen that she would be quite so pugnacious, but at least she was honest in her own way. Baldwin was sorry he wouldn't be able to show her off at the Valentine Cotillion, but maybe it was just as well. Maybe he'd stay away himself.

The Lord knows how many such dances he had sat through in his thirty-two years, actually more like sixteen years since he was old enough to attend dances. Last year, he had invited a young lady from Robinette, whom he met at a family gathering to honor his younger brother's engagement.

Had that ever been a disaster. She couldn't dance. She was stiff as a board and had absolutely no sense of rhythm. Henson had almost sworn off dancing after that. In fact, he didn't attend again until he met Ellie. Then the urge to check her out at the dance last September was too strong to ignore.

Lord, she was beautiful that night. It was the Christmas dance though, when she had worn that emerald green gown with the low neckline, that he had experienced a dull ache in his loins, one he had been trying to satisfy ever since.

"Tonight sure wasn't the night," he thought to himself, as he mounted his horse and trotted off into the darkness.

—

After weathering the storm of Clara's scolding for being late and wandering around on the streets of this awful town in the dark, Ellie marveled that Clara had mellowed somewhat. She actually stopped short of spouting about Ellie's reputation being at stake or warning her that she might as well advertise as a common streetwalker. Still, Ellie felt a need to vent her anger, but common sense bade her hold her tongue. Instead she was impelled to ask, "Do you think Rebecca will be very busy this month?"

"Rebecca?" Clara responded in surprise. "Oh you mean my sister. I don't suppose she's any busier than usual. Still she might be for the next week. I suspect some of the ladies will want new dresses for the Valentine's Day Cotillion

"Why?" Clara suddenly perked up. "Are you planning to go to the dance? I'm sure Rebecca could find time to sew a gown for you. She surely isn't that busy. Besides the ladies who planned in advance would have delivered their fabric to her well before Christmas. They know how difficult it is for Rebecca to get that backroom she calls a sewing room warmed up these chilly days. It's practically impossible if the wind is blowing, even just a little. I don't know how that man she calls a husband could go and nail up a few boards and call it a sewing room."

Clara lost steam for further comments about her sister and leaned forward across the table to peer closely at Ellie, while she daintily sipped hot soup from the edge of her spoon. "Well are you?" she demanded sharply.

As usual, Ellie had almost lost track of the original topic of conversation. She remembered in the nick of time, sidestepping the need to implore, "Am I what?" Instead, she said, "No, I think not this dance, but maybe the next one after that."

Clara rose from the table and began rattling the dishes she had set to soak. As she strode from the counter to the stove and back, carrying the teakettle to warm the dishwater, she reminded Ellie of a strutting peacock, or at least of a young tom turkey.

"Well, it's about time," Clara sniffed. "You haven't been out of this house since that creature left town. I just can't imagine what you . . ." Ellie put her hands to her ears to shut out what she knew would be a ten-minute diatribe on the faults of "that Williams fellow." She also knew she could no longer refrain from crying. Rising rapidly, she knocked her chair to the floor just as Clara was spouting. "Why even after that man practically abandoned you in the wilderness, did you stop seeing him? Oh no, you went . . ."

The clatter of the chair brought her up short. Hurrying across the room to seize Ellie's arm as she was straightening herself and the chair, she fretted, "Are you all right?" Clara peered into Ellie's face. Realizing that the younger woman was definitely going to cry, she sniffed, then turned back to her dishwashing chore.

Ellie pulled her skirts free from the top of her shoes and fled up the stairs.

George looked up from the magazine he had calmly perused throughout the whole encounter between his wife and their boarder.

"I hope you're satisfied!" he remarked.

"Well, well," Clara huffed. "I'm just stating the facts!"

"Did you know that Henson Baldwin escorted our Miss Delaney to the door tonight?"

"He did!" Clara beamed. "So that's it."

"That's what?" George asked.

"Don't you see?" Clara cried happily, "she's on the rebound!"

George didn't reply, but went back to his reading.

Clara attacked the dishes with renewed vigor. She even began to hum a few bars of "Let Me Call You Sweetheart." Finally things were starting to look up for her young charge.

Folding the tea towel into a meticulous fit for the round-ring hanger dangling from the wall near the stove, Clara announced, "I'm going up to check on the children."

"Umm," George murmured. He was well aware that she had other things on her mind. It was a full hour before the children's bedtime.

When Clara reached the top of the stairs, she headed straight for Ellie's door. Knocking softly, she called. "May I come in."

"Yes," Ellie replied. "It's unlocked."

Clara observed that Ellie had indeed been crying, but she was sitting in her chair now with a magazine lying across her lap. She seemed to be recovered, but just in case, Clara went to her to pat her shoulder.

"I'm sorry," she apologized. "I didn't mean to upset you." She paused momentarily, then went on, "Why didn't you tell me you spent the evening hours in Mr. Baldwin's company? You could have brought him in to continue your visit, you know," she said softly.

Ellie considered setting Clara straight on the issue of Henson Baldwin. Then she remembered her plan to work with him on the assembly program several nights during the coming week. She might as well let sleeping dogs lie, she thought, or at least not direct their wet noses in the right direction.

Rather she launched into a conversation about the new gown. Folding out the pages of a January issue of *Vogue*, she held the magazine up for Clara to see.

"I like this gown. Do you think Rebecca could construct it just from the picture, now that she has my measurements practically memorized?"

"Yes, it's quite likely she could do that, I think. Especially since you are practically the same size as she." Clara glanced down at Ellie's bosom, but decided not to mention its greater fullness, compared to that of her sister. Instead she laughed, "She's not at all like me, perfectly round."

When Ellie didn't respond, she went on, "But what color and what fabric would you use?"

"I think I'll try to obtain some more of the velveteen that I used for my Christmas gown, only in a blue, a little darker than sky blue, but much lighter than navy, I think."

"Yes," Clara agreed. "That would be lovely. A nice match for your eyes, much like the brocade you wore last fall."

Actually Ellie was more inclined to reflect on how it would mirror in Cord's eyes as he swung her around the dance floor. And she was spitefully happy to realize it would not enhance Mr. Baldwin's skin tone at all. Henson did not look good in blue. Rather he usually wore tans and browns. Yes bright blue would be a perfect mismatch, she smiled to herself.

"Then did you want to call on Rebecca tomorrow?" Clara inquired. "I can accompany you if you like."

"Thank you," Ellie answered graciously, "but I think I'll give it some further thought. Maybe a nice satin magenta gown would be more satisfactory."

"Oh my," Clara breathed, "I don't think so."

"No," Ellie feigned surprise. She had known in advance what Clara would say. "Well in any case, I do need to see about fabric before visiting Rebecca. So tomorrow will be a little soon, maybe next week."

"All right, dear," Clara said, almost squeezing her eyes closed in an attempt to shut out the image of Ellie's curvaceous figure slinking along in a magenta-colored satin gown. "Well good night, then," she murmured, as she turned to leave.

"Good night," Ellie responded. She decided it was time to write to Cord. Otherwise she might go mad. Clara was acting just too strangely.

General Delivery
Copperfield, Oregon
February 14, 1914

Dear Lottie Fern,

I am quite exhausted today, and I've managed to catch a cold, perhaps from the children. It is very likely that for the first time in forty-two days, I'm actually thankful Cord is far, far away. On the other hand if he were here, I might not feel so out of sorts.

As I mentioned in my last letter, I've been very busy preparing for the midwinter school assembly, otherwise dubbed Oregon's Birthday celebration. I'm looking forward to your next letter that I hope will be filled with details of your work and social calendar, especially for today.

I also mentioned that Henson Baldwin had issued an invitation for my company to the community dance, which I refused at the time. As it turned out, Mr. Baldwin, who insists I call him Henson, was about to invite me to the Valentine's Day Cotillion. Being desperate about the assembly, I managed to kill two birds with one stone, so to speak. I offered to go to the dance with him at the last of this month if he'd appear in the assembly program. He wasn't terribly happy about the bargain, but I was pleased to get his help, especially in view of the way everything turned out.

The crowd was every bit as large as it was at Christmas, maybe even larger. Now that there are no saloons to frequent, a number of the men from the work crews attended. For the most part, those fellows are rather presentable and pleasant when among ordinary folk. They were so polite, I can't imagine a one of them deserving the reputation of being a troublemaker.

Anyway, the program went off very well. After presenting the flag and giving the flag salute, Helen Carpenter, who is in the eighth grade, recited the opening prayer. Henson led the whole assembly in singing a medley of patriotic songs. The children were all smiles when they realized that the audience knew all the same songs that we had practiced for weeks.

Then the sixth grade presented the Oregon flag, marching it from the foyer to the display area beside the Stars and Stripes. They dressed in blue and wore gold scarves to match the flag colors. After that, each of the children gave a recitation of poetry, or an essay, or an explanation of their own artwork to show what they have learned about our State.

At the end of the student presentations, Henson sang a number he was inspired to write after watching the children practice on Wednesday. He calls it, "My Oregon." It was truly a marvelous rendition. He has a wonderful tenor voice. The words made me stop to think about my loyalties, and I believe I'm beginning to see myself as an Oregonian now. I had not given the idea a whole lot of thought before last night.

I was very happy with everyone's performance. Success was ours in spite of the fact that there are only 23 students remaining since the continuing exodus of families from the town. People were reluctant to leave after the program without first congratulating Henson on his talent. He told them that he usually sticks to the lighter side, but has enjoyed this more serious challenge. He also rather gallantly kept referring them back to the opportunity he encountered because of my unique assembly.

Now, lest you begin to believe that I have relinquished a degree of my aversion where Henson Baldwin is concerned, I have to tell you I have not. In fact the reason I am so weary today, I believe, is because I don't like being around the man. My feeling has nothing to do with his treatment of me. He is an accomplished dancer, and I've enjoyed every minute spent with him on the dance floor; but off the floor, I feel very uncomfortable. He has made no secret from the first that he disapproves whole-heartedly of Cord, whom he considers a beneath-contempt saddle bum.

I have been quite amazed that Henson would attempt to take up with me so quickly after Cord left, understanding as I'm sure he does, how I feel down deep. I haven't told him that Cord may return here early in the month of March. As a matter of fact, Cord's name has not come up in our conversation at all.

All together, I am quite relieved that I did not for a minute entertain the idea of going to the dance tonight. I can't imagine why, in a place like this, they call it a cotillion. I'm quite sure it is no more or less formal than any other dance. But perhaps the matrons in the community feel it gives them an opportunity to dress a little more expensively. At any rate, it provides them an excuse to wheedle a new gown from their husbands, or at least some new yard goods.

Speaking of yard goods, I was able to order yardage from one of the stores in Baker City for a blue velveteen gown. I'm hoping it reaches me today on the afternoon train. If so, I shall deliver it to Rebecca along with the picture of the design I hope she can create. Then I'll be able to relax for a while. Maybe I'll get over this fretful feeling I have experienced all week, being around Henson. Actually, he only dropped by on Monday and Wednesday. But I still feel my nerves jangling every time I have to think about him.

I hope this finds you rested and in good spirits. You didn't mention your English friend in your most recent letter. He hasn't' returned to England already, has he?

Please write soon.

My love and good wishes for a happy Valentine's Day.

Your cousin, Ellie K.

P. S. I'm sending a copy of Henson's song so that if it might be of interest, it can be used. Maybe you'd have to hear Henson sing it to be as impressed as I am, but I really think it's quite special.

My Oregon

Far in the West, beyond the Rocky Mountain ranges
There lies a land, where long the Red man roamed
Where days are bright, the climate sunny, mild, and changeless
A land of wonders, land of health and wealth unknown
With towering mountains and mighty rivers,
With forests green and valleys e'er in bloom
A land so fair, that all who come remain to build a home
Queen of the West, land I love best
        My Oregon

Since time began, this Paradise beside the western sea
Lay peacefully, unknown to the world
Then came the dawn, the white man's coming wrought discovery
And there the pioneers of old our flag unfurled
To add a jewel to our nation; with work and strife,
An Empire there was won
Here let me live and prosper and then rest eternally
In the land I love, blessed from above,
        My Oregon

Some years have passed since Oregon became our grandest State
And I relate, the future's brightest star
Its church spires rise, its schools and factories and cities great
Speak peace and plenty are the lot of all who are
Its happy people looking forward
To greater heights and better things to come
So launch your hopes, where dreams come true,
And by the setting sun
Find all you've searched for 'long life's trail
        In Oregon.

The Red Ball Gown

Ellie couldn't help smiling and being joyful again when Cord's letter came on Saturday. In order to share its contents she rushed to the Kellner's where Bridget welcomed her warmly, despite being in her last few weeks of pregnancy.

Sharing the contents of Cord's letter, they visited about his news that he would leave Lapwai the same day he wrote the letter. A friend had sent word to him about work in Walla Walla that would last for about three weeks. If that panned out, he would be taking the borrowed horse back to Agency Valley around the 10th of March, then be back in Copperfield by the 15th. If the job didn't work out, he said, he might be back even sooner. "Surely by this time," Cord wrote, "the sawmill is or will be starting work again."

When they finished rehashing Cord's letter for the third or fourth time, Ellie rose to say, "My goodness, I'd better be getting dressed for the dance tonight."

Bridget didn't rise from her chair, but waved merrily and said, "Well, deary, have a good time."

Back in her room, Ellie stared at herself in the mirror. "What in the world am I going to do?" she fumed. Her reflection clearly revealed that something had gone terribly wrong since her final fitting with Rebecca on Wednesday. They had both agreed that the bodice needed to be lengthened about two inches. Apparently Rebecca had removed the basting and rearranged the fabric in the wrong direction. Instead of lengthening it to provide more fullness for Ellie's bosom, she must have shortened the front pieces even further. The result was that there was not nearly enough room for her to be decently clad if she pulled the garment toward her waist. To let the waist ride upward looked even worse.

Ellie's first inclination was to cancel going with Henson to the dance tonight. But that wouldn't be practical because she had promised him, and she couldn't postpone. Cord was bound to return before the next dance, which would be in observance of St. Patrick's Day.

When Rebecca's husband dropped the dress by the store just this morning, she had merely taken it to her room and laid it across her bed. She hadn't given it another thought until she had washed and styled her hair. Now standing in her undergarments, she felt betrayed by everything that had happened since Cord left two months ago.

Ellie thought about unearthing her brocade that she had packed away in order to free up closet space. But she feared that it would require airing and pressing, maybe even some light repairs. The peach gown was a summer gown, as were the cotton frocks, in reality.

The only gown still hanging in her closet was the red one. While she wanted to show up in a new dress because she had protested her lack of anything to wear to Henson, she could find no solution other than the red dress. The longer she stared at it, the more certain she became. Suddenly a gleam came into her eye as she thought about it.

"Why not?" she asked aloud. Continuing her thoughts, "Henson will be here to escort me. Clara will not be able to march me back to my room ordering me to change my clothes like some young girl. And I will, at last, be able to defy her." Her hands trembled as she removed the dress from its hanger.

Ellie experienced a perverse pleasure as she climbed into the ankle-length red taffeta skirt. Drawing it up from the floor to fasten the closure at her waist, she giggled before drawing the delicate overdress past her already coifed hair.

Its sleeves were of white net embroidered with a wreathed rose pattern along the edge. The roses were repeated at the garment's lower edge, which struck at mid-thigh. Red netting was gathered over each hip and around the upper bodice. A large rose created from the red net decorated the lowest point of the plunging neckline where the white and red netting joined. The belt, cinched tightly at the waist, contributed to the appearance of alternate layers of delicate, frothy, easy-to-crush fabric almost blending into the more alluring slinky expanses of red taffeta that drew the eye to her every move.

Slipping on her black patent leather shoes, she felt the pinch of the narrow toes. Still, she felt wonderful to be freeing herself from the tight reins of Clara's control. She smiled into her mirror as she touched up her hair-do and applied face powder along the lower edges of her neckline.

When Clara called out from the bottom of the stairs, "Miss Delaney, your young man is here," Ellie happily grabbed her white lace shawl and draped it gracefully across her back then over each arm as far as her elbows. She allowed the remaining expanse to drape along the sides of her dress.

"I'll be there in a moment," she called, then spun around in front of the mirror to check her total image one last time. "Pretty nifty," she murmured.

When she entered the lighted area in the kitchen where Henson and Clara stood talking, Henson stopped in mid-sentence to stare. He gave his head a very slight shake as he recovered from his reverie. Then he came resolutely forward to take Ellie's hand and place it firmly on his arm.

Ellie watched Clara recover from a rigid look of horror in time to acknowledge Henson's announcement of their departure. They had barely stepped on to the boardwalk when Henson declared, "Your landlady is apparently not as delighted by your appearance as I am."

"Apparently not," Ellie laughed softly. Then she inquired anxiously, "Do I look all right?"

"All right!" Henson exclaimed. "You look wonderful. Even the look on your face is one of pure joy."

Ellie laughed again and prepared herself to act as impious as possible without incurring the wrath of the school board for flaunting the rules of her teaching agreement. Being in the company of a school board member, she thought she could chance being a little outrageous.

It was just after nine o'clock when Henson and Ellie spun on to the dance floor. The band was still playing their first number. Ellie knew that she and Henson always attracted the audience's attention when they danced. But usually their conversations continued without interruption. Not so tonight. Both men and women delayed their intended remarks to turn their heads and stare as the couple twirled by.

Observing Henson watching the onlookers, Ellie remarked, "This must be the kind of attention audiences lavish on Theda Bera."

As for Henson, he was quite satisfied with himself. Ellie hadn't disappointed him at all. While the red dress would have been perfect at the Valentine Cotillion, it was actually drawing more attention tonight because of its inappropriateness. As they danced one number after another, his grin widened to become a permanent fixture on his face.

Eventually, well after the Hoffstetters arrival, Ellie's shoes began to pinch rather severely. By eleven o'clock, she finally begged to sit down for at least one number. Henson wasn't at all gallant about her request. But he did grumpily consent to fetch her a glass of punch after Clara declared that she, too, would very much enjoy some refreshment.

While he was gone and George was engaged in conversation with a fellow seated next to him, Ellie knew that Clara was prepared to attack. "I hope you're satisfied with your little performance, missy," she growled. "I don't know what you think you're doing. I'm just glad the Willoughbys and the Halvorsons chose not to attend tonight. If they had, I'm sure you'd have to answer for your audacious conduct."

By this time, Henson was returning. Ellie could think of a million things she wanted to say in her own defense. Instead, she leaned forward to receive the glass of punch, then turned to Clara to remark, "I imagine Henson is glad too."

Clara's face grew bright red, knowing that Henson would want an explanation concerning Ellie's remark.

"What am I glad about?" he wanted to know.

"Oh, nothing," Clara insisted darkly.

Ellie, too, decided to postpone the explanation, so the three sat, sipping their drinks throughout another entire dance number.

Besides beginning to tire when she and Henson resumed dancing, Ellie had long since realized that Henson was far more interested in her performance than in her. If judged by the number of compliments he paid her, one could suppose she had chosen her dress for his pleasure alone. The whole situation was becoming intolerable to her. She resorted to looking past Henson and back over her shoulder if at all possible in order to avoid eye contact with him.

Suddenly, Henson flung at her, "You're looking for him, aren't you?"

"For whom?"

"You know for whom," he retorted. "You have that same hungry look in your eye as when you first saw him"

"Maybe, that's just the way I look," Ellie claimed.

"I don't think so. Come on, admit it; you're in love with the guy," Henson accused.

"I'm not either," Ellie denied hotly, thinking to herself that it was none of his business in any case.

"Yes you are. Come on, tell me something. How come you two didn't make a go of it while he was here? Too much chaperoning, what?" Henson persisted.

"How could I do anything to make a go of it?" Ellie contested bitterly. Forgetting herself, she added. "All he can ever say is, 'I can't.'"

"Well then, have you considered taking him at his word?"

Ellie drew back to look at Henson's face. "What do you mean, his word?" she snapped.

Flippantly, Henson replied. "If the guy says he can't, maybe he can't."

Color crept up Ellie's neckline to her face. She was not totally naive, even if she was a virgin. But Henson's grin did not betray his motives. Ellie let it go without upbraiding him, or, as she would rather have done, slapping him for his smart mouth. But her evening was ruined.

Determined not to spend another minute dancing with this man, Ellie deliberately kicked her heel into the hemline of her skirt, then stumbled slightly against Henson. As he tensed his muscled arm to support her, she drew her foot downward into her dress with all her strength. The dress tore several inches at the hemline.

"Oh dear," she cried. "I've ruined my dress." Henson guided her to a chair along the wall, and she seated herself quickly, ostensibly to survey the damage to her skirt.

She was just beginning to plead that she must return home immediately when she happened to turn her attention toward the door. There, to her amazement, stood Cord. She wanted to run to him to greet him. But her predicament of having consented to let Henson escort her for the evening plus her insistence that she must return home had her stymied. What could she do?

Henson heard her gasp when she spotted Cord, and his eyes quickly followed her line of sight. He wasn't surprised when Ellie reversed her opinion on her need to go home. She abruptly declared, "Maybe there's a needle and thread of some sort in the cloak room. I'll just go check."

Before he could object or offer to accompany her, she fled. Being certain that she was practicing subterfuge, he rose to amble along after her. He was greatly surprised that she purposely slipped past Cord, pretending she hadn't seen him. Henson, on the other hand, knew that Williams had seen her. As he came abreast of the small knot of men Cord was visiting, he nodded in greeting, then continued on his way out of the hall. He was just in time to meet Ellie coming out of the cloakroom, her shawl wrapped securely in place.

"And what do you think you're doing?" Henson demanded.

"Oh," she blustered. "There's no one in there, so I was just coming back to get you to take me home."

"Umm, I'll bet," Henson snarled as he entered the cloakroom to retrieve his hat. "Well come on," he said. This time he didn't attempt to pull her hand in place on his arm. He simply followed her down the stairs, then held the door for her to exit.

Ellie tripped along like a scared rabbit with a dozen hounds in pursuit. Henson remained a polite distance from her side. When they reached the back entrance of the General Store, he again held the door open for her. Henson tipped his hat and said, "Thank you, Miss Delaney for a most pleasant evening for as long as it lasted." He did nothing to disguise the anger in his voice.

"Good night," Ellie muttered and continued through the door. She felt no compunction to engage in any polite conversation about enjoying herself. She also had no idea why he was so steamed, nor did she care. If she never spoke to him again, it would be too soon.

Misery thoroughly encompassed her as she wanted to go to Cord, to explain herself. She couldn't stop thinking how hurt he must have felt, seeing Henson follow her out of the dance hall.

Ellie slowly prepared for bed. Once there, she tossed and turned trying to imagine herself in Cord's company again. What would she say? How could she expect him to understand? "Just another Bonnie Jean," she murmured to herself as she finally drifted off.

General Delivery
Copperfield, Oregon
March 7, 1914

Dear Lottie Fern,

I really must apologize to you twice before I even begin my letter. Once, for not writing for so long, and a second time, for heaping a report of my misery on you to read.

I have just spent the worst seven days of my life, but there is a chance that things will get better soon. You see, it's all because of my red ball gown and Cord.

I thought my life would get so much better and become filled with happiness again once Cord returned. That is most assuredly not the case, and it's all because he arrived back in Copperfield about two weeks and fifteen minutes ahead of schedule.

You remember I was having a gown of blue velveteen made for the dance last week. It is quite beautiful, but in making adjustments, Rebecca decreased, instead of increased, the bodice size. So when I went to put it on, it did NOT fit. Well, I had nothing left to wear but my red taffeta. To spite Clara, after all the remarks she made when she first saw it, I decided to do just that.

You also might remember that I promised Henson Baldwin that he could escort me. In the two weeks following Valentine's Day, I could not forget my promise for one moment. The dance itself would have merely become a bad memory by now, but in order to get Henson to take me home before the dance ended, I stuck my heel into the hemline of my dress and ripped it. Yes, I was that desperate.

The worst part is that just when I was within moments of succeeding in that endeavor, I looked up to see Cord standing near the exit door. Lottie, I couldn't think straight. I attempted to slip past him and away from Henson so I could run home. I didn't speak to Cord; I just acted as if I hadn't seen him. But I didn't escape Henson. He followed me out of the hall.

Henson was steaming mad. I don't really know why, and I don't care. After all, I fulfilled my obligation by going to the dance with him in the first place. But once I got home, I only slept a few hours, then tossed and turned the rest of the night worrying about Cord. That's pretty much what I've been doing all week.

I did decide last Sunday, when there had been no message from him, I would try to locate him. I went over to The Golden Star to see if he was or had been there. He had just ridden out a few minutes before to go to the sawmill to get his old job back. Marty assumed he'd be back by suppertime. So I stayed to visit for three or four hours.

Bridget is getting so anxious. Her delivery date is drawing very near. Nevertheless, she was glad for my company. I washed down the kitchen woodwork and did a few other chores for her that she can't manage right now. But suppertime came and went, and no Cord.

I suppose, down deep, I was relieved because I had no idea what I would say to him. As things turned out, he did get his job back. This time, he will not be staying at the camp. He will ride his horse to and from work and stay at the boarding house. But his hours are such that he strikes out before dawn and returns after dark. Under those circumstances I did not see him once all week. He may as well have been back in Lapwai.

Yesterday evening, though, I stayed at school until after dark, then stopped to see Bridget on the way home. Sure enough, he was there. He stood when I came into the room, but after that, it was as if we were strangers. He kept watching me for the few minutes that I visited with Bridget. All the while, my mind was spinning, trying to decide about what to do next.

I couldn't stay long without incurring Clara's wrath, even though she may very well have thought I was "spending my evening hours" with Henson. She's been bubbling all week about how great we look as a couple when we dance.

When I turned to go, I still didn't know what to do. So I just said, "Well, Cord, aren't you going to see me home?"

He didn't exactly jump at the chance. In fact he blinked a couple of times and looked as though I had slapped him or something. But he did get up and come with me.

Oh, Lottie. He is more handsome than ever, if that's possible. Anyway, we walked about a half a block, and he hadn't said a word, so I turned to look into the window of a little store, and he had to stop.

I said, "Aren't you ever going to talk to me again?"

"I don't know that there's anything to say," he replied.

I asked, "How about, 'How are you? I missed you.'"

He propped himself against the column in the entrance of the store, pushed his hat back on his head, and said, "All right, Ellie, let's have it." If he hadn't looked so sad, I would have put my arms around him and tried to laugh the whole thing off. As it was, I started to cry, and I just said, "I'm so sorry if I hurt you, Cord. I wrote to you after Valentine's Day and told you about Henson helping me with the assembly program. I just didn't mention that I promised to go to the dance with him." Then I went to him and laid my hand on his arm. "Can you forgive me?"

"I don't know Ellie. I felt pretty much the fool for riding all that last day and half that night to get here as quickly as I could. Then when I find you, you're with another man. That I may have taken in stride. But when you walked past me without speaking and headed on out the door with him, well to say I was dumbfounded doesn't begin to tell you how I felt."

"Oh, Cord. I'm so sorry." I tried to put my arms around his waist, but he pushed me away. I wanted to be angry and tell him he wasn't being fair, but I managed to keep my temper and go on to tell him everything, including why I wore the red dress. When I got to the part about ripping my hem loose, he laughed a little.

Then when I told him how testy Henson was and how we parted company, he brightened a little more. But all he said was,"C'mon, I'd better get you home." And we went on.

When we got to the kitchen door, he rubbed his knuckles under my chin and tilted my head up. In spite of my tears, I was getting ready to close my eyes to prepare for a long and wonderful kiss. Then I realized that was not his intention. Instead he said, "By the way, you were pretty spectacular in your red dress." Then he dropped my hand and walked away.

I wanted to run after him and yell and scream for him to please, please, forgive me, but I have a feeling he will take his own sweet time to give in, if he ever does.

Oh, Lottie, I am so unhappy. I wish I had stayed East. My life would have been more like yours. I'd be caught up in my career, and that would be enough. Instead, I am here feeling so alone, doing nothing more important than waiting for a cowboy to get over his anger.

I just hope my next letter will include a little ray of hope for Cord and me getting back together. Or if that's not possible, then I hope he can at least not feel so betrayed. But I guess whatever will be, will be.

I was happy to hear that since Governor West is certain that he is not going to enter the primaries, he is concerned enough to find a position for you in State government before the end of his term. I don't know if I find it as hilarious as you do that he would support you for Oregon's next governor. It seems like a peachy idea to me.

Write soon.

All my love,

Cousin Ellie K.

Martial Law Continues

George was sitting quietly at the dinner table on Friday night. He was avidly reading from one of the three Baker *Herald* papers stacked before him. Ellie and the children had gone up to their rooms, and Clara was finishing drying the dishes.

"Well?" Clara inquired after a long while of no conversation. George peered over the top of his newspaper at her. "Well, what?" he asked.

"You know what," Clara accused. "Is there news of ending this confounded martial law anytime soon?"

"No, there isn't," George said emphatically. "And I'm of the opinion it won't end anytime soon."

"I certainly can't see why not," Clara stormed. "What good are they doing here I ask you. They are just a nuisance, keeping everyone stirred up all the time. People are staying away from our store in droves. If it weren't for the fact that you picked up the Mercantile inventory when the Morgans left, and we've sold a few piddly dollars from that business, we'd probably be packing our things and moving on as well."

"Oh now, it's not that bad," George soothed. "As far as people staying away, that's going to continue no matter if the militia stays or goes. Hell this town is down to half its former size now. If we didn't have the militia around, the saloon families would pretty much move on too, which they will do when they find out that a lot of their customers aren't here anymore.

"As for our customers, we can depend on the farm trade to keep us going in any case. Those people don't want to take time to go out to Huntington or Baker City to buy supplies, or even up to Halfway. And thirty or forty of them are a heck of a lot closer to us than they are to any other suppliers."

"If a bunch of farmers are all we'll be catering to, we'll be down to scrambled eggs, potatoes and beans before you know it," Clara grumped.

"Oh yeah, why's that?"

"Because," Clara flared. "They don't bring money. They bring eggs and butter; and in the summer, they bring garden vegetables. You can't take that stuff to the bank."

"You let me worry about the bank," George ordered. "You know, I've been thinking that I need to bring in a supply of some more hardware items. You know, nuts and bolts, tools, nails, things like that."

"Oh, that's just swell," Clara said sarcastically. "I've truly always wanted to count out rivets and sell barbed wire."

George shrugged his shoulders, "It's a living," he muttered rising from his chair. He went to the window and drew back the curtain. Light from The Painted Lady was streaming into the alleyway in front of their kitchen door.

"Must be some goings on with the mayor tonight. He's got the whole place lit up," George remarked.

"Oh really," Clara chirped. "Are you sure there's nothing in the papers? Maybe he's getting ready to re-open."

"Hardly," George retorted. "Tom Partlin won't even consent to bring their liquor supply back from Baker City."

"Who's Tom Partlin? And what has he to do with anything?"

"Tom Partlin is Harvey's brother-in-law and his silent partner in the saloon. When Lucille, wanted to buy the ranch they have so she could move away from town, Tom put up the money for her. But instead of partnering on the ranch, he took a share in the saloon business."

"Oh, well why won't he consent to bring the liquor back and get started again?"

"It just isn't that simple," George said, returning to his seat at the table. "I told you, besides the Council refusing to resign so they could legally open their doors again, Harvey and Duane Wickert brought suit against the governor and others including Colonel Lawson. They want $8000 in damages."

"So?" Clara interjected.

"So," said George, "If they take the liquor back, that interferes with the damage suit, bringing it down to $1500 according to Harvey. Besides, Tom says the governor hauled it out of here, he can just haul it back. At least that's what Harvey tells me he says. Tom lives over in Ontario. I've never met the man myself."

"The whole thing still makes me furious."

"Well, I'm sorry sweetheart, but personally, I'm rather glad for the peace and quiet. Also for the fact that Jeffrey and Cecile can be out playing with the other kids now, and we don't have to worry that Jeffrey is being invited off the street to some madame's bordello. Or the boys aren't trying to sneak liquor, or worse yet, moonshine, like Davy Wickert evidently did with that Lawson boy."

"George, you know we never have to worry a minute about Jeffrey. He just wouldn't do those kind of things."

"Really! I guess I forgot to mention when the deputy sheriff was over here Tuesday getting some smoking tobacco, he served me with a subpoena. I'm going to be testifying next week before the Grand jury about those two kids having bottles of beer in the alley behind The Painted Lady. If you recall, Jeffrey was headed right toward them when I noticed him and called him back. Boys will be boys you know."

"George," Clara practically shrieked, "Why didn't you tell me about the subpoena? Or better yet, when were you going to tell me? You know you can't testify in that business. I won't allow it."

"And just what am I supposed to do when I'm sworn to tell the truth, the whole truth, and nothing but the truth? Tell me that," George demanded.

"I don't know, but you have to do something. I've drug you back from the brink before, I'll drag you back now, as soon as I think of something."

"Thanks a lot, Clara. You just stay out of it."

"I will not," Clara yelled. "You have no right to jeopardize our business that way. We simply can't afford to lose any more customers right now."

"When you think of something," George said, rising from his chair. "Let me know."

"There's one thing I have thought of," Clara announced.

"What's that?"

"It's that you don't know and have absolutely no proof whatever that there was beer in those bottles. Those kids could have just filled them with water."

George stared at his wife in total disbelief. "You would let those mangy bastards go right back to doing business as usual for the sake of a few lousy dollars, wouldn't you?"

"Yes, I would. I just don't believe it's any of our business. There was nobody hurt, and our front door was in constant motion with people coming and going. Now I could take a nap between customers if I had a mind to."

"Hell, maybe you better plan to take a whole vacation in the near future." George walked over to take Clara by the arm. "That light at The Painted Lady, you see out there," he continued. "If I had to make a guess, I'd say that's our deposed mayor meeting with his Town Council hashing over what their lawyer had to say. He came in on the train today for a while. He was probably here getting his act and theirs together to defend them after they're indicted next week."

Clara gulped, "You think that will really happen?"

"Yes," George said forcefully. "I think that will really happen. In spite of the Baker County people, more or less, taking sides against the governor, it's the sign of the times to be in favor of prohibiting fellows like them from profiting in the liquor trade. You know as well as I do they practically rob the working men around here, thereby denying families the support they deserve. That fact will not be lost on any of the politicians, including the judge, who has to be re-elected." He paused, "Or on that one-armed district attorney for that matter."

"Well, I still don't want you getting involved," Clara sniffed. "It's dangerous in the event that those saloon men do start up again. That fire at The Golden Star was just awful last fall. I absolutely don't know what I'd do if something like that happened to us."

"Oh, so now it's because you're afraid," George growled. "You're the damnest woman I ever saw," he grumbled. Letting go of her arm, he turned to go upstairs. Clara meticulously folded her tea towel, draped it through the wall hanger, and turned out the light. Then she meekly followed her husband up the stairs.

General Delivery
Copperfield, Oregon
March 21, 1914

Dear Lottie Fern,

    Good News! It has happened! Bridget had her baby last night. She's a darling little girl. They named her Deborah Kathleen. I can't tell you how excited I am.
    You see, that's the other good news. When Bridget's water broke, Cord came racing over to get me. Fortunately the store was still open, so Clara doesn't know a thing about it. She may not know yet until I go to tell her after I mail this letter.
    When Cord came, I just grabbed my coat and told Sissy to tell her mother I went to see Bridget. I've stayed at their house twice overnight lately when Marty had to be gone on business. He didn't want her to stay alone, you know.
    So anyway, Cord was very excited. You should have seen him. He grabbed my hand, and we practically ran all the way there. Dr. Hunsaker was there. He had already checked Bridget and was preparing to leave. He told us it would be a while yet. He said he was glad I was there and that he would be teaching me how to help him when he returned. He said, ordinarily, he'd have Alice help. But she has a cold right now.
    I'm usually not overjoyed if someone else is sick, but this time, I truly was. I just hope Alice gets well right away.
    Anyway, Bridget was so brave through it all. I became rather anxious when Dr. Hunsaker didn't come back right away after supper. It seemed to me like something might happen at any moment, and Marty was scared to death.
    Dr. Hunsaker laughed at all of us when he returned. He said at the rate we were going, not only would Marty wear through the soles of his shoes, Cord probably would too. He checked on Bridget, then ordered the three of us to sit down at the table to listen while he explained what would be happening.
    "In about an hour, or an hour and a half," he said, "Cord can fill the big kettle there with water and get it to a boil. And you, Ellie will come to the bedroom with me to help keep the sheets straightened and changed when necessary. I'd say that in about three hours, we'll have a new little Kellner for your laps. In the meantime," he added, "we may as well play cards."
    I was surprised that Marty consented to sit still and play cards. But I suppose in a man's mind, if that's what the doctor ordered, that's what should occur. For my part, I went to sit with Bridget. It seemed to me that she was getting awfully tired in just the time I had been there. Another two or three hours seemed out of the question.

For a while, she just wanted to get up and walk. Marty had been insisting she stay in bed. She said the bed just made her back hurt worse, so I asked the doctor if it was all right. He said, "sure, anything the lady wants, the lady should have."

So Bridget and I paced the floor through the house, through the ice cream parlor, and back again. After a while, when the pain got worse, the doctor handed me his watch and told me to keep track of the time between contractions.

The next thing we knew it was 10:30, and Cord was building up the fire. Dr. Hunsaker came to give Bridget a powder for her pain. He said it wouldn't put her to sleep, but she'd be able to relax better between contractions. He did have her lie down. Marty sat holding her hand and sort of crooning to her. He told her that he was so sorry and that he'd take her pain away if he could. His eyes were so big.

It wasn't very long until Bridget was in almost constant pain. Dr. Hunsaker told her how to breathe, and that seemed to help. The next thing I knew, the doctor was yelling for Cord to bring his tray of instruments after he sterilized them. He told me to get Marty out of the room and to come right back. So I did.

Lottie, I watched the baby's head crown and everything. Then I dropped one of the doctor's instruments as he was handing it to me. He had just said, "Here's where we play catch," and he told Bridget to push. Well, he had already told me the instruments had to stay perfectly clean, so while I ran to the kitchen to get a new tray of hot water, the baby came.

That's when my work really started. I held the baby while the doctor tied her umbilical cord. Then he took care of Bridget while I dried the baby with the towels.

Then it was clean-up time. It wasn't too bad. Bridget has a motorized washing machine, so she told me to just dump the whole batch of sheets and towels in the washer, pour cold water over them, and let them set until this morning.

Marty came in just as soon as the doctor would let him. By that time, I had Deborah diapered and wrapped in a receiving blanket and had laid her across Bridget's chest and tummy.

Dr. Hunsaker told Marty to go ahead and hold the baby. He wouldn't do it. I guess he thought she might break. He just took Bridget's hand and was stroking her arm and crying. Pretty soon I looked toward the door, and there was Cord watching with a dopey look on his face.

After I got everything cleaned up and Bridget was resting, Marty turned out the brightest light. He finally picked Deborah up. He wrapped her in more blankets, but he didn't hold her for long. He went ahead and put her in the cradle and laid her the way the doctor said.

It was just past midnight when Doctor Hunsaker said he'd check his new patient in the morning, even though everything was fine, and he didn't anticipate any trouble.

Cord and Marty went to the kitchen to have another cup of coffee, and I began worrying about whether to stay. I knew I could borrow a nightgown from Bridget's supply, and I wanted to stay. But I couldn't very well get undressed and go to bed in the living room while the men were sitting there.

Cord noticed my predicament or something because like a bolt out of the blue in the middle of their conversation, he said, "How about a short walk, Ellie? I'm pretty wound up myself."

So we went out on a cold Friday night in March to wander to the schoolhouse and back. Oh yes, we sat down there on those steps, and he told me he forgave me. I cried, and we held each other for the longest time. I wanted him to tell me more about his Lapwai visit, but I was crying so hard, I was practically sobbing.

He told me to be quiet. So I laid my head on his shoulder and almost went to sleep. When he told me we had the rest of our lives to catch up, and we'd start the first thing this morning, I began to hope he has resumed his promises to me.

I'm waiting anxiously right now for him to show up. I've washed the baby and dressed her. She's just like a little doll. I've helped Bridget change and get comfortable, cooked Marty's and my breakfast, run the washing, and hung it out to dry. Bridget didn't want to eat, but she drank two cups of hot tea and ate some toast. I've also washed the dishes and will return shortly to The General Store.

Ho, Ho, here comes the lazy bones now. So I'm also anticipating spending most of the day with Cord after I let Clara and George know that Deborah Kellner has arrived. I'm going to tell them too that I'll be gone today and maybe tonight.

Marty says he'll get Esther Carpenter to come on Monday and every day until the end of the week as necessary. He thinks he'll be able to handle the ice cream trade and take care of Bridget and the baby most of the time until Bridget is able to be up and about. But he doesn't want to wash diapers or give the baby a bath or dress her.

Bridget asked him about changing diapers. He says he can do that if he has to. Men!

I hope you are getting along fine. Please write soon, and tell all. Your out-of-town excursions just seem to keep happening. I'm glad none of them have been quite like Copperfield.

Write soon.

My most sincere love,

Cousin Ellie K.

PART III

April, 1914

Sunday	Monday	Tuesday	Wednesday	Thursday	Friday	Saturday
			1	2	3	4
5	6	7	8	9	10	11
12	13	14	15	16	17	18
19	20	21	22	23	24	25
26	27	28	29	30		

"... WHITHER THOU GOEST, I WILL GO
WHERE THOU LODGEST, I WILL LODGE
THY PEOPLE SHALL BE MY PEOPLE,
AND THY GOD MY GOD."

—BOOK OF RUTH 1:16

To Jail or Not to Jail

Floyd Nelson hurried along the boardwalk to The Painted Lady. A brisk April breeze threatened to carry his hat aloft into the low hanging cloud cover. Hence he held one hand over his hat, while trying to control his brief case as it hammered against his leg with every step he took. To make matters worse, his jacket button had fallen under the railroad car just now when he disembarked. His jacket was flapping in the wind like a sheet on a clothesline. He was rather glad that no one was in sight to watch his pitiful approach.

When he entered the saloon door, he was out of breath. His glasses had fallen forward on his nose so that he was unable to identify the five men sitting around the table in the middle of the room. He was ready to apologize for their being inconvenienced by his tardiness. Of course, he could hardly be blamed for a late train arrival. He wasn't prepared, though, for the barrage of questions being hurled at him without so much as a "How do you do?"

"What the hell happened, Floyd?" demanded Harvey Sullivan. "When you were here a couple of weeks ago, you said everything was under control. Now here you are with your hat in your hand telling us we have to come up with a satchel full of money or plan on going to jail?" The others chimed in with various degrees of complaint.

"I can't say that I can tell you what happened, Harvey. I came here two weeks ago, having just spent several hours with the district attorney assessing our position. You fellows know about the grand jury hearings. You probably know they weren't especially happy to be called into session over this thing."

"You know, too, that C. R. sure as hell put on a show. That first day, like the newspaper reported, he took off his coat and vest, rolled up his sleeves and tore around like a bulldog. He managed to take only a little testimony before he shut off that string of witnesses lined up against you fellows. Then by insisting on going to another case in the afternoon, it worked out that most of them went home. Like the paper said, his hair was even rumpled." None of the men so much as smiled at the image being painted of the District Attorney, even if it was entirely out of character for the man they knew to be calm as a summer day and smooth as silk at Court.

"Then, too," Nelson went on, "he tried his damnest to bring Colonel Lawson back over here. He said he had several ways to get the acts of the militia on record if he could just get Lawson up there on the stand. But when West insisted on sending Snodgrass with those pictures of nudes and refused to let Lawson be subpoenaed, we were cut off completely from that defense. Even then, C. R. thought we had it made when West launched his rather vicious attack on me.

"Deschinger had shown me the opinions he was going to release to the press that afternoon on the part of the grand jury, in which they would be bringing the governor up on charges."

"Yeah, I know," Wickert interrupted. "I was just reading to the boys here about the grand jury and what they were supposed to say. I was just getting to the line that says the report will contain '. . . a severe arraignment of Governor West.' It goes on to say what a helluva good job you Baker County fellows have been doing in cleaning up vice, especially in Copperfield. Maybe you should read the whole story, and then tell us what happened." With that, Wickert shoved his copy of *The Democrat Herald* across the table to Nelson, where he had seated himself.

"I'm just as mystified as you fellows are," Nelson whined. "All I can tell you is that before that account even went to press, the grand jury had already returned their sealed indictments against you fellows."

"So what happens now?" Sullivan wanted to know.

"That's what I came to discuss with you today. The judge has issued bench warrants for all of you for your arrest," Nelson replied.

"Jesus Christ," Charlie Thatcher swore, "You mean we're going to have to do jail time?"

"No, no, that's what I need to talk to you about. If you fellows will get your bail together, you can come on out to Baker City, be arrested, post bail, and probably return home all the same day."

"How much are we going to need?" Alan Greene inquired.

"I can't say for sure, but probably in the neighborhood of a couple hundred dollars each."

Wickert winked at Sullivan, "That $8,000 is sure going to come in handy, wouldn't you say, Harve?"

"I'd say, since we seem to be losing on all the other fronts, we'd better win on that one."

"Oh, you will, you will," Nelson chirped. "That one's a sure thing."

"I sure hope so," Sullivan said darkly. "So let me get this straight. You want us to come to Baker City, be arrested, pay our bail, then sit here another month or two until the case goes to Court. Is that the situation?"

"You don't necessarily have to sit and wait," Nelson offered. "Once the trial date is set, you can do whatever you want until you have to appear in court."

"Jeez," Charlie spouted. "Isn't there any justice in this thing somewhere? Damned governor comes in to make trouble, and we just might as well all roll over and play dead."

The train whistle sounded in the distance. Nelson began collecting his things saying, "I'm awfully sorry fellows. I've got to make that return train. But be assured this battle isn't over yet. We've got the damage suit in the works. The appeal on the injunction is winding its way through to the State Supreme Court. Then if we can manage to topple one of those witnesses swearing you sold drinks to kids, we'll be able to pull through this thing too."

"Damned kids," Greene swore. "People get all excited if they buy any liquor. But if they sneak it from the pantry and drink it, then it's just a childish prank, no harm done."

"Yes, them being kids and all," added Charlie, "it'll likely be touchy, especially when that bastard, Hoffstetter, joins in the complaint."

"He will?" Harvey uttered in shocked surprise.

"That's one of the witnesses all right," Nelson agreed. "Why, who's he?"

"The storekeeper, and now he's the Mercantile owner, as well," Wickert replied.

"Hmm! That is bad. As long as it was just some women, we probably could have discredited them as being hysterical," Nelson said haltingly. "Well fellows, I have to go," and he made a very hasty departure.

When the door clicked behind him, Frank Lawrence leaned back in his chair shaking his head. "You think we have the right man representing us in all this, Harve?"

Sullivan shrugged his shoulders. "I don't know how we could have done any better, his connections with the D. A. and all. That's why you picked him the first place, wasn't it, Duane?"

"Sure was," Wickert agreed. "Besides he's a helluva speech maker. Even the govenor's advocate, that Collier fellow, said he made 'a very cogent and convincing argument,' I believe it was."

"And we still lost," Lawrence said bitterly. "Martial law is the order of the day. Then we lost a second time trying to get that injunction enforced."

"That was just an exercise for the benefit of the Court so we could take the fight to the Supreme Court," said Sullivan. "There's a good chance we'll get satisfaction from them."

"I hope so," Lawrence muttered drearily.

"I don't know," Charlie Thatcher threw in. "It almost seems to me like there's more here than meets the eye."

"What do you mean?" asked Greene.

"Think about it," Charlie returned. "Our lawyer does a fantastic job presenting our case, and it looks like, by all newspaper accounts, that we will win, hands down. But we don't."

"Then the district attorney tells us the evidence on gambling and prostitution will never hold up in court. In fact it will never surface as long as we go after the governor instead of letting him come after us. So we do that. The next thing you know, the grand jury is called into special session, and the district attorney assures us the only particular that's going into the record is the sale of liquor to minors. He says there's nothing to worry about because every kid in the land will drink if given a chance. And it's up to their parents to keep them away from saloons. At least that's what Nelson reported to us on what the D. A. said.

"On top of that, they even get it in the press that the governor is completely out of line, that they were on top of things here in Copperfield, all the time, that every one of them is doing and has been doing one helluva fine job upholding the law. No neglect on their part, they say. Yet here we are, arrested and ready to pay our bail. Makes a man wonder who the hell is in charge, doesn't it?" he finished.

"I'll say," Greene acknowledged. "There's some pretty heavy pressure being applied somewhere."

"What gets me," Wickert added, "is what the hell is wrong with our system of government when one man can flat walk in, shut down licensed businesses, confiscate and destroy property, and arrest the proprietors on some trumped up charges made by old women and preachers. They're bellyaching about safety and law and order when not a one of them has ever been on the receiving end of so much as a flying bottle. Furthermore he does it all completely outside the action of the courts."

"You got it, Duane," Sullivan said. "He can't. We'll come out all right in this thing in the long run. You just wait and see."

"I don't know," Alan Greene observed. "Somehow I get the feeling that our big talking lawyer is just along for the ride and that he isn't going to do a damned thing for us. Look at how he took the governor's slam about being a lawyer for pimps, gamblers, and whores. Why he didn't so much as write a letter in protest."

Sullivan answered. "You don't know that. He could have. Not everything gets in the newspaper, you know. Somehow I think Floyd has an ace up his sleeve. He'll be playing it before too long."

"Let's hope so," Wickert grumbled. "I'm getting sick and tired of setting around here doing nothing."

"You're right about that," Lawrence agreed. "We've got to do something. I've thought about it quite a lot. If that son-of-a-bitch of a governor had just come over here and poked his head in the door, we could have sat down, talked it over, maybe compromised on a few things, then celebrated a little before he went back to Salem. That way we could have gone on about our business. But no, he hides behind a woman's skirts and sneaks an army in on us."

"I'll just bet you would have sat down to talk things over with him," Sullivan laughed.

"Well maybe not then, but I would now," Lawrence concluded.

"Like I said boys, everything will be all right in the end. Just you wait and see," Harvey concluded.

General Delivery
Copperfield, Oregon
April 14, 1914

Dear Lottie Fern,

This letter will be a little later in the week than usual. I decided to hold over writing until after Easter, and I'm glad I did. It was such a wonderful day.

The Methodist minister came down from Huntington on Saturday afternoon by train. He held a sunrise service along the River bank this morning, then rode on horseback to his evening service in Robinette. He is a very dynamic man and quite a leader against gambling and prostitution, they say.

His message today, though, was about our risen Lord. He met with all who wanted to attend before sunrise to re-enact the scene on the Road to Golgotha. He asked for volunteers to tote the cross up the hill here behind Marty's. None came forward willingly, but Marty started chanting for Cord to do it. I didn't think he would, but he gave in. When I was praising him later about being so gracious, he looked at Marty and said he just didn't want some other fellow to hurt himself while making the effort. We had a good laugh about that because even Marty said he was 100% right on that score.

The cross the minister constructed was a full eight feet long with a six-foot cross bar. It did make me think about how wonderfully strong Jesus must have been. He had to carry the burden of the cross a far greater distance than Cord did. On top of that He had been so badly beaten and abused.

The service at sunrise with all the ladies and the children in attendance was beautiful. I'm still humming "Shall We Gather at the River." Henson sang "The Old Rugged Cross" and "In the Garden," a cappella. Both are new gospel songs and very inspirational if you haven't heard them yet. That was really special. When we all sang, I vow the hills rang with the echoes. Just a little bit of heaven, I guess. The minister's message was one of hope. I believe that's quite appropriate for Copperfield at the present time.

At any rate, the minister surely made folks of the saloon crowd squirm in his sermon. He made a point of informing them how criminal they were acting when they plied their trade on the Lord's Day.

Even Clara remarked later at breakfast that he had certainly made an impression on her. When the construction workers were so numerous here, they were forever knocking at the back door of the store on Sunday wanting some kind of product—usually soap to wash their clothes, she said. She added that she'd often considered just unlocking the door and doing business as usual, but she was thankful that she never did. She says that's one less sin she has to worry about. George just laughed at her.

Anyway, after breakfast, I met Cord again, and we went walking. It was such a beautiful day. The sun shone; birds were chirping. The mountainsides are green now, though not for long, they say. We saw buttercups, and the bitterroot brush is coloring. Little streams of water were pouring down the sides of the road banks. Sometimes, we could even hear the tinkling of tiny water falls. Cord says they're playing the song of the season. This time we walked through the tunnel and went down to Homestead and back. We sang and laughed and had a very good time.

I made up my mind that since it was a special day, I wouldn't talk about the future to Cord. I didn't want to risk ruining our renewed relationship. So we never touched on the topic at all until we were almost back to Copperfield. We had stopped to rest. While we sat on an old log, he asked me what I was planning for the summer. I asked him what brought that on, and he said, "Well school will be out in early May, won't it?

I said, "Yes, it will be out in three more weeks, and I will have nearly four glorious months to entertain myself in any way I want."

"So what are you going to do?" he persisted.

"What are you going to do?" I asked, being coy.

He laughed and said that depended on what I was going to do. His tone was just a little fresh, I thought, so I told him I was planning to travel.

"All summer?" He sounded positively worried.

"Maybe not all summer," I answered. "Actually I should probably go to Normal School for the summer session. There's a school with a rather good reputation at Monmouth. That way I can see my cousin, attend some theater, go to church every Sunday, things like that."

We were standing by then. So he put his arms around me and said. "Ellie, you don't need any teacher training. You're the best there is, now."

I wriggled free and started walking. "What would you know about my teaching ability, Mr. Cord Williams?" I hedged.

"Maybe nothing much," he admitted. "But I'm willing to take the word of others. That's what they all say."

"They do, huh?" I was so happy. I threw my arms around his neck and kissed him. Then he kissed me back and knocked my bonnet loose so that it fell off my head.

I probably never mentioned it, but I had Rebecca make two bonnets to match the cotton gowns she sewed last fall. They're really quite attractive, and I don't have to pin my hair so securely. I just love wearing them.

Anyway, Cord untied my bonnet and let it fall on the ground. We couldn't seem to disengage ourselves and stop kissing for a time. I could have stayed there forever. Nevertheless, I decided we should probably get back to Copperfield to find a chaperone. We went to Bridget and Marty's. Cord even held the baby and cooed at her. He amazes me more every day. Of course, it didn't help that Deborah started crying right away. She was hungry. To end the day, we had a big dinner with Marty and Bridget.

Clara was not at all happy when I finally went home. It was after dark, and she was quite sure I had been out and about without being properly chaperoned. But she doesn't know for sure. It is very easy to walk around the perimeter of Copperfield without being seen. Some of the married men and all of the recently departed ladies have been doing it for years. Besides, women like Clara don't really want to know what they might see out there, so they are careful not to look. One afternoon, last year, a group of "the girls" decided to walk to the post office in the nude to get their mail. Despite the vivid and probably very successful advertising, the mayor had to put his foot down on that activity. It just goes to show how really uncivilized this place is.

I was not at all surprised when our out-of-favor Town Council along with other saloon owners were indicted after the Grand Jury hearing. I was somewhat unhappy, in that regard, when I read the newspaper account that they are going to be charged with nothing more than selling liquor to minors. Of course, that's the only real issue of importance for me. That was my personal reason for getting involved in the first place.

As for the gambling, since all the equipment has been burned, I suspect the practice will not be reinstated any time soon. I heard that a third large group of ladies of the night left by wagon before dawn one morning last week. That is supposed to be the last of them. Supposedly, they went back to Nevada.

Looking this letter over, I do believe I've chattered long enough. It is getting quite late, and tomorrow is another school day. I hope this finds you well and happy.

Please write soon.

My love and best wishes,

Cousin Ellie K.

P. S. I am truly considering doing the eight-week summer course at Monmouth. In that event, I'll be looking forward to spending time with you. Please take a close look at your busy schedule and let me know when you will have some time. I have a letter from the college that gives me a choice of two sessions. One begins during the last week of May and goes until the middle of July. The other begins the third week in July and lasts until Labor Day.

Getting ready to Come Out

"My goodness, Miss Delaney, you're off to an early start this morning," remarked Clara as Ellie came from her bedroom dressed for departure. "You must have something special on the back burner today."

"Not exactly today," Ellie hedged. How much should she share with Clara? Anything she might say to her landlady would undoubtedly be common knowledge in the town within the hour. "It's just that the children are so excited to get prepared for their final assembly a week from Friday, I can hardly stay ahead of them."

"Yes, well children do get quite excited about summer vacation, I suspect it is rather difficult to hold them in line."

"Oh no," Ellie exclaimed. "There's no question about holding them in line. It's more a question of getting them into the right line. You see, we began this challenge to 'show your best side' about two weeks ago, and now, we're inching toward the finish line—with spelling bees, calculations, recitations, essays, art work, debates, the 'whole ball of wax.' I'm getting as excited about it all as they are."

"You mean the children are going to do presentations at the picnic?" Clara asked in surprise?

"No, no. We're going to have a 'coming out party' on Friday night when the students will come out showing their best sides."

Clara extended a hand to place it on Ellie's shoulder, then reached to adjust the hat Ellie had chosen to place rakishly off center instead of straight on top of her head. "There," she declared. "I'm sorry, Ellie dear. Did I hear you say Friday? Well, I wish you the best. I thought we were grandly surprised at the children's improved behavior and skills at the Christmas assembly. But I suspect with an additional four months in your care, we saw only a glimmering of what your coming-out party will be."

Ellie turned away in frustration over the hat incident. "You're so right, dear lady. You're so right," she said softly between clenched teeth. Pulling her gloves on, she reached for the door, saying, "I'll probably be late this afternoon, so don't worry please."

"It's okay. I'll send Sissy for you about a half an hour before dinner. Bye, now," Clara said as she watched Ellie descend the stairs from her room.

Ellie walked at a brisk clip to school. She had so much to do. Put the calculation exercises on the board for practice. Those could stay there pretty much unchanged for the next few days. Get the progressive lists for the spelling competitions jotted down, prepare the history bee, start thinking seriously about the awards she wanted to present. Of course, she couldn't fill in the names for the spelling or arithmetic competitions. But she could begin to observe little details in the recitations, the "uhs," the sighs, and their voice quality in their speech delivery.

The children had agreed to let school board members judge their handwriting samples. Ellie would also relinquish judging their crafts and their building projects to board members and their wives. After all, she still had the power of the grade, but she did hope the judges could be objective and tuck their prejudices into their hats and bonnets for the evening. She hadn't made the final choices yet on who would judge what, but she intended to avoid having anyone deal with his or her own children's work. Since each student was limited to only one exhibit other than the class competitions, it would be possible.

"There's so much to get ready," Ellie murmured to herself as she removed her hat and gloves in the school foyer. She was glad she didn't have to contend with lighting the stove. The weather was really getting warm these days. Just lift a few windows, draw the window blinds down as far as possible without shutting out the light entirely, and place the handwriting practice pages on each desk.

It was not yet 7:30 when Ellie could hear children's voices laughing and squealing, and Billy came stomping up on the porch steps. She had told him on more than one occasion, "Your horse is not allowed in the building, Billy. Please tether him in the barn." Billy had just laughed. Being excited invariably found him stomping more loudly than ever.

"Billy," she greeted him. "I'm so glad you're here. You can help me take down the maps on that wall and start putting up the art projects this morning."

"Aren't you going to have the fifth grade compete in world geography contests the way they've been practicing?"

"You know, Billy, I've been thinking about that. I think instead of using the stick and pointer with the maps, we'll just let them spin the two globes. Jake and Laura can compete against Jerold and Emma the first round. Just a speed race to correctly place a finger on the globe locating world capitals and other places of interest. I think the four of them could handle that. Then the winning pair can finish it off with a contest against each other. What do you think?

Billy busily rolled up the paper wall maps. "Probably work just fine," he agreed. "Sure save wear and tear on these old maps. I bet some of these maps are nearly as old as I am."

"So?" questioned Ellie. "Countries don't change their shape, form, or even their names very often. And as far as I know, they've never relocated on a different continent."

"I guess not," Billy replied. "So am I supposed to use thumb tacks to put up these water color paintings, or what?"

"Yes, I think so. I rather hate to puncture Wade's painting of Ballard Landing. It couldn't be more perfect if it were done by Albert Fitch Bellows."

Billy glanced over his shoulder to a small water painting hanging between the chalkboard and the wall at the front of the room. "It isn't really that good, is it Miss Delaney?"

"Well, yes I think it is. I think that Wade may just become famous some day. By the way, how are you doing finding information for your Prohibition debate with him?"

"I can't really tell yet. I could sure use some help though to counter the idea of the individual's right to drink in the pursuit of happiness as well as the saloon keeper's right to do business without governmental interference."

"Yes, I know," said Ellie. "My cousin, Lottie Fern, plans to put the governor's point of view on those issues in the mail. That information will be in the mail tomorrow I believe. Have you and Helen and York been thinking of good arguments for the importance of the historical events' defenses? You never know which of the six topics you will be drawing from the hat that night."

"Yes, I know," Billy replied. "I sure hope I draw the invention of the Gutenberg press."

"Oh, why is that?"

"Because," Billy answered, "That argument is so easy. All I have to say is," Billy reached down for a deeper tone of voice, "Look around you people. Yes, look around you very carefully. The fact is, without the benefits of the Gutenberg Press, none of you would be sitting in this place at this time, being free to think what you are thinking. No, without the Gutenberg Press, you'd all be somewhere in Europe—that is, if your ancestors had survived the bubonic plagues, the London Fire, and other great catastrophes of flood and famine. You'd be hoeing and digging the gardens of some fancy Lord, or maybe you'd be spit-polishing his shoes."

"That's good, Billy. That's really good. If I thought I'd have time to read and grade them before summer vacation, I'd have all of you write out your thoughts on each topic. But I'd never get them done," Ellie sighed. "Maybe next year."

Billy finished placing the artwork on display. "What now, Miss Delaney?"

"Hmm, I don't know about this morning, but I intended to ask you and Helen to demonstrate unfolding and raising the flag for the 6th graders when school takes up. Then Jimmy Lawson and York can demonstrate the process of retiring the flag this afternoon. Tomorrow, we'll let Wade Swinyer and the other 7th graders take over your good office of leading the flag salute. They can practice seating dignitaries and escorting you four to your place of honor for the awards program."

"Okay. Is Mr. Baldwin going to perform that night?"

"I don't think so," Ellie replied. "I'm determined to stick with just student talent. I think Cecile will be ready with her piano recital, and Jeffrey can do "Taps" for the flag retiring ceremony. That reminds me, I need to give music awards too." Ellie stepped back from the almost completely covered chalkboard saying, "Why don't you take a break Billy? I need to go through the penmanship exercises again and choose the final practice for the 4th, 5th, and 6th grades for exhibition. I don't know where I'm going to find room for them—maybe in the windowsills. I know the foyer will be full, especially when we load up Martha's spinning wheel and bring it over for her demonstration."

Ellie clapped her hands together, rubbing them lightly to remove the chalk dust. "I guess I'm about ready for today," she declared.

As Billy turned away to take up his self-imposed duties on the playground where he would referee the contests and games of the bigger boys, Ellie knew he would keep a watchful eye out for the younger children to see that none were being bullied. He generally accomplished this task from his observation post on the school porch. Mostly, he had only to say, "Hey!" to the offenders, and peace and harmony were quickly restored. Ellie would never forget the day though that he got his nose bloodied when he broke up a fight between the Riley twins from down-river.

So now in the few moments before bell-time, she drifted into reverie, imagining the 8th grade graduation ceremony. She would present Helen with the outstanding young miss award, rattling off her attributes as one with a ready smile, patience beyond the call, and a willing hand in teaching the primary students. Her inspirational qualities in engaging youngsters in singing and playing group games on the playground, and her readiness to take on responsibility beyond her 13 years would be additional praise. While Ellie would add that she would be a fine teacher in her day, she knew in her heart of hearts that Helen was much more likely to choose the path to motherhood. Maybe it was just as well. Her spelling skills as well as her ability to do her arithmetic were no match for York or Jimmy, to say nothing of Billy, the other three 8th graders.

Then she'd present York with the outstanding athlete award. She had been amazed at his abilities the first thing last fall as she watched him pitch or hit a ball, but for the last three months, hardly a day went by that he didn't spend his free time sprinting. For York's benefit, Ellie involved the entire school in a distance measuring exercise one day last month from the post office to the school. The first grade pushed the wheels. The second grade counted the revolutions. The third grade used chalk dust and a string to draw a straight line on which to push the wheel. The fourth grade was responsible for tallying every tenth revolution. The 5th grade carefully measured the two wheels to determine the circumference and the diameter. The sixth grade calculated the length of the distance covered by each revolution. The 7th grade multiplied the revolutions of the large wheel, and the 8th grade, that of the small wheel, to verify results. It turned out to be just 120 revolutions or 220 yards on the 21" wheel, and only fifty-two and a half revolutions on the wheel that was four feet in diameter. Through using several algebraic formulae, the 8th grade discovered that a forty-two inch wheel would require 60 revolutions.

York could cover that distance in just 45 seconds in test after test. This gave him a speed of 6 minutes to the mile. But he admitted he's never run a whole mile in less than 8 minutes, and that was on flat ground. It took him a good ten minutes and sometimes more, he said, to cover the mile from his house to the school.

As for Jimmy Lawson, Ellie still had concerns about him, although he was beyond a doubt, entitled to the Most Improved Student award. This was not only in the 8th grade, but also in the whole school. He had entered last fall with an attitude. He was often late. Or he was so tired that he spent his time with his head cradled in his arms on his desk unless Ellie called on him to recite or solve a problem on the chalkboard. He actually went to sleep several times that first week. Then he missed school for three days after the Friday incident that had been primarily responsible for the shutdown of all the saloons in Copperfield.

Nevertheless, after his father returned from the wheat harvest, and Ellie had a heart-to-heart talk with Mr. Lawson, Jimmy began coming around. Now he was achieving at least at the 6th grade level in all subjects, and 7th in some. According to testing done by the County School Superintendent a few weeks ago, his reading test showed his comprehension at the 10th grade level. That was quite a jump from the fall testing, in which he barely achieved a 4th grade reading level. It was the kind of result she was keeping a closely guarded secret until the big day. Of course that kind of gain had been achieved by most of the children who were nine years of age or older.

"Then there is Billy," Ellie thought fondly to herself. "Billy is the most self-motivated, intellectually curious individual she could ever hope to meet. Although he could be quite sociable and seemingly commonplace in his conversations, his sharp senses were cataloging every fact and every event he encountered. He listened with an intensity she'd never before observed, whether it was to music, a birdcall, or just conversation. He remembered as if he recorded every sound, and he read voraciously.

Ellie questioned herself, "How many sixteen year olds could you find who could recite orally or in writing the history of the Kings of England from the Tudors to the Windsors, naming their major conflicts, reciting where and when they fought, and the outcomes of each conflict. He knew them all. He could talk of American history as if he had lived it; and Greek history was of endless fascination to him. His one true champion was Socrates.

And when it came to the Bible, Billy had announced just the other day, "Such wisdom will never be clearly understood by mere mortals." Ellie had no doubt that Billy Mitchell deserved the "Best Student Award."

General Delivery
Copperfield, Oregon
May 1, 1914

Dear Lottie Fern,

Just a quick note in the midst of all the chaos. Tonight is the Coming Out Assembly, and then there's the end-of-school-year picnic on Sunday. I intend to use Saturday finishing up here at school. I've already tidied and packed my books and winter clothes away at the Hoffstetter's.

I have my ticket to begin my vacation and will leave on the train on Tuesday, the 5th. As you suggested, I'll be staying over in Portland on Wednesday night and I plan to go shopping on Thursday. I'm going to believe you that I'll be perfectly all right if I take a cab from the train depot to the hotel. My steamer trunk will go on ahead of me to Salem since I don't care to claim it in Portland.

I'm so glad the hotel in Portland is located in the midst of the big department stores and small dress shops. I wouldn't be at all hesitant about wandering around Philadelphia, but in a completely unfamiliar city, I'd rather not get too far away from base. I'm sure all will go well in Portland though. After all, I'm from Copperfield. That must count for something.

Cord is going to help by seeing me off Tuesday afternoon if he can. I don't know if he's very happy about my going. I can only hope that absence will make the heart grow fonder. So far he has still made no move to keep his January promise to "take care of me."

I have to go now. I'm really quite excited to get started on my summer sojourn. I will be so happy to see you on Thursday. I just can't believe this is really happening.

Love and best wishes,

Cousin Ellie K.

P. S. I hope you don't miss my usual line too much. You know, write soon.

The Best of the Best

The Friday night "coming out" party and the eighth grade graduation was a resounding success. Of course it had its moments of levity, especially when Carrie Alderson had a front tooth fall out as she recited, "The Gingham Dog and the Calico Cat."

Ellie hadn't been surprised either by the giggles among the children and the outright laughter of several parents when Billy deepened his voice in the presentation of his defense of the world's greatest invention. He made it to the very last sentence, then practically squeaked as he finished, "So it is my conclusion that the most important invention ever to influence the history of the world is the Gutenberg Press."

All day Saturday, parents and local citizenry paused as they shopped at the now renamed General Mercantile Store. If Ellie was not in sight, they lauded her anyway and asked that their praise be delivered to her.

Today was a landmark in Ellie's personal history. She had completed her first year of teaching. When she rose at her usual early hour this Sunday Morning, she smiled at her reflection in the mirror. Then she dressed, and hurried away to Kellner's to prepare her specialty, a double-layer chocolate-mayonnaise cake.

She felt a little guilty about the noise she made in Bridget's kitchen. But Marty was banging around anyway, and she hadn't been entirely responsible for waking Baby Deborah. She was only too glad to entertain the baby while her cake baked and cooled so that Bridget could rest for a time.

Although the school population had dropped by thirteen students in the last few months since the declaration of martial law, the crowd at the picnic was every bit as large as any other she'd seen in Copperfield. George and the mayor had to haul in extra sawhorses and boards to erect more temporary table space to hold all the food.

After their meal, the men played a game of baseball. The River Rats (everyone who lived along the River) beat the Rollicking Ranchers by three points when York hit a home run at the bottom of the 9th inning. In the process, he pushed three runners, who were on base, in ahead of him. They all tumbled into a heap at home plate.

As the community began dispersing about four o'clock, Chairman Willoughby announced that the schoolboard members would hold a brief meeting inside the school as soon as all had picked up their belongings. He said they merely needed to clear up a few points on a vote they had taken at their last meeting. Then he added that they would also need Ellie's presence.

Ellie was just finishing wrapping Kurt Riley's ankle with sheet bandages to protect it from further aggravation until he could get home to soak it. He had turned it badly when he slid into home base a scant second ahead of York in the final victorious play.

When she heard her name, Ellie's heart skipped a beat as she assumed she would be offered a contract for the next school year. She began immediately composing her speech of acceptance and gratitude along with a list of goals she would set for herself and the students for the coming year. In her mind, she exulted, "Oh, how I love teaching!"

Cord approached her to ask if she wanted him to hang around to walk her home. She cheerily dismissed him saying she'd meet him for ice cream at The Golden Star to celebrate. She was sure it would take no time at all. Then she proceeded into the schoolhouse.

For some reason, Ellie was stricken with a sense of foreboding as she stepped into the foyer. She assumed it was the barren surroundings now that every scrap of student work had been expunged or removed. She felt a little better as she entered the main room where the afternoon sun was streaming through open windows; but she was puzzled by the quiet that reigned among the five men now standing in a semi-circle near the organ. Three were looking down at their shoes as if readying themselves for bad news. Only Abe Willoughby and Henson Baldwin were looking at her. She didn't know whether to take a seat or remain standing. She finally decided to simply stand a little to the right of the group of men.

"Well, we might as well get this over with. Miss Delaney," Abe began. "Overall I suppose you are to be congratulated for completing your first year of teaching. Not all instructors accomplish this feat, especially in our community. I suppose that in itself marks you as a good teacher. We, the members of the school board concur on that fact, but," here he drew a deep breath, "you will agree that you have not observed all the board's rules as presented to you at the opening of school."

Ellie braced herself for the scolding Abe would be delivering. What the exact content could be, she couldn't imagine. So even though she was somewhat prepared, she was shocked at her own outcry when Willoughby continued, "As a consequence," he said in what Ellie would always remember as a thunderous voice, "we have determined not to renew your contract for the coming year."

"What?" she shrieked. Overcome with anguish, she sank down in the nearest student desk, dropping her head into her hands. Her body began shaking, but she held her sobs until she heard the last of the men's feet shuffle out of the room. Or so she thought. As she continued to quiver, then began to sob aloud, she sensed a body lowering beside her and felt an arm enclose her shoulders. As she raised her head to peer through tears, she found Henson Baldwin squatting at her side.

Producing a handkerchief, he began dabbing at her tears. Ellie wanted to claw him, to scream, to demand information on how or what she had done to deserve this and to know who was behind this despicable action. But her voice wouldn't cooperate. She was finally able to squeak out a single word, "Why?"

Henson was too busy comforting her to give an immediate reply. "There, there," he soothed. "Everything will be fine."

If he had been Cord, Ellie would have sought his strong arms while she continued crying. But her grief was being taken over by anger with none other than Henson himself.

"What did he mean?" she asked wildly. "What rules did I fail to observe?" With this she leapt to her feet on the other side of the desk. With her hands on her hips, she glared at Henson.

"If looks could kill," he thought, "I'd be a dead man." He again tried to assuage her emotional outburst, saying, "None of the important ones, sweetheart."

Henson's endearment almost made her nauseous. "What is he up to?" she wondered. "Well, which unimportant ones did I overlook?" she snarled.

Henson rose to his feet, walked around the desk to place his hands on her shoulders. Facing her with what he hoped was a friendly smile, he murmured. "It's not important sweetheart. What's important is that I'm here, and I want to take care of you. I love you, and I want to marry you. I want you to put all this teaching business behind you and come make your home with me."

Ellie wanted to place her heel on his toes and grind, or at least slap the silly grin off his face, but she didn't. She just batted his hands off her shoulders, hoping he would get the message that she wasn't interested. As a further signal, she turned to walk along the aisle to the open windows.

He must have interpreted her move as one of unreasonable anger as he pursued her to the window. Again, placing his hand on her shoulder, this time from behind, he murmured, "Please Ellie."

Ellie spun around, eyes blazing, "Keep your damned hands off me," she commanded. "And if you have a decent bone in your body, you'll tell me what they think I did wrong." Then overcome by her own reprehensible behavior, she fell against him, "Please," she said tearfully, "what went wrong? How will I ever get another teaching position with this for a recommendation?" She started shaking again as she sobbed.

Henson, finally cowed by her reception of his proposal, decided to answer her. He enumerated the boards' reasons for letting her go. "Not that I concur," he said, "but certain community members stated that discipline was lacking. There were several fights on the school grounds, including one where a student's nose was bloodied. In fact that same student left the grounds not once, but on numerous occasions, and was seen entering a local business establishment during the noon break. A saloon, I believe it was at the time.

"Then your participation in local political affairs was extraordinary in spite of the fact that you as a lawyer knew you were prohibited from taking any action or even discussing such matters as a public employee. Whether or not you received any remuneration for the preparation of documents submitted to Governor West, it was your 'successful petition endeavor' that led to martial law being proclaimed, a condition not appreciated or approved by everyone in the Copperfield community.

"Further, although the Board did not discover the source of the funding, you were responsible for awards that were not first approved by the Board for questionable student work. The example given was a certain painting depicting the spirit of Death, I believe; a most inappropriate subject for young children to contemplate.

"Then, there is your behavior in public, usually in the company of one Cord Williams, which certain parents did not feel was exemplary in view of your influence on young children."

Ellie stood listening to the entirety of Henson's barrage, but at its end, she felt the need to sit down. Returning to the piano bench, she was able to snarl, "Is that all?"

"Oh, Ellie," Henson pleaded, dropping to his knees before her and taking her hand in his, "Please listen to me. I want to marry you. If you want to continue teaching, we can move somewhere else. As for a recommendation, Clara Hoffstetter won't be writing it. You'll have no trouble finding employment."

"So that's it," Ellie cried, jumping to her feet. "Clara is at the bottom of this. I might have known. Anything she can't control, she tries to destroy." Ellie began pacing the floor. Now that it was in the open, she felt she could cope somehow. First she had to send Henson Baldwin packing. She thought of blurting out the truth of the matter, "I wouldn't marry you if you were the last man on earth."

Instead, since he had chosen to linger, she would let him have it as the representative of those snake-in-the-grass school board members. "And you," she sneered. "I suppose you were right there to defend the little woman you want to marry. You and those mealy-mouthed sniveling rats who say, 'Yes, Mr. Willoughby; you're right, 'Mr. Willoughby. Your cousin Clara Hoffstetter and you were surely right in protecting the community from the most vicious female since Lizzie Borden. We must relieve her of her duties at once."

Shaking her finger at Henson, she continued, "No, not at once because all those offenses except one took place during the first semester. But no, you didn't let her go until the end of the school year, so you didn't interrupt the student's learning process.

"And as for Cord Williams, he's been defending and sheltering, and supporting me like the gentleman that he is since the day we met. Can you say the same?" she screeched.

Bursting into tears yet another time, she spun away to run out the door. Henson's lips twitched as he murmured to himself, "I guess I can safely conclude that she won't be marrying me anytime soon." He picked up his hat, went outside to get his banjo case, then made his way to the livery stable to pick up his horse. He planned to submit his resignation as a member of the school board to Abe Willoughby on his way home. That way someone else could be sought in time for the May primary. He had a feeling that at least two of the other three board members would also be resigning.

It had been one hellish fight the previous week when Abe had presented Clara's bill of particulars leading to non-renewal of Ellie's contract. In the end, Abe prevailed, saying, "Rules are rules, and if a teacher can't abide by them, how can we expect to produce young people who have any respect for the law?" Henson had remained relatively quiet hoping to move in as the handsome prince to rescue the damsel in distress.

"Henson, old man," Baldwin observed to himself. "You certainly flunked the romantic, charming, and chivalrous prince test . . ." He almost smiled at the fool he had made of himself.

General Delivery
Copperfield, Oregon
May 5, 1914

Dear Lottie Fern,

 I don't know how to tell you this. Since this letter will be on the same train with me when I leave this dastardly place, I debated about writing you at all. The fact is, I may as well just come out and say it. I was fired from my teaching position. Well not fired exactly. Euphemistically speaking, my contract was not renewed.
 I'll tell you the details when I arrive on Thursday night. I just don't know how I'll get any joy now while spending two days in Portland. I wish I were able to come straight through to Salem, but my reservations are made. I'll probably just sleep when I get to Portland. I certainly didn't for the last two nights, and I'll be riding the train all night tonight.
 My worst problem in the long run is going to be retrieving my things from my room at The Store. I knew I couldn't spend another minute in Clara Hoffstetter's company. It was at her urging that the school board acted on a pack of lies and half-truths so that they let me go. After the horrible experience of learning they were not going to give me a new contract, I went to The Golden Star to meet Cord. When I got there, I just fell into his arms and cried and cried.
 He and Bridget were so patient in trying to find out what was wrong. When I was finally able to get the salient points across between sobs, Cord wanted to beat Henson Baldwin within an inch of his life. Henson had been quite happy about my predicament. His solution was to propose marriage.
 When I said I just couldn't face Clara, Bridget said she wanted to go give the old biddy a piece of her mind. But Cord said, "No that would be unwise." She told him he couldn't throttle Henson, then, either. Between the two of them, they made me feel some better. I had to giggle as they bantered about the best way to even the score with Clara.
 Then they decided I had to move into the big room in back of the ice cream parlor. Both were prepared to go carry my belongings, lock, stock, and barrel from the Store.
 I certainly appreciated their support, but I finally realized that such a move wouldn't be prudent. After all, Henson shouldn't have told me Clara was behind the board's move to fire me. I guess he just didn't care if only he could get me to consent to marry him.
 I finally conspired with Bridget and Cord to fake a sprained ankle so I wouldn't have to go back to the Store on Sunday night. As it turned out, I stayed away on Monday too. I don't know what Clara is thinking, but I really don't care.

Honestly, the injured ankle isn't entirely faked. When I ran out of the schoolhouse to get away from Henson, I tripped and almost fell. I really hurt my toes worse than my ankle, but nothing is broken.

Bridget did go to Clara to get my small suitcase. It has the things for my stay in Portland. At the same time, she convinced Clara not to come check on me because, she said, I was quite exhausted and was already lying down to take a nap. Bridget hinted that I might have to consult Dr. Hunsaker, and he would likely order me to stay off my foot for a couple of days. Hence, I didn't have to go back there yesterday either.

The exhausted part is no lie. At least it isn't this morning. I've hardly slept since Saturday night. I'm so worried about what to do next. I can't make up my mind about Normal School now that I no longer have a job. My application for training has been accepted at Monmouth. They are waiting for me to remit the fees they require.

I think the only solution for the present is to stop worrying, at least until I am able to talk to you. I'm going to the post office to mail this letter. Then I'll go with Marty to the store where I hope George will help pack my steamer trunk down the stairs to put in Marty's whiskey cart. He will wheel it to the depot for me. Cord couldn't help because he went to work both yesterday and today.

When the trunk is taken care of, I will bid the Hoffstetters "good-bye" perhaps forever.

So I hope you are prepared to receive a somewhat hysterical woman in your company. Whether you are or not, I will see you on Thursday evening.

With love and gratitude,

Your Cousin Ellie K

Salem Visit

It was 6:30 p.m. when the Oregon Electric train screeched its brakes and halted at the depot in Salem, Oregon.

Charlotte Fern Hobbs stood watching anxiously for her cousin to disembark. When at last Ellie came into sight, Lottie was shocked at her appearance. Her ever-vibrant cousin, whom she called "little" until Ellie reached her sixteenth year, appeared quite bedraggled. Strands of her honey-blonde hair fell across her forehead from beneath her hat, which looked as if it might tumble to the ground at any moment. If Lottie didn't know better, she'd accuse the younger woman of being inebriated. That being only the very remotest possibility, Lottie rushed forward ready to catch the tottering woman in her waiting arms.

"Ellie," she squealed. "What's wrong?" Attempting to deliver a welcome hug, she was startled when Ellie pushed her away.

"Lottie, don't" she wailed. "I've been quite sick."

"Oh dear," Lottie said in alarm. "Well, we must get you home right away. Come I have a cab waiting."

"I need to claim my baggage," Ellie whimpered.

"Yes. Look we'll pick it all up tomorrow," Lottie decided. "I can send someone for it. In the meantime, I have anything you may need tonight." Gently placing her arm through Ellie's, she led the way to the cabby who assisted both ladies into their seats.

It was a very short distance to Lottie's gleaming two-bedroom apartment. If she were feeling better, Ellie would have happily toured every nook and cranny admiring the wall hangings, the comfortable love seat and matching over-stuffed chair, and the oval oakwood coffee table in the living room. What-not shelves would have caught her attention for long minutes. The two ladies would have eaten a light supper of salad and soup or a sandwich, and they might have turned to Ellie's two most profound concerns, her career and Cord.

As it was, Lottie immediately consigned her guest to the spare bedroom. She laid out an almost new white gown, a blue robe and slippers and ordered her ailing cousin to get ready for bed while she fixed tea and Melba toast.

The girls visited for a very short time. Ellie told of ordering fish for dinner on the train on Tuesday evening after leaving Baker City. She said she had settled in her berth in the Pullman car for a good night's sleep, but had awakened during the night to be violently ill. She smiled a little at the poor conductor's predicament of cleaning up after her. When she reached Portland, she had gone straight to the hotel and hadn't even gone to the dining room all day on Wednesday. On Thursday morning, she ordered poached egg, which she barely touched. Then at noon, she had tried again to eat a little soup. She no longer felt nauseous, but in spite of the many hours spent in bed or just lounging yesterday and today, she was still exhausted.

She became fearful that she might become sick all over again when she smelled food as she boarded the train in Portland. But so far so good.

"You poor dear," Lottie murmured rising from the chair beside the bed. Placing the back of her hand on Ellie's forehead to check for signs of a fever, she announced. "If you are not greatly improved by morning, we shall have to seek the services of a physician."

"Oh no, I'm quite sure a day in your care will find me one hundred per cent improved."

"Well, we'll see," Lottie said. "For now, unless you'd like more to eat or drink I'm going to leave you so you can rest."

Ellie handed her cup and saucer to Lottie, leaned her head further back on the pillows she had used to prop herself upright and said weakly, "Nothing more to eat. I'm not sure I shall ever eat again, at least not like I did Tuesday night." She brightened a little to add, "It was very tasty at the time, but I think I'll avoid fish forevermore."

"All right then, good night my dear," Lottie said as she left the room.

It was Saturday morning before Ellie rose from her bed to bathe and fully dress. Her trunk and suitcase had been delivered on Friday afternoon from the depot, but she didn't feel up to making an effort to dress. She still did not feel completely recovered, but she was certainly improving.

As she came through the hallway to Lottie's kitchenette, she was not surprised to see her cousin lost to the world around her while she studiously read from the front page of *The Morning Oregonian*. "Oh," Lottie said jumping up as Ellie smiled at her. "Do come sit. I have coffee if you'd like some. I also have fruit cut up in the icebox. I planned to fix French toast and bacon. Do you think that will be all right?"

"Sounds delicious," Ellie agreed. "I think it will be all right. I don't feel so sore this morning. I'm pretty sure I'm well now."

"You certainly look much better. Maybe it's because you've done your hair so prettily. I haven't seen that comb you're wearing since I came East. Was that four years ago already?"

"Actually, it was five," Ellie laughed. "You had applied to take your Oregon bar exam, and you were consulting with Father on how to proceed."

Both girls sobered for a moment, thinking of the loss they had suffered in Attorney Leon Delaney's passing. Lottie was the first to return her thoughts to the present. She quickly poured Ellie's coffee and served it. "You sit here and relax. I'll have breakfast ready in a jiffy. Everything is set out on the counter waiting for me to pop it into the pan."

Later when they had almost finished eating, Lottie mentioned that she had originally requested the use of the Governor's touring car today to go sight seeing. But in view of Ellie's illness, she'd simply postponed until next week.

"I realize," Lottie said, "that you need to go to Monmouth to arrange for your room and board for the summer session, so I'll just absent myself from work on Friday, and we'll go together to take care of all that. Then on Saturday, we'll try to seek out some historical points of interest. I may just put in to represent the Governor at the celebration in Champoeg next week. I don't believe he's planning to go.

"In the meantime, there is going to be a special Mother's Day celebration in the rotunda at the Capitol tomorrow. The President has declared it a national holiday, you know." Ellie knew. She had considered having her students make gifts for their mothers during school, but the project had gone by the wayside as the last day of school loomed ever closer.

"After the serenade by the Willamette University men's choir, I can take you on tour all through the Capitol if you feel up to it." Lottie glanced up as she was placing her coffee cup back in its saucer.

Ellie's eyes were brimming with tears. She rose quickly to rush to her room to get a handkerchief. Coming back to the dinette table, she sat before she said, "I'm so sorry. I've been thinking about it all week. I just can't make up my mind about Normal School. When I think that I'm not going to be with my students in Copperfield next year, I almost can't bear it.

"Oh Lottie, when Father died, I had things I needed to do, so I moved through the days and made my decisions slowly. I'm not sorry about any of those decisions. But now, I feel as though I've been left with nothing. How can I look forward to another school year when I'll have to pick up and establish myself in some new community? I will have to give up the few friends I've made." By this time, Ellie was sobbing. "There . . . there must be a better solution."

Lottie rose to put her arm around Ellie's shoulder. She pressed her cheek to Ellie's wet face. "Of course, there is," she said softly. Then she stood, "and I think I know exactly what that is."

"What?" Ellie pouted, loudly clearing her nose into her handkerchief.

"We'll go gown shopping, maybe even wedding gown shopping today," Lottie announced.

"That's stupid," Ellie said, placing her handkerchief in her sleeve. "Why would I want to try on wedding gowns?"

"Because you need to see how beautiful you are and realize that you are a very important person in the scheme of things."

"Hmmmp!" Ellie grumped. "I wish some other person would think I was important."

"It sounds to me as if somebody already does."

"Who?" Ellie growled.

"I think his name is Cord Williams," Lottie teased.

"I wish," Ellie sniffed.

"Oh come on now. You know he loves you. It's only a matter of time, and he'll come around."

"You really think so," Ellie brightened.

"Trust me. I know so. I think all you need is a beautiful wedding gown to show him. He's sure to know that you will want to wear it someday soon."

Both girls giggled. Ellie began clearing the table. After dishes were washed and replaced in the cupboard, the two groomed themselves to go shopping. Setting out with umbrellas in case of rain on the cloudy overcast day, they went out to visit the several bridal shops in the nearby area of downtown Salem.

To say they had a good time would be an understatement. Returning to the apartment in the late afternoon, Ellie seemed fully recovered.

"I can't believe I just chose a wedding gown," she giggled when they had settled themselves in the living room with a cup of tea.

"Not only chose it, but fitted it, and ordered alterations," Lottie agreed. "There's no turning back now, and it will be ready in just one week."

May 10, 1914
Dearest Cord,

    I hope this letter finds you well and happy.
    As I mentioned in the postal card I sent from Portland on Thursday, I was quite ill. I didn't recover to be well enough to get out of bed until Saturday. Although as I said in my message to you then, I did come to Salem on Thursday evening.
    Lottie has been such a dear. She took such good care of me in spite of having to be at work by 7:30 on Friday morning. She's spent every minute while here at the apartment trying to cheer me. I think she's pretty close to her wit's end! I haven't told her yet, but I'm going to pass on going to Normal School at Monmouth. I just cannot see the point.
    We had quite a wonderful day yesterday. We attended services at the fabulous Jason Lee Methodist Church near the Capitol in the morning. It is so beautiful. I can't make up my mind which is more special, singing out in the mountains of the Snake River and hearing the echo, or being enclosed with a heavenly sounding organ, singing in this magnificent church. Despite my inability to decide, which is more beautiful, I have no doubt where I'd rather be—if you are there.
    After lunch, we returned to the Capitol to be entertained by the Willamette University men's choir in honor of Mother's Day. The rotunda where they sang is spectacular. I wish you could see it.
    Lottie is planning an outing for us at the end of the week. Specifically, we'll be using the governor's touring car. We'll be going north toward Portland to a historical place called Champoeg, where they have erected a monument in honor of the men who voted for a Provisional Government in Oregon in 1843. The monument has become a very popular tourist attraction. I'm quite looking forward to it.
    Lottie and I went gown shopping on Saturday. I think you'll be very surprised, and I hope pleased, when you see what I have chosen.
    I so miss my daily dealings with the children of Copperfield. I don't know how I can face the future without them. But I know I must. I rack my brain every waking moment and pray fervently before going to sleep each night for a solution.
    I have postponed my conversation with Lottie about Normal School until it is getting disgraceful. She thinks she is taking the day on Friday to accompany me to Monmouth. She believes we'll be taking my things, finding living quarters, and making arrangements for board in addition to officially enrolling for classes. But as I said, I see no point in going, although I will surely have to seek employment for the fall.

So that brings me to my most important question. Will you come with me to the new community where I am able to secure a teaching position? I will have to begin making serious inquiries in various communities by July.

I have the feeling that you are not so very happily employed at the sawmill on Pine Creek; yet that kind of job would be available in almost any community in Oregon. If you will consent to follow me, we can make certain you can find work. I know it is shameless of me to ask you such a question. Yet, after my teaching experience in Copperfield as far as the children are concerned, then to have things end as they have, I just can't go some other place by myself to start all over. I suppose the children would be much the same and equally as enjoyable. But I don't believe I can face another community of adults by myself, not knowing what they expect, or which of them might turn on me.

I didn't get to talk with you after I bade the Hoffstetters goodbye. George was as apologetic as could be. Neither he nor Clara was in the least evasive about knowing I had lost my job. In fact, Clara seemed almost contrite when she said she was so sorry to see me go, meaning from their household, I'm sure. After all, it did put $10 per month into her household budget.

Sissy ran to me and put her arms around my waist when we got the trunk on to the cart. I bent down to hold her closer because she was crying. The Hoffstetter conversation on Sunday evening and Monday must have been filled with the news of the board's action. Otherwise, I don't believe Sissy could have understood the issue. She was already aware that I would be away for Normal school for a time, and she hadn't reacted to that idea before.

Jeffrey accompanied Marty and me to the station with my trunk, and even he seemed sad as he shook my hand and said, "I hope you will return soon, Miss Delaney."

So much for my problems. Do you miss me? While Lottie is here, I succeed fairly well in putting you out of my mind. But you come racing in as soon as I am alone. I can't wait for you to hold me in your arms.

My sincerest love to my only love,

Ellie K.

P. S. Don't bother to write. It is quite likely I'll return to Copperfield before another week has passed, although I'm getting quite spoiled here. Lottie hovers over me and waits on me hand and foot. Then, having cab service available and being within walking distance of the finest shops and restaurants has caused me to miss my childhood home just a little. But I miss you more!

At Champoeg

Saturday morning finally arrived. It had been a long and almost unbearable five days for Ellie as she whiled away the hours. She read books until she grew restless. Then she walked for miles thinking about Cord, wondering how he really felt about her, what he thought of her proposal, and how she could honorably keep him by her side.

She had told Lottie on Monday evening after mailing Cord's letter that she would be returning to Copperfield rather than going to school.

Lottie looked at her steadily to see if she was dissembling in any way. Realizing she was not, Lottie went to massage her cousin's shoulders as she sat slumped over the edge of the kitchen table.

Ellie managed to hold back her tears for a very long time, but by the end of their conversation, she realized that she was no nearer to a solution than ever.

"Ellie," Lottie called from the kitchen, "our car will be here in a half an hour or less."

Ellie continued to sit at the vanity table, pulling her hair this way and that, finally giving it a wrap into a chignon. Satisfied with the result, she called, "What should I wear, do you think?"

"Something dark," Lottie called back. "The ride will be pretty dusty."

"Do you think the black broadcloth with the bolero that you gave me will be all right?"

Lottie peeked in the doorway. "Sounds perfect," she said. "Did you bring a good pair of walking shoes?"

"I have my brown ones," Ellie said doubtfully. "They won't look so great with black, but my black ones are more for dancing, if you know what I mean."

"The brown ones will be fine. We won't be in a fashion parade," Lottie returned. "I think I'll pack a picnic lunch right quick. Perhaps some ham sandwiches from our leftovers last night. I have lettuce, pickles, onions, and a very tasty relish in the icebox. I think there's still some cheddar cheese too."

"Sounds wonderful," Ellie said. "By the way, who is driving today?"

"A friend of the governor's, Richard Littlejohn, will be driving us. He often drives the governor to Seaside for his vacations. Be sure you wear the wide-brimmed hat we chose the other day. You'll need to tie netting over it to protect you from the dust. I have extra netting if you need it."

"I wish I had one of my bonnets," Ellie lamented.

"Oh, that's so provincial," Lottie commented.

Ellie laughed. "So I'm provincial!"

A few minutes later, the cousins were hurrying out the door, picnic basket in hand, to be assisted into the back seat of the touring car. Ellie had a feeling that her hat would surely go flying as they sped across town. When they came to a stop before turning north on the main thoroughfare, she untied and retied the huge net bow beneath her chin, tightening it until it pulled, but didn't irritate her neck.

An hour later, they reached the site of the Champoeg monument. Smiling Lottie said, "This is the site where the State of Oregon was born. The monument lists the names of the fifty-three men from throughout the region who voted yes to form a Provisional Government. It was built in 1902.

"But for the votes of two rebellious British subjects from Canada, who voted yes along with the Oregon settlers, the ground we're walking on might very well be Canadian," she continued.

"Or there would have been a few pitched battles," remarked Ellie May. Having stared at the monument for a while, Ellie noted: "This is really fascinating. Who were the real leaders?"

"According to what we can learn," Lottie replied, "a man named Joseph Meek was instrumental in achieving a majority when the vote was taken, though ever so slight. You see, there were 103 persons participating in a rather raucous meeting that day in 1843. Forty-nine of them voted against the idea of a Provisional Government. Many of the nay-sayers were there at the behest of the British according to people's belief at the time. They weren't settlers at all, at least not from the surrounding valley."

After their picnic lunch, the trio went for a walk along the Willamette River. Mr. Littlejohn was most helpful in identifying the names of a dozen varieties of songbirds including the western bluebird. The springtime melodies of the birds' chirping was tantalizing. All the while, hawks circled lazily overhead.

The ground area was no less magnificent, especially when Ellie compared it to Copperfield. Flowers dotted the landscape in their pretty pinks and blues. The predominant color was yellow, but clumps of white dogwood appeared at intervals to add further variety. There were trees of all kinds, Douglas fir, birch, alder, willow, and oak. The one thing Mr. Littlejohn could not be certain about was whether or not there was poison oak, so he warned his charges not to touch the branches overhead unless they bore coniferous needles. He was quite certain those would be safe.

Returning to Salem, Mr. Littlejohn offered to drive the ladies through town to tour some interesting points. Among the places where he slowed or stopped were the Jason Lee house built in 1841, and the John D. Boone house built in 1847. When the tourists finally returned to Lottie's apartment, they were quite weary.

"The automobile may become a popular mode of transportation, but I really find it hard to believe," Lottie remarked. "Give me a train anytime," she said, as she stood in the foyer shaking dust from her hat and brushing gray particles from her skirt."

"But you have to have a track available. Considering where we drove today, the automobile wasn't so restricted," Ellie protested.

"Well, I'll just have to stick with where the train goes for my travels. I'm so thankful that you can travel by train from Copperfield."

"If there hadn't been train service, I would never have gone there," Ellie laughed. "I had also considered Ayrock in Malheur county where there was a position open. But guess what, no door to door train service."

"So see?" Lottie pursued the subject. "The dust would have been unbearable. And the continual bouncing about over the roads, especially after they've been soaked by rain, then dried. That and the odor of gasoline fumes takes all the joy out of the so-called joy-ride as far as I'm concerned."

"Hmm! You're sounding as if you wished we hadn't gone today."

"No, not really. I'm just getting old I guess."

"My, my, a whole 30 years, and you're ready for the rocking chair."

"That does sound so good. I believe I'll fix us a cup of tea and sip it while I sit in my rocking chair and relax."

"Forgive me," said Ellie. "But I thought today was supposed to be relaxing. At least I found it that way."

"Not for my feet," Lottie complained. "Give me the city streets for walking any day."

"I suspect I would have said the same a year ago," Ellie remarked. "Right now, I think if I were back in Copperfield, I might even climb one of those high mountains just to take in the view."

Lottie was handing her a cup of tea. "You're crazy, Ellie, you know that?"

"I guess so," Ellie replied. "Or I wouldn't be spending my time trying to find a way to have my cake and eat it too. Anyway, thank you for today. I believe I can find a very good use for all I learned. I may just prepare a skit for Oregon's birthday to show how it almost wasn't."

Lottie laughed.

Sitting in the rocking chair in their living room on Sunday afternoon, George Hoffstetter was turning the pages of Friday's newspaper. Ellie's subscription was still arriving in the mail and would continue until the first of June.

"I wonder where she is," he commented.

Clara was seated on the couch busily rolling yarn from a skein draped over Jeffrey's outstretched hands. Jeffrey was tiredly shifting his weight from one foot to the other as he stood in front of her.

"Do you have to go?" Clara demanded. "We'll be through here in just a minute." Without changing tone of voice or inflection, she asked, "Where is who?"

Turning another page, his chin resting on his chest, he glanced over the newspaper, "Miss Delaney," George replied.

"I suppose she's in Monmouth in readiness to attend classes tomorrow," Clara said unconcernedly.

"I don't think so," George said, leaning forward now, the paper folded in quarters as he read.

"Oh, why not," Clara pursued.

"I believe she'll be returning long before those summer classes are over. I'm somewhat surprised she hasn't already arrived for that matter."

Clara finished the last flip of the ball of yarn, and Jeffrey almost ran from the room. She still had five skeins to go, and he had no intention of being pressed into further service today. He was grateful that she thought he needed a toilet break. That provided him the perfect opportunity for slipping outside to see if he could find Davy or Billy. As he descended the stairs, he could hear his mother assailing his dad.

"George Hoffstetter, you've heard something you're not telling me."

George looked up quizzically, enjoying the annoyed look on Clara's face. She was standing before him, hands on her hips, ready to do battle for his negligence in not telling her the latest gossip.

"I may have heard something," he said. "Particularly regarding Miss Delaney's choices now that the school board saw fit to relieve her of her duties."

"You're still blaming me for that, now, aren't you? I told you I didn't ask Abe to fire her, I just thought that as chairman of the board, he should know exactly what has been going on over the months she's been here. After all, she was put in my custody at Abe's request."

"That self-righteous, over-educated, dirt-farming prig," George growled. "And as far as you are concerned, I believe you were directed to advise her. I didn't hear anything about reporting her activities to the school board."

"I only did what I thought was right and good for the community."

"Oh really. I suppose it was for the good of the community that you managed to get rid of the best teacher this school has had or could ever hope to have. What I'd like to know," George said rising to tower over Clara while she was tidying the yarn supply and picking up items from the floor "is why?"

"Why? Why?" she shrieked. She stopped. Her hands on her hips, she stared up at him. "After the foolishness at that 'Coming Out Assembly,' you can ask why!"

"You're still smarting because our precious children didn't bring home the most prestigious awards, aren't you?" George adjured.

"Well, aren't you?" Clara retorted.

"Not particularly. Their grades are better than we could have hoped. Jeffrey's ability to do arithmetic has improved ten-fold. And Sissy does very well for a seven-year-old. Besides, most of those awards were determined by school board members. The ones Ellie decided for herself were entirely correct I thought." George returned to the rocking chair and picked up another page of the newspaper.

"Oh you did, did you? Billy Mitchell, a nobody, an orphan, The Outstanding Student." Clara sniffed.

"That was just among the 8th graders, for crying out loud. Who would you have chosen? Jimmy Lawson, who just last fall had never read one whole book in his life? His own mother told you that at Christmas time, you said." George adjusted his spectacles and looked more closely at the paper before him.

Clara still standing with her hands on hips, replied. "So, that's water under the bridge. What I want to know is how do you know Ellie is not going to Normal School?"

"I don't know," George returned. "I just know that she is coming back here sooner or later, and I want to make sure you behave yourself."

"What's that supposed to mean?" Clara flared as she took a step closer to George. "You know yourself if it weren't for her and that uppity cousin of hers, we wouldn't have soldiers parading up and down the streets outside, ruining our trade."

George came to his feet to stand toe to toe with his wife. "Oh I see. Well let me tell you a thing or two." George's eyes were blazing. Clara turned to retrieve the ball of yarn that had dropped to the floor in front of the couch.

George snatched her arm as she bent over and spun her to face him. "You consider yourself a Christian woman. Well you and that asinine cousin of yours are as self-righteous as any Pharisee. You both sit around and wait for a chance to cast the first stone instead of giving consideration to helping others."

"There's no help for Ellen Delaney, as far as I can see," snapped Clara.

George continued to grip Clara's arm. He was almost ready to shake her. "And just where are you looking? What has she done that's so unforgivable?"

"She's a sneak, that's what she's done. You can tell by looking at her after she's been with that vile creature that they have spent a great deal of time together—more than I was ever aware of. It wasn't until that ice-hauling incident that I figured out they had been sneaking off to be alone all the while. Is that the way you want your daughter to behave when she's a grown woman?"

"Better that than to turn her into a mouse like your sister, Rebecca." George released Clara's arm and trudged back to the rocking chair.

Clara untracked her handkerchief from her sleeve to blow her nose. Her reaction hit George with a twinge of guilt. "What I don't know, George, is what you expect of me. I work hard. I try to be a good wife and mother. Yet ever since the day I insisted you go to Baker City to meet with that Hobbs woman, and you came back with your tail tucked between your legs saying there was nothing you could do to stop her, you've been engaged in unending criticism of me. It's almost as if she robbed you of your manhood or something."

"My meeting with the Hobbs woman, as you call her, has nothing to do with it. She was doing her job. She did it, and that's that. If I have any regrets, it's not that I couldn't stop her, it's that I wasn't up there with her on that platform calling for those bastard's resignations. You know that's all it would take, their damned resignations, and we could have our town back."

"Oh George, you're such a fool!"

"I am, am I? Well you wanted to know what I expect of you. I don't know if I expect it or not, but I want you, the next time you're ready to put your nose where it doesn't belong, to stop and ask yourself, 'What can I do to make the situation better?' instead of going off half-cocked trying to keep yourself in control of everybody and everything. In other words, 'Do unto others as you would have them do unto you; turn the other cheek' and all those words we are supposed to live by. You might be surprised how much nicer the world would be for you." George rose from his rocker and stomped downstairs.

Sissy came quietly into the room. "Is Miss Delaney coming back here?" she asked timidly.

At first Clara was ready to snap, "I should hope not," but some glimmer of compassion for her lovely little daughter caused her to hold her tongue.

"I don't know dearest," she said quietly reaching to pull Sissy to her. "But if she does, we'll all be happy to see her, won't we?"

Sissy looked up at her mother's face, studying it closely. Her eyes were shining, "Oh yes, Mommy, we'll be very happy." Then she threw her arms around her mother to hug her fiercely.

—

Ellie's baggage was being transferred from the cab to the baggage truck for loading to Portland. It was 6:30 on Monday morning, and the two cousins stood face to face, their outfits immaculately pressed, their hats fastened securely, their lily-white gloves tidily covering dainty hands.

"Lottie, I can't thank you enough. My visit with you has been absolutely wonderful. I don't know how you've managed to put up with me for nearly two weeks. But I'll never forget our shopping trips, Church, Mother's Day, our trip to Champoeg, and your heavenly salads. Our tours through the Capitol and the State Library have quite possibly changed my life."

"I'm just glad you came, and I do hope you'll come again soon. It is such fun to sit and reminisce the year I spent with you and Uncle Leon in Philadelphia." Lottie smiled saying, "You were such a bundle of energy when you were 18. But that was before life got entirely serious for either of us."

"Oh, I'm so sorry, Lottie. If I hadn't been sick when I came, I would still have been energetic, I'm sure. I hope you didn't wear yourself out taking care of me."

"That's quite all right," Lottie assured her. Placing her hand on Ellie's arm, she said, "Now you have a good trip back, and I'll get a wire off to The Golden Star just as soon as I arrive at work this morning. I wish we knew if someone can meet you when you arrive in Copperfield. But then, such uncertainty is to be expected when one makes last-minute decisions."

Ellie looked sharply at Lottie, but could detect no hint of criticism. She moved in closer to give Lottie a farewell hug, saying "Goodbye, I'm sure we'll be together again soon. After all this is the second time in five months that we've seen each other. That's quite an improvement over five years that elapsed previously."

The conductor approached, calling, "All aboard."

"Goodbye dearest," Lottie murmured. "I truly hope you're right, and while you consider re-locating, think about moving in this direction."

Ellie stepped up into the passenger car entry. "We'll see," she promised as she waved a final goodbye with the handkerchief she was clutching tightly in her hand. She was sorry to notice that Lottie appeared a little downcast. Her own mood was one of pure joy. In less than 36 hours, she would see Cord again. There didn't seem to be anything else of any great importance at the moment.

In her two weeks away, her anger toward Clara had faded. As Lottie reminded her, "Whatever Clara hoped to accomplish, she evidently thought she was doing it in your best interest. If it weren't for Cord, and the way you feel about him," Lottie advised, "it would probably be best not to return to Copperfield at all. However, under the present circumstances, you are practically making yourself sick. You will just have to go back and ignore Clara, if necessary. It couldn't hurt if you can bring yourself to forgive her. It would be for your own good."

"I don't know," Ellie had replied, tears streaming. "I only know I can't be anyplace else, at least not until I know for sure that Cord will never marry me."

So, it had come down to that. Ellie wasn't able to pick up her wedding gown on Saturday because they had departed early for Champoeg, and had not finished seeing the sights of Salem until after closing time. On Sunday as the two of them conversed about what to do next, Lottie concurred that Ellie would be better off going back to Copperfield. She needed to work things out rather than sit around ten hours a day while Lottie was at work. Being remorseful wasn't accomplishing anything at all.

That had required Ellie to pack quickly this morning while Lottie arranged for a cab to arrive at six o'clock to whisk them off to the train depot. The two decided Lottie would pick up the gown and send it along by parcel post as soon as she could manage. Thankfully, Ellie's ticket had already been paid when she purchased a round-trip fare earlier in the month.

The first forty miles of Ellie's return trip practically flew by. The rails fairly sang on the short jaunt to Portland. Ellie planned to eat breakfast at or near the train depot while awaiting the eastbound passenger train. She would have preferred to go straight through and not have to stay over in Baker City. But at least she'd have no trouble in catching the Tuesday run to Copperfield

Once on the train, Ellie reached into her handbag and pulled out a copy of *The Scarlet Pimpernel*. She had selected it at a bookstore in Salem a week ago when she was posting Cord's letter. Then because she had already immersed herself in reading Lottie's copy of *David Copperfield*, she had forgotten all about her own book until she was repacking her things.

Lottie had insisted she borrow her copy of Jane Austin's *Pride and Prejudice*, which she was reading for the fiftieth time. Ellie had misplaced her own copy somehow while coming West last summer.

Life could be so wonderful when one was able to get such enjoyment from the pages of a good book. She intended to make the most of the fact that Lottie pressed her to enroll as a patron of the Oregon State Library. Wherever she would be teaching the next year, she could borrow books not only for herself, but also for her students.

Since Lottie used the State Library frequently on behalf of the governor, it took only a few minutes for Ellie to become a patron. The librarian, Cornelia Marvin, had impressed her beyond words. The woman was reaching toward her middle years, yet her complexion was flawless. Her smile was infectious. And nowhere in Ellie's brief years had she ever met a person so devoted to the betterment of others than was Miss Marvin. Such a handsome woman, in physique, in spirit, and in action.

Ellie often daydreamed of becoming just such a person, serene, and joyous. She had only one problem. The world and the people in it often interfered. A prime example was Cord Williams.

Perusing her book, and following the adventures of the Pimpernel, she realized that Sir Percy Blakeney had a great deal in common with her own hero. He was brave and resourceful, and handsome. She just wished she had the fortitude to discover Cord's true identity. At the end of the book when all was solved, Ellie closed her eyes and listened to the thrumming and clacking of the train wheels carrying her back to the love of her life.

General Delivery
Copperfield, Oregon
May 21, 1914

Dear Lottie Fern,

    I successfully reached home on Tuesday afternoon. Your wire arrived, as planned, obviously. Although it was quite a different reception than the one last September, it was nonetheless heartfelt. Marty, Bridget and the baby, Billy Mitchell, and Cord were all there to meet me. Billy is staying in the loft at The Golden Star now.
    After hugs all around and a whistle-provoking kiss from Cord, we proceeded back to The Star. That was Billy doing the whistling. I had to laugh.
    I asked Cord right away why he was not at work. He said he stayed home to help cart my trunk and assist me in unpacking. It seems that George and Marty arranged on Saturday to haul the rest of my things from the store. That was after Cord revealed that I would not be going to Normal School.
    Marty said Clara was away for several hours on that day visiting her sister, and she knew nothing about their moving my things. In fact, he thinks, she is probably still in the dark since she had closed my bedroom door and told the children to stay out, awaiting my return. I wonder how she'll react when she discovers the empty room. She'll, no doubt, be furious with George.
    Bridget told me she is still aching to give Clara a piece of her mind, and she just might do it yet. Marty told her that in view of how decent George is acting, it isn't necessary. He believes George can handle it, but I'm not entirely sure, judging from what I know of them.
    Anyway having my things here has postponed the necessity of my going over there right away. Marty says Mr. Gorman of the Gorman Pharmacy, wants to talk to me about working for him, beginning the first of June. He particularly wants me to audit his books. I'm not sure I'm qualified to do that, but I'm planning to talk to him to see if I can learn.
    Have you mailed my gown? I hope it arrives while Cord is at work. I can probably slip it past everyone else. Now that I am back here, I'm a little embarrassed by the whole idea of having chosen a wedding gown. Fortunately, I have plenty of closet space for hiding just about anything. Marty has walled in the staircase and put a door on it, which exits into the small hallway leading to the ice cream parlor. The closet then consists of the area under the stairs so it extends at least twelve feet along that wall. For the rest of the room, I am planning to shop for a single bed, a bureau, a desk, an overstuffed chair, and a vanity. Right now Bridget is loaning me the essentials such as a sleeping cot, a chair from the dining set in her kitchen, and a small table.

She has placed a handsome rug on the floor, one she braided herself last winter while they were staying with the Carpenters. She also sewed the curtains and some flower patterned drapes which are quite lovely. There are two practically floor-to-ceiling windows in the room. I can only wish my room at the Hoffstetters had been this spacious. Or, better yet, that I could somehow get my job back and live here while teaching.

Marty has been telling me about the school board shake up. Henson, Carson Swinyer, and Joe Halvorsen all resigned. Abe wasn't able to get anyone to consent to run in the primaries because everyone he talked to was more than a little upset about him letting me go. They told him he either has to hire me back or get off the board so someone else can.

Alice Hunsaker told me when I went to pick up my mail that she didn't know what they were thinking, but she is pretty sure that by the end of summer it will all work out.

So here I am back in Copperfield in a beautiful room. Cord is bringing me a set of bookshelves that he is constructing himself. I have a job, maybe. I'm living with my closest friends, and all is right with the world. Well, almost all. Cord still hasn't mentioned matrimony, and I'm not officially hired to teach school. But who knows? There's still three months to go. In Copperfield, that can mean a lot of change. It's not quite that way in Philadelphia.

I'm sorry I was such a wretch and a problem on my visit. I promise when we see each other again, I will keep things in perspective. After all, God does take care of me. As they say, when one door closes, He opens another.

Write soon.

Your cousin

Ellie K

The Mayor is Down

Cord and Ellie were walking along the boardwalk from The Golden Star on Tuesday morning. It was a beautiful summer day, but they were oblivious to just about everything including the chorus of birds that were twittering and flitting along the streets and alleys as they captured and carried food to their squawking offspring. Neither was paying attention to the thud of construction hammers and the sounds of machinery clanging in the distance. The sound of someone whistling a merry tune might have caught their attention except for the fact that both were preoccupied with their own thoughts about the future and what they would do about it.

At the same time, Ellie may have been trying to hurry to her new job at Gorman's Pharmacy. Because the teaching job was still in limbo, she tended to exercise considerable discretion concerning her public image in the company of Cord Williams. Clara had just remarked to George calling attention to that fact. The Hoffstetters were busily arranging fresh produce in the bins along the front of their store. Whatever the reasons for Ellie being several steps ahead of Cord, she was not prepared for being shoved roughly off the sidewalk and into the street, then pushed down into the dirt.

In fact, even after a gunshot rang out and she heard Cord command her to stay down, she couldn't comprehend what was happening. When she contrarily began to raise herself, she could see Cord running at full speed toward the Painted Lady. Then she heard the second shot, and her body reacted even if her mind could not. She screamed louder than she thought possible, then cringed in fear, clasping her hands over her head, even as she peered in terror at Cord's receding back.

George Hoffstetter, following the sound of the first shot, jerked his head to the north, catching a glimpse of metal protruding from the second story window in the Red Carpet Hotel. He began running in that direction when the second shot rang out. When someone shouted, "The mayor's been shot," he looked sharply to his left to see Harvey Sullivan thrashing on the boardwalk just outside his saloon door. Changing directions in mid-step, he dashed to the ex-mayor's side. The four militiamen on duty, two from each end of town, converged on the scene, running like the wind. In seconds, at least a dozen men were at Sullivan's side.

Clara stood, as if frozen, for a lifetime. She continued to stare at Ellie, who was again attempting to rise to her feet.

"Stay down," a militiaman yelled. His voice was quickly followed by a crisp order from another soldier, "Clear the streets."

A third man was pushing his way through the crowd to assist Cord in pulling the downed mayor through the door. Once Sullivan was inside, Cord rushed back to Ellie to crouch beside her, clearly shielding her from further gun shots from the direction of the hotel. "Are you okay?" he panted as he noted the two militiamen kneeling, back to back in the middle of the street, rifles at the ready.

Feeling an urgency to get Ellie safely away, he grabbed her hand, pulling her up, then dashed with her to the nearest doorway. Cord was looking intently at her when Ellie finally got around to answer, her voice trembling. "Yes, I'm okay."

"I'll be back" he announced as he turned and raced like a madman into the street. He was just in time to see two riders spurring their horses into flight toward the Pine Creek road.

"There they go," he yelled. The militiamen followed Cord's hand signal, dashing along the street between the Hotel and the General Store. But by they time they reached a vantage point from which to shoot, the riders were curving out of sight.

Two other men, whose horses were tethered at a hitching rack along the street, ran for their mounts. Another five or six pounded to the livery stable to secure their horses, and the chase was on.

Clara's eyes finally relinquished their hold on her stunned brain, and she scampered across the street to reach Ellie.

In the meantime, Doc Hunsaker, for all his exposure to wild nights in Copperfield was not certain that the loud popping noises were really gunfire. He thought, "It's possible that some of the town's youngsters have begun to dip into a supply of firecrackers from last 4th of July and are commencing an early celebration."

When he did step outside to see men running wildly and shouting for him at the top of their lungs, he whirled back up the stairs to his office to grab his bag and made the 100-yard dash to the Painted Lady in record time. He saw Cord pulling Ellie to her feet and noticed the militiamen kneeling in the street, but his attention riveted immediately on the door of The Painted Lady where men were yelling "Over here Doc." George Hoffstetter and the militiaman who was kneeling by the ex-mayor both rose and asked what they could do.

"Not much," the doctor ventured after a quick preliminary check of Sullivan's heartbeat. He noticed the mayor's mangled right hand, as he juggled his bag for scissors to clear Sullivan's shirt from a badly bleeding chest area. Quickly placing layers of gauze over the wound and applying pressure to staunch the flow of blood, he also realized the mayor's pant leg was rapidly turning blood red.

"That looks bad," the janitor for the Painted Lady gasped as he approached from the rear of the building.

The doctor glanced up; "Eldon can you see that somebody goes to the ranch to get Mrs. Sullivan? She's needed here."

"Yes sir," Eldon said, flipping his cleaning cloth over his shoulder. "But what do I tell her?"

"Tell her," the doctor said quietly, "that Harvey's been shot three times."

"Yes sir," Eldon replied and hurried away to accomplish his task.

As the doctor was rising and organizing some men to carry Sullivan to his office, George approached him. "Are you sure he was shot three times?"

"Right now, I'm not sure of anything," Hunsaker replied, "Why?"

"Well, because, there were only two shots."

"Maybe so," the doctor acknowledged. "But he has three wounds, one in his hand, one in his hip, and one in his chest."

"Must have had his hand in the way of one of the shots," George observed.

"Maybe so," Hunsaker replied, buckling the closures on his bag. Stepping around George, he fell in behind the men carrying their hastily constructed litter.

George, experiencing a let-down after minutes of fear, rage, and now helplessness, pushed out of the semi-darkness through the swinging doors and into the bright sunshine.

Little knots of people were gathered here and there along the street, chattering wildly about what happened or about what they thought had happened. Hoffstetter returned to the store. Entering the kitchen, he was not surprised to see Ellie sipping from a cup of hot tea. But he was surprised a few moments later when Cord came knocking at the back door asking Clara if Ellie was all right.

As far as George knew, those were the first words ever spoken between Clara and that "vile creature," as she often referred to him. George was even further amazed when Clara rather graciously invited him in to see for himself.

Clara quickly poured another cup of tea from the teapot setting in the middle of the table and carefully handed it to Cord where he squatted beside Ellie. His hat, though not removed, was rakishly pushed high on his forehead.

Clara was too excited and too caught up in the moment to stand on ceremony. In seconds she was interrupting the review of events and trying to absorb all the details. George joined in from his position near the doorway. He grinned with amusement as Cord slid on to the bench along the back wall so he could tenderly stroke Ellie's hand and arm. Clara didn't so much as raise an eyebrow. Rather she turned to him to inquire, "What do you think is going to happen now?"

"I guess that depends on whether Harvey lives or dies," George commented.

"Do you really think he might die?" Ellie gasped.

"Doc Hunsaker sent Eldon Landers right away to get his wife," George replied. "That's not exactly a good sign."

"Oh dear," Clara lamented. "I just don't know what I'd do if that happened to you George." She rose from her place at the table and sidled over to him, wrapping her arms around his waist and laying her head on his chest.

Cord's mouth shaped into a lop-sided grin upon seeing the color of embarrassment creep into George's face.

Not wishing to contribute further to the older man's discomfort, Cord squeezed Ellie's hand and also rose from the table.

"I think I'd better get on out of here and report back to Bridget that you're okay Ellie. Then I'll see if there's anything I can do for the Sullivans."

"I guess it's a good thing the mill is closed until after the 4th of July," Ellie commented. "It looks as though you'll have other fish to fry for a while."

Cord grinned down at her, "I'm going to be frying some of them with you if you'll let me."

A cloud of misgiving descended on Ellie as she remembered their continued disagreement over whether or not he had the right to propose marriage if he didn't have the wherewithal to fully support a family. "How long, O Lord," she thought to herself, "will it be until Cord either surrenders, or I bring myself to give up on him?"

She experienced the same old twinge of fear about her future without Cord. Also the throbbing in her temple and the choking feeling in her throat reminded her that there must still be some other reason for Cord's everlasting reluctance to go through with marriage.

Ellie rose from the table too, saying, "I may as well go on to work."

"Are you sure you're all right," Clara asked anxiously, releasing her hold on her husband. "You were so pale when I first saw you standing in that doorway."

"Do I look pale now?" Ellie demanded from Cord.

Cord cupped her face in his hand, turning her head from side to side. "I can safely say that I've seen brighter cheeks," he admitted.

"Oh, I'm all right," Ellie groused. "C'mon," she said as she tugged on Cord's arm and they went out the back door, both of them calling back, "Thank you for the tea."

"I guess he might not be so bad, after all," Clara remarked staring after them. "He certainly was brave in the face of all that gunfire."

"And I wasn't," George implored.

Clara turned back to embrace him once more. "Oh darling," she breathed, "You were wonderful. One just doesn't know what's important in life until there's a crisis, does one?"

"I guess not," George grinned. "I have to go find my glasses that must have dropped on the ground in front of the Painted Lady. Then I think I'll go see how Harvey's doing," he said extricating himself. "If he lives, somebody is going to have to go with him and Doc to Baker City. Maybe Cord can do that. I'll make sure The Painted Lady gets locked tight so that he doesn't lose any of his recently recovered inventory over this."

Taking his hat from the coat pole by the back door, George left Clara to tend the store.

General Delivery
Copperfield, Oregon
June 24, 1914

Dear Lottie Fern,

 This is going to be very short. I'm writing it on my lunch hour because I know you'll be reading the newspaper account about the shooting here today before I can take time to get a long letter to you.
 Mainly, I just want you to know I'm all right in case they happen to put a great deal of detail in the news report. I was terrified; I had no idea what was happening when the first shot sounded. But when the second rang out and I saw the mayor fall, I screamed. I think I was yelling because Cord was almost exactly beside him by that time.
 People came running from everywhere. Even Clara came to get me after Cord returned to help me get inside the rooming house doorway. I've never been so scared in my life. Clara's traditional cup of tea was very welcome.
 I'm going to have to sign off for now and give this to Jeffrey. He is here at the pharmacy right now to pick up some things for his mother. So he will mail it for me. The doctor will be taking the mayor to Baker City by train for surgery. There is no certainty that he will live, but it's been about four hours now.
 I'll write more of the details at the end of the week.

Love,

Cousin Ellie K

By a Twist of Fate

By departure time for the train that afternoon, Doc Hunsaker decided that Harvey Sullivan would be stable enough for the trip to the hospital in Baker City. The citizens of the town had rallied around to take care of things at The Painted Lady, and several in the business community offered to accompany the doctor and Mrs. Sullivan on the train ride.

George Hoffstetter named Cord as the best candidate, to which Marty Kellner heartily concurred, saying, "Hell, Cord can pack old Harvey and three others just like him, all at the same time."

Cord ducked his head, then assented, saying, "I'll be glad to go." It was a subdued group who assisted in putting the ex-mayor on the train, while expressing their wishes to Mrs. Sullivan for her husband's speedy recovery.

The doctor and Cord placed the patient on a stack of blankets in the aisle of the train's single passenger car. Mrs. Sullivan, having broken into tears repeatedly earlier on was now holding tight control on her emotions. Seated at an angle so she could closely observe her husband lying along side, she leaned over to murmur assurances in response to his groans. She told him quietly that he would be okay, all the while clinging tightly to his uninjured hand. Doc Hunsaker sat across the aisle, also watching his patient's every move.

Cord asked if there was anything he could do. On being told "No thank you," in a tight-lipped fashion by Mrs. Sullivan and being assured by the doctor that there was really nothing he could do, he settled himself at the rear of the car. It was going to be a long ride with no one to talk to and the only sounds being the rhythmic clank of the wheels and the almost continuous groans of what might be a dying man.

Cord reflected on the day's events after he had last seen Ellie this morning. By noon, the self-appointed guardians of the law who had ridden hell-bent for leather to catch the perpetrators of today's tragedy began drifting back into town. Two had followed in what they thought was hot pursuit in the direction of Homestead. After three hours, they concluded the pair could be anywhere, holed up among the rocky ledges, or hiding out in the heavy brush along one of the creeks. They added that the gunmen could probably successfully hide out there for the rest of the summer, eating fish or rabbit and deer along with berries and wild roots.

Two searchers had gone up Pine Creek, but were unable to find any sign of newly made horse tracks in the dusty roadway. When they got to Jim town, old man Coulter assured them that he had been working in his garden and resting in his rocker on his front porch since eight o'clock this morning. "Nobody," he told them," has ridden past on the main road to Cornucopia today."

Two others had doubled back thinking the gunmen had circled Copperfield and headed out for Robinette where it would be easy to go up through Richland and points West. They, too, were unable to pick up a trail. Riders they met along the way declared with certainty that they had met no one. The only way the men could have escaped the attention of the riders would have been to swim the treacherous Snake. To their knowledge, no one had done that and lived to tell about it in this particular section of the River because of the deadly undertow.

Some surmised they might have attempted to climb out over the shale rock mountainside, towering almost straight up by fifteen hundred feet or more above the River. If they had done that, they would be taking a mighty big chance on being seen because the view was wide open from the road in either direction. It being summer, there had been at least two hearty souls driving this stretch of road in their new automobiles already today. The motorists had come in from Baker City to Richland, down to Robinette, then turned north toward Homestead, planning to take the Kleinschmidt grade over into Idaho.

If either had spotted a rider on the mountainside, they reflected to the searchers, they would most assuredly have stopped to watch such an impossible feat.

"So much for their avowed intent," Cord thought, "when one of the searchers had shouted, 'C'mon, let's go get the cowardly sons-of-bitches.'"

After changing coach cars at Blake's Junction, Cord relaxed a little more. The smoother ride, along with the doctor's administration of more painkiller made it possible for Sullivan to rest for minutes at a time without moaning or crying out.

Cord crossed his left ankle high over his right knee, tilted his head back, let his hat fall forward over his face, and assumed a position of dozing. But he was far from actually sleeping. His darkest thoughts conjured up images of Ellie somehow being struck by one of those bullets this morning. His pulse began to throb and pound loudly in his ears as he contemplated the grief he would have experienced. Being almost two full strides ahead of him on the boardwalk, she could easily have stepped into the line of fire of the second bullet if he hadn't reached her to shove her to the ground. God, he was scared at the time.

Having turned his reverie to Ellie, Cord drifted back to his same old quandary. What if? What if he were ever to be identified as the Indian who sold the horse to Locksley? What if a grand jury found evidence to indict him? What if he had to stand trial? Even if he located the two cowboys, and they along with the bartender established an ironclad alibi for his whereabouts at the time of the murder, and he walked away a free man, his name would still be sullied. He would be marked a half-breed after the attending publicity, and no amount of moving around the countryside would ever change that in spite of his blue eyes.

And if all that happened after he committed to Ellie by marrying her, she too would be the subject of speculation on how she could associate herself with him. She'd be the victim of gossip wherever they went. He twisted in agony in his seat. He just couldn't do that to her, in spite of her pleading, the most recent of which was, "I love you Cord. You can't continue to break my heart like this. I don't care anymore why you think your doing this. Your reasons just won't stand in the light of day."

Tears were streaming down her face as he had tenderly enfolded her in his arms and promised to love her for the rest of their lives no matter what happened. It was getting increasingly difficult to convince her on the basis of finances alone that they couldn't marry.

When the train slowed to a stop at the Baker City depot, Cord sat up to view the scene. The ambulance, attended by two men, was parked beside the tracks, ready to receive their patient. Cord was dismayed to see the sheriff standing a few feet closer to the train track than even the ambulance attendants."Questions, more questions," he muttered as he rose to assist Doctor Hunsaker in transporting Harvey Sullivan out of the rail car.

Ted Yargo peered at the man being loaded into the waiting ambulance, satisfying himself that Harvey Sullivan was in no condition to talk. As one of the driver's assistants held the door for Mrs. Sullivan to enter the vehicle on the passenger side, the sheriff tipped his hat and said, "I'll be around to the hospital tomorrow to check on things." He nodded to the doctor, who had climbed in beside his patient.

Turning to Cord, he said, "In the wire from Copperfield, it said you'd be able to fill me in on the details."

Cord felt his skin crawl, as he replied, "I guess so." He hadn't known before now that dealing with the law would fall to him.

"Let's go to my office then." The two men were silent as they boarded the streetcar to ride the six blocks toward the Courthouse. Once inside the sheriff's office, Yargo remarked. "I'm somewhat at a loss Mr. Williams in that every time I start digging into a problem lately, you turn up at the bottom of the barrel."

Cord's breath caught. "Here it comes," he thought, but he managed to mumble, "What do you mean?"

"Well they call me to Huntington where a man's been murdered after you sell him a horse." The sheriff observed the visible cringe of the man who was sitting before him. But he continued, "Then I find you badly burned when they want me to investigate a fire at Copperfield. Now here you are with blood on your hands that comes from an avowed enemy of your former employer. Now wouldn't you say all that's rather strange?"

Cord glanced down quickly at the palms of his hands to note that they did indeed have blood on them. "I don't know sir," he gulped. He fidgeted in his chair as he considered that this man, with whom he had tried at all costs to avoid contact, knew more about him than Cord thought possible.

"Well, we'll try to put everything in perspective about you in a little while. In the meantime, what the hell took place in Copperfield this morning?"

Cord told him what he knew of the event, leaving out the details of Ellie being in front of him when the shooting started.

"You don't think the sons-of-bitches could have been shooting at you, do you? I understand you're a hard man to take out without an equalizer."

The corner of Cord's mouth lifted ever so slightly in an almost grin, as he said, "Well if they were, they are sure as hell in need of target practice. As I said, when the shooting started, I was about fifteen feet away from The Painted Lady where their bullets struck."

"They said in the wire that you saw two guys ride out and that several men pursued them. Did you recognize either of them?"

"No sir. Actually I didn't see anything but one man wearing a dark hat and the other with no hat. They were both spurring their horses into a high gallop. They were at least 150 yards from me when they caught my eye. Other than wearing regular work clothes like the miners down there, I couldn't tell anything except that the one with no hat was blond."

"What about the horses?"

They were a pair of matched bays. Neither of the livery stable owners could identify them. When I asked John Miller his opinion after he talked to the men at the blacksmith shop, he said they must have ridden in, probably from Idaho, shot the mayor, and continued on back where they came from. He thought somebody ought to be watching the Kleinschmidt grade day and night.

"Is somebody watching it?"

"The clerk at the depot wired a message for the section hands at Homestead to keep an eye out, but I don't know what good that will do. There won't be anybody watching after dark."

"Damn." Yargo swore. "A helluva lot of good the governor's dutiful militia is doing in this situation. Were they big men?"

"Probably about average," Cord replied. "About five ten or eleven, I'd guess, weighing between 160 and 180."

"Hmm. Anything else come to mind that I should know about?" Yargo paused. "If not, I'll be riding out first thing in the morning to get another man hunt under way."

"I can't think of anything Sheriff." Cord had no choice but to rise to his feet as Yargo prepared to leave. "I guess there is one other thing, sir," he said as Yargo came from behind the desk.

"What's that," the sheriff said looking sharply at Cord eye to eye.

"How long have you known?" Cord asked staring back.

"Known what?"

To Cord it was perfectly clear what he was asking, and he was surprised at the sheriff's lack of understanding, "About me, who I am I mean."

"Oh, you're talking about that Locksley thing. Well I've known from the beginning that you didn't kill the guy if that's what you mean. As for whether you're the Indian the Carter boys are accusing, I haven't made up my mind. Are you?"

Before Cord had time to craft an answer, Yargo went on. "You see I went on over to Weiser last November following up on a lead about some black hair hanging in a barber shop there. But when I talked to the barber, and he let me examine the hair, we decided it wasn't coarse enough for an Indian. Then too, the barber couldn't seem to remember any of the details about the guy or just when he did the haircut. So like I said, are you the guy the Carters are looking for?"

By this time, Cord made up his mind. "Don't see how I could be," he replied. "Like you said, he was an Indian."

The two men stared at each other like a pair of bulldogs deciding whether to take up the challenge.

The sheriff broke first, resuming his motion of pulling his hat on tight. He chuckled, "I guess I did say that, didn't I?"

Cord was not sure how he found himself in the street walking toward the hospital just a block away. But he wanted to run, jump, shout, "I'm free, I'm free!" The cloud he'd been under for the last nine months had lifted. Now he could make plans for the future with Ellie. He couldn't wait to get home to tell her.

General Delivery
Copperfield, Oregon
June 25, 1914

Dear Lottie Fern,

I know I promised yesterday, was it only yesterday, that I'd write a full accounting of the shooting. But I'm hoping that you will satisfy your curiosity through reading the newspaper coverage because I have news that is ever so much more exciting, I just have to tell you all of it now!

It's eleven p.m., June 25, and I'm so happy I could cry. If you were here, I'm sure I would. As it is, I just have to sit down and write without delay.

Just two short hours ago, I sat down at my vanity table and began to cream my face. I was trying to decide how I'm going to plan a program for the Grange picnic to be held here on the River bank at Copperfield in mid-July. Mrs. Cox, the Grange lecturer, asked me if I would do it, and dumb me, I said, "yes."

I had just covered the area around my eyes and across the bridge of my nose, when Lo and behold, Cord came bursting through the door. He didn't pause for even one second. He just ran and picked me up, one arm under my knees and the other around my shoulders. Then he stood me on my feet. He was so excited, I thought he would drop me, but I recovered my balance with his help. Then before he even kissed me or anything, he said, "Ellie, Ellie, we can get married now."

I was so shocked I finally managed to cry out, "Cord Williams, have you gone daft? What are you doing here anyway? I thought you'd be coming back on the train on Friday."

"No, no," he said. "Doctor Hunsaker and I took the stage to Richland, and rode the rest of the way on horseback. We just got in."

I couldn't quite grasp what he had said, so I stammered, "I thought Doc was busy with Mr. Sullivan. How is he anyway?"

"Oh, he's all right. I mean I saw him this morning, and he can talk and everything. Doc said he's got a good chance of recovery if he doesn't have a set back. But Ellie, that's not important. Didn't you hear me, we can get married!"

"I suppose we could," I replied, "but, when, why, what has happened?"

"What happened is I'm a free man," he answered.

My thoughts began spinning. After all this time, was I to discover he had escaped from prison or what? "So when weren't you a free man?" I demanded.

"Well I've always been a free man I guess. But ever since I came here, I've been a wanted man. At least I thought I was, but now I'm not," he announced grinning from ear to ear.

"That's not true," I said with as much coyness as I could muster. "I want you, but I thought maybe you'd ask me to marry you first."

"Oh, Ellie," he groaned. "I'm sorry." Guess what, he even took his hat off, all the way, not just shoved back like he usually does. He got down on one knee, took my hand between his palms and looked up at me. "Ellie darling," he almost whispered, "Will you marry me?"

The situation was so ludicrous, I burst out laughing. I mean, just picture it. I'm standing there in a full-length cotton nightgown, buttoned to my chin. My face is smeared with face cream. My hair is tied back off my face with a piece of yarn. And this man is kneeling at my feet asking me to marry him.

I knew right away I hurt his feelings. But you should have seen him, Lottie. He looked so serious. Then it struck me, he is serious. I pulled him up and put my arms around his neck. Ever since he was burned there, I've been hesitant to caress his neck like I wanted, but not this time. I stood on tip-toes, closed my eyes, and aimed the biggest kiss I could manage right on his mouth. I had never exactly done that before. The next thing, we kind of wandered out of my room into the darkened living room and fell across the couch. I don't know what would have come of it if Marty and Bridget hadn't come bursting in the door through the kitchen. They had been to a birthday celebration, and they were laughing and talking.

I was mortified. But Bridget and Marty turned their laughter on us. Marty boomed out so half the town could hear, "What the hell's going on here?"

Cord and I jumped up, and he grabbed my hand, stammering. "It's okay, we're engaged."

"You are," Marty bellowed. "Well by hell it's about time is all I have to say. But you still have to explain yourself, Mr. Williams."

I pulled my hand loose from Cord's and ran to my room for my robe. I ran back still tying my belt. "Yes Cord," I said when I reached the door. "You were telling me you are a free man. Free from what? Explain please."

Cord looked at me, then at Marty and Bridget. He was wearing his dark blue shirt. He is so handsome. The Kellner's had returned to the kitchen to seat themselves at the table. Cord pulled up a chair, straddled it, propping his arms across the chair's back. I stood by his side, with one hand on his shoulder. He had barely begun talking when he reached across to hold my hand so tightly I thought he'd squeeze it in two.

By the time he finished, I just wanted to cry for him, Lottie. He has tormented himself uselessly for all these many months. Anyway here is what he told us.

"You remember that Locksley fellow who was killed over in Mormon Basin last fall? Well, there were a pair of guys, the ones who found him, who were telling the sheriff and everybody they met that an Indian had done the killing. They said the Indian was trying to steal the horse back after he sold it. Well I'm the one who sold Locksley that horse.

"I found out when I went to Agency Valley that those two guys had taken off to find, me, come what may. They were referring to me as "a murderin' Redskin." Cord paused to look up at me.

"So what happened? Did you run into them or not?" Marty asked.

"No, but I found out from the sheriff that he knew who I was all the time—knew my name and everything." Cord was awestruck. "So when I was reporting on what happened here yesterday, he tells me some about his murder investigation. He tells me he knew I didn't kill Locksley, but then he asks me if I'm the man those two guys are talking about?

"I said to him, 'You said they're looking for an Indian.' So he just stares at me. I figure the jig is up, and he's going to arrest me or hold me for questioning or something. Well, I stare back at him. Then he starts to laugh, and says, 'So I did, so I did.' And he turns and walks away.

"Thing is, I know that he knows I'm the guy those bounty hunters are searching for, but probably since there's no reward out, they'll give up sooner or later. At least I hope so. Anyway they can't do anything to me if the sheriff believes I'm innocent.

"Now," he said, rising to his feet and pulling me into his arms, "I want to marry Ellie if she'll have me."

First Marty smiled, then he got mad. "Jumpin' Jehosophat," he shouted. "Why in hell didn't you tell anybody, man? We're your friends. We could have done something to clear the thing up!"

"What?" Cord challenged. "Contact the sheriff?"

"Well, I don't know, but among us we'd have thought of something."

Cord tightened his hold around me, and Bridget poked Marty to remind him they needed to check on Deborah. So they left. About fifteen minutes ago, Cord left too. I didn't want him to, but he said he couldn't stay all night under another man's roof without a proper invitation, even if it was with the woman he loved. He promised before he left that we'll spend all day Saturday planning our wedding.

Oh Lottie, I'm so excited. I don't think I'll ever sleep again, well maybe after I'm Mrs. Cord Williams.

I apologize for writing every little detail, but it feels so good to write it all down so I can believe it really happened. I hope you will be taking your vacation soon and can come assist me with the most exciting time of my life.

All my love,

Cousin Ellie K.

P. S. Even though I wrote this several days ago, I didn't get it in the mail. The big day, the day we will marry will be August 16, that is if we can get everything in place, specifically a minister, the songs, and you.

The Grange Picnic

Alberta Cox dismounted from the roan mare that their daughter, Emily, had ridden to school all year from up-river. She was an attractive woman wearing a brown print full-skirted dress with bonnet to match. She smiled and delivered a spirited greeting as she handed the reins to the liveryman.

She headed first to the post office where she bought postage stamps, then backtracked across the roadway to The Golden Star. Marty was engaged in washing the outside windows. He hailed her cheerily and held the door for her to enter.

"My what a nice place you have here. This is my first visit since the day of the raising. It's so cheerful with the tiny checked tablecloths and matching window curtains. Reminds me of my mother's kitchen."

"Well thank you. Bridget and I are very proud of it. I'll get Ellie for you. I believe that is why you are here."

"Yes," Alberta answered. "if she has a few minutes."

Alberta was amazed at the quantity of sparkling glassware behind the counter, the bud vases with flowers on each table, the silverware's rich reflection gleaming in the huge wall mirror along the back counter of the bar. She was tempted to slide on to one of the barstools just to see how it felt. But perhaps that was too daring, even in an ice cream parlor.

Marty returned saying, "She'll be out in just a moment, Mrs. Cox. Why don't you have a seat at one of the tables?"

"Thank you," Alberta replied, "I don't mind if I do."

Marty drew two glasses of water, used the ice tongs to reach into the freezer area for several bits of ice for each glass, and was carrying them to the table Alberta selected.

She was almost compelled to laugh at his appearance. He looked like a different person than he was six months ago. He had developed a full-blown handlebar mustache along with sideburns kinked tightly in front of his ears. The effect was to divide his upper face from the lower half. His hair was parted in the middle and lopped to each side of his forehead. To add to his aplomb, he was wearing a white bib apron over black slacks and a white shirt. A tea towel dangled from one of the strings used to tie his apron. His waist had noticeably expanded, and his cheeks were filled out. He was the picture of health. "It must be the ice cream business, or is it the new baby that makes you look so well?" Alberta inquired looking up at him.

"Probably a little of both," he grinned. "Oh, here's Ellie now. So what flavor do you want your sundaes to be?"

"Oh I couldn't," Ellie groaned.

"Oh, but you must," Marty countered. "How else can I advertise but to serve some of my product to the good citizens who visit so infrequently?"

"Well, if I must, I must. But please, just a very small portion. I admit I can't get enough of those delicious strawberries you shipped in from Richland the other day."

"Fine," Marty boomed. "How about you Mrs. Cox?"

"Call me Alberta, please," she replied. "The strawberries sound really good, but I grow them myself. You know what I'm so very fond of, butterscotch. Do you have that flavor?"

"You bet!" Marty exclaimed happily. "Coming right up."

Alberta turned her attention to Ellie. "My you're looking fetching today. The color pink is quite flattering to your face. Or, maybe it's that you're very close to becoming a blushing bride, and you're practicing! Your hair is just lovely."

"Thank you," Ellie's cheeks burned. "Bridget and I have been experimenting with ways to wear it under my veil."

"When is the big day again? I know I marked it on my calendar, but I never look more than a week ahead."

"It's August 16, just a month from today."

"My, that is getting close isn't it. Well I'll try not to keep you. I just stopped off to see how the program is coming for the picnic."

"Nicely, I think," Ellie replied. "As you said, the theme of peace is very apropos. It just so happened that Cord and I went to Huntington to see our minister to arrange our marriage ceremony. You know, he's the one who did the sunrise service at Easter.

"I happened to mention that I would be in charge of the program for you on Sunday, and that the theme would be peace. His eyes lit up, and he said, 'Grange picnic, huh?'

"Then I was suddenly inspired to ask him if he'd care to be our speaker, and he accepted. I told him it would not be a religious service, and that the speaker would be competing among the sounds of the River, the birds, restless children and satiated adults who might be quite dull and ready for a nap. He said that would be no problem. He could easily impart the message of our Lord on His peace in twenty minutes or so. You know how he starts his presentation, always with something humorous and ends with a song. So I thought that would be quite satisfactory. He will sing, "A Mighty Fortress Is Our God," in that deep voice he has.

"Just a minute. I'll get my notes from my room and give you a general idea of the rest of the items on the program," Ellie said, jumping up.

When Ellie returned, paper in hand, Marty was just serving the two sundaes.

"That's a small portion?" Ellie gasped as she gazed at an oval serving dish piled high with strawberries served over three scoops of vanilla ice cream. Whipped cream topped the berries.

"Oh, you know you can handle that," Marty scoffed.

"I don't know," Ellie groaned as she took her place at the table. Between small bites of her sundae, Ellie said, "Billy Mitchell will read a selection from Baroness Bertha von Suttner, winner of the Nobel Peace Prize in 1905. Her book is called, *Lay Down Your Arms*.

"York Fields has located a newspaper article on the origin of the Oregon State capital's name, Salem, and its meaning. He will be prepared with that. And Jeffrey Hoffstetter will present "Ring Out Wild Bells," by Alfred Tennyson.

"Then I located a skit about 'Keeping the peace at the hearthside.' I believe I sent a copy along for Emily to practice her part. Sissy Hoffstetter and Helen Carpenter will be acting with her as the main players.

"After that I thought I'd work in the minister's sermon and his song.

"Then I believe you wish to explain the position of the Grange on matters concerning caring for our war Veterans, who, for those in the Civil War, are getting on in years.

"You also said, the Grange Master would be speaking on the peace-time economy and how it affects ranchers and farmers.

"Then I have just a few short comments about teaching our youngsters the importance of maintaining peace in the world.

"Finally Henson Baldwin will perform whatever musical numbers he has. You have spoken with him, haven't you?"

"Yes, I have," Alberta replied with a smile. "He wouldn't tell me exactly what his songs will be, but he said they will be original."

"Oh, that's good. My cousin and I are quite taken with the Oregon song he wrote. When you see him again, please convey my appreciation and ask him if he'd care to favor me with the lyrics to whatever musical numbers he plans to perform."

"I believe that can be easily arranged," Alberta agreed, "since he is our closest neighbor."

"Does the rest sound all right?" Ellie asked anxiously.

"Oh yes," said Alberta. "It sounds just fine." She was scraping the bottom of her ice cream dish, finishing the last little bit of butterscotch sauce.

Ellie hadn't devoured even half of her serving yet. But she was not sure she was going to if Alberta chose to leave, which she did. She stood, drew on her gloves, and thanked Marty for his wonderful hospitality. Ellie was only too glad for the opportunity to clear the bowls and glasses from the table.

When she apologized for not eating all her treat, Marty assured her it was all right. "But," he said, "What kind of advertising would that have been if I brought you two teaspoons of ice cream with a strawberry on top?"

Ellie laughed, then returned to her room where she went back to trying to set her hair just right under the long white veil. She could hear Marty rattling the dishes and humming, "Here Comes the Bride."

General Delivery
Copperfield, Oregon
July 20, 1914

Dear Lottie Fern,

 The picnic is over and the wedding plans are firmly in place. I'm sorry that it will be impossible for you to be here because of your new appointment. I'll be more sorry that you will miss my big day, but we can't make it any sooner, because the minister will be away attending a conference from today until the 10th of August, I believe.
 The final plans are for us to marry in the ice cream parlor at The Golden Star. Marty will clear all the equipment away from the counters so the big mirror will form a backdrop, at least from my shoulders up. We think this will be rather unique because guests will be able to see whether we smile or frown, while we stand before the minister. I like the idea though because the candlelight reflects so beautifully. With the curtains drawn on the windows, and no light on in the room, the setting is so romantic.
 Esther Carpenter will be playing the organ. Cord and Marty will either move the school organ temporarily, or if we can find a larger one from someone else, we'll borrow that.
 Cord is fretting that there won't be seating enough or room for everyone who wants to come. I told him not to be silly. After we take the 15 tables to my room, there's chair space for a 100 if we want to borrow chairs from the City Hall. There are 60 here already. If more people than that show up, they'll just have to stand. I don't know where all these people will be coming from. Cord says all the men from the sawmill will be there. Some have wives, so he thinks that will be at least 35. We'll just have to see.
 Bridget will serve the punch for the reception, and Clara has agreed to cut the cake. Can you believe that? Clara Hoffstetter cutting the cake at my wedding reception. Sometimes I still hurt when I look at her. But she's certainly been nothing if not nice for the last few weeks. I thought about asking Lillian Lawson or one of the other student's mothers, but Cord says if I'm at all serious about wanting them to offer me the teaching position, I had better have Clara. I'll hate it down the road someday if she reverts to her old busy-body self.
 The picnic was wonderful. I'm pretty sure Bridget went around giving everyone an invitation to the bridal shower she's planning for the 26th of July. She's so funny! She always wants to surprise me in some way or other. If I could choose a sister, and it couldn't be you, I would choose her.

I can't bring myself to ask Henson to sing or participate in our wedding in any way even if there isn't anyone else. Well, I could ask the Copperfield band, but all of them except Marty are among the deposed members of the Town Council. I don't think they'd be interested since several were fined for selling liquor to minors, and in the end, they've had to pay all court costs. But, of course, you know all that. The bad part is, when they are through blaming you for blind-siding them, they blame me.

Mayor Sullivan would probably be magnanimous and agree to participate, but he's just now getting out of the hospital. He is improving, but slowly. The chest wound injured his liver and his right lung.

Then there's Marty, but he's giving me away. The only other musicians that I know of are the people in the dance band. They come down from Halfway, and I hardly know them. So that won't work. That leaves Cord. I think I have him talked into singing 'O Promise Me.' When I asked him, he wanted to know what I'd be singing to him.

I told him that wasn't part of the bargain. I said, "All I'm obliged to do is look pretty and say I do. And there might be a big risk in that if I have to sing first. I'd be so nervous, I'd be bound to lose my voice."

But back to Henson. He sang two original numbers at the picnic for my program. One was about Cord and me. I think you'll get a kick out of it, keeping in mind that I've not ridden horseback since I was ten years old. Not that that counts for anything. The whole thing is a spoof anyway.

As usual, I was not at all prepared for the response Henson got from the crowd. They laughed and clapped and cheered. It was a little embarrassing, actually. So I tried to set the record straight, but the harder I tried, the more they laughed. Ben Lawson shouted, "The lady doth protest too much, methinks." So I gave up and asked Henson to continue.

His other song, he says, he wrote because of the assassination of the Archduke of Austria. It's called, "Raise High the Flag." I'd bet if Henson were to make a move to get it published, it would be around for a while, especially in view of Bible prophecy.

In any case, it was quite appropriate for ending the program. As we all know, maintaining peace requires vigilance and sacrifice. I just wish Mr. Baldwin would find a nice girl who can dance so he would marry her. He still makes me shiver to be around him. Anyway, I've enclosed the words to his songs.

I guess I've about run out of things to write about, and I am quite tired. Now that everything is settling into place between Cord and me, we're almost like old married folks. We sit in Bridget and Marty's living room and go to sleep in each other's arms. The trouble last night was that after Cord got up to go home, and I *prepared for bed, I couldn't get back to sleep for the longest time. I couldn't get over how much I wished he were there. I hope that doesn't happen again tonight.*

Please write, and please tell me you're doing something more interesting than following the governor from one meeting or conference to another on your weekends. It was so exhilarating to walk around the grounds at Champoeg Park, and to see the sights in Salem. I can't believe you don't do things like that more often.

My love,

Cousin Ellie K.

The Schoolma'rm's Sunday Ride

Miss Ellie was on vacation when she came here to the West
She told us all she had a theory she couldn't wait to test.
She said she likes the climate, the sunshine and the rain
She also likes the singing birds and riding on the plains.

Now that is so peculiar, coming from her ruby lips
Before you decide on what to think, just listen to these tips.
Think about that theory and believe it if you can,
Then check out her real reason. It was to catch a man.

Our Cord was just a cowhand she met at a country-dance.
But he was lean and lanky and so ready for romance.
They danced a few, then sat one out; the hour was getting late
When he finally became courageous and asked her for a date.

She looked so shy and rather coy as he begged her make it soon.
So, she promised to go riding on next Sunday afternoon.
On Sunday Cord came calling, dressed in his very best
His white ten-gallon hat, and red embroidered vest.

Ellie too was decked out in her brand new blue jhodpurs.
Her shiny satin long-sleeved blouse. It matched her silver spurs.
She topped her head with floppy hat; and she was oh so cute.
Cord gave a long low whistle. She surely was a beaut.

Cord came ridin' Rocket, the best cow-horse he owned.
He was leading Old Red Pepper, a gentle horse, it's known.
But those spurs were their undoing, as shortly you will see.
Yet the outcome, it still puzzles Cord. For him it's a mystery.

Now Pepper was a single-foot with lots of good cow sense,
But carrying a pretty school ma'rm was a new experience.
Still he was fine and dandy under gray-blue skies above,
As they spoke of this and of that and finally talked of love.

Well Cord got so excited, he began to sidle near
Tried to hug her gently, as if to 'dog a steer.
She just laughed and pulled away, waving the olive branch.
She cried, "I dare you cowboy to race me to the ranch."

Now Ellie in her excitement applied her silver spurs,
And what then happened next could never have been worse.
Red Pepper balked, then bowed his head, leaving solid ground
He bunched his feet, then flew up high and turned himself around.

Now Ellie's hat sailed skyward, then gently floated down.
But alas, our poor Miss Ellie had no time to frown,
When the earth came up to give her an awful, awful thump
So hard that she turned black and blue right there upon her
     —uh backsides.

Well Cord was quick to reach the spot where our Miss Ellie landed
Mindful that she might think he was being too high-handed
He fell right down there on his knees and put his arms 'round her
When she raked his smoothly shaven chin with a tiny silver spur.

Then Ellie 'gan her homeward march as fast as she could trod
It was plain for Cord to see that she was clearly on the prod
He was feeling helpless now as snow in the month of May
'Cuz Ellie, she was marching home in the absolute wrong way.

But Cord is quite persistent, and though he made no sound,
His hat in hand, he ran to turn her half again around.
Thus it was we saw them as they came grimly walkin' in.
Though neither has ever told us just where it was they'd been.

Raise High the Flag

Raise high the flag, our country's calling
    To arms all men who live on freedom's soil
That we shall not, nor e'er be victims falling
    To life in bondage, nor in slavery toil
Raise high the banner others bore before us
    And carry on for freedom's cause anew
Join in a song. We know that God is for us
    Raise high the flag; our own red, white, and blue.

Raise high the flag, the flag our fathers
    Bequeathed to us with this our blessed land
And let us show the world that we like brothers
    Will join free men and lend a helping hand
To lead the world to happiness and freedom,
    Proclaim the Brotherhood of man anew.
The Nations call America to lead them.
    Raise high the flag; our own red, white, and blue.

Raise high the flag, the day is dawning
    When we must fight that all men may be free
When storm clouds gathering in the east give warning
    To draw the sword and guard our liberty
For we must show the world that truth and honor
    And love of justice to all men is true
We'll win this fight, so gather round the banner
    Raise high the flag; our own red, white, and blue.

The Bridal Shower

Bridget's living room buzzed with conversation. A dozen ladies were seated, eagerly engaged in catching up on the latest. They were thrilled with their tumblers of punch served with ice. When Ellie made her entrance to be honored, they all stood and clapped and cheered.

Bridget, Marty, and Cord had escorted her from this very room a scant two hours earlier, demanding that she stay away until she was called. In that time, the room had been transformed from ordinary living quarters to a setting out of a fairy tale. A white latticework archway was raised handsomely over the upholstered chair at the far end of the room. A silver-toned piece of cloth was draped over the chair to better represent a throne. Ellie was pretty certain Cord had constructed the archway during his off-hours at the mill. Each opening in the latticework was alternately stuffed with light green tissue paper or a pink rose.

A serving table brought in from the ice-cream parlor sat to each side of the throne. Both were draped with pink and lavender bunting. The one on the left held a mound of beautifully wrapped gifts. The table on the right had only a lace doily on the top at the moment. A smaller table suitable for playing cards was placed a little forward to the right with one chair for someone to sit. On it were a cluster of game playing items and several prizes.

Either side of the living room was lined with chairs from the parlor. The only other furniture was the sofa, where Alice Hunsaker, Grandma Cox, and her daughter-in-law, Alberta, sat.

Bridget came from behind Ellie to escort her to the place of honor, then turned to officially greet those assembled. There were fifteen in all, including Clara and Sissy Hoffstetter. Sissy was the only youngster in evidence. She, it turned out, was to have the honor of presenting Ellie with each gift when unwrapping time came.

But that would be after several games. The first game required passing tiny amounts of common spice around the room in a sauce server. Each lady was to identify the spice by smell or touch only. "No tasting, please," Bridget ordered.

Clara won that round, which wasn't surprising considering that she was not only a good cook, but also had any spice available that she might want to use.

Another game consisted of concocting a favorite recipe for Ellie's future use. The first lady was to write her choice ingredient for her favorite kettle soup on the top portion of a sheet of paper. She then folded the paper downward, hiding what she had written and passed it to the next person. After each guest completed her entry, Sissy came forward to hand it to Ellie to read aloud. Laughter prevailed as ingredients were announced. Several ladies guessed at the identity of the contributor according to the entry.

When Ellie finished reading, Bridget challenged her to add one last ingredient to the mix that would make it perfect for Cord. Being caught off guard, Ellie took a moment to try to think of something humorous, then blurted, "I don't know, water I guess."

"Yes, water," echoed Lillian Lawson, "to wash the whole mess out of the kettle and cook something decent for Cord."

After a good laugh, Bridget announced it was time to open the presents. Then she asked who wished to record the gifts and their sources for Ellie's future thank-you notes. Esther Carpenter offered and rose to take a seat at the small table where pencil and paper were now provided.

Clara rose at the same time to say, "Well, I want the honor of being Ellie's mother for today. I'll sit to her right and receive the gifts after they have been passed around the room." Ellie was speechless. Bridget quickly arranged the chair for Clara beside the empty table.

So many beautiful things were hiding in those packages, large and small, that Ellie was almost in tears as she opened one after another. It turned out that not only had the ladies in attendance brought gifts, but they also brought items from neighbors who couldn't be at the shower. From tea towels to kettles to quilts and blankets and linens, each became priceless to Ellie.

At last came the largest gift of all. It had been under the table and thoroughly obscured from Ellie's view. As Sissy began to crawl under the table to get it, Clara jumped up to assist her. Instead of handing it to Ellie, she placed it on the tabletop, now empty of gifts. Ellie stepped down from her throne to consult the gift card, then remove the ribbon without breaking or twisting the bow. Hanging it from her left wrist as she had all the others, she proceeded with the unwrapping. She was astonished to behold a twelve-place setting of Haviland China imported from Limoges, France on display before her eyes. She was so overcome by their beauty that she hurried to Clara to give her a hug, laughing through tears the whole time.

Then she took Sissy's hands in hers so they could dance around the room. Everyone was clapping and cheering. Ellie, feeling a stab of guilt about the simple thank yous she had murmured to the other ladies as she opened their gifts, dropped Sissy's hands and went to each lady in the room, taking her hand and expressing her gratitude for the present received. It was quite a feat to remember each person's contribution, but she did it without error.

Esther Carpenter threw her hands into the air and remarked, "I don't know why I've given myself writer's cramps to record all this if your memory is that good."

Ellie smiled and said, "I doubt the list will be straight in my mind tomorrow when I begin writing thank-you notes." With that she bent down to give Esther a hug.

When Ellie came to Bridget, who was standing near the throne, she was overcome with emotion. Realizing that there had been no gift from the Kellners, she still embraced Bridget tightly, then reached quickly for her handkerchief to dry her eyes. She said nothing because Marty came into the room at that moment, announcing that all the ladies were invited to the parlor to partake of ice cream dishes and sodas of their choice. "You will be served," he continued loudly, "using Ellie and Cord's new glassware and C. Rogers and Brothers silverware."

"First come, first served," Marty went on as he bent to assist Grandma Cox from the sofa to join in the parade of ladies into the parlor.

Ellie was stunned when she saw the display of glassware and silver on the counter in the ice-cream parlor. She looked at Bridget who was whispering, "I didn't have time to wrap them. They just came on the train yesterday."

As ladies were seated, Billy, with pencil and paper in hand, began taking orders. Marty was still dissembling with Mrs. Cox convincing her that a small serving of fresh strawberries served over ice cream would be just what the doctor ordered. Alice and Alberta, who were seated at the same table, agreed wholeheartedly, smiling at the old lady's reluctance to try something new.

Eventually with Bridget, Clara, and Esther's help, everyone was served. Marty insisted on making each dish himself, and Billy was kept busy placing glasses, dishes, and silverware in readiness.

Ellie gasped when Billy almost knocked one of the twelve berry dishes to the floor. But he recovered it as it slid toward the edge of the counter and flipped it in the air as if it were a mere toy or something. Ellie had slipped up to the counter to admire the elegant reproduction of English "Prism" cut glass. She knew from her days in Philadelphia that the real thing was valued in the hundreds of dollars. But these looked so nearly real that she sat blissfully staring at the pitcher, the punch bowl, the vinegar bottle, and the many other items she hadn't dreamed she would own so soon in her young life. Although her father had given her everything she ever begged for and more, she was never so pleased as she was today, receiving these gifts out of friendship and respect from the ladies of Copperfield.

Now, if only the school board would get its affairs in order. But she had to face the truth; that might not happen. Cord had received a letter from his friend in Agency Valley telling him to come back. There was a good chance he could take over the operation and maybe even the ownership of one of the ranches there if the details could be worked out. Ellie didn't know what to think, but she agreed to accompany Cord once they were married to see what might come of it.

General Delivery
Copperfield, Oregon
July 30, 1914

Dear Lottie Fern,

    I'm here to tell you that you must get married at some time in your life. The bridal shower alone makes it all worth while. I am suddenly in possession of so many nice things, I just sit and drool. I unwrap them, then rewrap them. Then I do it all again.

    Cord, the silly goose, groaned as though he were thoroughly put out at having to move all our gifts from Bridget's living room through the ice cream parlor to my room. But after Billy and he toted the last of them, he came back to watch while I looked at every gift at least twice. I will be writing over four dozen thank-you notes in all. In addition to the Copperfield ladies' gifts, we are also receiving something in the mail almost every day. I had written my good news to Tessa, one of my sorority sisters. I guess she and several others who are married figure it's payback time for the gifts I contributed to them the last several years.

    I can't tell you which gifts are more pleasurable. But I was stupefied when I opened the Hoffstetters' gift of a 12-place setting of French china. Then Bridget and Marty gave us a complete silverware set for 12 as well as a glassware set that is just beautiful, also for 12.

    I can't wait for you to see it all. There isn't a thing we're going to need for setting up housekeeping, except a few groceries. Since I must get started on the thank-yous right away, I'll make this short. It's barely two weeks until August 16. I'm so happy! I'm so excited, I just want to squeal.

My love,

Cousin Ellie K

Up in Flames

Ellie was dog-tired, having worked from early morning on one of the hottest summer days. Her goal had been to try to balance the pharmacy's books. She finally concluded that the differences in quantity were too great between the invoices for purchases and receipts for sales to be a mere bookkeeping error.

As a result, she zeroed in on several of the most common purchases, like rubbing alcohol, aspirin, ointment for bites and burns, and bandage material. She not only checked the paperwork, she went into the backroom to take inventory. Her conclusion was that discrepancies were far too numerous.

Forty per cent of the most recent receipts were for aspirin. But they accounted for only sixty per cent of invoice purchases made during the same time. Five per cent or more of the aspirin were missing. Rubbing alcohol revealed a similar shortfall. She had detected a very insignificant difference in the quantities of cough syrups, tonics, and laudanum. Of course, the latter products usually required a doctor's prescription before sale. Meticulous records had to be kept of their dispersal.

Ellie dreaded facing Mr. Gorman, having correlated the inventory check with the presumed discrepancies, a chore that had probably never been done in the four years the pharmacy had been doing business. Still the records should convince her employer that he should stop handing out products, then neglecting to record the fact that he had done so.

His reply would probably be that the charges he had allowed, but failed to record, would be paid for as soon as the men got their paychecks. "Clara," Ellie mused to herself, "would be horrified if she knew that anyone would call himself a business man, yet trust in the basic honesty of his customers to pay for unrecorded purchases."

Ellie would bet her life on it that these same men whom Mr. Gorman believed would remember and pay up sooner or later were the more notable patrons of the area's thriving bootlegging business. Otherwise, they would have had little need to charge the cost of a bottle of aspirin in the first place.

The problem Ellie needed to solve was whether these oversights were the result of laziness on Mr. Gorman's part, or whether he was being overly generous with men who couldn't manage their financial affairs because of their drinking habits. Ellie did believe that it was alcohol consumption that led these men to their need for cures for excessive pain and injury. But since the closure of the saloons and the ever-present exercise of martial law on the town's streets, Ellie knew she couldn't comment in public on that issue.

After all, it was a man's constitutional right to drink all he wished in pursuit of his individual happiness. Even the brawls in the streets, which had fallen off dramatically in the presence of the militia, were, according to some, a matter of freedom of speech.

Still how many times had Mr. Gorman been roused in the middle of the night to dole out bandages and pain relievers to somebody who had caught a fist in his eye. It was probably little wonder that he didn't write such items into his records of the day's transactions.

Nevertheless, he had hired Ellie for the summer to determine why he was increasingly unable to show a profit or actually have enough cash to pay for new inventory. She was supposed to recommend price increases on the products that would halt the over-expenditures he was experiencing. She was to determine if he had overstocked his shelves, or if his mark-up was too low in relation to his overall expenses. What would a careful audit show?

So now she had to show him the audit and disclose the facts. Among his most often sold products, he was only making a profit on an average 50% of his inventory. The rest was somehow escaping the process. He would deny it at first. He would want to know how much money had come in marked on account without any record of designated sales. Well, she was prepared with that figure too. It was not more than a paltry two per cent of the total shortage. So, unless he wanted to continue losing money, he would have to keep better records of his sales. Even Mr. Johnston, the town's banker had suggested such a remedy when Gorman requested his latest loan in June.

Being exhausted, Ellie decided she would settle for an apple for her evening meal. It was only 7:30 when she poked her head through the door of the sitting room where Bridget was nursing Baby Deborah. "Don't set a place for me tonight, Bridget. I'm turning in early."

"Already," Bridget responded. "I thought it being Friday night, Cord would be showing up."

"I don't think so," Ellie said tiredly. "We're planning to go to the dance tomorrow evening. We agreed Wednesday evening that since Cord is staying at the mill site now, and he has to work tomorrow, we'd turn in early tonight."

"Oh well, have a good night's rest, deary," Bridget said.

Ellie took only minutes to settle into bed in the rapidly descending twilight. Her sleep was so intense that sometime after midnight, she felt a need to turn her logged-down body to a new position. Relaxing, she fell to dreaming. The first part of her dream was of riding a buggy through the lush green hills and occasional widening valley areas. Fruit trees were in bloom, and, of course, Cord was at her side. Snuggling under the covers, she turned to her opposite side, making a conscious effort to be able to recall this pleasant dream for daytime reverie.

Her eyes fluttered briefly, and she noticed an orange glow being reflected in the mirror over her vanity. At first she simply closed her eyes tightly and tried to resume full sleep. Then she heard a loud yell coming from the direction of the Hoffstetter General Store. A man's voice was yelling, "Fire."

Ellie jumped to her feet to realize that the orange glow was indeed caused by fire. She flew to the window to note that flames were leaping from the dry needle grass between the General Store and the hotel. She glanced around wildly for something to put on. Her dress from earlier that day was draped across a chair. Grabbing it, she began screaming. "Fire! Everybody, get up!" On her second call, she could hear Marty stomping into his boots. She could also hear Billy making a noise in his room above hers. The yelling in the street was getting louder as men came running. Ellie had pulled her shoes on and quickly looped the laces around her ankles for a fast tie.

She opened the door to see Marty bounding toward the front exit. He turned briefly to yell, "Get everybody out, then go house to house. If you can get the women and children past the fire, get them to the school. The fire will probably hold along the Main Street." The door slammed on his last words.

Now Billy was flying down the stairs. Fear clutched at Ellie. "Billy," she yelled. "Where are you going?"

"I'm going to get a horse and get Cord."

Ellie had no time to react as the door slammed again. But it didn't stay shut. She felt the hot wind whipping in from the street. Bridget, still in her nightgown, was carrying her screaming infant into the night. "Ellie," she called, "Grab my diaper holder. I have a blanket." Ellie returned momentarily to her own room to snatch the top coverlet, which turned out to be her mother's cherished quilt. Then she hooked the diaper holder filled with diapers over her wrist as she whipped past the washing machine. She double looped it to make certain she wouldn't drop it. The bag was a creation of her own making. A pillow-slip with heavy twine drawstrings threaded through buttonhole openings along the top made a perfect transport for the clean baby napkins.

Ellie made it to the street, then stood for a moment to get her bearings. Men, including the militia were running their hardest. The hotel and the General Store were ablaze.

"Marty said go to the schoolhouse," she called as she rushed to Bridget's side. "Here's a bigger blanket. I'll be there shortly with the diapers." She didn't want to take time to undo the tightly secured bag.

"Where are you going?" a frightened Bridget squeaked.

"I'm going house to house to get everybody out and to the school. With the grass burning and the wind blowing like it is, there's going to be no putting this fire out before it spreads."

Though Ellie was running like a deer, the actual alarm had already been heeded. People were pouring from their houses. Men were grabbing shovels. A few ladies dashed to their clotheslines for clothing that had not been removed earlier in the day. Children were being ordered to get their shoes on and bring blankets.

Men were shouting that a bucket brigade from the livery trough was their only chance. The pipes in the hotel were bursting from the heat, releasing the town's water pressure, and running water from other buildings was draining uselessly away. By this time, the wind was sending burning debris across the street. It was only a matter of seconds until that side of the street too would be ablaze. When that happened, the whole town would be lost.

Ellie directed each woman and any children she met to go to the schoolhouse since it might be the only building out of range of the fire.

By the time Ellie started back from the River to go there herself, Cord was pounding into town on the horse Billy had taken to him. He stopped first at the livery. Since every able-bodied man had rushed to the fire to see what he could do, no one had released the horses, now in the direct path of the oncoming wildfire. Seeing him, Ellie ran to him, the flames a scant hundred yards behind her. Cord was thumping each horse on the rump, after jerking the halter from its head. Along with the sound of running horses, Ellie could hear dogs barking their dismay. It was a nightmare.

Spotting Ellie by the door, Cord left the halter on the last mare, leading her at a dead run from the building.

"Cord," Ellie cried, "It looks so bad."

"I know. I think it just hit the boardwalk on Independence. In thirty minutes, every building in town will be on fire. Here, Sweetheart, see if you can keep these two safe." He handed her the lead ropes of Bell and the last horse he had untied. Then he was gone.

Ellie was still carrying the diapers, so she twisted one rope twice around her hand. The fire was ungodly hot by then. Flames were leaping up the sides of buildings and high into the air. Women were screaming at their husbands to come back. The wind was so strong and the heat so intense that fear gripped her even though she was pretty sure all the women and children had done as they were bid and were now at the school, up-wind from the inferno.

She knew she didn't have a prayer of leading the horses anywhere near the fire. The flames were racing through the grass on all sides. Even though the wind was beating against them, flames were slowly retrogressing toward the river bank.

More men were coming now from the sawmill camp on Pine Creek, having been alerted by Billy. But the fire was completely out of control so that all they could do was fight their way along the perimeter and join the townspeople in watching the ghastly leaping, dancing flames.

"Miss Delaney," Ellie heard Billy call. Then he was beside her. She had traversed about half the distance from the livery to the school making her way behind the buildings on the west side of the street. The heat was getting more intense with every step. She was getting into heavy smoke, and her nostrils and eyes were stinging unbearably.

"Miss Delaney," Billy pleaded. "We can't go this way." The terrified horses were pulling back, and Ellie lost control of the lead rope in her right hand.

Fortunately Billy grabbed it, but before he could get the other rope disengaged from her left hand and arm, the horse reared and pulled back, throwing her to the ground. She could feel the yank on her arm. Her hand suffered a stinging, tearing rope burn on both front and back. But before it worked loose, it twisted firmly around her wrist as well as the dangling diaper bag.

Billy grasped the rope. "For God's sake," he cried, "unwrap the rope." At first she thought she couldn't. Her arm was still being pulled with all the strength of a thousand-pound horse. While she had hit the ground face down, she had been pulled hard enough to flip her over on her back, and her captured arm was now drawn straight above her head. The pain was excruciating. Billy did seem to be getting the horse calmed a little, and Ellie was finally able to free the rope from the diaper supply using her right hand.

When she was finally loose, Billy had all he could do to get the horses under control. Although she hadn't been aware of it, Billy had been shouting at the top of his lungs. "Cord, Cord, Miss Delaney's hurt." So while she cried out in pain from the rope burn and the injuries to her shoulder and arm, Cord was rushing to her side. Billy was babbling. "Her arm was caught, she was dragged. She couldn't get loose. She was dragged."

Cord barely hit the ground beside her when he cried out, "Oh my God," then slipped one arm under her knees and the other under her shoulders. He had her in his arms, when he commanded Billy to take the horses and go back toward the stable then down to the River's edge to circle back to the townspeople.

Cord was running full tilt when he felt Ellie slip into unconsciousness. He slowed briefly pleading, "Ellie, Ellie, say something." Realizing that flames were encroaching from the south, he resumed running toward the stable. He could see Billy was outdistancing him with the running horses, but he hadn't the strength to call for him to bring help.

Crossing to the wagon road leading to Pine Creek, he circled to his left and labored on breathing raggedly. Ellie was groaning in pain and seemed to be trying to say something. Reaching temporary safety, Cord almost dropped Ellie as he fell with her to his knees. Looking back to see the flames voraciously licking up the sides of the jail, Cord knew that it was not likely anyone was coming this way.

Cord figured Ellie was in shock even if she wasn't completely conscious; so he picked her up again and headed further up the wagon road. Though he was no longer running, he was progressing rapidly to the creek's edge. Laying her gently at the bank's edge, Cord stood up. He spotted the diaper holder for the first time. Removing the diapers in a heap on the ground, he grabbed one, dipped it in the creek, and wrung it out, then laid it across Ellie's forehead. Kneeling beside her again, he gently lifted her injured arm, then decided to remove his shirt and pull it around her. He hoped it wasn't too despicable with dirt, ash and smoke from the fire. She was coughing and wheezing intensely as it was.

Ellie began shaking violently. Cord cradled her in his arms whispering his love and concern. But she was not responding, only groaning piteously. Cord hoped Billy might come back, but the fire being as bad as it was, it might be that no one could make it through right now. The brightening glow delivered its message that it had consumed the jail and was lapping at the Miller Livery stable. "Well that's the end of the town to the north," Cord surmised. It remained to be seen if the houses along the River bank would survive. The wind, dying down, would actually work in their disfavor since the flames could make their way back now in the opposite direction.

Cord was fairly certain that the children and their mothers had reached safety. Just before he heard Billy calling him, several of the men decided they couldn't do any good trying to put out flames. They went on to the schoolhouse to check. He just hoped they'd notice Ellie's absence and make a sweep to find her. Or Billy should be getting worried by now. Cord huddled closer pulling Ellie's skirt tightly around her legs.

At that point, he could hear a speeder approaching from Homestead. He supposed the clerk had sent distress wires from the depot as soon as he could. Considering the men would have spent valuable time getting dressed, getting organized, and gathering tools, then running the speeder up river for a distance of four miles, a half an hour at least must have passed since the alarm went out.

Even though there might be as many as 15 or 20 men on the speeder, he didn't suppose he could begin to yell loudly enough across the distance to get their attention before they reached the tunnel. On the other side of the tunnel, they'd be almost as far south as the depot. But he had to do something to help Ellie, who continued to shiver and groan.

All at once, he could hear the rapid approach of a team-drawn wagon rattling down the Pine Creek Road. He had thought the sawmill crew had been right behind him to a man, but whoever it was, he was grateful. He laid Ellie back to the ground and jumped up to run to the road to stop the driver. The horses on seeing him frantically waving his arms, jumped to the side of the road, almost upsetting the wagon, but the driver managed to get the animals under control. "Whoa!" he shouted. "Whoa!"

"Cord," he yelled recognizing the blackened face appearing above a bare-to-the-waist creature before him. "What in hell's name is going on?" He was triple wrapping the reins around the wagon brake and readying to jump to the ground.

"Don't stop," Cord yelled. "Ellie Delaney has been hurt. Bring your wagon over here." Cord led the way closer to the embankment where Ellie lay.

The fire had stopped its northeasterly progression now and was doubling back, so it was practically dark along Pine Creek.

"Is she burned?"

"I don't think so!" Cord was breathing so hard, it sounded as if he might be sobbing. "Do you have a blanket?"

"Yes, as a matter of fact. I had my wife load as many as she could find."

The two men took a blanket and carefully placed Ellie in its folds. Then they picked her up and placed her in the back of the wagon.

"How'd you know to come?" Cord asked. Cord was addressing Stephen Underwood, foreman of the sawmill, and the only man living at the site with his wife and family.

We heard the shouts and saw the men running. Figured something was up. I told Margaret to get some blankets and drinking water. We could see the glow from the fire, figured it was a grass fire. Here," Underwood said, "Let's cover her a little better."

Ellie was now installed on a pile of several quilts and covered with two of them. Cord carefully pulled his shirt loose from around her and shrugged into it. He didn't want to leave Ellie's side, but somebody had to go for the doctor.

"What's taking place anyway?" Underwood asked again.

"Town's burning," Cord said simply. "Look, somebody's got to find Dr. Hunsaker. He's undoubtedly up at the school. Fire started a ways north of there, and the wind was hitting full force until a little while ago. Anyway that's the designated meeting place. Can you go?" he pleaded.

"Well sure," Underwood replied. "You don't think we can make it through with the wagon?" he asked in surprise.

"Don't think so. I suppose we can drive as close as the horses will go. The fire isn't coming this way any further." Cord hopped up beside Ellie, and Stephen climbed back on the wagon. The puffing horses had recovered from their wheezing, and snorting. Their breathing was fairly calm as Underwood drove them slowly forward.

As soon as they rounded the bend in full view of the town, Stephen was awestruck, "Oh my god," he breathed, "You ain't just a whistlin' Dixie, the town is burning!" He wrapped the reins, but then warned Cord.

"You better step down and make sure this team stays put," he directed.

Cord didn't want to leave Ellie's side, but he said, "Okay."

Stephen jumped down and headed north around the livery stable, then to the east hoping to circle toward the schoolhouse without having to go through the 1,000-foot tunnel. It would likely be filled with smoke by this time in spite of the prevailing wind.

Cord paced beside the wagon like a caged lion. Ellie's breathing slowed and her whimpering groan practically ceased. Cord began to imagine that perhaps she suffered injury to her ribs and possibly punctured a lung. Becoming more distraught, he unfastened the harness tugs from the single trees on the wagon tongue, thus disabling the horses from being able to run away with the wagon in tow. Then he climbed in the wagon to cradle Ellie in his arms again.

He immediately regretted his action because Ellie resumed groaning more loudly than before. "Ellie, Ellie," he urged. "Talk to me." But if Ellie was able to hear him, his pleas went unanswered.

For Cord, time was out of whack. By the time Dr. Hunsaker jumped into the wagon, his black bag in tow, Cord felt that at least an hour had passed. Actually it had been twenty minutes. Stephen had almost made it along the east bank when the fire flared in front of him. He'd had to make a hasty retreat and a four-block detour, then edge along the River bank again, gingerly passing the flames on his right as if they were a rattlesnake.

When he gained the school playground and began shouting for Doctor Hunsaker, several men came with the doctor to meet him, then accompanied both the doctor and Underwood along the bank, carrying shovels to make sure they made it through. A glistening covering of morning dew remained on the grass that had not yet burned. It was slowing the flame's progress somewhat. The sky was beginning to lighten with the dawn, but was hardly noticeable because flames were still leaping skyward each time the fire encountered a new fuel source.

Several houses along the River as well as the school barn and the school house still stood; and, ironically, were able to survive along with the town's only remaining business establishment, The Golden Star.

Dr. Hunsaker made a check of Ellie's breathing and her heartbeat with his stethoscope. He wished his gentlemen assistants, especially Cord, were at a more polite distance, but after checking twice, he concluded, "She's fine internally. You know, young man, you should have left her flat. There would have been less pain. Now help me turn her a little, and I'll see about that arm.

"Billy said her hand was caught in the rope, and she was dragged," Cord informed the doctor.

"Yes, I know," said Hunsaker. "Billy told us what happened as soon as he got there." The doctor was probing Ellie's shoulder and inspecting the top of her arm, then under her arm.

"If you knew, why in hell didn't you come?" Cord demanded in anger.

"We didn't know where you'd be," the doctor answered calmly. "Billy said she was conscious. We thought you'd probably carry her to safety and wait for the fire to die down. I'm sorry, old boy," he said compassionately. "If I'd had any idea, I'd have been here. But it wouldn't have made a lot of difference. There isn't anything I can do until we can get her to a hospital. My place is burning at the moment."

"And just how do we get her to a hospital?" Cord asked. "How badly is she hurt anyway?"

"Well I can't tell for sure," Doctor Hunsaker replied. "Her breathing and her heartbeat are strong. She may have a broken collarbone, but her shoulder blade and arm bones are all right. I don't want to push hard enough to check the collarbone out completely. So there are a couple of things to worry about."

He went on, "I don't like it that she's not coming around. Even smelling salts is not working. As nearly as I can tell, she isn't wearing any constrictive garments, so her being unconscious is not from lack of oxygen. So that means one of two things. She could have hit the back of her head or the back of her neck on a rock or something, which means she's suffering a concussion. Or her tendons in her upper arm and shoulder have been badly injured, perhaps even torn loose, and the pain is unendurable. Unfortunately, I don't dare give her morphine for the pain until we can determine which it is for sure."

Dr. Hunsaker paused, "As for getting her to a hospital, there are two choices. We can take her up Pine Creek Road to Halfway, where the facilities are probably adequate. Or we can take her by train to Baker City. If I could be sure there's no concussion, Halfway would be the better choice because it would ultimately be quicker. She could have painkiller, and we could begin treatment to her injured arm. I also see her hand has been mauled pretty badly. I can treat that now." The doctor reached for his bag.

The day was brightening in spite of the heavy pall of smoke, which was beginning to lay low along the River now that the flames had begun to die down.

"So you're saying what?" Cord pressed.

"I'm saying," the doctor replied, "I wish for the sake of the moment, that she were Mrs. Williams. But since she isn't, I'll have to field this one myself. They're sending a special train up from Huntington with emergency supplies, food for people who lost their homes, blankets, and things to hold the place together until some sort of organization can be managed. The train should be here in the next hour or hour and a half.

"Since Miss Delaney is apparently the only casualty, I am going to wait right here another 30 minutes or so, try some more smelling salts, and then if there's no change, we'll hitch up the wagon and make our way to the depot. I'll be going out with her."

"I'm going too," Cord announced.

"I figured you would," the doctor replied. "I have a piece of advice though."

"And that is?" queried Cord.

"You go back to your tent, gather up a towel, clean yourself up, change clothes, and even shave. The nurses at that hospital in Baker City will be a whole lot easier to convince that you need to hang around if you look presentable. In the meantime I'll be here if there is any change," the doctor assured him.

"I, I suppose you're right," Cord stammered.

"Go on now," the doctor ordered. "If she comes around, so much the better, if not, we'll be able to take her to the women shortly and maybe they'll have some way to clean her up some."

"Okay," Cord glanced up the street toward the school to notice that the fire was dying out in some locations. But the livery stable behind the Painted Lady and the post office, probably the last two places to catch fire, were still burning.

Jogging back toward the mill site, Cord spotted one of the horses he had released from the livery standing along the creek bank. But he didn't even have a halter rope, so he continued on. He had never actually bathed in a horse trough before, having always had access to a wash tub, a public bath, or if worse came to worse, a river. But tonight, or rather this morning, he knew the water in the horse trough would be cool, but not as cold as the creek.

After gathering clean clothes, his razor, soap, and a towel from the tent he shared with three other fellows, he made a bee-line to the horse trough, hoping Mrs. Underwood might have returned to her bed, or at least hadn't noticed him come into camp. Fortunately one or the other turned out to be the case. Otherwise, she would have been right there to find out what was going on.

Not that he blamed her. In this instance, he probably would have been more than a little curious. In spite of no wind coming up the draw, the smell of smoke permeated the air.

Cord felt refreshed after grooming himself, but he was anxious to get back to the train depot to make sure he'd be there for Ellie whenever she came to. So he was only too glad to be able to avoid an encounter with his boss's lovely wife.

The Columbia Hotel
Baker City, Oregon
August 28, 1914

Dear Lottie Fern,

I have a few minutes by myself, so I thought I would write for the first time as Ellen Kathleen Williams because the change does take some getting used to. I've been practicing my new signature for a little while. I asked Cord to leave me for a bit so I could write you and so I could prepare for the evening. He laughed at me. Then he said he'd take Marty up on his invitation to meet in the lounge for a drink.

After you left on the train, the Kellners and Billy accompanied us for our evening meal. We considered going to the Geiser where you stayed. The accommodations are much more elegant, I know. But we were fearful that we might encounter friends of Mayor Sullivan and the Council. Not knowing yet what they might make of the fire since Marty's place didn't burn, we remained cautious and out of their clutches.

The hotel we're staying in is just across the street from the train depot. We had a nice dinner, then Cord and I went walking to the north. I wanted to see the archway up close. That is a very nice welcome to a rather attractive city, just as you had told me. The same goes for the invitation on the City's side for people to return, as they make their way north to LaGrande and points west. I'm so glad you brought it to my attention. Cord had seen it several times he said, but he was happy to just be with me. We did enjoy watching the sun set behind the Elkhorn Mountains. It is absolutely wonderous to me that mountains are practically vertical here as they rise up thousands of feet above the valley floor.

Marty and Billy decided to tour the town to the east, across Powder River, where I understand there is a nice picnic area along the river bank.

Bridget took the opportunity to go to their room and rest with the baby. All our various rooms are on the second floor. None have a view, just dry sagebrush hills to the south of town. But we do have the benefit, at least this evening of a cool breeze.

I hope Governor West has been able to get along satisfactorily in your absence. I'm glad he has decided against running for office again. In this area, half the people think he overstepped his bounds, denying "respectable" businessmen their right to conduct their legitimate trade. Another fraction doesn't know what to think, only that several suits have been brought during his tenure, so something must be wrong. Then the rest of us are sure that he's a caring person trying to do his best for everyone.

I know you went on the 15th to interview for your new appointment. When will you begin there?

My shoulder is a little painful tonight, but I'm so happy to have all the bandaging off.

So again, I want to thank you from the bottom of my heart for being here with me this past week. You certainly made our wedding a memorable occasion in spite of the tragedy of the fire at Copperfield. Your voice is so beautiful. That Cord and you could sing "O Promise Me," was a dream come true. Of course, like always, I envy you your wonderful talent of piano playing and singing as you do. I wish we wouldn't have had to put you on the train practically the moment we were pronounced "man and wife." But I guess we couldn't very well take you on our honeymoon.

Besides having you here for our wedding, I'm eternally grateful that Bridget and Marty's place didn't burn, and we didn't lose anything except the few items Cord still had at Winona's Boarding House. I feel so guilty sometimes that we lucked out. But then I tell myself, "Bridget and Marty had already lost everything to fire twice. They certainly didn't deserve to do so again. I'm very sorry about the post office. Somehow they saved the mail, which was good. I was just glad I didn't have to watch when some wind-blown debris or something lit the fire. There were so many valuable artifacts in the lobby there.

The Star being so close, just across that roadway, it was surely a miracle that the fire stopped before consuming it. Cord says it's because the wind died down. But I say, it is because, "God works in mysterious ways."

I'm sorry I neglected to tell you in July that I had run into Mr. Moore. But I trust you had a good visit with him and other friends while I was frantically getting ready to be married. Just to set the record straight, this is what happened. I had come to the City with Bridget to do some shopping a few days before the Grange picnic. We stopped for lunch at that little shop across from the Grand. As we sat down, I noticed Mr. Moore sitting nearby. I wasn't entirely certain it was he, since I had only seen his picture in that newspaper clipping you sent me when you thought I might wish to engage legal counsel over the loss of my job.

Then I happened to mention to Bridget that you definitely wouldn't be coming for our wedding because of your new job appointment. Actually what I said was, "I'm disappointed that Lottie Fern can't come for our wedding because of her new job appointment. I was hoping we could go shopping in preparation for the wedding."

Bridget didn't seem to remember your name, so she said, "Lottie Fern, Lottie Fern, who?"

I said, "You know, the governor's secretary, Miss Hobbs?"

"Oh, my goodness," she said. "How could I forget? I guess it's just that I always think of her as Miss Hobbs."

I was about to launch into a speech about you being my closest living relative, when Mr. Moore picked up his hat and his check and came past our table.

He told me to send you his best and remarked that if you ever want your old job back, it will be available. I'm sorry it slipped my mind at the time. I hope it didn't make things awkward for you when you contacted him while you were here.

And now, I am thrilled to begin my life as a properly married woman, honeymoon and all. Cord and I will pick up the rental horse and buggy in the morning. By eleven, or so, we should have our supplies purchased and be on our way. We'll either stop at North Powder tomorrow afternoon; or we'll keep going as far as Union. The days are getting shorter, so it will be a stretch to get to Union before the liveries close for the night.

Then the next day, we will press on, taking as short a route as we can, probably through Cove to Elgin and on toward Wallowa. I am so anxious to finally see the Lake and the place where the older Chief Joseph is buried. Cord says, "It's beautiful beyond words." But he still doesn't understand my fascination with going there. He teases me, saying I am becoming more Nez Perce than he is.

So I tell him, "Why not? This is my native land too, and I intend to see that our children learn their true heritage. Besides, you're only an adopted Nez Perce. They could adopt me too, you know."

He just shakes his head and says something like, "I just hope you feel the same way when we return from Lapwai." He always gets such a sad look when he talks about Lapwai.

But I tell him, "I will, I will, you'll see." And yes, dear Lottie, I am trying hard to ignore my qualms about moving to Agency Valley. In some ways the letter from Mr. Barstow about the release of land for settlement on the former Indian Reservation was heaven sent. I assure you, though, Cord has promised that if I don't like it, we will move on. Maybe we will even come back here to Copperfield. We'll see what they have decided when we return from our honeymoon next month. Right now, they are not even sure they will be opening school. It would quite likely be just for the rancher's children if they do. Still, it might be possible for all the students to squeeze in at Robinette or Homestead, at least temporarily.

Cord still stands on his right to make a living for us without the help of my trust. I respect him immensely for that, so I intend to make every effort to accommodate his wishes. In any case, should we decide to settle in Agency Valley, it won't be the same as being raw homesteaders trying to eke out an existence from between sagebrush roots in some dry canyon. The ZX Company has already constructed modern ranch buildings at several locations. We will be acquiring one of those. Cord vaguely remembers the one that Mr. Barstow will be holding for us. If we like one of the others better, he is quite certain we can make the trade either now or in the near future.

Mr. Barstow says of the people who settle there now, fifty per cent will probably move on in the spring after they have put in their first winter. It frightens me to hear him say that; still Cord says it's not so bad. Then he assures me that he not only knows how to keep himself warm, he can handle keeping me warm also. Hmmm!

So now dear cousin, I bid you adieu. I'll write again in about a month.

Forever your cousin,

Ellen Kathleen Williams

Epilogue

The following note appended to the letter of Ellen Kathleen Williams was as follows:

January 3, 1964

Dearest Ellie,

As I observed at the time, your honeymoon must have lasted considerably longer than a month. As I recall, I received one postal card from Lapwai, dated in September. There was nothing again until about December when you began telling me about your pregnancy.
Since the election was past and the Supreme Court had cleared Governor West, and since I was still getting settled in my new job, I did not save any further of your later missives. I rather wish I had.

Love forever yours,

Lottie Fern